BOONDOCK BOUNTY

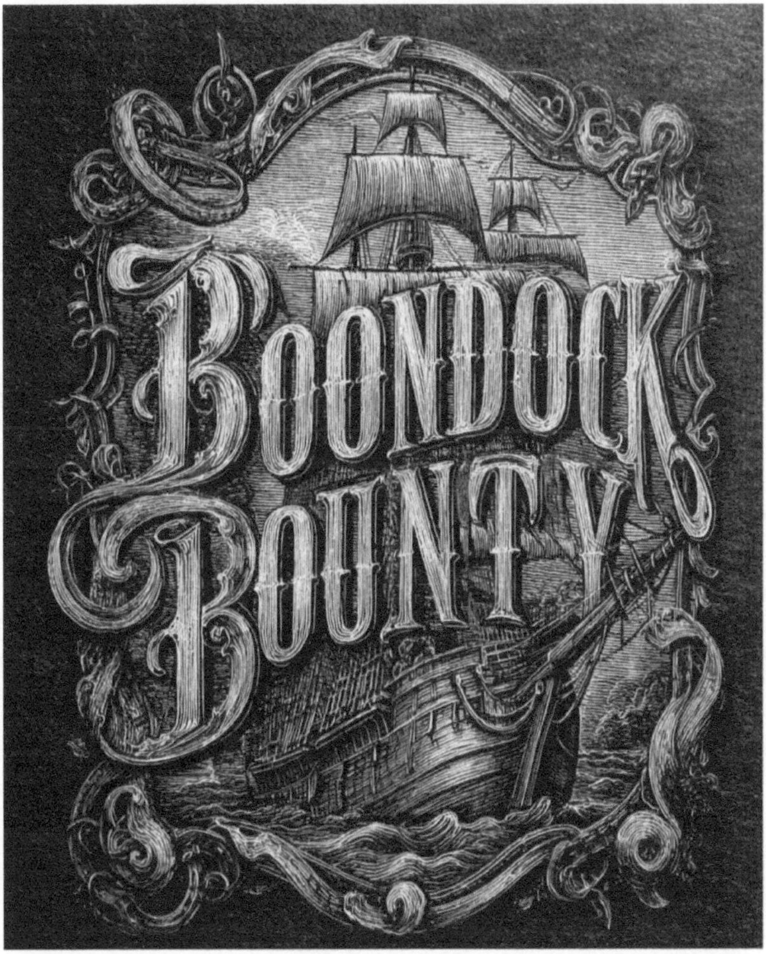

MORGAN GELLER

A Morgan Geller Book

Published by Morgan Geller Company

ISBN 979-8-218-89128-2 (trade paperback)

Illustrator: Ramile Imac

(instagram.com/lalunadraw/)

THE PINWHEEL ISLANDS

KLEPPENWITZ

The Boondocks

Vista

Prego

Caldo

Forza

Chapter 1

The Unopenable Chest

The bodyguard looked down triumphantly at the man he'd just shot. He'd heard for months a famous bounty hunter was coming to steal their new prize, and there he was sprawled out on the cold ground in his black leathers stiff as a board. He'd gotten close too, the man-sized sapphire chest he gave up his life for was perched just a minute's walk away, stuffed up under a canopy of wilted palm trees.

He could already hear the bar halls cheering his name, singing songs about how he took down the man no one else could. His boss Knox wasn't known for compassion, but he would have no choice but to reward him for this.

"...Is that Ra… Radish??!" his partner said out of breath as he sprinted over.

"Better believe it."

"*The* Radish?!?"

The man grinned and nodded.

"The Radish that was partners with the Rogue, the man who stole Quicksilver, is in front of me, takin a dirt nap? And you of all people killed him?!?"

"That so hard to believe?!" he asked sweeping the dust off his crumbling wool overcoat.

"With all due respect, I'd sooner believe monkeys ruled the Five Islands…"

"I'll remember that when I give you orders after this, now go and fetch Knox before I kill two people tonight!"

The bodyguard tucked his rifle back over his shoulder as he watched his sidekick scurry away. He could see his companion's eyes flutter and tone of voice shift; it only took half a second to figure out what this meant. The respect he'd never been given around here would finally come his way.

The man donning shoddy wools didn't show it, but he could barely believe it himself. Though the scars across the corpse's face, speckled black hair, dusty old eyepatch, peculiar necklace, and maroon sword on his hip left no doubt and matched the description to the letter. *A shame* he thought, *a legend gunned down with no glorious battle or martyrdom, only a single unseen shot from a no-named smuggler.*

The roar of spouting thunder in the distance filled the air, as the stars in the night sky illuminated their glowing trails. The pools of hot ash and black, mountainous terrain made this small island all but uninhabitable to most life in the Pinwheel Isles yet provided the perfect cover for an operation like Knox's. They were a group of known smugglers around Otto and its surrounding islands, if you needed a banned substance or even better banned person in or out of the Boondocks, they were the ones to see.

They'd made quite the name for themselves and snuffed out most competition by either undercutting them or more commonly deadlier means. It was a booming business, until they got their recent cargo, the chest Radish just lost his life over. Not a one of the men knew what the sapphire chest contained, but Knox had become obsessed with it, ceasing all smuggling operations to focus on finding out how to unlock it.

Knox approached along the mountain path purposefully with his Grey Wolf snarling at his feet. His uneven face made grown men shudder, and his near rotting skin hardly helped the matter. The Brigadier seemed to float like a ghost on the dirt underneath his feet as his eyes never broke from his hireling and the corpse below him.

The bodyguard wasn't sure he even needed the Grey Wolf he called Hugo, after he'd witnessed Knox kill a man with his blade, then seconds later kill another man with the same blade two-hundred feet away, most other men in his company were sure he wasn't even human.

"Hello old friend." Knox said speaking to the motionless body, "Looks like Radish wasn't as clever as he would lead you to believe. Shame, thought he might've been the one person in the Five Isles that knows how to open our chest… What's your name soldier?"

"Be-Benedict. Sir." the words would barely come out, he was so confident moments ago, but his superior had a way of tearing that down without even trying.

A grin flashed across Knox's face.

"I'd hope to have the pleasure of killing him myself, never thought one of my sstuttering guards would take him out." he laughed as he looked Benedict over, his black eyes looking right through, "How'd you do it? The old fool trip or something? Fall on his own pistol?"

"He was ju-just standing there, I took my time, steadied my aim just like I was taught and hit him dead center."

Knox gave a suspicious glare. He bent down and took a closer look at the body, looking first at the corpse's maroon cutlass and tattered old pistol. He wasn't looking over the body long, but to Benedict it felt like time stood still.

Knox's body stiffened where he stood. Something wasn't right…

The grin from seconds ago sank into an unexpected rage.

"Tell me Benedict, did this dead man'ss face not look odd to you?!" the all too familiar tone of unfettered rage revealed itself as his face was now inches away from his shaking soldier.

Benedict's heart sank as his glowing mood from minutes ago sunk into desperation. "I-uh, I…Sorry sir I was …I…erm… I don't understand."

Knox's hand was now clenched around the Bodyguards throat. He held up the corpse's unsheathed maroon sword in his other hand and squeezed it. With little effort it shattered to dust in the moonlight. It was a fake.

"That man you shot isn't Radish you twit!" he said as he gazed maniacally into the man's eyes he was about to kill. "That dead man you just shot works for me!"

Benedict could feel his heart slowing as his vision steadily turned black. He took one last look at Otto's lights glowing in the distance, from this view it was breathtaking, at least something amazing would be the last thing he ever saw.

His journey would end here, it was all over it seemed, until…

A piercing whistle came from behind them, so loud that both men nearly fell over.

Sitting atop the sapphire chest was a man with a soggy old eyepatch, speckled black hair, and maroon cutlass on his hip. Except now the sapphire chest wasn't lying under the wilted island trees, it was carefully secured into the back of the man's small wooden ship.

"RAADDIISSHH!!" Knox howled the veins throughout his face looking like they were about to burst.

Unsheathing his two pistols he began firing wildly at the fleeing ship, the sparked ejections of his shots looked like a hail of fireworks exploding below the canvas of stars. The lead shots came close, but by now the ship was already gracefully sailing away into the midnight waters, too far to hit.

Almost too far away to see with the naked eye, Radish winked and waved goodbye smugly, still sitting daintily on his new sapphire throne. His faithful old ship was now a distant haze, heading for Otto a few miles ahead.

Onboard his ship Radish could just barely make out Knox kicking over wooden boxes lined along the beach shore and shoving all the soldiers that began gathering around, ramrods in hand, black feathers poking out of their wool hats, attempting to reload for a target that was clearly too far to hit.

"The old numpty thought he could catch the Quicksilver Thief!" he said in a mocking tone. Arms flailing and feet turning, he jumped in his very own celebration until he stubbed his toe on a nearby wooden ship wall and proceeded to writhe in pain.

Figuring this called for a special celebration he grabbed a bottle of his favorite rum, just as he kicked back and started to relax, sprawled out on the deck of the ship, his Captain Kersey rushed in, looking like all the blood had pooled out of his face.

"Ehm, Sir! What are you doing?!"

"What am I doing? Relaxing. Till we get to Kleppenwitz. Where I intend to explore one of the cities many fine dives and get tight as a boiled owl!"

"Sir… Knox has one of the fastest ships in the Pinwheels, along with the best captain on this island or the next. There's no way we'll outrun them before we get to the Boondocks!!" Kersey was rife with anxiety as he glared at Radish who was still trying to figure out how to get his rum open.

"Well I could agree with you, but then I'd be wrong too…" he snapped a finger at him.

"I don't think you're taking this near serious enough!!"

"Mate, mate, mate... keep your hair on, what's wrong no faith in your glorious leader?" Radish's voice was relaxed with its normal raspy and edged tone, as if he'd had the perfect thing to say to calm his captain, "When you sailed in and met me at the rendezvous spot, as you lazily watched me drag this sapphire wonder up into the cabin, we saw that poor soul get shot... Do you know who that man was?"

"Why would it matter? Just some decoy... I don't think you understand the gravity of this situation!!"

Radish paused like he was about to show the grand finale of his best magic trick, "Dead men sail no sails... that man, may he rest in peace, that man... was... their captain." he slouched back onto the ship wall into a tranquil position, "There's not a man on that uninhabitable rock that can captain a ship as complex as theirs, besides the one kissin dirt right now... Unless Knox's gotten so strong he's the first man to bring blokes back from the dead... I'm feelin real comfy. Now if you'll excuse me, I'd like to have a drink..."

"Uh... well then... that does make me feel better... Right... I'll get back to it." Kersey gruffed, finally feeling like he could breathe again as he headed back towards his Captain's Wheel on top.

"Any chance you'd be useful for once and help me figure out how to open this thing?" Radish said as he pointed at the chest.

"Not a fishey's chance on Caldo I'm goin near it. Don't know how Knox got through the Monsoon, an to be quite honest I don't care to. There's a term for treasure that came from a cursed isle... it's called cursed treasure."

"Don't know why you're a captain, with that kinda bravery you'd make the finest knight in the land! Makes me question what I'm payin you for."

"You can't threaten my pay if there never is any!" the captain hooked back sarcastically.

The ship was quiet as its crew raced towards Otto or the Boondocks as most people called it. Now at full sail as it peacefully glid through the calm waters, the only sounds coming from Kersey tapping on his wheel and Radish sat on the deck below, rummaging around for a second rum jug.

The mass of land ahead was surrounded by crystal blue waters you could see a doubloon in ten feet down and capped with emerald green forests and trees of all sizes slouching like they had a bad back.

Most prominently in front was the port city of Kleppenwitz, with its many thousands of housewall torches illuminating miles of cobblestone streets and hodgepodged districts of white cottages. They were close enough to the big city now it took up most of their view and Radish was delighted knowing it would provide plenty of cover from Knox, for a time at least.

"Don't know why they call it the Sober Sea, I never been sober on it..." he murmured leaning on the bulwark and looking out over the open ocean, "And what do we have here? Treasure from the cursed isle..." Radish said curiously.

Bending down he ran his fingers across the top of the chest. It gave him the strangest feeling.

The chest was unlike anything he'd ever seen. Massive and other-worldly. Bulky and heavy in look yet somehow was moved with ease. It was faintly cool to the touch with hand-carved intricacies of an undecipherable language, and if you looked at it long enough from the right angle it almost looked like it was giving off a blue glow. Even if the thing was empty, he could've sold it for a fortune to any fence on Kleppenwitz, *not bad for an hours work* he thought.

Radish still wasn't sure of what was inside, but he knew it was the next piece of the puzzle.

Suddenly, and inexplicably, he felt the necklace around his neck tremble. He heard a crisp clack like that of a distant door opening very quickly and looked down at his pendant hoping it had opened, only to be disappointed to see it still locked up tight as always.

When he looked down even further however, his newfound treasure chest was now gaping wide open.

With eyes halved and mouth puckered, he hovered towards it like it was toxic sludge. Slowly and carefully, he peeked inside perhaps

7

expecting to see a heap of golden doubloons or maybe even some prehistoric artifact that would make him rich enough to buy his own Island. However, it wasn't a *what* that was inside the chest… it was a *who*.

Chapter 2

<u>The Boondocks</u>

Jack Tripleleaf watched a snowy owl dance across the night sky as he looked up at the gaudy stars.

He felt like he could breathe again being back in his hometown, something about the fresh spring air here brought him instant peace of mind the minute he waltzed off the ship with his captive in hand. Their destination, the golden city of Kleppenwitz was hallmarked by its white cottages, many of them stacked two or three homes high and leaning on the neighboring structure, red bricked government buildings that looked far too professional for the city they inhabited, and its famous crystalline turquoise canals that separated most streets along their winding and uneven paths. With people from every corner of the Five Isles, it was said to be one of the busiest and most lawless places in the Pinwheels. As long as you had the doubloons, there was little you couldn't do here. Naturally, bounty-hunters, thieves, and smugglers who flocked from all over took a liking to the place, especially with how far away it was from other, more law-abiding island countries.

He carried a short stubby man in steel chains along the crowded city streets finding it difficult to carve out enough space to move his captive. Though there was little to fear now that they were in home territory, Jack's mother Riley was right behind them still instinctively watching his flank.

The smell of fresh pork in the air was intoxicating. The Boondock's satellite islands where this mission had taken him weren't exactly known for exquisite cuisine, it was all he could do to not drop his captive and pig out. *Almost there* he told himself.

There was always something interesting to look at in Kleppenwitz no matter the time of day. Jack couldn't help but admire the famous Laughing Monk in the distance still so prominent so many miles away. Tonight there were two stars right behind its massive stone head, which made it look like it had two giant glowing ears.

Many of the cities' castles were impossibly tall, but somehow the monk managed to look down on them all, with his throne the sprawling trees and gardens in the Municipal Park below him. The Laughing Monk was a feat of engineering, and a symbol of peace and good fortune in the region, created after the eight brave women and men who had settled the area many hundreds of years prior.

The cities' kaleidoscopic torches hung by rope above illuminated merchants, dealers and city folk crammed into the streets like sardines, as it seemed like every salesman in the city wanted to sell exclusively to Jack.

"Forzian Wild-Geese here! Tastes so good Magnus outlawed anyone eatin it but'em, had to be smuggled in! Handsome boy like you deserves my best price, only cost ya four copper centimes." one merchant said.

"Got a double-barreled hunter's pistol here once belonged to the Rogue himself, your marks will beg for mercy when they see this!" another said.

Jack kept toward their destination paying them little mind, dodging pushy salesman was an art in this city.

"Think I should take his blindfold off? Take the rope off his mouth? May get him to stop shaking trying to get out, and least give'em one last look at the stars before he's locked up forever…" Jack yelled back at his mother.

He took a second look at them himself, admiring how no two night skies were ever the same on the Boondocks.

"I can't imagine why you'd want to hear his mouth again, but you're the one who caught him. Just be careful…"

It was only the third bounty Jack had ever captured, Riley had only in the past few years come around to the idea of him working on bounties instead of being cooped up in the inn while she went off on some grand adventure.

Maybe it was a weak spot but watching how pitiful the prisoner looked bumping into poles and wood tables, part of Jack felt sorry for the man. His mother had always tried to stress that, in this line of work, weak spots would get you killed. Jack was only sixteen, possibly even seventeen, with an outside chance of eighteen. He had no way of knowing given how Riley found him. In his mind he figured he still had plenty of time left to grow out of his weaknesses.

Carefully he removed the ropes from the criminal's eyes and mouth and felt instant regret.

"Sneakyyy Sneakkkyy Jaaaaaaaack!!!" he said with a wide-mouthed, dumb smile showing off all his missing teeth and halitosis.

Jack winced, "Hello again Morty, have a nice nap?"

"I did! Say… what are the odds you… take off these cumbersome chains? My poor little wrists… I could chafe!"

"Odds aren't good Morty!" Jack jeered keeping up his brisk pace while trying to keep Morty from bumping into pedestrians. "Don't think the police here would appreciate me giving a bomb-maker free hands."

"Mate… A bomb!" he lied as if he was shocked. "What's in a bomb besides stuffs in the ground all around us? Is that wool tunic around your back a bomb? A little gunpowder and a fuse, and it could be! Hear me out, what's the bounty on me one-hundred doubloons? Maybe even two with my good looks?? I'll pay you double that if you free me right here and now no questions, got fifty fresh sparklin doubloons stashed in a sewer not ten miles from here!"

"Good thing he picked bombs over becoming a mathematician..." Riley laughed.

Feeling desperate Morty broke down and began to cry in the middle of the street, making onlookers stare wildly, "Think of the children Jack! Growing up without a father!!"

"We read your file Morty… you don't have any children…"

"Well… yeah…" he sobbed, "But I still could!"

Beginning to realize his miserable pleas weren't effective he shouted again. "Jack please!! If the lads hear I got taken by a boy with a pink sash and his mum, I'll never work again!"

"Don't worry, where you're going there's a whole slew of men I've taken in, they'll understand..." Riley chortled.

The term pink sash Morty had used was an exaggeration. It was more of a reddish pink. The sash had a devilish looking one-eyed monkey as a fastener and everyone in their fellowship received one when they joined. The brighter the color, the newer the member.

"Ok hope you had a good look around… rope's going back on!" Jack could still smell the man, but at least now he didn't have to hear him.

"Told you." Riley said delicately.

For what felt like the hundredth time today, Riley was right and Jack found himself in the wrong. As frustrated as it made him, he had to remind himself he wasn't a fully fledged bounty hunter yet, and still had plenty to learn from her.

Riley wasn't his real mom of course, he had no clue who was, but as far as he was concerned, she was all the parent he ever wanted or needed. Ironically, they both had features so similar, people often mistook them for a real mother and son anyway. Besides the length, Jack's wavy dark hair matched his mothers, they both had snubbed noses, sharp jawlines, and like most good bounty hunters they had athletic builds that came in useful when chasing down marks that liked to flee.

They approached a clearing known as the Flagpole Market with its hundreds of flags from every city Jack had ever heard of and many he hadn't and so many lanterns strung up on lines along the roofing it was almost brighter now than it was in the daytime. Jack walked past a young mother and her tiny daughter and heard the toddler yell,

"Uhhhhh!!! His Hand!!"

The mom quickly grabbed her daughter and darted to the opposite side of the street attempting to hide her embarrassment.

He must've forgotten to put his gloves back on when he took the ropes off Morty. It was hard to blame the little girl for reacting like that. His right hand had been blackened and disfigured since Riley had found him, not far from the age of the girl that had just screamed. He'd felt like he had moved passed it, grown to accept his disfigurement, but if he was being honest with himself, situations like these still stung and would linger around for the days to come like sorrowful little daggers stabbing at him when he least expected it. Still, he kept on walking with his best stone face, his prisoner in tow. He didn't dare let Riley see, he knew it would break her heart.

The once wide and congested city streets began to narrow, and the city of lights darkened as they approached their destination. A red brick wall so big it looked like it kissed the sky stood directly in front of them. By this point Jack knew the drill, he took out his pistol and beat the wall three times with the butt of it.

"**PASSWORD??!**" a solemn deep voice retorted.

"A gift for the Blackwater Cantina!" Jack yelled back.

As if by magic, a perfectly symmetrical legion of bricks in front of them created a crease in the shape of a door, and with a shove gave way to an opening with a behemoth of a man standing behind it.

"Evening Gunter!" Jack said.

"Hello Gunter!!" Riley said cheerfully.

He nodded back emotionlessly.

Knowing this non-response was completely normal for Gunter, they followed down the abandoned old alleyway until they came upon a hanging sign with a sleeping monkey. Underneath the marquee in lettering almost too worn to read was the phrase, *'Tight lips build ships.'*

Riley removed a key that was hidden in her body armor and opened the massive wooden doors.

The tunnels leading down to the inn were always the worst part of the trip. They were part of an abandoned old mine shaft that had been repurposed by the Gibbons into a backway tunnel. There was a front door of course, however most Gibbons given their secretive nature preferred the tunnels as a quieter option.

The Gibbons, or Jolly Gibbons if you wanted to be technical, was a unique group of Bounty Hunters that only took bounties for the worst of the worst. The men that anyone on the Boondocks would agree were no-goods. Where many bounty hunters were mercenaries only after riches, the Gibbons took pride in their work, not only did they get paid, but also felt a sense of good taking murderers and thieves off the streets.

Jack witnessed a record high seven bugs on his way in when they arrived at two giant wooden doors with 'THE BLACKWATER INN & CANTINA' written in bold red letters on a sign above. Finally, after a long and grueling mission they were home.

"Is your shirt tucked in? Pistol holstered? How's your hair?" Riley said trying to dab off some dirt on Jack's cheek. Look sharp you'll be sharp she liked to tell him.

"I'm fine…." Jack droned, though he knew her worry was logical, didn't want anyone to think the Tripeleafs had lost a step.

"Remember to stand up straight, be cool yet confident, and keep your wits about you."

"I know, I know…." Jack said extremely happy no one was around to see this.

"I can't wait to see Matilda's face when she sees you come through the door with him, she's going to be so proud!!"

"It's not that big of a deal…" Jack droned again, "He's probably not even on the board… This isn't Knox we're talkin about here…"

"Why don't you tell that to the person his next bomb would've blown up? It doesn't matter how big the bounty is, be proud of what you've done and the tidal waves it will send through this city."

Riley's work had earned her a real reputation at the Cantina, men much bigger than her had a habit of scattering when she walked past. Jack often noticed Gibbons attempting to buy her a drink or recalibrate her pistols free of charge, wanting to get on her good side. Some even went as far as offering doubloons for her to stay out of their way. It wasn't always like that of course; it wasn't until a few male members ended up in the alleyway they'd just come from with broken arms and fingers that attitudes quickly changed.

The wooden doors gave way to Hangman's Hall, the sprawling wooden chamber that was *the* place to be if you had any sort of business at all in the Cantina. The space was as lively as ever, with men swinging on the elephant-sized chandeliers, throwing empty bottles of rum at one another seeing who could knock who off first. The vibrant array of swooping lights opposite pinewood walls was somehow just as spectacular as the city lights of Kleppenwitz. Even though the wood inside was hundreds of years old, the smell it gave off was still both pungent and delightful, and the rustic stone pillars along the walls every dozen feet or so looked like they belonged to a castle's tower instead of their current purpose which was acting as the structural foundation of the entire building.

Lining every bit of free space were wood and stone statues of the Gibbon's Emblem, the always wily monkey. Hundreds of them, all a different shape and size were hung along walls, underneath tables, and lining the chandeliers. The biggest of them all, and the only one without full vision, was the one-eyed monkey sitting directly in front of the always lit fireplace that was only a touch smaller than the monkey himself.

"Pardon me… Scuse me… Comin through!" Jack said as ducked, dived and jumped over patrons.

"Ahm!" A simple clear of the throat was all Riley needed to help clear the path.

In the center of the room was a circular maple bar big enough to seat a king *and* his castle. Directly above the bar, was what most people best remembered about the space - the infamous Bounty Board, a golden bronze and fanciful brass clockwork behemoth of a metal slab that held all the names of people that were wanted by the Gibbons, as well last known location, height and weight and other details… and most important how much gold they were worth. When a band wasn't playing, the typewriter-like sounds of the Bounty Board switching letters up and down filled the hall, as all the members dreamed about one day capturing whoever was at the top of the board.

Tonight, hundreds of men and women were singing and dancing along with the nightly band, while others were tucked away in dark corners, scheming and planning out their next mission. Jack was attempting to guide his zombified prisoner through the crowd and trying even harder to get around passed out patrons having a nap on the floor, when he saw a familiar face.

"Jack and Riley Tripleleaf! Thank the heavens you're still in one piece!" the woman said excitedly, like an old friend they hadn't seen in years, "And would ya look there you've even brought us a friend!" she gasped with wide eyes and fingers clenching her nose, "Is that Morty the Skunk???"

"Matilda!" Riley said embracing her with the biggest hug she could manage, "Were you worried about us? Think old Morty had blown us up?"

"The only thing he's blowin up is my nostrils!" Matilda cackled in her deep sing-song voice while slapping her giant hip. If you didn't know her, Matilda might've looked like the most intimidating one there. Of all the cities and isles Jack had visited, he'd never seen a woman so big, big in stature but even bigger in heart.

As a result, the three of them had become fast friends over the years, sharing meals together at the best local dives around the city and her filling them in on all the latest happenings in Kleppenwitz.

Matilda always wore the same type of ruffled black dress along with an oversized black leather belt repurposed from a saddle that she used to tuck in her pistol and cutlass. She wore *running boots* as she called them and put her often gray rarely brown hair in a vice-like series of buns, she didn't want them getting in the way each time she had to carry some unruly patron out through the main doors.

The Jolly Gibbons and the Blackwater Cantina were all she'd ever known, she was raised among these pine walls and dormitories, just like her father before her, Siegfried Baum, who amusingly had his portrait hung right behind them. She'd gotten to know the place like a dog knew fleas and had risen to the top ranks of leadership. Not a single person in the pub could tell her where she could go or what she could do. She was in 'Management'.

"How'd you get him Jack? Snipe'em in the leg then put chains on'em? I was tellin the boys at the bar all about how good you've gotten with that pistol!"

Riley patted his back like the proud mother she was.

"None of'em believed me, said there was no way a boy that age could outshoot them. Then I said OK, put your money where your crusty mouth is rats. We'll test it when he gets back! HA! Somehow right at that moment they all had somewhere else to be..." Matilda looked tickled with herself, "...anyways he put up much of a fight? "

"He was just sleeping, found him holed up in a bar on Isla Mercado one of the satellites smugglers used to use to sell their wares, identified him, threw some chains on his wrists and that was that."

"He's being humble!" Riley said proudly, "He forgot to mention the eight or so booby traps that he had to disable to get to him..."

She turned her head with raised brows and started clapping for Jack, "Riles... Jack very well may be giving us the orders pretty soon... Welp, I imagine the two of you are pretty exhausted then, you'll be happy to know I had Chef Greene whip up some wild Pregorian Beets we just got in, super rare those, first time we've had'em. I tried'em the other night and had no idea sleep could be that good, slept thirteen hours, and felt like I could run a marathon the next day, and with all the weight I got to carry that's sayin somethin!"

After such a particularly long and grueling trip this may have been a better reward than the bounty they were about to receive given what a chef Chef Greene was.

As Matilda continued probing them on all the details of their successful mission, Jack couldn't stop looking at the parrot swooping around the giant room. He'd learned fast to always keep an eye on the sly creature, as he was likely the biggest thief in the hall, always on the lookout for doubloons or jewelry he could quickly swipe up and take back to his hiding spot.

"… Spose you'll want to turn that louse in then…" Matilda said, "JENKINS!!!" she let out a piercing howl, and a frail young man appeared so fast it was as if he was there the whole time, hiding behind a chair or something.

"Mince Jenkins, take this man to the cells, and be quick about it!!"

Jenkins looked over each of them, slowly… as if he was ignoring her. Being a relatively new employee, it was the first time he'd met Jack since he'd been off chasing Morty… And when he did a scowl crossed his face.

"Miss Baum with all due respect, the Blackwater Cantina is no place for a boy! And a deformed one at that!" Jenkins murmured like he was far more important than he was.

Matilda's face was beat red as she puckered up full of air, trying and failing to keep her anger in check, "THAT BOY HAS BEEN TAKING MURDERERS OFF THE STREET WHILE YOU CAN'T EVEN FIGURE OUT HOW TO CLEAN THE LOO!! IF I EVER HEAR SASS LIKE THAT FROM YOU AGAIN YOU'LL BE SHARING A CELL WITH MORTY HERE… IS THAT CLEAR???"

"Yes miss, I-I uhh… was out of line apologies…" the pale and boney assistant said terrified, as he ran away, scared she may pounce.

"Real sorry bout that Jack," Matilda said with a soft voice, "I've had my fair share of assistants," she said watching the young man sulk away strangely, "but Jenkins… can't tell what to make of'em, hope he makes a turn around. Would hate to kick'em out. Not sure he's got anywhere else to go."

Unfortunately for Jack, this was far from the first time he'd heard a comment like that growing up around here, luckily Matilda and Riley wouldn't ever let those comments just slide, so if anything *was* said nowadays it was mostly behind his back.

"So, what'll Morty be then, fifth… sixth successful bounty for ya?" Matilda said, attempting to change the subject and take Jack's mind off the rude comments that were just made about his hand.

"Actually only the third!" he said cheering up a bit.

"Wowww…" Matilda said trying not to yell, yet somehow even when she tried to go quiet, she was still very much the loudest of the three, "You'd better watch out, word'll get around you're a talent, n' these louses will try to split bounties with you. Problem is most times that means you do all the work, and they'll happily keep half the doubloons!"

"A few have already tried!" Jack smirked, "I just told them they'd have to run it by Riley first, funnily enough, they stopped asking after that!"

"You may not have her blood, but you sure did get Riley's brains! Give a few years and your sash'll be darker than mine!" Matilda howled.

Riley and Matilda took to discussing which decorations they would use for the Concord this year, and if history was any indicator, they'd be chatting for some time. Jack decided now was a perfect time to mosey around Hangman's Hall and catch the latest, one of his favorite pastimes.

He spoke to some picaroons by the bar, they were outsiders here, but it wasn't uncommon for non-Gibbons to be in the hall at least. They were from the neighboring Isle of Vista and had been working with some members on tracking down a fugitive, thought to be hiding somewhere on the Boondocks.

After spectating two men with hooks for hands attempt to arm-wrestle he watched the band on the oversized stage and all the people on the dance floor circling rhythmically to their harmonies. The band had more fiddles than members and were wearing matching top hats which when combined with their skilled playing put most of the audience into a delightful trance.

For a while he watched Plunders the Parrot circle around the whole cantina with a gold necklace in his beak, eventually landing high up on one of Hangmans Hall's giant rafters to store away his misbegotten goods. Patrons consistently tried to swat him down with brooms, swords, and on more than a few occasions, pistol fire, but the bird was as cunning as he was agile. The shots taken were all so far off, the shooters were humiliated, and even if they did eventually manage to corner the bird, he'd bore out enough small holes in the roof he'd make his escape, and come back inside the next day, with his head high and feathers sprawled out as if he was taunting them. The only real solution was to keep your valuables hidden while in Hangman's Hall.

It was still a matter of hot contention on just who exactly trained the bird to steal valuables so they could later go climb up and collect them from the ceiling rafters. The bird was so old though, whoever had done it, could very well have been outlived by his mischievous parrot.

As Jack got towards the back of the hall, by the old wooden booths just barely lit by candles, Gibbons were so gabby and loud Jack could hear them over the band. He heard one man talking about seeing a woman at the Flagpoles so beautiful she could've brought the Mercurial back, and another man he'd met a few times known as Willow Turtleby bragging about how many names he'd 'taken down' from the Bounty Board.

Next he happened upon a few of the men that'd helped him and Riley trace and pinpoint Morty's last known location and was thanking them when he overheard a very interesting conversation coming from the table next to him.

Sitting there was a plump man with fire orange hair and more freckles than skin with stubby feet that didn't touch the ground from his chair. Like many in the Cantina, he wore a tricorne hat with a silver one-eyed monkey stitched into the front. The hat, along with his burgundy sash and silver pistol on his hip were the only parts of him that weren't covered in filth. He was speaking to a crew of other ruffians with arms flailing wildly and eyes like planets,

"He's as mad as a Caldorian Warlord that one," he said with a crotchety voice, "To steal from King Magnus, as unhinged as he is, then somehow manage to keep his head on, *then* have the stones to go and steal from the one man who could contend with Magnus's rapidness. Cept fer Knox ain't busy trying to take over a whole country, he's got all the time in the world to look for'em."

The small crowd gathered around the man's table was hanging on his every word when another man added,

"Word I got was some of the lads saw him asleep in an alleyway on the north end above the big monk, somehow he could manage stealing from Magnus and Knox but couldn't manage to find his bed!"

The table erupted with laughter as another man asked,

"You think he's hidin out on the Boondocks then, stowin away on Kleppenwitz?"

"Aye, that's the word," the red headed man said, "Wanted to get as far away from the Forzians as possible, an there's no better place than the Boondocks for that!"

The man took a big gulp of ale and cleared his throat,

"If you lot mean to keep your heads on, I'd steer clear of any gangly, pale, and boney men with blisters adornin their faces. There's good reason why he's been on top of that board so long… He ain't the type to sit back and let a Mercenary take from him… he'll be here, and be here fast. Nuthin I'm more certain of…"

Jack tried to lean in and hear the rest of what the men were talking about, but it was no use, they'd splintered off and were whispering now. He wasn't sure what to make of it, but it sounded horrible, he was eager to hear what Riley and Matilda would think when he told them in the morning.

It was past midnight when Jack finally got back to his room. It wasn't a Forzian Palace, but it was quiet and cozy, a comfortable respite away from the craziness of Hangman's Hall downstairs. His goose feather bed never felt so good after the week he'd just been through. The aches and pains of being cramped up in a tiny old sailboat and dodging lead swooping past his head gracefully faded into his mattress. Jack stared at the fat sack of doubloons he'd just earned and excitedly pondered the possibilities. Of course he offered to let Riley keep whatever portion she saw fit, but she always enthusiastically refused, she would accept nothing less than a fifty-fifty split. Maybe he'd go down to the market tomorrow and buy a new cutlass that could hold an edge, or if he was smart, he'd take it to the local bank to start saving up for a ship of his own one day.

In a trance he watched all the candles in his cozy wooden dorm flicker with the draft from the open window. The lights danced along with familiar sounds of horses clocking on cobblestone and drunken scoundrels yelling unintelligibly from the city below as it lulled him into a deep slumber.

He was fast asleep until a shattering noise from outside that sounded like an explosion jolted him upright. For a few minutes he sat up with a sweat-covered brow, waiting for something more, and peeking out his window, but saw nothing. Gibbons must've been holding another late-night shooting competition outside in the alleyway again he figured. It wasn't long until Jack was again comfortable and cozy, fast asleep, dreaming of what wonders the Flagpole Market may bring tomorrow.

Chapter 3

A Shake in the Night

When Jack awoke the next morning he felt his leg tremble, which usually meant a storm was brewing.

His leg was in decent shape now, but when he was younger, he was close to a cripple. For years he stayed inside the Cantina and saw other kids go play tag or swim in the canals while all he could do was stand by and watch. It broke Riley's heart to see him like that, so much so she'd blown through most of her savings, probably enough to buy a new ship on paying gypsies from all over to heal his leg. The gypsies weren't cheap, but that was because they were effective. A mound of different balms, preserves, elixirs, and potions had left his leg purple and burned, but eventually, after a period of years he was running almost as fast as the other kids his age.

Never quite able to shake the guilt off, for how much he'd cost Riley, and how much she'd given up just so her boy could live a normal life, he wanted nothing more than to fix the damage caused. Deep down he knew it was a farce, naïve even, but the rumors he'd heard last night had him thinking, maybe taking down the infamous man from the top of the Bounty Board was one way of paying her back.

The blackened and charred right hand was an entirely different matter, however. Unlike his leg, it was much harder to hide. No amount of potions or elixirs could do anything to bring back his real skin color, not from even the most renown healers. And what made it worse, it looked eerily similar to a particularly infectious and deadly disease that had been in the Pinwheel Islands for a millennia known as the Black Molder. No matter how many times he told people it wasn't infectious, and the hand had been like that since childhood, most folks weren't willing to take the chance. On the rare occasion when he forgot his gloves at home, he felt like the lowest form of low, at best he'd been yelled at and spit on, and at the worst a man near the Flagpoles once swung a sword at him, nearly taking out his eye, for the crime of walking beside him.

Jack walked down the long winding and cavernous staircase back to Hangman's Hall. It was a completely different scene now compared to last night, the clinking of forks from breakfast tables and light chatter felt normal and somehow peaceful in a place that was anything but. If not for the four of five men still passed out in the back booths it could've almost passed for a regular dining hall on Kleppenwitz. The wood walls, wood ceilings, wood chairs, and wood almost everything else gave off such a magnificent smell and gave Jack a happy start every time he was lucky enough to notice it. Matilda liked to brag about it, about how her family was a crucial part of Hangman's Hall's construction, how they slaved for years over picking the perfect blend of one-hundred and three different types of wood from all over the Boondocks, and not just a random assortment, according to her they discovered a powerful blend of pleasant aroma and staying power to create the perfect 'wooden' smell that would last for centuries. Matilda had been known to embellish a story or two but given how amazing the hall still smelt, Jack was sure this wasn't one of those times.

On the way down the stairs, he passed the dark-haired and even darker clad Jenkins decked out in leather scrubs and busy sweeping up after someone who had lost their lunch the night before. The young man would barely look his way either due to embarrassment, or fear that Matilda would have him clean the chamber pots today if he had another outburst.

"Really sorry about how things went down yesterday Jenkins, maybe we got off on the wrong foot?" Jack said sincerely as he approached him. "Name's Jack Tripleleaf, grew up in these halls and dormitories, so I know the place pretty well if you ever need assistance. Though it's so ancient there's still plenty even I haven't figured out yet!"

Jenkins just stared back at him blankly.

"Matilda can get a little heated sometimes, but she means well, she'll set you up here really nicely if you're willing to do some grunt work for a few years…"

"I didn't ask for any advice from you." he said back coldly.

Taken aback by his unexpected snark he replied, "I only meant to help?" now with a morsel of fire in his voice.

"You could help by leaving me be! Some of us have to earn our sash instead of being coddled our whole lives. Some of us have to actually go through our trials instead of being born into the place!"

"You saw me take Morty the Skunk in, what more proof do you want?!"

"I saw you bring Morty through the doors in chains. Whether you were the one to put them on is a different matter entirely. You know I'm not the only one around here who thinks a bright sashed boy doesn't belong here right?!

"Let me guess, you and Lucas Geist? Am I missing anyone?"

"Hmph! Lucas Geist is the finest bounty hunter the Gibbons have ever seen, just be happy he even knows you exist!"

"Did Lucas tell you that?!" Jack said, unable to hold back a smile.

Jenkins exhaled angrily and took a step toward Jack trying to intimidate, but when he noticed Jack wasn't even close to backing down, he turned around and stormed off gangling like a windblown young maple as he moved.

How strange. He'd only just met him and already he was this upset. It wasn't something he'd dwell on however, he would find out eventually who or what led him to this strange gripe, emotions that strong were a difficult thing to keep hidden.

After putting away all the supplies Jenkins left behind he leisurely strolled along Hangman's Hall and took a trip down memory lane when he noticed the rickety old table where Riley first reluctantly taught him how to reload a pistol, just behind that he could see the loose wall planks that when he was a tyke his hand was small enough to fit inside and stash the rare candies Riley had forbidden, as he got to the bar in tiny handwriting he spotted his initials and remembered how bad of a scolding Matilda had given him for carving it up when he was seven or eight. He then learned precisely why anyone with their marbles preferred to be on her good side. Every dusty chandelier, wobbly old wooden table, or worn bronzed fireplace of the room had a bump, scratch, or carving along with a wild story to back it up, Jack felt like he could keep at this all day if he wanted.

Finally, he gazed up and looked over the Bounty Board, clicking and clocking away in all its massive glory. The wanted's names went up and down day and night, the clockwork feat of engineering was the size of a small ship and never took a break, always ticking just like a clock of similar make. Names shifted up and down without warning with their black wax lettering, but there was one name that didn't move. The only name that had never moved, at least that Jack could remember, was the one at the very top of the list.

Gazing up at it like he did most mornings, his eyes fixated on the reward. It was ten thousand golden doubloons. Just the thought of that much money made his mouth hang open. It'd be enough to retire. Enough for him and anyone else who wanted to live on some immaculate Vistan Beach and spend the rest of his days surfing its famously long waves or lounging beachside drinking out of a pineapple. Enough money to buy a top-of-the-line ship and circle the cursed waters of Allora. Enough to try out whatever amazing new idea came to his head.

The name at the top of the list printed in a haunting bold lettering was Carneld Knox. The smuggler 'Born anew between cursed Alloran Meadows', a man so cruel he had to blackmail or enslave his hirelings because no other criminal on the isle was dumb enough to go near him. Matilda once told him the tale of the Firing Five as the newspapers nicknamed them, titled so because they had a renowned bounty hunter from every one of the world's five inhabited island countries. They decided one day that with their skills Knox's bounty was all but assured. Searched every satellite island off Otto expecting to find fame and fortune when they brought him in. It wasn't until a year had passed that Matilda had to admit to herself what she knew to be the truth, that Knox found the Firing Five before they found him. No one had seen or heard from them since.

After that most folks at the Cantina had given up, figured this job was impossible and wasn't worth the effort. He was said to have some sort of ancient Mercurial Power that most wouldn't risk fighting for all the pearls in the Sober Sea. Maybe it was naivety, perhaps it was foolishness, but Knox never struck fear into Jack's heart the way he did to most. There were things that made him nervous, but not bounties. Riley told him this would change the minute he took a lead shot to the chest, but for now he remained as confident as ever.

Many people had doubts, of course, about the veracity of Knox and his Mercurial Powers. But somehow those same people never dared to take on the bounty, not after the stories they'd heard.

The Mercurial hadn't been around in Jack's lifetime, though they may as well have been with the amount folks around the Five Islands talked about them. Entire professions had been created for the sole purpose of tracking them down or finding any information on why they disappeared so suddenly and with no warning. In the end, they were no closer to finding answers now than when they started. Most just figured they'd smartened up and abandoned them, that a group of people so perfect could never truly coexist with a race as flawed as humans, despite many years of trying.

Jack looked toward the double doors exit and made his way. He was always more of a morning person and consequently felt excited about the start of a new day, especially for the rare opportunity when he had extra doubloons in his pocket.

Just as he reached the exit, he noticed Matilda and Riley having breakfast in a darkened side booth with another Gibbon, Willow Turtleby. Jack sat down beside them and attempted to exchange morning pleasantries until he noticed terrified looks on each of their faces.

"Happened in the middle of the night, before anyone knew what was goin on men was fallin down dead as daggers…" Willow said shakily.

Lazy-eyed Turtleby looked like he'd just been in the middle of a hurricane, he was bruised and bloodied, and his usual confident demeanor was now shaken and skittish, even the gold he had on every other tooth looked demure.

"We was just goin for an evenin stroll in one of the alleyways not far from the back entrance, takin in the moon and stars, tryin to figure which one of us was smart enough to remember their names… wh-when some explosion happens knocks me clear off my feet… I look up with blurry eyes and ears ringin and saw just about the last person I'd be wantin to have a midnight tussle with. I knew who it was immediately, with them popped boils oozing down his face and those horrible eyes… It was Ca-Carneld Knox and his men, and that horrible overgrown wolf… recognized the crew by our sashes… said he was coming after us bounty hunters…"

The look of fear around the table was palpable.

"Like'd to see'em try and take the Cantina," Matilda said enraged, "We'd have one heck'ofa sursy waitin on'em! This may be the most fortified place on this isle or the next, no one's ever gotten through our tunnels, and if they did, they'd have a few hundred pistols to deal with after!"

"He's not that dumb." Willow said cautiously, "But what he does got is time and a lunatic's rage, he'll wait us out till he can pick us off one by one. Someone in the Boondocks made him so mad his face looked like it'd been dipped into the sun itself."

28

"I'll kill the rat!" Matilda said with embers in her eyes.

"Can't be killed, not by the likes of us mere mortals at least. He's Mercurial… a Ghost." Willow said back matter-of-factly, "I know what my plan is, did a few favors for the guys down at the docks a while back, gonna sneak onto a cargo ship headed for Vista. Hear they got a few hunters there hidin out, still somehow able to dodge the Freeboots tryin to send them to war. Won't be like Kleppenwitz course, ain't much is, but it sure beats dyin a slow death to some psychotic Mercurial."

"No one's seen a Mercurial in a hundred years, you don't honestly believe that rubbish do you?" Jack said louder than he meant.

"If youdda caught me yesterday I'd be on your side of the table," he said with wide eyes, like he was much wiser than he was, "But I ain't on your side of the table anymore, cause I saw it with mine own eyes! Was always skeptical bout the stories of him goin under the storm, to that cursed rock Allora. And then hearin he was the first one to return with heart still beatin, practically a god to boot. Hogwash I thought, some jab nonnas tell their young'ens to get'em to sleep at night. 'Go to your bed or Knox will come for you!' But what I saw that man do last night… it ain't no tall-tale" Willow gave a drawn-out sigh.

"Well go on man! Don't leave us hangin!" Matilda shouted.

"Saw poor Crowfeet get a jump on Knox with those lanky arms o'his. While his back was turned, Crowfeet was hidin behind a boulder that'd been upheaved minutes before by the bombs, any other man they'd soon be pushin daisies with him in such a prime spot, he stabbed Knox right in the center of his back. A thrust like that could've pierced a ship's hull. Clean as ya like. But Crowfeet's blade… it… it snapped right in two as it hit. Knox didn't budge. Not even a muscle. Looked like he'd need one of his men to tell him it even happened…." Willow said in a scared whisper, "Needless to say Crowfeet didn't last long after…."

"You sure it wasn't body armor? I've heard of Pregorian Steel Armors snapping swords before." Riley said.

"He wasn't wearing any, just a cotton shirt and a long black cloak. Guess when you've got stone skin you don't need no body armor."

29

Jack had never seen a man so pale faced before, and watched as Willow chugged any bit of liquid he could get his hands on, though it didn't seem to help the sweat that was dripping out of every pore on his body.

"And just what were you doin the whole time?" Matilda said narrowing her brow.

"That hulk of a Grey Wolf had me pinned durin the whole thing, sittin on top of me like I was his chew toy, slobberin like I was a juicy steak. Tried to get a shot off but it just grabbed the pistol and bit it in two. You imagine that? An animal breaking wood and steel with just its bite!" he paused to try and regain composure, "I grew up in the north not far from Dunkel, Grey Wolves used to take people all the time, just for the fun of it. Never went out in the forest with less than four men clasped with the biggest rifles our village could afford cause'a them. Nasty animals the whole lot, feral to their bones. I know that cause a few folks was foolish enough to try'n capture'em then train'em... but they just turn up a few days later with a missing appendage or worse! This wolf in particular though... he was different... only answered to Knox... he was obedient... like some kinda farm animal." he started his whisper again, "Obedient like he didn't have a single thought of his own in that wild brain of his, like Knox had replaced its brain with his own! Turns out there is one man out there that can tame the beasts, well... if you consider a Mercurial a man that is."

Matilda was still on fire while Riley remained composed, looking through the man inquisitively.

"A man that can move like lightning, with steel skin, and has that kinda hold over wild animals..." Willow paused to catch a breath then continued, "... doubt it if you like... but that's the definition of'a Mercurial... and the only Mercurial anyone's ever heard of who kills for the thrill of it. Not much on these islands scarier than a living breathing god that's gone mad." Willow shuddered, "If I was you... I'd be looking for ways off this island sooner rather than later."

It was a lot to take in. They were all used to being the ones hunting the bad men, not the bad men hunting them.

"Welp, I best be off, got a date with a galleon to get as far away from here as I can."

"Wait!" Riley commanded stopping Willow in his tracks, "One last question… how did you escape? Why would he not just kill you too??"

Willow inhaled anxiously, like he was hoping to get away without having to answer this one question in particular,

"He fr-freed me… I-I couldn't believe it myself. I'd already made peace with my maker and said my goodbyes, well in my head I did at least. Sa-said to tell the others. Said to tell the others… he'd be killin every thief, smuggler, and bounty hunter one by one till he found the man who stole from him…"

"And who stole from him?" she said carefully.

"Not a Gibbon… scoundrel type, a picaroon I hear. Heard so many drunken cadet's tales about him thought he was made up. Someone even told me he killed a Caldorian Worm that had swallowed one of his marks, then pulled the man from the worm's stomach with his bare hands. Never believed it until now…" Willow Turtleby paused and sunk his head, "Man goes by the name Radish."

Chapter 4

Boondock Flatfoot

Detective Konrad walked out of the moss-covered alleyway onto the chaotic streets of Kleppenwitz. A few men dashed into the crowd trying to hide when they saw him, it was a regular occurrence for him. *More of the criminal infestation plaguing my fine city* he thought, he could spot them by the way they dressed, though most times he felt he could tell just by the way men carried themselves. Just the sight of them drove him mad, but for now he'd have to ignore it. There were more important matters to attend to today.

It was a nice day out, the first he'd been able to enjoy in weeks as it had been a shy spring. In his eyes the perfect weather for investigating a murder scene.

The detective's face looked like it meant business without ever having to move it. His clothes were immaculate without a single wrinkle; he had a pointy nose and a flat top soldier's haircut that complemented his well-groomed appearance. He was dressed in typical police attire on Otto with baggy wool pants, a cotton undershirt, and standard issue steel-rung black chainmail over his chest and shoulders, and he had his golden seven-pointed badge pinned over the heart of his wool black overcoat with the lettering 'KONRAD' in black ink underneath the star.

He noticed a crusty old beggar passed out on the street near the crime scene with a stained and smelly sack by his side, he tried his best to ignore it as he had somewhere to be, but the man was being so flagrant and out in the open about his vagrancy, he couldn't help himself. *I'll have to make this quick.*

"You there! Wake up!!" he kicked the sleeping man hard in the stomach and as he did the man let out a guttural cough as bits of spittle and blood launched from his lips, "Loitering isn't permitted here, pick up your things and go to whatever shanty you call a home or you'll be sleeping in jail tonight!"

The beggar winced in pain, "I wasn't sleeping, just meditating…" he was somehow able to groan out words through the pain, "You never heard of it mate?" he said sarcastically as he dug at his eyepatch awkwardly... it always itched.

"I've seen a million men like you. Polluting our streets, scamming the good people of this city into giving you their hard-earned money, while you lounge around doing nothing all day… Not on my watch! Just another drunk looking for handouts."

"Not drunk... feel fine sir… just so happy to see fine men like yourself keeping us so safe." he proceeded to hiccup and fell over as he tried to get to his feet.

Grabbing his shoulder he forcefully pulled him up, "Maybe you can try being smart with your new friends at the Stalhaus Prison… to your feet!"

"Wait wait wait!" he said slurring, "Gonna need to see some identification first mate. How do I know you're not some weirdo trying

33

to kidnap me back to his personal dungeon?" the beggar said as he tapped him on the shoulder sloppily. "You certainly look the part mate..."

Infuriated the detective ripped the badge from his overcoat and gave it to the man.

"Ahhh Detective Konrad... got a nice ring to it. My old plumber was a Konrad..." the beggar said, he had a way of snapping his fingers when he spoke, as if they were drumbeats for his sporadic manner of speech.

"Enough talking scum... Let's go!" Konrad said violently, shoving him up against the wall with a thud.

The vagrant did a very good job of looking like his back was broken, "Wait! If you're gonna take me to jail for being drunk what about the six men across the street somehow drunker than I am. Prolly couldn't even tell what island we're on." he pointed directly behind Konrad.

Right as Konrad looked back the beggar slipped something into his pocket and pulled something else out.

"There's no one there!"

"Course there isn't! Must've gone. Sorry mate you know how sneaky those drunks are... Oh and here's your badge back..." the vagrant said as his eyes flickered up and down like silent waves in the ocean.

Detective Konrad snatched it back as he looked annoyed enough to kill the vagrant long before they ever got to any jail.

"One last thing... musta been the rum... I sorta forgot to mention I was mugged earlier, it's why I was laying there all sad like, wasn't sure if you'd understand after breaking one of my ribs n' all... I know I shouldn't loiter about on your lovely streets, but surely a mugger takes higher priority."

"You lie... Just like all the other punks before I put them away!" Detective Konrad said coldly, "You're not about to talk your way out of this one."

"Your police friends they saw the whole thing, even went after him down that street, they'll confirm it I'm sure..."

"Really?!" Konrad said smugly as if he'd just caught him in a trap. "Then what were the officer's names?"

"Let's see... it was Nuster, and Schmidt, and Speck was the short round one looked like he never missed a meal. Wouldn't bet on him bein the one catching the perp... eh cap?!" the man laughed to himself as he gave the detective an elbow nudge.

In sheer disbelief he looked him up and down, these were the exact names of the new police officers he was supposed to meet today.

"Tell me... What's your name?"

"Friends call me Radish, but if you let me go you can call me Daisy if ya fancy..."

"Listen Radish..." he said with suspicion like he'd heard the name somewhere before, "You may have just caught the luckiest break of your life... if I ever catch you sleeping out here again, you'll do worse than jail, that clear??

"Kristal Sir!"

"And take a bath sir, you smell like a goat!"

Konrad finally removed his vice-like grip from Radish and rushed in the direction he pointed him to earlier.

"Oh, and detective!! Thanks for protecting and serving!!" Radish yelled with a smile that looked anything but genuine. As he was a half block away Konrad looked back and shook his head with confusion as he continued chasing.

Radish pulled the shiny new badge out of his pocket he'd just acquired and admired it. He then began rummaging around in his sack, moving around several trinkets and hand-written letters, careful to avoid the golden ones. Finally, he pulled a black wool overcoat out of the stinky old bag and put it on along with the stolen badge over top of it.

The very real pain he was feeling from almost having his rib kicked in was somehow overshadowed by the sense of victory he felt as he posted himself against a greystone cottage and watched what looked like a swordfish hunting down a baby redfish through the nearby canal.

Something about the man he'd just duped reminded him of the Rogue, the man Radish had worked with all those years ago. Maybe it was Konrad's intimidating stature or perhaps it was his self-confidence, he couldn't be sure. Though unlike Konrad, the Rogue's self-confidence was anything but misplaced. Not in a million years would that trick he just pulled have worked on him. It was said bounty hunters and criminals alike had a holiday dedicated to the day that the Rogue left Otto to pursue politics on Vista. The criminals celebrated because the Rogue put them all out of business, and the bounty hunters celebrated because by the time he was done... there were no bounties left.

The buildings of Kleppenwitz looked completely different during the day when sunshine lit them up, while the most common structure was a white cottage with reinforcing wood boards lining the exterior, every one of them was interesting, because every one of them was different.

Whether it was the colorful plants lining the windowsills or sprouting trees in the front gardens hiding vine covered walls, or the red tiled roof versus the salted black variety, some flat, some as steep and winding as a treacherous mountain path. Porches were common and in various states of slump, and bronze ornaments lined roofs and gardens depicting symbology meant to ward off evil spirits. Many even had a smoking brick chimney and most were worn down to almost rubble from the fatigue of smoke and sea salt.

With the sun out in full force and not a cloud in the sky, very few people remained inside. The city was alive, even more so than normal, businesspeople with their cravats walked through the crowds with a purpose, like they were all simultaneously late for something, while vacationers could be easily spotted looking around awkwardly blocking the flow of foot traffic as they searched for wherever it was they were supposed to be going.

Radish made the short walk over to the alleyway that had been roped off where the investigation was taking place, and saw officers Nuster, Schmidt, and Speck searching the scene for evidence. Nuster and Schmidt were preoccupied with the crime scene examining particles and leftover scraps of clothing, while Speck was preoccupied with the snack he was having.

Radish whistled an old cadet's jingle completely out of tune and strode towards the scene like he didn't have a care in the world. Speck spotted Radish and his eyes jumped wide.

"Detective Konrad! It's really you, heard so much about you sir." Speck said eagerly as he wiped some crumbs off his shirt, "We all heard they was sending you and feel much better knowing you're helping. Can I get you anything? A cold towel maybe? There's a store nearby that's got a pot of coffee sposed to be illegal soon it's so good, one sip'll have ya jumpin out of yur skin for hours then crash so hard you can't even stand."

"As a man of the law I'd expect you to be avoiding things that could be illegal soon!" Radish said sounding very angry, but after a few moments had to bite his lip.

"I... Uh... uh... C-course sir! Just thought it'd help is all..."

The other two policemen rushed over to greet him as Radish looked over them with hands crossed behind his back and squinted eyes, like he was judging them and didn't like what he saw.

"Officer Schmidt here sir! So nice to finally meet you," he said with googly eyes, Schmidt could've been mistaken for a broom and had long strands of hair so thin most people wondered why he still kept it, "I heard about how you caught those alpaca thieves using just your nose... I just gotta say sir, I think I speak for all of us when I say you're an inspiration to the force..."

"Quiet!!" Radish barked as the officers instinctively stood at attention beside him.

He examined the men trying his hardest to be intimidating as he looked each of them up and down.

"You there! What's your name?"

"Officer Nuster sir!" Nuster had a nose like a Dutch Monkey and teeth that would make a claustrophobic wince.

"And you? What's your report?" Radish pointed at Speck who was shaking slightly, amusing Radish.

"Sir! Bodies are gone now, but we looked them over before the medics brought them out, the armor was bounty hunters alright. Looks like they're having some sort of turf war or something." he chuckled slightly as if this was of no importance, "Seems like a pretty open and shut case, I assume orders from above still stand, don't get involved helping any bounty hunters?" Speck continued laughing as blabbering out words seemed to help his nerves, "Seems to me we can just cleanup and leave, no one's gonna cry about this lot gone missing."

The thief was momentarily offended but remembered who he was supposed to be and continued. He pointed at Nuster,

"And what's your take? You catch a strong scent or something?"

"What's that sposed to mean?!" Nuster sputtered out clearly offended.

Speck feeling confident decided now was a good time to speak his mind, "Say sir, I don't mean nothin by this but I always heard you was a younger man, you've got grey in your hair sir?"

Radish's knees buckled for a moment surprised, as he regained composure, he angrily grabbed him by the collar "Are you questioning your superior??"

"No sir, just not what I had heard is all!"

"Hunting down thieves for a living and..." he stumbled, "... Chasing down... uhhh... Alpacas can age a man. Just look at Detective Abdullah."

"Whose Detective Abdullah?" Schmidt quietly whispered to Officer Nuster.

"No clue...?" Nuster responded confused.

"If you plan to keep your job, you'd do well to remember your place." Radish said inches away from Speck's face, "Now! The three of you keep looking for evidence, we better be sure everyone involved was some no-good bounty hunter!"

The men did as they were told and scurried off to different corners, while Radish was relieved he could finally take a look for himself.

The random bits of cloth spattered about, and blood-trails looked gruesome yet deliberate, the hallmark of a professional's work. There was a massive crater in the center of the cobblestone street from what was obviously some sort of bomb, and bullet holes in the surrounding greystone alley walls from misplaced pistol shots.

Radish spotted something and bent down to take a look, he had his suspicions, but this all but confirmed it. He stared at the broken ground in front of him and noticed a handful of some sort of animal fur. Picking it up he gave it a lick like it was some sort of candy. *Grey Wolf…* he whispered to himself with a furrowed brow.

Carriages rumbled and merchants shouted out names of their wares, as the hustle of the thousands of people in the vicinity made the noises the city was famous for. A few vacationers were at the rope on either side of the alleyway rubbernecking and trying their best to figure out what'd transpired, though something about the way Nuster was shooing them off had an incredible effect.

"Konrad Sir!" it was Speck again, Radish looked up at him like he was very annoyed, "This case… standard operating procedure I presume?"

"Yes of course!" he responded without looking up from the cobblestone he was examining.

Speck just stared at who he thought was a detective awkwardly for some time.

"I know you fancy me but are you just going to stare at me all day?!"

"Sir standard operating procedure says we need a course of action from the detective, code one through thirty sir… what'll it be?" Speck said hesitantly.

"Uhhh… erm..." Radish's face was awkward like he'd just eaten something extremely sour, "Right of course… this case…. ahh… definitely a ten. Yup ten through and through with this lot…"

"A ten sir? You want me to call pest control? I don't understand. There's no bugs…"

"You thought I said ten? Need to have your ears checked mate, I clearly said this was ahhh… uhhh… thirteen?" Radish said the number with a high-pitched voice like he was asking a question where he didn't know the answer.

"Thirteen sir?" Speck was bewildered, "You want me to call a plumber sir? There's still room for cleanup, but not what a plumbers used to handling…"

"You know what, fine young aspiring detective like yourself. I want you to pick on this one… I trust you'll make the right call. You've got the brains of an ox!" Radish winked and put his hands on both the man's shoulders like he trusted him.

"An ox sir??"

"Yes of course! An ox! Now, run along… much still left for the detector to detect…"

Speck ran back to the other two men never having been so confused.

Radish continued looking over the scene, pacing back and forth using his right hand to itch his long unkempt speckled hair. He looked over at the officers who were now grouped up conversing with one another and looking over at him suspiciously.

As he was glancing back at them trying to keep up the charade, he stubbed his toe on a pear sized rock that had most likely gotten lodged into the ground in the explosion. Given the contrasting stories they heard, the officer's mouths were wide open when they saw Radish on the ground holding his toe and screaming expletives incessantly.

Eventually, after realizing his face was red hot because of an inanimate object, he composed himself. And what he saw underneath the now unearthed rock flabbergasted him. There were hundreds of little orange crystals coating the rock, each a bit larger than a grain of sand.

Isn't that something? he said as he held a bunch in his hand, he recognized it from a very peculiar location not far from where he was now.

Right as the pain in his foot had begun to fade, he heard an ear-shattering yell. Just behind the officers, was a man with a flat-top military haircut and a face that was the same shade of red as Radish's was only moments before. He was running towards Radish, arms flailing wildly, like his life depended on it.

"RADISH!!!!!!" Detective Konrad screamed, looking like he may pop a blood vessel.

"My time to go then!" Radish said looking at him in the distance and giving half a little wave, he quickly darted off towards the opposite side of the alley where hundreds of city folks still lined the streets. Radish nabbed some unlucky passerby's cocked hat, and he was off. He couldn't help but chuckle after he got a few hundred yards away and saw Konrad and his motley crew of officers shoving people out of the way going in the complete opposite direction.

Now all that was left to do for today was to get back to the hideout, to Kersey and his new friend. Maybe by now she'd have something to say.

Chapter 5

<u>A Dream of Jack</u>

Riley Tripleleaf slept that night better than she had in years, which was ironic given she'd just found out one of the deadliest men in the Five Isles was coming after anyone who shared her job title.

She dreamt of her younger life, distant memories of exploring the hidden deserts of Caldo and Kristal mines of Prego with her old crew, she dreamt of Knox and the horrors he may bring. But mostly she dreamt of Jack, and the day she had found him. Chained to a hollow tree all alone with his little burnt hand and mangled leg, on death's door with bones clearly visible through skin, and buzzards patiently waiting beside him to finish the job.

Her once captain Amal Stout looked at her looking at the child and could see her pain, he felt it too,

"On Forza, they leave'em like this if they're deemed too weak. One of their weird codes… Poor kid musta been born a cripple or something." he grumbled, "You'd think it gets easier after seeing them like this a few times… it doesn't."

Amal's upbringing in the harsh deserts of Caldo had hardened his skin and made his mannerisms short. He was a massive man with bulging muscles, and a quiet confidence that naturally garnered respect, and made him an easy choice for the leader of their crew the Gallowsmen.

The mission had been a success, the team had been hired by the Forzian Council to find an escaped slave. It seemed they wanted to make an example of him to the others, and as a result were willing to pay handsomely for his return. The slave had built a clever little cottage that blended into the earth, but in the end it didn't matter. He had chains on now, and in a few hours he would most likely be breaking his back in the Kristal mines, that was if they decided to go easy on him.

Their appointment had taken them to a mountainous desert-like environment, that was so hot it made drinking water every few minutes a necessity. There were random patches of grass and shrubbery, and odd trees with trunk-sized branches going in every direction that seemed to not just survive in this harsh environment but thrive.

Riley had been the one to find him. She noticed animal carcasses nearby that had been picked clean, too clean for any animal, they always left at least something behind. She figured there had to be a stowaway close, and much to the chagrin of her crewmates she was correct.

Five of them in total, six if you included the slave, were at water's edge almost back to the ship when Riley looked back at the dying boy.

"Captain, I don't feel comfortable just leaving him out here!" she pleaded, "Surely there's something we can do!"

Seeing that boy abandoned much the same way she was made it feel like her chest was going to cave in. The tyke couldn't have been more than five or six, laying there semi-conscious, heaving, desperately trying to draw air.

"Don't think the Forzians that hired us would take too kindly to saving a boy they meant to kill…"

"There's reason we're the Gallowsmen and not the Gallowswomen." one of the short, pudgy crew members chortled, "Told ya she wasn't cut out for Forza cap, too sweet for a world like this. Thinks every helpless creature she sees is some cuddly little dog."

"Throw your pistol to the ground and I'll show you how sweet I really am…" Riley said without skipping a beat, "Captain you can take my cut, but the boy is coming with us."

Itching his chin he thought about the proposition.

"Your cut we'll split amongst the crew… After we turn in the prisoner. We can come back for him after the ship gets repairs and supplies in The Seven Cities."

"He won't last that long sir…" Riley said hopelessly, "he needs water now or he'll die!!"

Amal looked disappointed but knew the rest of the crew would never forgive him if he didn't stick to his guns,

"Listen Riley, I realize it's tough, but this is what you signed on for. This is what we all signed up for. I don't like it either but remember none of us ever started this to save the world. And we didn't start this to save some random kid fate decided to chew up and spit out." his deep voice attempted the best it could to sound understanding as he put a hand on her shoulder, "I mean, for all we know he's too far gone already, and there's nothin we coulda done."

He wasn't used to seeing her like this, prior to today she'd been the absolute pillar of his crew, quiet, kept to herself, but tough as nails, with a laser-like focus he knew was irreplaceable. He'd grown to become quite fond of her over their time together, even admire her as tough as that was for a man like him. Which is why when he expressed his sorry, it was obvious he meant it.

It wasn't until he felt something cold pressed against his temple that his sympathy faded.

Riley stared coldly at the three other crewman who had their pistols and rifles pointed at her head, while she kept hers pointed squarely at Amal's.

"Looks like we've got a standoff…" she spoke calmy.

"Gonna be so much fun killin miss know-it-all! Reckon you didn't know enough to not take a four verse one fight though… heh-heh" yelled the short one who insulted her earlier.

"Considering we're in a desert with no civilization for a hundred miles, and the only ones bright enough to captain a ship for more than a hundred miles is me and the man I've got a gun pointed at… Doesn't seem like the best idea…" she pressed her gun deep into Amal's chest as she carefully hid her body behind his. She pointed at the short one, "Go uncuff the boy and bring him to the ship, you act weird or make any sudden movements I'll make this wasteland your grave."

The man was furious, but he wasn't dumb enough to try and cross her with the leverage she had. Not that he'd have a clean shot if he tried.

As she got towards the ship with Amal still at gunpoint, she looked at the slave they'd originally been hired to find. He was elderly with stringy grey hair and a piercing set of different colored eyes, one sky-blue and the other a glowing purple. He looked meek; the kind of frail that scavenging tended to cause. He would have one more shot at a meaningful life at least. With her free hand she gently opened his chains and he sprang to life.

"You're free to go…" she said as the man looked like he couldn't find the words to say what he felt, "Any chance you want off this awful island?"

The former slave still couldn't manage to find words, he just bowed before her with incredible gratitude before he made a break towards the trees nearby.

"Make sure you bury your leftovers this time!" she yelled just as he disappeared.

"I want you to know I'm really sorry about this Amal, if I have to travel the entirety of the Five Islands to find you, you'll be repaid for this…" Riley said with a sprinkle of guilt.

The mountain of a man just hung his head quietly, same as he'd done ever since she put steel to temple.

As she escorted her captive to the top deck the rest of the crew had blood in their eyes, like they may forget their senses and fire off a shot at any moment. Still her aim never strayed from the captain, he would take them to Kleppenwitz, or they would all end up finding a permanent home somewhere at the bottom of the Abyssal Sea.

The boy was taking water, but still not conscious. Her, Amal, and the kid in rags sat on the top deck awkwardly as Amal resentfully guided the ship off towards their heading. She had to be careful to split her eyes with one on Amal and the other tending to Jack.

"You know the ships in no shape to make it back to the Boondocks…" Amal said lowly.

"I checked the hull and rudder before we left, even patched the sheets; With wind in our sails we'll be fine." Riley said nervously, knowing all too well he might be right.

The largest island of the Five Isles Forza was now in their rear view, as they got a clear view of the Seven Cities on their way into deeper waters. It was more city than a field of vision had room for, and the word lavish didn't feel good enough, with its seven castles or more like palaces, looking over the hilled villages and blue rivers like giant wardens in the sky. Riley always felt it was unbelievable that a group of people so crazy could build something so beautiful.

The sea was a rare sort of calm, especially for these waters, as the full sun above them warmed any chill winds. The boat rocked up and down peacefully as their black sails guided them along. Riley had put the boy in her lap and held him tight. *Maybe the warmth of another would help him pull through* she thought, cling on to life just a few more days until she could find a way to get him to safety.

The insulting crewman from earlier approached the top deck like he was the captain and poked his tub belly out like he thought it would be intimidating,

"Want you to know me and the boys are watchin every move you make... even takin shifts." he said coldly as he got in very close to her face, "Wouldn't sleep if I was you. You take that pistol off his head for one teeny tiny little second and you're dead!!"

Riley without hesitation cracked him over the head with her pistol and then pointed it right back at Amal,

"Not dead yet..." she murmured.

As they set a course at full sail, the vast sea on all sides became a blur, and it would stay like this for fourteen days... that was if their ship held up.

She was thankful when the captain slept, so she could tend to Jack in the corner and try and force some more water down his throat. Looking down at his mangled leg she knew exactly why the Forzians had left him to die. The leg looked like it was put on the wrong way, and the arm was so full of blisters he must've been in constant pain.

Time passed excruciatingly slow for her, while her pistol stayed firmly on target. By day three without sleep she had started hallucinating, seeing many old friends and distant relatives trying to motivate her to stay awake. A few of the other crewman had tried to creep onto the deck in the middle of the night, and 'correct' the situation, but somehow, she stayed alert and stared at them blankly with her pistol up to Amal's head.

For fourteen days she barely slept, she'd been spit on, called the worst things she could imagine, and had her life threatened over and again. Yet for fourteen days her pistol never wavered.

She couldn't be sure if it was real or not when she saw the Laughing Monk statue peering above the clouds, with steam coming off its head from the rain.

"I want you to remember what I said." she said wearily to an ever stoic Amal, "You and your crew will be paid back for this. That much I promise."

The ship made port in Kleppenwitz as she crept out with young Jack still unconscious at her side. She made her way out of the ship into an old alleyway near the dock, now too weak to keep her gun pointed at the crewman who stared at her.

Seeing she was vulnerable the short one lifted his rifle and went for a kill-shot, but Amal shoved the man so hard into a nearby ship wall his rifle flew in the air as high as the top mast and then sunk down into the crystal waters below.

Hope welled as she saw her former ship and the Gallowsmen with it fade away into the sea mist. Unable to stand any longer she collapsed to the ground with Jack just as weary at her side.

Now penniless with no crew and a little one to look after, she had no clue how she would make it from here.

In her delirium, with rain crashing down on top of them, she looked up to a sign with a sleeping monkey that happened to be right above her.

The city she'd grown up in might as well have looked like a foreign planet. She laid there for what might've been hours or days, until a very tall woman in a ruffled black dress came to her and Jack's aid, a woman big in height and even bigger in heart, a woman that neither of them would ever forget.

****

Riley woke up in a sweat, she was amazed she still remembered it so vividly, like it wasn't nearly as long ago as it was.

For a time, she laid up in bed and stared out her window, marveling at the big laughing monk in the distance, looking down on the sprawling Municipal Park below like a doting father, with the flower like trees of the park appearing to garnish his robes. Like the Sullenmoon of Caldo, or the ever-burning fires of Prego's Blazing Mountain, it was an anointed wonder of the Five Isles, known as The Great Wonder of

Otto officially, or Big Brother Boondock unofficially. Many of the Gibbons even took it a step further and referred to him as Big Billy, named after William Ordassian, one of the founding eight members of Otto.

Much closer than the park, she had a wonderful view of Pigly Harbor, or Port Pigly as some liked to say, nicknamed for all the island piglets that liked to rest under the docks and bask in its clear waters. The port was the natural endpoint between two massive strips of land, mountain, palm trees, and sand, and was one of Kleppenwitz's biggest docks. Ships of all sizes were pouring in and out throughout the day, with sails of every color you could imagine. Most, especially the bigger ones, even had intricate designs, like the flag of their home city doubling as sails, or stone mermaids hoisted above their bow. One in particular caught her eye today, with sails as large as she'd ever seen, and black with faded white etches all throughout, almost like it was designed to look like cobwebs.

Tidying up always seemed to help get her mind off things as she looked the place over and searched for anything out of place. The room was tiny and intimate, just the way she liked it. For years Matilda had insisted that she upgrade to a bigger suite, something more lavish, bigger even, with a double bathroom or some fancy cabinets, but she refused. She'd grown accustomed to the place and couldn't imagine going through the chore of having to fill up a bigger space with more stuff she felt she didn't need.

On her desk was a ripped green woolen jacket from her childhood she was currently learning how to resew. Beside the desk were two piles of books, one taller than she was of books she had read, the other only slightly passed her ankles of books she had yet to read. Atop the desk's chair was her blue bonnet with a bill so oversized Jack used to refuse to sit next to her on their trips to the Municipal Park he was so embarrassed.

It kept the light out of my eyes! she laughed remembering.

While most Gibbons decked their interiors with exotic off island paintings or bespoke furniture, Riley's had none of this. Her favorite of what little décor she did have was a picture on her bedside table of her and Jack when he was much younger at the Ghost's Farewell celebration and parade on Kleppenwitz. Jack was dressed as a pumpkin and still young enough to not be embarrassed holding his mother's hand in public, while Riley had a smile on her face that said she'd never known real happiness before this moment.

The corridors leading to Hangman's Hall downstairs always had a pleasant smell to them, like they'd just been cleaned. They could've doubled as an art museum with all the antiques and portraits of famous Gibbons Members on either side. There was a framed long-rifle that killed Comandante Magnus II King of the Seven Cities, a replica of the Kraken's Cutlass with wormlike steel tentacles for a guard, a single strand of Mercurial hair framed in glass with a plaque that read 'stronger than Pregorian Steel', and a portrait of Mattias Baum 'The Unclean' who famously defeated the Codwater Pirate leader Blackcrow by hiding in a clever spot in his outhouse.

Looking over all the oddities, she took her time heading downstairs, she noticed a double-barreled pistol on the wall that had a twisting snake plated in silver along the barrel, she could've sworn it was the exact pistol her former Captain Amal had used. *It must be a copy, probably even the same maker as his*, even still it reminded her of him. And how he knocked over the short stubby would-be assassin, saving her young son's life.

She wondered where he was now, and why he'd never reached out again, if for nothing else than to collect the bounty she promised to repay. It took some time, but she did get the money, yet all these years later the big sack of gold doubloons sat quietly underneath her mattress gathering dust.

When Riley made it to Hangman's Hall it was a very different scene than what she was used to. Two days ago, it would've felt like a party from the moment she stepped in, but now it felt like everyone was about to walk into some serious business meeting. The usual cheery faces were stern and suspicious, drunk men were sober, and menacing guards were posted at each door in their unsorted mix of black leathers and chainmail with wood steel rifles at the ready. There was an eerie quiet about the place, that didn't feel right at all. Her anxiety fluttered as she thought of others abandoning such a special place so quickly in the same way Lazy-Eyed Willow Turtleby did.

The Bounty Board was clicking and clocking away as it always did as she could clearly hear Matilda firing off orders from the balcony, even when enraged it was difficult not to be first thing she thought of whenever she saw Matilda. Her mind jumped to that day so many years ago when she hoisted both her and Jack over her massive shoulders and took them in for good.

"You!! I saw them eyes close, what use is a guard that sleeps on the job?!!" Matilda yelled at one, "You! Tuck that shirt in, if we're all goin to be turned to dust by a mad Mercurial at least we'll look good doin it!" she yelled at another.

Riley approached her cautiously careful not to get in the way of her hands that were swinging around like a windmill,

"Anything I can help with Matilda? You look a little overwhelmed..." she said lightly.

"Wish dad was still here," Matilda pushed her hand into her forehead in frustration, "He'd have these guards doin jumpin jacks till they couldn't stand... sleepin on the job... the nerve!" there was a worry in her eyes that gave Riley a real pause.

Embracing her old companion with a warm hug, needing to stand on her tippy toes to do so, she said, "Don't worry... we'll get through this just like we've always done. Do you remember when the Codwater Pirates had some silly revival and wanted to take revenge on the Gibbons? We made it through that well enough, didn't we?"

"The Codwater Pirates were barely out of diapers an' throwing sticks at us... far different from a full blown Mercurial coming after ya."

Seeing someone so typically fun and animated, so cold and somber tied a knot in Riley's belly.

The two of them walked together out of Hangman's Hall downstairs into the dungeons where the prisoners were held so Matilda could make her rounds.

"What about Barney LeBlanc, surely you think he was a formidable opponent? Remember when he tried sinking us after losing the Concord Race around the Boondocks?"

Her face looked brighter as she throat-laughed at the thought, "Barney LeBlanc the old dingus, you know some people got all the luck, some get none of it. Barney was the latter. Never knew you could cut a ship in two with just a hull and a prayer… that may've been one the best ideas you ever had!"

Matilda was doing her duties and quietly wiping dirt from the stone cell walls while Morty the Skunk was staring at them from his cell with wet eyes and a pitiful face, "Don't forget Morty the Skunk, you caught him too!" he said, "And I'm as vicious and bloodthirsty as they come!"

The pair got a big laugh out of this, so much so Riley almost forgot he'd tried to blow her up a few days prior.

"You're real kind Morty, a fine addition to the Stalhaus Prison you'll make! Maybe I'll put in a word to the warden, tell'em you only need one shower a week." Matilda said as Morty looked giddy at the thought.

"Well even if Knox is a Mercurial… we don't know if that makes him invincible… do we? Maybe he's just really tough to kill or something?" Riley said positively, "The Mercurial have been gone longer than I've been alive, so I'm no expert, but surely they have some sort of weakness, has anyone ever been crazy enough to try it?"

"Welp there's the one everybody knows about…"

"Butternut?"

"Marius Butternut the warlord that sailed outta Caldo with a death wish. Sure would hate my name to be immortalized as the biggest idiot in the Pinwheel Islands."

"Fellas two cells down won't stop callin me that, whose Butternut?" Morty butted in.

"Wudya, been livin under a rock?" Matilda huffed.

"Yes…" Morty said back unemotionally to confused stares.

"A-alright. Man was a Caldo Warlord that got into a huff about Ghosts being the peacekeepers of the Pinwheels n' all, not letting him or anyone else start wars with the other island countries. He figured since no one on Caldo could challenge him, they couldn't either. He ignored the warnings and sailed him and his giant fleet out to Allora, was possible then o'course cause it wasn't covered by a giant monsoon yet." Matilda shook her head in befuddlement, "I heard from Chef Greene you can still see bits and pieces of their ships floatin around Allorian waters if you're type crazy enough to get close."

Matilda continued walking past the rusty stone cells with the prisoners giving them pitiful glances, "Here I was thinkin the Rogue goin missing, and the Forzians havin the nerve to start up the first multi-island war anyone alive today can remember was our biggest problems. That woulda taken years to show up on the Boondocks… at the least, and that's if Prego laid down easy which I sure couldn't see."

"You said it yourself, we're in the safest place that we could possibly be, even a Mercurial wouldn't be crazy enough to barge in here. The Gibbons are older than both of us combined, and these walls will still stand when we're both long gone. We'll get through this just like we always have, even if we have to spend years inside these walls…"

When they arrived back up to Hangman's Hall the big wood and stone chamber looked at least a little less somber than it had earlier as the bounty hunters who called the Cantina home had started to wake up. Matilda jutted off upstairs in a whirlwind of a sprint towards the Hanging Gardens after she'd gotten wind someone had stolen several wild monkeys the night before and released them inside as a goof.

Riley Tripleleaf spent the rest of her morning being productive looking after Hangman's Hall as best she could to help Matilda. She dusted the hundreds of monkey statues around the space having a good laugh at one that appeared to have one arm behind its back ready to throw a mysterious substance, assisted a few patrons who were still sleeping from the night before in finding their quarters, helped a few of the guards properly clean and calibrate their pistols, and even had time to check the four she kept on her. But most of all she ruminated on why Jack wasn't up yet.

****

Jack made his way towards the Flagpole Market, making sure to look over his shoulder as much as possible. Riley would've been livid if she found out he snuck out, but one way or another she'd have to accept he could make his own decisions. He'd taken all the proper precautions, he replaced his bounty hunter's armor and sash with some crusty old ascotted suit he found in his closet from years ago and carefully tucked his sheathed blade and pistol into the back of his belt.

Upon entering the Flagpoles, the first thing he noticed was a pearl the size of his hand encased in glass atop a concrete podium, the space so prominent reserved for the annual winner of the Concord Pearl Diving Contest.

Behind it, there were thousands of beautiful vibrantly colored flags all swaying in the wind and changing direction in unison. He spotted the northern city Dunkel's flag with its frightening snarling Grey Wolf, Kolsch's flag which was many hours south had some sort of tropical bird with a beak longer than its body, and the Kleppenwitz Flag with Big Brother Boondock towering above the clouds. There were so many flags from all the different isles and cities that Jack was ashamed he recognized so few of them.

With monasteries ringing their church bells, fledgling thespians putting on acrobatic cobblestone theatre, the market felt so alive and diverse. People from all over the Five Islands came here to sell and purchase goods, switching in and out so frequently you could find a new array of goods each day of the week.

There were a pair of merchants from Caldo dressed in sandworn robes and tiny little hats, offering free samples of some sort of sweet-looking cake that looked too delicious to pass by. Once Jack popped one in his mouth, the tart liquified to sludge and reminded him of spoiled milk. Striving to remember the manners Riley tried her best to instill in him, he held the rotten morsel in his mouth for as long as he could, but eventually the ooze came spewing out as he darted away hoping they didn't see.

The rows and rows of cobblestone houses fat with ivy and presenting shoddy wooden tables alongside wicker baskets melded together, though the flags at their tops were so unique you could use them as markers for places you'd already been. He spotted one podium with zero goods which at first struck him as odd, and as he got closer immediately knew why. Two stern looking men were sitting upright in their military regalia with long navy wool coats patched up with military honors, steel toed polished black shoes, and chainmail poking through white linen undershirts. They had a sign that read **'THE GALE COMETH - FIGHT FORZA'** in bold letters underneath their stand. Men like them were an increasingly common sight in the city. They were recruiters for the Freebooters, a group mostly comprised of Vistan Military and the people of Prego, fighting against Forza for control of Prego and all its bountiful natural resources.

As he passed them, he heard one of the men yell,

"Join the Freeboots and maybe you can buy a shirt that fits!"

Instincts kicked in and he had the urge to spit back at the man but after he looked down and saw that his ankles were showing, the recruiter probably had a point.

Most people on the Boondocks, including Jack, supported the Freeboots. They weren't perfect, no army ever was, but anything was better than the Forzians who treated their people more like slaves than civilians. When the Mercurial were still around there really was little to fear from Forza. But now that they had disappeared, and for so long, there was no telling what could happen. And it wasn't like Jack needed even more of a reason to hate Forza, his arm and leg were a constant reminder of their brutality. But at least he could stuff that away, deal with it in the background, and settle up when the time felt right. But now with the war the talk of the town, and details of their skirmishes in all the papers that was all but impossible.

Continuing along his stroll, one of the tents had the strangest glass bottles glimmering at him as he passed, fire in a bottle they called it, a type of Kristal that had been set on fire along a toy-sized ship's sail, or cutlass's steel, or the end of a model pistol. Depending on how much Kristal was used, the fire could burn for years and was as beautiful as it was dangerous if you ever let it slip out its glass enclosure.

"My friend! My friend!" the merchant yelled loudly giving him a start, "Come purchase one of my lovely fires. For you I give special price, so cheap you will have enough left over to buy clothes that fit!"

Embarrassed now he was thinking maybe he should look around for a tailor, when he nearly stumbled over a man sitting in the middle of the street. It was lucky he didn't hit him; the man was a monk, and monks were considered sacred on the Boondocks. The man was donning their typical dusty brown robes, as well as the bald haircut minus a few stray grey hairs along his freckly head.

Several baskets of golden roses decorated the monk's burgundy mat, a symbol of rebirth and prosperity on the island. Excited to finally find some, Jack picked up two of them,

"How much?" he said.

When the man turned his eyes were closed in such a way Jack could tell he'd been blind for a very long time, yet somehow, he was still able to locate and stare directly into Jack's eyes.

"Five copper for the two of them." he said in a tranquil voice.

He paid the man double what he asked and kept walking along, these would make a great gift for Riley and Matilda, maybe it would calm their nerves after Willow's retelling of events.

Looking back, he noticed the monk was still staring at him, but instead of the tranquil look he had previously, he had a terrified look on his face, like he just witnessed a murder, as his gaze never moved from Jack no matter what direction he moved. A harrowing and physically uncomfortable feeling took him as he tried to bob and weave through the crowds to somehow escape his gaze. Even as he got far enough away where he could just make out the man, the monk's head inexplicably moved right with him.

He could still feel his heart racing but didn't know why, it came on so suddenly. Someone staring at you shouldn't have been the end of the world, but this felt different. Jack needed something to calm his nerves. Luckily, he was just passing the food section of the Flagpole Market.

This section was long his favorite and brought back fond memories of coming in and sneaking free samples with one of his old friends Roy Gerling back when he didn't have a single doubloon to his name. He bought the first thing he spotted which was a whirlwind cake that had such a different array of flavors like peach, apple, and tart it was said to make people spin.

The altering taste counteracted his anxiety, and his nerves began to calm. He sat on a nearby bench gorging down the sweet and pondering what just happened with a cooler head. He'd never seen or heard of any monk acting so strangely… so why him? And why now?

While enjoying the scenery and the calm it brought on, he watched the seagulls eye his treat. These weren't your average seagulls, they had bulging eyes that rarely moved in sync, a beak that looked like it was laughing at you, and an uneven blue stripe down their backs. They were unique to the Boondocks and were just as annoying as they were clever.

The heart palpitations stopped as he settled into a groove and took in the nice spring weather, trying his best to forget about what had just transpired. *Probably just some old monk who's out his marbles, that's why he's out here and not in his monastery* he told himself.

"Pirate Lord, Captain Davey Scrimshaw escapes from Stalhaus, his sixth prison escape in six years with the help of his loyal and ravenous crew! READ ALL ABOUT IT!!!" Jack heard a nearby paperboy shouting, with his hand-me-down gray woolen cap that looked to be about eight sizes too big, "READ ALL ABOUT IT IN THE MAROONER'S HERALD!! Sources close to Davey say he escaped to Stormsong, home of the pirate kings, a buzzling metropolis that can float on open ocean, leaving the authorities puzzled as to its whereabouts! A police spokesman declined to comment but did say the Stormsong was just some nonna's tale pirates made up to keep police off their trails! READ ALL ABOUT IT!!"

As Jack tried to stop his snickers after spotting a nearby seagull trying to eat some poor woman's bonnet it mistook for fruit, he spotted an old friend he was very much hoping to see today.

"Roy Gerling!" Jack shouted, hardly able to believe he was lucky enough to catch him.

"Is that a monkey on my back?!... Tripleleaf?!" he embraced Jack with a bear hug so big it took him off his feet and expelled most of the air in his lungs, "You haven't changed, not even a bit! Is that body armor I felt underneath there?!"

"Never can be too safe these days..."

"Word around the cobblestones is you're almost a full-fledged bounty hunter now." Roy said with a big voice like he was meeting some celebrity, "I think there may be about five active bounties on me if you need some work..."

"Always happy to help out a friend!" he chuckled assuming he was joking but not entirely sure.

They had been thick as thieves growing up in Kleppenwitz, spending most of their time climbing up roofs and through forests and getting into more mischief than either of them wanted to remember. He wasn't Jack's only friend growing up, but he was certainly the dodgiest as Riley loved to say. It was a wonder to Jack how he'd even managed to live this long after he'd once seen him jump into one of the city canals onto a reef shark that was bigger than he was, almost drowned while pearl-diving in the Sober Sea, or the time he had to talk him out of sneaking onto a pirate ship.

"How's the hand doin?! Saw something recently that I thought may be of interest to you."

If anyone else had asked this question, Jack would've quickly changed the subject, but for reasons he didn't fully understand he was completely comfortable sharing with Roy.

"Eh, it's ok. Not as painful these days, still looks like it got runover by a carriage though..."

"When I was on Prego recently, avoiding all the battlefields of course, on business ya'know, I heard about a preserve sposed to work wonders for burns. Thought about you immediately, I'll reach out to some contacts, see if I can't get a tub shipped to the Cantina..."

"Sounds amazing!! What do I owe you??!"

"Your money's no good here, Tripleleaf." he said putting his head to the sky and shaking his brown locks in confidence, "Know it's been a while, but rules still stand!"

The past year had been a blur for him, doing nothing but chasing bounties had made him almost forget his school years, made him almost forget how nice it was to have friends that were looking out for him.

"And is the Jack Tripleleaf Roy Gerling ban still in place?" he said pushing the strands of his hair back, "Or did Riley forget?"

"Think I've gotten a little too old for her bans… least I hope!"

After turning up from hanging out with Roy with something bruised or broken too many times, Riley had forbidden Jack from seeing him. Even going as far as telling Stono the Caiman his son Glasgo should watch out for him as well. But it didn't much matter to Jack, after seeing him get into a few schoolyard scraps with the kids that called him *Deadhand*, he knew he was a true friend, even if a little rough around the edges.

"And what about you?" Jack said, "How's everything in your world? Snuck onto any ships lately?"

"Ha! In my defense it was a pirate's ship. In all likelihood they'd just stolen it from someone else, wasn't even theirs to protect! But my world's been clear skies and full sails, never any shortage of schemers, plots to uncover, or conspiracies to dismantle in the Five Isles. Heck even Kleppenwitz has been a hot bed lately!"

The two boys had shaggy hair though Roy's was a great deal shaggier. Roy was shorter than most, stocky, and always had a twinkle in his eye, like he was up to something. He was unassuming in nature and was exceptional at blending in and fitting in no matter what his environment. He was ever curious and every bit as charming as the best con man on Kleppenwitz and never shied away from putting these skills to use. From what you could see on his clay table he was selling mineral herbs from Prego, but Jack knew better. While he had entered the intriguing world of hunting bounties, Roy had entered a field equally as interesting, the field of selling secrets.

"Didn't know you were so into Pregorian Herbs... thought you had other... talents." Jack said coyly.

"You'd be amazed at the sorts of things people say when they think you're a commoner. Just a humble herb peddler payin them no mind. Talk of corrupt cops, a corrupt mayor, even heard Knox was coming after bounties. Which I gather explains your suit."

"Ever heard of a monk giving you a death stair?" Jack said still a little chilled thinking about it.

"Now that's bad luck!"

"He was back that way..." Jack pointed trying to see if he could still spot the man but couldn't.

"Got Knox comin for Boondock Bounties, and now it sounds like you're cursed.... maybe I should step away from you." he chuckled, "Wouldn't sweat it Tripleleaf, sounds to me like he may've been havin a little too much fun at one of their breweries!"

The idea comforted Jack but something about the way the monk moved, the way his blind eyes tracked him... felt genuine.

"You mentioned Knox... What exactly did you hear?"

"That he was comin for any and all bounties till he got his man. And since the police leave bounties to their own business, he ain't got too much in the way of worry either..."

"That it?" Jack was a little disappointed, it seemed he didn't have any new information like he normally did.

Roy itched his cheek and thought for a while, "I did also hear he ditched one of the satellites where his operation was, sposed to be hidin somewhere here indefinitely until he gets the guy he was looking for. The most important part was he's got a real nice hideout somewhere in Kleppenwitz, and a little birdy he told me... it's *a few* of the police who've been helpin him keep hidden. Spose the rest is up to you to find."

Now that was useful information Jack thought.

"You know you really oughta let me start payin you!"

He and Roy spent the rest of the morning discussing the latest happenings on Kleppenwitz, old friends and classmates and where they'd gone off to, and trying to plan a fishing trip.

Not realizing they'd spent so much time chatting, he looked up and saw the sun at high noon. It was time to get back to the Blackwater Cantina and get a stern talking to from Riley for leaving when there was a killer on the loose. Saying his goodbyes to Roy, he took a few last quick glimpses at all the merchandise as he strolled along.

"Ghost's Farewell Ball expects ten-thousand guests this year!! READ ALL ABOUT IT IN THE MAROONERS HERALD!!" Jack could just barely hear the paperboy shouting as he walked, "Event to be held at the Muni's south entrance, and this year's theme is animals. Eight giraffes, seventeen elephants, four baboons, and two apes to be in attendance, men expected to wear furs, and women to wear printed dresses with animal masks! READ ALL ABOUT IT!!"

As he got back to the entrance of the Flagpole Market, a spike of pain flashed in his shoulder as he turned to see who was grabbing him.

Terrified he looked behind him instinctively reaching for his pistol. Before him, was the monk from earlier with the same terrified look on his face.

"FOLLOW... FOLLOW YOUR NEW COMPANION... OR YOU WILL DIE!" he said with a ghostly voice.

It was all he could do not to pull his pistol with the man grabbing at him, but he knew he wasn't a threat.

"AS SURE AS THE TIDES TURN YOU WILL FOLLOW YOUR NEW COMPANION... OR YOU WILL DIE!" he said again, somehow more terrible than the last. His voice was like nails on a chalkboard.

With not too much effort Jack jumped away from the man and scurried off towards the Cantina. In the distance he could still hear,

"AS SURE AS THE WIND WAILS, FOLLOW YOUR NEW COMPANION... OR YOU WILL DIE!"

Chapter 6

<u>The Blackwater Cantina</u>

Jack could breathe easy not having to look over his shoulder anymore as he walked through the giant wooden doors of the Cantina. Hangman's Hall wasn't back to its normal self, but it was certainly more alive than it was in the morning. He even saw one man with a shabby bandanna and buckled black leather boots so big he looked like he may fall out of them attempting to jump on one of the chandeliers and promptly fall down, an alarming thing to most but oddly reassuring to Jack.

Riley immediately approached him looking like she could've boiled him alive with just her eyes, "Where have you been??! And what in the Five Isles are you wearing??" she said furiously.

"I- uhh – I needed to take in some fresh air, ac-actually ended up doing some investigating of my own…"

Her frown persisted.

"Ended up at the Flagpole Market, figured I'd pick up a few things and ended up learning something..." he said with nervous defiance.

"You do realize a Mercurial, who can move through the air like lightning is trying to kill us?! Honestly Jack have some sense… people are dead!"

Jack knew it was coming but hated this feeling, he had gathered very useful information and risked his neck to do so and here he was getting scolded like he was still a child.

Luckily Matilda had overheard them and came over to try and smooth things over, "Ooohhhh…" she said in a high-pitched voice, "Whos' this handsum man in the suit? Believe it may be time for a new one!" she said laughing. "And look Riles, even brought us flowers! Golden roses even! Maybe the one thing that could brighten the mood round here!" she grabbed a nearby vase and placed them inside delicately, "So how was the Flagpoles?"

Still seeing the man in his mind's eye giving him that awful stare, as if he was looking down on him from a perch somewhere oddly enough. He had to tell them even if it made things worse,

"There was this monk… h-he looked like he'd lost mind. Was just following me around and… and he wouldn't stop staring."

Matilda grabbed the wooden table next to her and spit on the ground several times, her way of dispelling bad luck.

"A monk??" Riley said bewildered. "Is it possible he was just some crazy old man and not an actual monk?"

"He had the robes and everything, even the hair…"

They both grimaced. "That's a monk alright…" Riley said shakily.

"Don't worry Riles, I'm sure the monk just went crazy is all. Not like monks are somehow free from losing their marbles just like the rest of us…"

So confident on the way over, confident in how he'd stand his ground and have his voice heard and respected. Somehow that confidence was never quite as strong in the moment, only a fraction of its imagined self. Hundreds of the deadliest men for miles dwelled inside the Cantina, and not a one of them could hurt Riley, not a one but Jack, who felt he did it all the time without even trying.

Riley looked right at Jack, and he was overcome with emotion when he saw her wobbly eyes, "Please don't leave without me again… not until this is over…" she said solemnly in a way that was asking not demanding.

As much as he wanted to fight it, he had no choice but to agree, the look she gave told him everything he needed to know. He'd expected to tell them the scariest of what the monk said, "FOLLOW YOUR NEW COMPANION… **OR YOU WILL DIE!**" but after seeing their reactions thought better of it, it would have to wait.

After Chef Greene brought over some lunch tempers cooled as the three of them sat down. The meal consisted of leaping fried lizards so crunchy Matilda once broke off a tooth on one, Codwater Octopus Eggs seeped in butter and the size of grapes that were a very common appetizer on Kleppenwitz. Usually referred to as the last first course because people filled up on them so easily. There was a green potato hash and some sort of fish from Vista that was so big its eyes were the size of Jack's fists. Between lizard bites Matilda was busy reminding them of the time they took a fish watching trip to Glowater Bay, a small port town on stilts overlooking its bay where each tiki-like cottage kept their biggest catch above their front doors.

"Heard Captain Seabone is still in Glowater bumming around taking odd jobs, apparently he initially stayed for the rum but seeing the Lumineers do their dance made him never want to leave." Riley remembered fondly.

When it was breeding season the Lumineer fish would light up their whole bodies to attract one another, making the whole fishing village of Glowater shine an electric blue in a symphony of swirling lights.

"Old fool always was a better drunk than he was a captain!" Matilda made her peculiar throat laughs, "Bet y'all forgot how many times he got lost sailin there, place ain't even a day away! Silver linin I spose, glad he's landlubbin and not on the open ocean!"

Matilda shifted her focus as she dabbed some octopus egg goop off her cheek and turned to Jack, "Forgot to ask, didn't you mention findin somethin else out at the Flagpoles?"

"An old classmate Roy Gerling told me…" he tried to sound elegant but eventually just blurted it out, "The police are working with Knox."

Both of them were stunned; Matilda bashed her hand on the table with a thunderous thud.

"Knew they didn't love us…. but working with a killer? They've done it now!" Matilda said lowly, "I got half a mind to show up to that dinky station of theirs and remind them exactly why they don't bark up our tree, why they don't want monkeys on their back!"

"Did he say it was the whole police force? I did a favor for the mayor many years ago… he may be able to help." Riley said.

"All he said was it was a few of the policemen."

"Well that's a relief!" Matilda said, "I'd put money it was that detective with the stick in his rear Konrad… He'd fit right in with the residents of Pigly Port out there. Came round few years back sayin the Gibbons oughta pay for them keepin us safe n' all. I told'em to go pound sand and don't come back without a judge's signature. That sure shutt'em up quick!"

"It makes sense." Riley said, "Konrad hates bounty hunters because we do his job better than he can, there would be no bounty hunters if they weren't completely incompetent."

First a Mercurial was after them, and now a corrupt flatfoot, the high Jack had gotten from catching Morty was now sinking into a new low.

"Heard he lives over in the Rhineland District," Matilda continued, "Maybe our next stop is going to pay him a visit."

"Do you honestly think it's a good idea to barge into the home of a sitting policeman? Even if he is corrupt, they'd have the entire force in here in hours looking to take us to Stalhaus."

"Point taken sister!" she said as she rubbed at a few chin hairs, "But there is someone who ain't got the full force of the city behind'em... heck the police may even help us get to'em. The feller Willow was talkin bout who killed the big worm on Caldo."

"Radish..." Jack said with a sternness.

****

The Concord was only a few months passed. A holiday time of gift-giving, spending time with family and loved ones, and remembrance for when the Mercurial hailed in a new age of peace to the Five Isles.

Jack still remembered studying the Mercurial in school, about how they tore down uprisings on Forza and Prego without firing a shot, their presence alone was enough to dissuade an army. If only they were here now to deal with the one they'd forgotten.

At Matilda's direction the three of them were taking down the last of the wreaths and garland imported from the north that were still up. The decoration's smell was invigorating, like being deep in the forest just after rainfall.

The wanted posters of nasty looking men and women that lined the walls of Hangman's Hall slowly reappeared, as Jack started removing candles that were shipped in from the Vistan city of Alexandria. They were beautiful shades of red, orange, blue and yellow, and the colorful lights they emitted bobbed gleefully up and down the walls like a spider in its web. It was almost a shame to see them go.

Just as he had almost finished up, he saw a face that put a knot in his stomach, it was Lucas Geist, another one of the managers of the Jolly Gibbons. He had an air of superiority and order about him, a personality type almost unseen in the Cantina. He was flat, calculating, and always rude even if he seemingly wasn't trying to be.

Today he was dressed in his usual decadent garb with polished body armor rimmed with fanciful gold and a blood red cloak that matched the auburn stripes in his long blonde hair. He had a zombified prisoner with him donning massive chains so big Jack shook at the sight of him.

"Mmmm, Mr. Tripleleaf!" Geist said sternly, he tended to belt out deep hums when he felt he was saying something important, "So good to see you in one piece."

Nodding back while trying not to acknowledge him and looking busy with the candles, he hoped the man would just move on.

"What's with all these stupid lights??" Geist muttered.

Hardly able to stand it anymore, Jack bit his tongue.

"Heard you captured Morty the Skunk... did he even put up a fight? Or did he just let you put chains on him?" he laughed condescendingly.

"You do know he was a skilled bomb maker?? He had booby traps set by his bedside, rigged to explode with one wrong move."

Geist yawned, "Mmhmmph, very impressive. Golian the Vistan Menace here killed over one hundred men in Alexandria for the sport of it, been on the run for years of course, hiding in the salt marshes of Vista. Wasn't much of a match for me and my men though."

Jack gave back an awkward smile, half attempting to look impressed.

The giant prisoner gave a jolt as if he was waking up and Jack could now see Mince Jenkins right behind him.

"Amazing job sir! Not a finer man in the Cantina!" Jenkins said with his crispy-creepy voice. He seemed to have taken quite a liking to Geist.

The idea that Lucas Geist was the finest bounty hunter at the Cantina with his mom and Matilda so close by made Jack cringe, but still he kept his tongue and worked on taking down lights.

"And what's this I hear about Gibbons being attacked? Knox, was it? Makes perfect sense he'd wait till I've left on a mission before he attacked..." he gave a belting laugh, "I leave for two weeks, and the place is in shambles, what kind of ship is Matilda running? Afraid I'll have to escalate this after I collect Knox's bounty."

Unable to hold his tongue any longer he started to shout, but before the words could come out, he saw Riley over his shoulder with a look that could've killed.

"Don't you have some underlings to harass? Maybe even more men to hire to do your job for you?" she sputtered out coldly, "Thought I told you not to mess with my son?"

"My dear Riley," he spoke more delicately now, "I was simply trying to get information on how under you and Matilda's watch you allowed Gibbons to be killed?"

"They were outside the Cantina, outside of our control. Being a bounty hunter is a dangerous job... you know this. And unfortunately, they weren't the first nor will they be the last that met a cruel twist of fate. Now, unless you want a repeat of what happened last time, I suggest you leave myself and Jack alone and turn in your prisoner."

Pruning with embarrassment he muttered, "Last time was a complete stroke of luck, if I hadn't been wearing the wrong shoes..."

Riley cut off his speech with a quick, interrupting laugh. She confidently placed her hand over the hilt of her sword and smiled, "We've always got tonight Lucas..."

"I am a MANAGER," he said with a puckered face, "And I won't be talked down by the likes of you! Or your bright sashed snot-nosed boy!"

By this point Matilda had rushed over to see what the fuss was all about.

"**OUT! OUT! OUT!**" Matilda said with a face just as red as Geist's as she towered assertively above him and even his giant prisoner, "We ain't doin this again Lucas, you hear me?! If you have a problem with either one of my friends here you'll go through me first... that understood?! Don't speak to'em, don't even look at'em. If that gets yur drawers in even more ova bunch tattle to whoever you need!"

The man still looked furious but knew he couldn't pull rank with her and darted off towards the dungeons with Jenkins in tow.

"JENKINS!!" Matilda screamed, "Where do you think yur goin?! Straight to the kitchen for you today, Chef Greene's got fish guts with your name on'em need haulen out!"

Geist was another one of the five managers that ran the Cantina, and by far the most annoying. Like Matilda, his family came from a long line of bounty hunters, Jack knew this because most times he had the misfortune of walking by him in Hangman's Hall he was regaling a crowd about the time his grandfather Lenox had saved some execrable village on Vista, or how his father Liam still had Forzians looking for him years after he outwitted them.

He'd never been particularly fond of Jack and Riley ever since Matilda brought them in. Nor particularly fond of any newcomer for that matter. Wanted to keep the Gibbons 'pure', as if it were some elite club only he and his friends could join. Luckily, none of the other managers ever saw eye to eye on the issue.

"Sorry bout that pepper-head." Matilda said to Jack, "You'd think after me n' Riles here whoopin him so many times he'd sink back into whatever hole he crawled out of. Guess some folks never learn…"

"Just giving you warning Matilda, another outburst like that and he'll be missing a few fingers instead of getting off lucky with a few bruises…" Riley said incensed.

"Won't blame ya for that! Heck I can even cover for ya to the other managers… Don't think I'd need to, but I'd make somethin up if I had to."

Bright Sashed, Snot-Nosed Kid. Jack thought, is this how the Gibbons saw him? Just a shadow under his mom's wing? He didn't think it was the case but still it was hard not to let thoughts intrude.

After Matilda and Riley took to arguing over how to best 'deal' with Lucas, he decided he needed to blow off some steam and headed down to the basement beneath the dungeons that housed the shooting range. The journey felt quick as his mind was on other things but was happy to see the place so alive when he arrived.

The gun range was surprisingly big given how far underground it was and went back far enough the pellets from the rifles and pistols took seconds for the crackle of shot to be heard hitting the back wall. It always had a new and unusual theme; it felt like every time Jack saw the room, he hardly recognized it. Today the range looked like a spitting image of the Kolsch Rainforests to the south, complete with a couple of parrots behind the stations chirping, vibrant man-eating flowers hung in vases through the range, and massive tree canopies shading the shooting stations.

The steel targets were equally impressive; they were disguised as Forzian Soldiers with their foreboding black and red armor and beaked hats. Perched behind trees, bushes, and flowers, if you hit one a loud 'TING!' like a symbol hit would sound across the whole room.

A few familiar faces poked out from behind wooden shooting cubbies as their silhouettes were lit up by the bomb like explosions pouring out of pistol barrels. Marcus A. was there, a former pirate now bounty hunter, who was so paranoid he refused to tell anyone his last name, and just used the letter 'A.' instead. He saw Old-Man Timmermans, who had worked with Riley on a few missions before he'd gotten too old. Jack was always impressed by his uncanny ability to bring up his knee problems in every single conversation he'd ever had with him.

He overheard Sarah Blitzen, one of the range's operators, yelling at Old-Man Timmermans from her podium,

"Mr. Timmermans, PLEASE STOP shooting at the ceiling!!" she yelled as nicely as she could muster.

"SORRY!! The KNEES made me slip again!!!" he croaked back even louder.

Sarah Blitzen was part of a small crew of people in the Cantina that were close to Jack's age, which made her a fast friend and a great person to talk to about the latest happenings around the Cantina.

"Look Out!!"

Jack heard a loud voice behind him and almost dropped his pistol when someone used their hands to cover his eyes.

"Hi Jack!!" Sarah said showing her big pearly whites between bright red cheeks.

"Almost gave me a heart attack…" Jack squeaked. She had already crept her way into his station and was checking out his pistol, she had a habit of not respecting personal space, but she was such a ball of sunshine most people didn't mind.

"Man, this grip is amazing! And the scope…. looks better than my own eyes… Cordaroys? No too light… Bombadiers then? Couldn't be anyone else."

"You guessed it! Got it in last year's Concord." Jack said as a pang of guilt entered his chest when he remembered Riley spent money that she didn't have to buy it.

The sidearm had rosewood grips with mother of pearl inlays that loved to shine when the moon outside made contact. It had dual hammers that felt like they would set if you looked at them too hard, and double barrels that looked oddly slender until it expanded at the muzzle. The body of the gun had monkeys etched on either side, and the underside compartments housed two steel ramrods meant for reloading, but since they'd been hollowed out, they made for an excellent hiding spot for extra copper, lead shot, or gunpowder.

"Guess the gun'll come in useful! Word around the Pinwheels is we've got a Ghost problem? I should know, Marcus hasn't stopped talking about it since he's been here." she said as she handed it back.

"Knox?... Thanks for bringing it up… Shooting is about the only thing that's been able to get my mind off it."

"It can't be," she said worried, "Are the Mercurial back? After all this time? Why would they leave one behind? Sounds like the race of perfect people weren't so perfect after all."

"Your guess is as good as mine, but if Willow were here, he'd tell you what he told us, he saw Crowfeet's sword smash into pieces when it touched his back. It was fine steel too, not just some glass from the Flagpoles."

"Wowwww, so he has powers? Can he fly around like a bird??"

By this point Marcus A. had heard them and joined in yelling from his station,

"Can he fly?" Marcus laughed confidently, "Why fly when ya can just zap around wherever ya want, whenever ya want. Even heard from a crew in Hangman's Hall he could sink the Boondocks back into the ocean with a flick of his wrist if he felt so inclined…"

"Erm… well he has a ship," Jack said boldly, "Doubt he would need that if he could just teleport anywhere, also I'm pretty sure knocking an island into the ocean is a stretch, even for Mercurial."

"Whatever you say, allz I know is I've been sleeping in one of the bomb shelters with as many guns and explosives as I can get my hands on."

"Aveline Nickel in the Starboard Pods told me she once saw him down by Big Billy. Said he had a face like a bulldog, but he wasn't flying or teleporting." Sarah said as she looked at Jack and then looked away again, "Do you have any idea what he wants? Why he's doing this?"

"There's this famous thief, he stole something from Knox and Knox is going on a killing spree until he gets it back. Man goes by the name Radish, and apparently, he's hiding out somewhere in Kleppenwitz."

"Radish!?" she said shocked, "Gave the Rogue his start Radish?! Stole Quicksilver right from under King Magnus' nose Radish?!"

"That's the one." Jack said assuredly, "And we've either got to find him and convince him to turn himself over…. which doesn't seem likely. Or take down Knox, which mom feels is completely hopeless. After looking at his bounty though, I'm starting to feel tempted."

"You could always hide in the bunkers with me!" Marcus shouted.

Jack ignored Marcus and kept going, "And the final cherry on top is, I have a source that tells me Knox is working with some corrupt cops in the city. Matilda and mom think it's someone named Konrad, as corrupt as they come from what they said."

Sarah's mouth was hanging open, "Is there any good news?!"

"We're safe inside the Cantina? That's all I can think of. I think Mom would love the idea of hiding in here until this whole thing blows over…"

She looked like she'd seen a Ghost.

"If you go out, I wouldn't do it with your sash or armor on. Knox attacked when he saw the others wearing theirs. Best to keep some kind of disguise… blend in with the city folk."

After answering about a hundred more of Sarah's endless questions, Jack quietly made his way back up the long series of stone corridors to get back to Hangman's Hall. He was supposed to meet with his mom and Matilda to once and for all make a plan on how to solve the Knox problem.

As he walked up the corridor stairs the cobblestone reminded him of the Flagpole Market, and the terrifying visage of the monk sprang into his head again. Follow your new companion *or you die*, the man's face and words were burned into his memory. Maybe he was referring to Morty the Skunk? It would certainly be odd to consider him a companion though. He needed to find answers, and fast if he wanted to stay sane. He'd made a mental plan for tonight to stop by the downstairs Monarch Library and look for any clues he could find on monks and if there was anything to their prophecies.

When he got back up to Hangman's Hall it was electric, he could see a group of men with doubloons in fists huddled around a dirt pit where two rats were charging each other. The fighting rats were all completely unique, no two were ever truly the same. One of the current fighters had a pink mohawk that made it hard to take seriously as a contender. The other was as plain jane as could be with brown fur covering its body and a feint white stripe running down its back. Riley referred to the practice as 'Brutal' and always scolded him for watching the fights, but it was tough to look away. Plus, the poor creatures were never gravely injured, which made it justifiable in his eyes to at least watch.

Walking towards the central bar he could see Lucas Geist yelling at a poor young barmaid for what looked like bringing him a drink with too much condensation. Matilda was at the bar giving him the stink eye, until she saw Jack and gave him a hearty smile with a big wink. He was about to make his way over until he ran into what felt like a brick wall. Looking up he saw Chef Greene,

"How yu likka de fish?" he said with his thick accent that was so deep it sounded more like murmurs than words.

"Huh??"

"DE FISH!"

"Oh sorry! The fish was excellent as always! Matilda was upset she can never cook hers quite like yours!" Jack said politely.

Chef Greene was built like a bull, a bit shorter than Matilda but more gifted horizontally. Jack always wondered why he'd become a chef when he could've made a fortune as a bodyguard.

"I have summon for yu to meet."

"Huh?" Jack said confused again, "Someone to meet?" before Greene could respond Riley had swiftly approached,

"Chef!" she said happily, "The fish was excellent! What's your secret??"

"Sauceeeeeeeee!" He said back deep and slow.

"I really hate to do this, but we've booked the Acclaimatory for this afternoon. I'm sure you can understand, Matilda will have our necks if we're late!"

Grunting like he didn't care the chef made his way back to the kitchen.

The pair made off towards the room, which was right beside Hangman's Hall. Jack nearly ran into a man with an eyepatch who was asleep sprawled out at a broken table beside their destination. He questioned if he should move the man, being so close to the Acclaimatory he may overhear something, but then when he saw the pool of drool on the man's jerkin, he supposed it wasn't an issue.

Inside the room was cozy, and intimate, yet it still managed to fill its walls head-to-toe with faces of different influential historical women and men throughout the Five Isles. Not just bounty hunters, but prominent traders, thieves, smugglers, politicians, soldiers, generals, and judges. The Caldorian Spice Kings hung up so high displayed mischievous grins while Vistan Queens returned glares with sapphires for eyes.

As they sat down at the central table Matilda marched in, sat down, and wasted no time,

"Right then, as I've got my duties to the Cantina, Riley will no doubt be the one leadin this charge, so she should start first. What'r your thoughts? What'r our options?"

Riley stood alert in her chair and inhaled calmy, "After speaking to some sources, each one of them confirmed Knox is a legitimate threat. He's a madman and a killer. Multiple people have recalled him moving just as Willow described and even manipulating creatures to do his bidding. The way I see it, we have three options. Hide in the Cantina hoping for this to blow over, kill Knox, or capture Radish and turn him in ourselves."

"Let's not gloss over the fact, that if we did manage to kill Knox, we could retire overnight." Jack said confidently.

"Hard to retire if you're dead." she said back bluntly.

"Mom we can do this! You've said yourself how good I've gotten with a pistol. Plus no one in the Gibbons can say they've beaten the men you've beaten, you're the best in the Cantina probably even the Boondocks."

"I appreciate the complement but even I know my limits. I know when to act. But more importantly when not to act. I've survived this long specifically by knowing which fights not to take. And I'm telling you I don't stand a chance against a Mercurial."

"You saw me bring in Morty the Skunk! Not to mention the others, you're not just a lone wolf sniping bounties now. You've got a team behind you!" Jack said passionately."

"Morty the Skunk and Knox may as well be a different species... you're not ready Jack... I'm not sure anyone is ready for someone like him."

Jack put his hands over his head as the faces adorning the wall looked through him.

Matilda chimed in after some time itching her whiskers, "What if we were to set some kind of trap? Lure'em in then blow the tunnels!"

"I can't risk that… I won't put you all in danger. For all we know he could just teleport out or in or something."

It was about this time Chef Greene swung the doors open with an oversized plate of freshly steamed octopus eggs, Matilda hadn't looked so excited this whole conversation.

Jack shoved a few eggs into his mouth in a manner that clearly showed his anger, "So what's the plan then?? We'll just sit in here till we all die of old age?"

"I don't hate it" Riley said sharply, "Based on the people I've spoken to, it seems our only real option is to find Radish and put chains on him. We know he's somewhere in Kleppenwitz… we just have to find him. My sources say to look for a man with salt-and-pepper hair, that wears an eyepatch and carries a maroon cutlass."

Something about the description gave Jack pause, but he continued, "You think Knox's just going to quit once we hand him over? If he's got the cops in his pocket, we're the only ones he's got to worry about."

"Maybe so maybe not, but it will buy us some time."

There was silence in the Room as the faces on the wall seemed to stare at them begrudgingly. The only sounds were the clinking of plates Chef Greene was putting onto the kingly wooden table.

"Let me get this straight." Jack cleared his throat, "You think Radish, the man who stole Quicksilver from Comandante Magnus himself is going to just waltz into our laps? For all we know Knox may be easier to deal with than him!"

"I'll take my chances with Radish the human, over Knox the Mercurial." she said back swiftly.

It was about this time Chef Greene's ears perked up after overhearing them.

"Radish??? Yu looking for him??" Greene said nonchalantly.

"Yes… Have you heard of him??" Riley said back with utter confusion.

"Heard o' him? Even better… know where he is!

Flush with excitement, Riley couldn't believe what she was hearing, she'd never known Greene to tell tall tales, but this was simply unbelievable.

"Well, where is he?!?!"

"He sitting right over there!!" Chef Greene pointed out through the open doors to a broken table just outside in Hangman's Hall.

There could be no doubt the man sitting there was Radish, with his unkempt black and white hairs, unhooked suspenders, and moldy eyepatch. He was passed out and snoring loud enough for them to hear and kept jumping up in his chair every few seconds looking like he was choking on something in his sleep.

Riley pulled her cutlass from its scabbard while the others looked on agog, unable to comprehend what was happening.

Before anyone could think she was at Radish's table with her blade at his neck as nearby patrons looked on in disbelief. Jack and Matilda darted along with her and put their pistols on the man as a small crowd of patrons gathered around.

She looked dead in his eye unwavering for what seemed like minutes,

"So you're the Quicksilver Thief?" she said slowly.

"Allegedly." he laughed, kicking his feet up. "And you must be Riley…. Pride of the Blackwater… heard a lot about you… Setting the Five Isles on fire one bounty at a time… spose I should be lily-livered right about now!"

"Your liver for once isn't your biggest problem. Give me one reason why I shouldn't kill you and take your corpse to Knox!"

He responded with a devious smile, "Cause that would mean death for both of us, love."

Chapter 7

<u>The Monkeys Imparted</u>

Radish sat there awkwardly furiously itching at his eyepatch trying to remove gunk buildup from underneath it while a room full of bounty hunters had their pistols pointed squarely at his head.

"I'll say it again, give me one *good* reason why I shouldn't kill you right now." Riley commanded her sword still at his throat.

"For the same reason rats dream of a world without owls." he still said itching at it. Without looking up he pointed at the Bounty Board clicking away, "You think that thing's some hidden jewel of the Boondocks?"

"What's your point?" she said coldly.

"Let's say you kill me," he said making a mocking death gesture and accompanying throat sound, "Do you really think Knox's going to stop? The police are too stupid to stop him and that's me bein charitable… why wouldn't he want to kill the only ones on this island that have a chance of bringin down his little… operation?"

Radish's expression just like the skin surrounding it seemed as if it were carved from stone, how someone could be brave, or rather stupid enough to be unbothered at a time like this was a mystery to every man and woman staring at him.

She lifted the flat of her blade against his chin forcing him to look up at her,

"Maybe he won't stop, but it may at least buy us some time. I'd take that well before throwing my hat in with the likes of a mercenary who would sell his own mother for a sack of doubloons."

"Don't sell her so short. She's worth at least double that love!" he laughed, "I'm quite sure that pie face Knox can't be negotiated with, he's too far gone, or sick, whatever you want to call it. But let's assume I'm wrong, to be honest with you the last time I saw him his head was so red it looked like it had been dipped into the sun itself, so maybe you're right."

"My thoughts exactly, so tell me again why I don't have chains around your neck yet?"

"Because getting rid of Knox won't solve your other problem…"

"Which is?" she said suspiciously.

"What do you think happens to Kleppenwitz, and by extension the Gibbons after Prego falls?"

"That's if Prego falls…"

"Corrrecto!" he said finger up as if he knew more than he was letting on, "What happens when Magnus has access to all of Prego's resources? Enough Kristal and doubloons to double the size of his army? What happens when the Comandante convinces Vista to fight against you?" his raspy voice now captivating an audience, "I've seen the Forzian Fleets turn crystal waters black, and I've seen the Forzian Armies turn the impregnable pregnable, and let's just say after that I had half mind to seek out some satellite hideout till the day comes I finally cash in my chips."

"Maybe if you had left we wouldn't be in this mess. You reconsidered I assume?"

"Hidings no fun, especially when you could be enjoying the finer things in life!" Radish winked at Riley who then shuddered immediately.

Matilda took her turn to sit down with her oversized pistol flat on the wooden table pointed straight at him.

"Your real sweet Mr. Mercenary man, but you ain't goin to talk your way out of this one."

"Well now! I would say that's exactly what I intend to do!"

"Uh-huh… So let me get this straight… not only can you take care of this Knox dingus, but also the greatest army the Five Isles have seen since the Ghosts left? Ha! Well you must be our guardian angel."

"And here I was worried this was going to be an unpleasant exchange!"

"You… do know the Rogue's been missin for months, right? The one man who had any shot at leadin an army against Magnus…"

He snapped his finger back at her like she had a great point.

"Well then, given you worked with'em, I'd guess you know the latest rumor is he finally figured he was way in over them fancy brisked boots'o his and ran as fast as he could to some forsaken desert in Caldo to try and hideaway from Magnus. The leader of the Freeboots… heh… poof… gone just like that!"

He nodded even more excitedly. The clinking of plates and glasses had all but died down as the audience of nosy Gibbons grew bigger. Jack stared at Radish intently through his sights, for a man he'd grown up hearing tall tales about he couldn't help but notice how unremarkable he was. From his tattered clothing to his knotted hair and dusty old boots, the man looked like he'd been living under a rock.

"So what's your plan then genius? You look like you couldn't even beat the washer, and you plan on beatin Knox *and* Comandanty Magnus?!" Matilda laughed.

"What if I told you we didn't need the Rogue?"

Several people in the audience laughed as he continued,

"Or suppose we do need'em. What if I told you the last place the Rogue was seen was right here in Kleppenwitz? Under our little noses…"

The crowd didn't laugh at this statement however, instead many of their ears perked up.

"You didn't think I'd just show up here empty-handed, did you?"

"That's it I've heard enough of this pirate's lies!" Riley interjected having more than she could stand, "I'm putting on the irons and finding a way to get him to Knox."

"Oh you can arrest me if you like…" Radish said looking over the crowd, speaking to them now instead of Riley, "But more of you will die, probably even most of you, just like the ones that died not too far from here… what was the fellows name? Crowfeet was it?"

"H-How did you know?" Riley said in shock.

"I'm the Quicksilver Thief, even kings stash their crowns when they hear I've made port. You really think it's hard for a man like me to gather information? Now, do you want blood on your hands Tripleleaf? The blood of all these good people around us? All because you can't stomach working with a man with a less than stellar reputation?"

"Less than stellar! Now that's what I call charitability!" Matilda howled.

"Your morality is a luxury, one I never had. I can assure you me and my contemporaries see the world much the same as you, but we all gotta eat, and we all got little birds in our lives mouths open lookin for grubs, so here we are…"

Riley was horrified to see a few faces in the crowd now looking at her sideways.

"Let'em speak!" one yelled.

"The man was partners with the Rogue…" another said, "And pulled one over on the Comandante. Mphm. We should hear his thoughts!"

She took her eyes off Radish for one second and noticed one of the men yelling was Lucas Geist.

"Lucas please don't start now; you know if we compromise our morals for any savage who decides to barge in off the street, we're no better than animals. We've got a code… a code I plan on sticking to, the Gibbons have never made a habit of scheming with low lives like him!"

"The Gibbons also never had a Mercurial murdering its members!" he yelled back louder with several of his cronies cheering behind him. "I didn't say we should initiate him, I said we should hear what he has to say…"

Radish pointed at Lucas with an approving smile, "Now there's a proper bloke! A bottle of rum on me!"

Jack was shocked this may've been the first time he'd ever agreed with Lucas Geist,

"I can't explain now, can't believe I'm saying this… but I-I uh agree with Lucas, I think we should hear him out…" he whispered to his mom.

She looked at Jack flabbergasted and unsure. Feeling defeated Riley took a seat beside Matilda,

"Go on…" she said face looking like it'd been folded into a million pieces.

The picaroon continued with his ever so slightly slurred speech, and a tone that no matter how hard he tried to be serious, always had a hint of sarcasm.

"Ah Yes! As I was saying I have good information from some of the finest pub enthusiasts on the Boondocks that the Rogue was last seen in Kleppenwitz. And given that he left an army which he raised and commanded, we'll I'd venture he must've had a very good reason to be here!"

"That all you've got...?"

"I believe the Rogue was looking for... some sort of weapon. And given he decided to leave all that was precious to him to go lookin for it, I highly doubt this was some fancy new pistol."

"What sort of weapon?"

"Hard to say really, in fact I've been spending most of my days pondering that exact question. But if the Rogue wanted it, I can assure you we do too."

"Let me guess, you'll want us to go on some wild goose chase to find it?" Riley sighed.

"I believe I've already found it! ... Or maybe I should say found her..."

Several audience members gasped.

"Well that's a relief, so why haven't you saved the Pinwheels yet?" she said sarcastically.

"I just haven't figured out how to *unlock* it yet, so to speak. Which will involve hmmm... what's the term?"

"A wild goose chase?"

He pointed at her with his confusing smile, "Yes yes! That's it exactly!"

"Ok I've heard enough, Matilda hand me the irons! I'd rather Knox kill me than hear another word of this dribble!"

Riley attempted to stand up, but Jack pulled her arm and whispered in her ear,

"Mom you can't do this! I can't explain now, it's-it's something I heard earlier in the market, he's right when he says we need him!"

"What's gotten into you?! What could possibly justify working with him?!" she whispered furiously.

"Well if the monk I spoke to was right, my life may depend on it…"

Riley just stared back at him with her mouth open.

"Ahem!" Radish blurted out loudly, "As much as I appreciate you lovely monkeys showing me all your fine weaponry, I've got more than a few people trying to kill me right now, so I'd rather not dally."

"Any other day you'd be a dead man Radish, I want you to remember that. By some miracle I'm not going to sign your death warrant… yet" Riley said coldly.

"By the grace of the monsoon! Well doesn't this sound like the start of a wonderful new friendship!"

"Don't push it… Let's say I don't change my mind… where can we find you?"

At about this time Chef Greene brought over the bottle of rum Radish had ordered.

"Ah yes, Marquise here can give you the particulars." he said as he pointed at Chef Greene, Jack was embarrassed to learn that this was his first name, he'd only ever heard him referred to as Chef Greene.

"One last thing," Jack finally got up the courage to speak, "Why do you need us? It sounds like you've already got a good plan without our involvement?"

"Was wondering when Jack would speak! It's simple, my short-toothed friend. I need Riley, I need the resources Gibbons can provide, but most of all…" he pointed up to the Bounty Board where Knox's name still rested at the top, "Most of all I'd like a big pot of gold!"

"H-how did you know my name?" Jack said utterly confused.

"You're a storm in a teacup! Your mum said it earlier kid…" he said as he poured a glass of rum for Riley and Matilda and pushed it towards them after taking a big gulp for himself. He then confidently got up to leave taking his rum with him.

"You gotta pay for dat!" Chef Marquise Greene yelled back at him.

"Ahhh… right… let's see… I seemed to have left my coin purse at home, Riley and… Matilda was it? You don't mind covering me just this once, do you??"

"Mister I can't tell if you're real real smart, or just real real stupid." Matilda laughed.

"Make no mistake, dark clouds are rollin, Jack, Riley, and Matilda…" he said to Jack politely as if he didn't still have a gun pointed at his head, "Do keep in mind, you need me just as much as I need you…"

Radish smiled and bowed and made his way out with a giant room of bounty hunters still staring at him, too dumbfounded to try and stop him.

****

The faces around the gritty wooden Acclaimatory had a way of following you around wherever you went, and even more oddly matching whatever emotion you were feeling. Matilda, Jack and Riley sat awkwardly trying to make sense of what had just transpired.

"Honestly, what in the Five Isles has gotten into you Jack? We just let the one man we needed to save our tails waltz right out the door after he gave himself up on a silver platter! What's this about the monk? Is there something you're not telling me??"

"He was right you know," Jack said slowly, "Knox won't stop, even if he gets Radish."

"Radish is a **Picaroon**!! A thief, and a scoundrel! What are you not understanding?? He's just as likely to sell us out to Knox as he is to help capture him. You're still young Jack, and new to the game. But if you'd seen how these men operate... they'll turn on you without a second thought. The minute you stop benefitting them. They're rotten, the whole lot of them!"

"Mom we can't know that for sure! The man was partners with the Rogue, how bad could he possibly be?"

"If he's even being honest about that, wouldn't surprise me if he got his reputation solely by telling tall tales in every one of his grimy bars, and just let word-of-mouth do the rest."

"Knox wouldn't be terrorizing every bounty hunter on Kleppenwitz if that were true."

Riley thought about it for a bit then realized he was right, if she wasn't so mad with him right now, she might've been impressed.

"So what about the monk? You mentioned you forget ta tell us somethin important?" Matilda said as she looked up over her boots on the table.

"I told y'all most of it already, just left the last little bit out is all. I-I'm sorry, I just didn't want to frighten you. At the Flagpoles he was chasing me around, incoherent almost, but as he was following, he kept saying something..." Jack felt a knot in his belly as he remembered it, "What he said was *Follow your new companion... or you will die...* and he just kept saying it over and over, like he'd gone completely mad. Even as I ran away, I could hear his voice echoing through the crowds.*"*

Matilda and Riley both gulped in unison, while Matilda fought off the urge to spit on the ground.

"And you think he was referring to Radish?" Riley said with bated breath.

"I don't exactly know of any other new companions..."

Riley sat with her hand over her head for what felt like forever, eventually Matilda spoke up,

"Riles, I'd hardly call that dusty feller a 'companion', we just met the guy. Jack you sure there's no one else you met recently, an old friend or? Maybe some new girlfriend yur hidin from us??"

Solemnly he just shook his head in place.

"I need some time to think on this," Riley said as she got up to leave, shying her face, "If you need me, I'll be in the library…"

The two giant mahogany doors made a thunderous thud as Matilda looked over at Jack.

"She just needs some space is all, time to process her emotions ya'know. She'd take a seven-day vacation to Allora if she heard you was there. Which is why she's been so stressed lately, wouldn't know what to do with herself if somethin happened to ye."

"I know… I know. It's just, I'm not a kid anymore. Sooner or later, I'm going to have to make my way in this world just like everyone else, just like she did all those years ago."

"Well son, given your monk situation, and Rile's reaction, sounds like you'll have that opportunity sooner than you think. Anywho, I gotta be off, gave Jenkins chandelier cleanin duty and I'm afraid he may fall off the rafters, wouldn't want that on my conscience. I'd get all your affairs in order, sounds like we're all in for a pretty wild ride!"

With that Matilda made her way out with her ruffled black dress dragging across the floor like it always did.

The faces lining the wall stared at him as if they were just as interested in finding out his next move as he was. Somewhere in the middle of the wall was a portrait of Radish with his red scars and leather eyepatch. If there was one mind he could read Radish's would be at the top of his list. What could he have been thinking? No one had ever been brave enough to waltz into the Blackwater Cantina like that, unarmed and without a plan, and even crazier, he miraculously made it out in one piece.

Back in Hangman's Hall Jack took some time to stand still and take it all in. It always amazed him how this spot for Gibbons might've been one of the liveliest places he'd had the pleasure of visiting and thought it unfortunate so few would ever get to see it. There were currently men hurling insults over which of their rats won a duel, a bar-maiden threatening to throw someone in the dungeon for not paying their tab, and when he looked up, he saw two men hanging from the rafters with a pile of silver eights in between them. Jack soon worked out whoever held on the longest got to keep the silver. Seeing as how it was such a long drop, Jack felt thankful Riley had instilled enough sense in him to avoid situations like these.

As he got to the bar and admired the Bounty Board above him, he was happy to see Sarah Blitzen sitting close enjoying some poached ostrich eggs.

"Evening Jack!! Monsoon's Mercy! What a day you've had!"

It was one of the reasons Jack liked talking to her so much, even when it was about something negative, she was always extremely curious and interested in what he had to say.

"I have a feeling this day is just getting started..." he said wearily.

"You've got your body armor ready? Pistols loaded? Hope you're not planning on fighting Knox just yet, are you??!" Sarah spoke with a yell, trying to speak over all the loud noise the hall produced.

"Not if he's lucky! What I wouldn't give to have him in my crosshairs..."

"You're not serious, are you?! I've seen you in the range I know you can shoot, but a full blown Mercurial that could set a pack of wolves on you?? Have a flock of ravens gouge out your eyes? Seems totally different from a still target!"

"As serious as a heart attack. He attacked Gibbons, killed some of our own, in home territory no less. No way we can just let that go."

"Ohh... I do hope you know what you're getting yourself into!" Sarah stood up in her chair, "I've been hearing rumors floating around all afternoon that Riley Tripleleaf and Radish may be teaming up against Knox. The Pride of the Blackwater and the Quicksilver Thief working together... feels like I should call the press!"

"She's still making her mind up, but at this point, with everything that's gone on today; I'd say the odds of that happening are pretty good…"

"Well, you'd better make it back in one piece, Old Man Timmermans can't keep himself awake past four p.m., Glasgo's always gone, and there isn't much else our age, unless you count Jenkins. And if he sneaks up behind me one more time, I have half a mind to make him a real-life target dummy!"

They both had a good laugh as he got up to leave,

"Oh, and one more thing," she said, "I forgot to mention it, when all the commotion died down earlier, right after Radish left. I saw Lucas Geist whispering into Chef Greene's ear with a look in his eye that gave me chills…"

"You think he's up to something?"

"When is he not up to something?!"

"Good point." Jack looked around the room and thought for a minute, "Now what would he possibly want with the Chef?"

"Didn't Radish mention Greene knew where Radish's hideout was? Maybe he wants to get to Radish before you can?! Maybe he wants to offer him a deal of his own?! I wouldn't put anything past him…"

"That little weasel! I knew he would stoop low, but not this low. I need to get this info over to mom and Matilda. See what they think." he said speedily. "Do me a favor and keep an eye on him while we're out, will you?"

"I'd be keeping an eye on him even if we never had this conversation!"

As Jack was making his way towards his destination, he spotted Marcus A. and gave a nod as he heard the man lecturing a group of young bounty hunters on his favorite hideouts around Kleppenwitz, and the best sailing routes to take to avoid pirates.

The old stone castle-like tower which led down to the Monarch Library was in the corner of Hangman's Hall and might've been one of the good hideouts Marcus A. was mentioning given so few patrons even knew about the place.

The windy staircase kept going for so long one could become hypnotized by them. There were stone carvings of all sorts of faces of men and women with strange features like bulging eyeballs and oversized chins.

Down he went, only able to tell he was making progress by the stone faces steadily growing smaller and smaller. When he finally got to the bottom, he looked over the tiny but portly stone door that hid at the entrance. It was the only door in the place shorter than he was, and you had to nudge it quite hard with your shoulder to even get it to open.

After getting in he grabbed his shoulder awkwardly and looked across the library. It was brighter than he remembered, and he recognized new bookshelves, which embarrassed him since it was a reminder of how long it'd been since he'd visited.

The rows and rows of worn wooden rafters on the ceiling gave the space a subtle charm, assisted even more by rows of teakwood desks which were interspersed evenly throughout the main floor. The centerpiece of the library was an exact replica of the Five Isles suspended fifteen feet high with a mixture of chains and glass. The suspended wood and canvas were meticulously maintained. Jack was always amazed when he read the news about a village, for example, being destroyed on Prego, that same village would be gone from the piece only a few days later.

Lining every inch of stone wall was a sea of motley old tomes and scrolls covered in dust and endlessly stacked on top of one another, with all the known and unknown classics from gypsies, historians, monks and scribes across the Five Isles. The thousands of candles that lined the desks and upper shelves were the main source of light within and perfectly set the mood for a night filled with studying or even better discovering secrets long lost. If one accidentally stepped out of the entrance hall, they could easily get lost in the place, with all its unchartered floors and unseen quarters, Jack was surprised he'd never stumbled into a skeleton while exploring.

The main bookkeeper Peg Odswald was sitting behind her desk at the head of the entrance hall just like she always was, with head buried in a book. Today she had her silky grey hair tied up in a suffocating bun, dull weatherworn wool clothes, and the same pointy glasses she always wore.

The book she was currently waving her arm over her head to page turn made him wonder how she managed to haul it over to her desk. She loved this place so much Jack wasn't sure if she had a pod of her own, or if she just slept behind her desk when everyone left. Of all his years in the Cantina, he'd never once seen her enjoying a band in Hangman's Hall or socializing in a pod chamber. It mattered little, however, because as long as you could keep quiet in her library, she was a great friend to have, most especially when you needed information.

An excellent source of all the vast histories and current mysteries of the Five Isles, in fact bookkeepers in general were renowned for their knowledge of all types of complexities. From average city folk to kings and queens, on matters of great importance many of them would never act until they had the blessing and wisdom of a bookkeeper. They were mostly found as the head of universities, but the Gibbons were lucky enough to have one of their own.

As Jack was passing by, looking over all the scrolls seeing if he could find anything that mentioned monks, he accidentally stepped on a loose floorboard and caught a wide eye from Peg. *Doubt that's the first time this happens today* he thought.

As he wandered, he noticed several old tomes that looked worth a read like *Forzian History: The Bedeviled Dynasties* by *M. Kutter* and *The Greatest Story Ever Told – Tales of The Rogue* by *Jean-Luc Aurus,* and *Steam Powered Engines via Kristal and other Mercurial Invention* by *Masink Koontz* and lastly *Choosing the right healer for you: Doctors, Monks, or Gypsies?*, he'd have to remember to try and check them out later if Peg would allow it.

Continuing to peruse as quietly as he could, he spotted Riley in one of the back cubbies, looking so interested in the book she was reading she might not've noticed a bomb going off.

"Back in your favorite place?" Jack said as he took a seat beside her, "I'm surprised they don't have a bookshelf here named after you!"

"They do, Peg just put up the plaque last week…" she whispered back, and they both snickered as she pointed at it.

"Why isn't Peg over here helping with any of this?"

"That would've made things easier, she would've found what I wanted in seconds instead of hours. I wanted to ask, but... well you know how she gets when she's disturbed. Figured I'd be better off trying myself, at least at first."

Jack looked down at the book she was reading entitled *Caldorian Monks: Pacificism, Parables, and Prophecies* by *Marc Lemmings*.

"Well the title sounds promising enough! Find anything Interesting?"

"Yes, actually," Riley said her face more concerned now, "I've been going over this passage again and again... it's called **The Legend of Caldo's Corazon**, take a look..."

The Fifth Tsar of Caldo strolled along the desert by caravan in midsummer where the temperatures got so high most dared not leave their dwellings. By stroke of luck, he happened upon a peculiar glowing green chest that a recent sandstorm had uncovered.

In all his years as a Trade King of Caldo dealing with the rarest of antiquities, he'd never stumbled upon anything that captivated him so much. His army of servants carried it the long distance back to his castle outside of Sullenmoon City, and when they arrived, he was amazed to see the locking mechanism that had previously been clamped down tight, found its way open.

Expecting to see riches beyond compare inside, like enough doubloons to build a second castle, or a golden crown to signify his great status, he instead found something unexpected. Inside, sitting by itself, and looking lonely with all the space there was to spare, was a piercing blue sapphire, with two prominent edges on either side jutting out in the form of a jagged heart.

It took no time for the Tsar to become obsessed with his new treasure. He slept with it on his bedside table, brought it as his guest to the castle's great feasts, and had even begun quietly whispering to the jewel, like it was a dear friend or confidant.

There was a secret to be unlocked within it, he knew beyond a certainty. Perhaps something that would help fight the other Caldorian Spice Kings who meant to seize his fertile lands and trade routes for their own.

On more than a few occasions the Tsar looked over at the jewel sitting by his bedside, as if it was calling to him, but nothing ever happened. He attempted baking it in the sun, dunking it in freezing water, and one night after much frustration, in a fit of rage he took his giant mace to it. Still nothing... the jewel was indestructible and immutable, it appeared now immaculate in the shape he found it.

Frustrations only grew and eventually the Tsar called forth his most trusted advisors, bookkeepers from all around Caldo gathered to try and figure its secret, but as old tomes were read, and interviews conducted, they were hurt to admit they had no answer to give.

For years the jewel sat on the Tsar's bedside table, slowly gathering dust, until eventually a young monk came along who called himself the Monk of Morregan and informed the Tsar that he knew the identity of his prized possession.

The monk confirmed exactly what the Tsar had expected. That this was no ordinary jewel, it was borne of an ancient Mercurial Magic, as old as the Pinwheels themselves, and as cursed as the Black Gale.

Still the Tsar insisted, and because he had been an honorable and trustworthy ruler to the monk's people, protecting them from raiders and providing rations when their crop yields floundered, the monk felt compelled to assist. The jewel was known as Caldo's Corazon and was designed to hold powerful Mercurial Magic within it. The monk again urged the Tsar that this was no magic for a man, even for one as impressive as himself, and that if he continued trying to unearth its secret... the jewel would soon destroy him.

The Tsar thanked the young monk for his time and sent him on his way, promising to again provide provisions should the day come his monastery required it.

It was only a short few years later the Monk of Morregan attended the Fifth Tsar of Caldo's funeral. There was no casket, no officiant, and no body. Only his prized possession had made the affair, strung along a dusky rope and being let down as if it were the most practical thing they could find in place of a body.

Many speculated of course, as to what happened to the great ruler. But none could say for sure. Some said he'd fled Caldo for Forza to escape his enemies, others said he'd gone to live the quiet life in some hidden desert oasis, but the monk however, had his own suspicion.

Happy that what he knew to be a cursed jewel was now being buried deep in the ground, where it couldn't harm anyone again, he gave it one final look before it was let down for good. The tortured face of the great Tsar was staring right back at him, looking through the glassy jewel like it was a prison wall, mouth agape as if crying out for help.

"Sounds like the monks aren't just puffing smoke..." Jack said wearily.

"No... no it doesn't...." she said flummoxed, her silver body armor showing his faded reflection.

"Does that mean you've made up your mind?"

"We'll at least see what he has to say, for the time being it seems pretty clear his interests are aligned with ours, so I doubt we have to worry about him trying to kill us, not yet at least..."

"Didn't think you'd be so easy to convince."

"Don't get cocky, if I see a way out of this that protects our family, I'm taking that option the first second I can..."

Feeling a little spark of inspiration, he nodded back assuredly.

"And another thing, I want to be Clear as Kristal when I say this... if we're going to do this, to try and kill the deadliest criminal the Boondocks has ever known... you follow my lead *every-single-step* of the way. No stepping off on your own to try and chase someone down. You do what I say... When I say it. Clear?"

"Yes mom... of course. But you know sooner or later you're going to have to let me spread my wings, right?" he said earnestly.

"I know that sweet, of course you're not a kid anymore. Pretty soon you'll be free to explore the Pinwheels and make all the dumb mistakes I made at your age. And if it was anyone else, I would be happy to let you fly. But make no mistake about what we're chasing. One or both of us may not ever make it back from this, I just really hope you understand the gravity of the situation..."

Back in Hangman's Hall underneath the Bounty Board they continued their conversation, thrilled to be in a place where they no longer had to whisper,

"You've got all your armor on? And on snug? You tested it just like I taught you right?"

"Yesss..." Jack droned.

"Cutlass? Pistol? Backup boot pistol? Food supplies, ammo?"

"Right where they should be."

"Make sure and order another basket of rye, you don't know when your next meal will be." she said shortly.

"Almost forgot to mention," he said wiping butter off his cheek, "Did you hear what Sarah Smiles saw Lucas doing?"

"Trying to get Radish's hideout from Chef Greene?"

"How'd you know?!"

"Matilda saw him do it too, I don't think she ever lets at least one eye off him. Anyways, like most people here Chef Marquise Green doesn't like Lucas very much. So, after Greene told us we told him to give him an address of our own instead. Not to where Radish is hiding, but to another very... *special location...*"

"What place would that be?" he smirked.

"The Landfill. If I had to guess right about now, he's waist deep in garbage, swimming through rotten chunks, thinking he'll have outsmarted us all when he finally finds the hideout." she could barely hold in her laughter while Jack couldn't help himself from howling smack in the middle of Hangman's Hall.

The pair was watching two ruffians in the Rat Pits still having a shouting match, most likely the same from earlier, when suddenly ahead at the bar, they were happy to see Matilda with a big grin serving them another plate of buttered rye bread.

"You two ready to make moves? Heck I hadn't put my armor on in way too long… I'd be shocked if it still fits." Matilda joked slapping her big belly.

"You sure that's such a good idea? Who's going to watch the Cantina?" Riley said, "Where are the other managers? Where's Agnes Beach?"

"Heck, I doubt Agnes even knows where Agnes is…"

"And Bartleby Storm?"

"With his monkey mind? Prolly doin the same thing he's always doin, wholed up in a dark room somewhere, monkey-wrench in hand tryin to discover all the secrets of the isles."

"What about Stono?"

"Stono the Caiman? Well… he'd keep chasin bounties even if we started chargin steada payin. With that little mirror image Glasgo of his holdin a rifle you didn't think was invented yet. You could guess just the type of place they're at, some marsh with reeds all over their heads, stalkin some murderer wortha lotta gold."

"Well, if that's the case someone has to watch the Cantina. Maybe Knox gets a wild hair and decides to attack here."

"You sure about that? I know some of these guards ain't playin with a full deck, but the rest ain't so bad. This place'll be fine without me for a few hours!"

"I'd rather not risk it, plus Jack and I will have an easier time blending in if it's just the two of us."

"Ha! That's a good point, I'm not exactly what one might call inconspicuous! So you've got a deal Riles… say, were ya able to gather anythin else on the weapon?"

"What weapon?!" Jack said with his cheeks so full he looked like a chipmunk.

"The weapon Radish spoke about," Riley said calmly, "I couldn't find much, he didn't really give us much to go off other than the Rogue was on the Boondocks looking for something. Something powerful enough to fight Knox and Magnus."

"Sounds like a dern dream come true!"

"Almost too good to be true… though this crazy island has been harboring all sorts of seedy types ever since the eight settled it. There's a long history of treasure hunters coming here looking for lost or hidden doubloons, some books even mentioned treasures greater than gold, though unfortunately they didn't go into much detail, there may be more to discover in the Monarch, but it would take me weeks instead of a few hours to pour through it all."

"Well I guess Radish'll have to fill us out on his little master plan then. If he's even got one. You think we can trust him?" Matilda said.

"Can we trust Radish? Absolutely not." she said, "What we can trust is that Radish will always look out for Radish. If we aren't getting in the way of his own limitless greed, I think he'll be manageable. Especially if I've got my pistol pointed at him."

"Sounds like you got it all figured out. You remember the instructions on where Radish is hidin from Greene?"

"Sure do."

"Well hope you two have fun at the Flagpoles then." Matilda looked over them each with a stern look now, "And remember to come back in one piece, don't think I could bear to be the only one here dealin with that doofus Lucas!"

Riley smiled and blew her a kiss from her seat at the bar.

"You ready kid?" Riley whispered to Jack.

"Just another day on the Boondocks…" Jack said with both timidness and excitement in his voice.

The pair marched towards the big wooden double doors, past the guards that were on duty. Jack took one big look back at Hangman's Hall in all its majesty. The last time he'd left like this to catch Morty the Skunk, he hadn't seen this view again for weeks, he hoped maybe foolishly this time around he'd be back in shorter order than that.

As they walked Jack put a hand over his eye to block the moonlight coming from the door at the end of the tunnel.

Riley pushed it open which made a big *creak* sound, as Gunter the doorman briefly looked up at them.

"Evening Gunter!" Riley said.

"Hello again Gunter!" Jack said.

Gunter just gave a nod so small his head barely moved.

The cozy Kleppenwitz white and woodboarded cottages looked back at them like they were old friends as the full moon brought their exuberance to life.

Just as they had passed the entrance to the crowded city streets Riley jerked Jack's shoulder back with her hand.

She was staring in disbelief at four men approaching them in policemen's uniform.

"Keep quiet…" she whispered as she stepped in front.

As the men approached Riley immediately recognized one of them.

"Evening madame," Detective Konrad said in a forceful tone, "We're here looking for a fugitive goes by the name Radish. And I've heard from a little birdie, that you're working with him…"

Chapter 8

The Boiled Witch

Knox's cave was a pool of stalactites and stalagmites with blends of fire and smoke pouring out of their ends, which left behind peculiar sand like orange crystals as the smoke evaporated.

Alireza Bale walked along the caverns slowly, her black leather suit was immaculate, held up by a battle worn leather belt sided with two pistols on either hip. She had imposing eyes, with bulging dull green veins scattered around them like jagged cobwebs. Her hair looked dry and wiry, and her fingers were scarred bone. On said fingers she wore her most prized possession. A white gold ring in the shape of a sunflower, which no matter what she was doing, never left her finger. She had an eerie sort of grace about her when she moved, a sort of confidence that came with being such an accomplished assassin.

She approached behind Knox who was busy interrogating an elderly man chained to the cave walls.

"And what color were the girl's eyes?" Knox said looking deeply into the man's eyes as he swatted at gnats feeding on his sores.

The man was too broken to speak, barely even breathing, in a foggy slumber.

"Hugo!" Knox said looking at his Grey Wolf companion, "Wake up our friend..."

With teeth on full display, the wolf that was bigger than the prisoner himself crawled inches away from his face. A few loud barks were more than enough to jolt him from his spell.

"I'll give you one more opportunity to answer before I give Hugo an early lunch. When you saw the girl being smuggled into the sewers, what color were her eyes?!" he said with thunder in his voice.

The man struggled desperately trying to get out the words, "Mixed sir, never seen anything like it..." he stuttered, "One blue.... the other b-brright b-beautiful purple..."

The Grey Wolf was still lurched over the man, sniveling like he desperately wanted Knox to give the order.

"That will do..." Knox said with a half-smile, "Hugo! Come!"

The Brigadier, his bloodthirsty wolf, and new assassin near chuckled when they heard the prisoner collapse again as they walked along a cavernous path with bits of steam sprouting out from the hundreds of geysers surrounding them.

Knox was wearing flowing white linen robes that covered his crooked and gangly figure, with cracked sandals that matched his cracked feet. He wore gold and aged jewelry on his face, neck, and ears that did a poor job of hiding the many boils and blisters along his face and body and did an even poorer job of masking the needle-like indentations circling his skull as if he'd worn a crown of thorns to bed every night. He had a bent nose that'd been broken more than once, which sat under his bloodshot, swollen, and unblinking eyes. His skin was pale, so pale he hardly seemed human, like the blood had all but disappeared and was replaced by something else entirely.

"You come very highly recommended Alireza, your master tells me you're one of his most capable young apprentices… I hope you'll enjoy my little hideaway as much as I do, I trust your accommodations are suitable?" he said his snake like voice slithering.

"It's a pleasure to be here Brigadier. And of course, sir, fit for a queen. Our Comandante Magnus said he's impressed with what the winds whisper of you… he hopes you'll be a valuable ally in the wars to come."

Knox nodded. "And I understand you're coming right from a battle on Prego. Some of the slavers tell me they're putting up a bigger fight than expected."

"They've got more grit than we anticipated. It's true. But Magnus will make quick work of them. In Forza you don't make it to the top without talent, and he's got it in spades. His prowess as a general is unmatched. It's just a matter of time until he moves on to Vista… and beyond…"

"Seems you aren't very worried about the Rogue?"

"What's there to be worried about? He put up a good fight at first it's true, the stories of the counter general weren't distorted. His armies were clever, flanking us and attacking when they had the numbers, and hiding in the mines when they didn't. But in the end, it made no difference, he did what all generals do when they see the full force of a Forzian Fleet coming for them, he tucked tail and… ran." she fluttered her bony fingers.

Knox towered over her with a malevolent look. While his words were filled with pleasantries an onlooker might've mistaken this for an interrogation much like the one they'd just come from.

"I've heard many tales of Aurarick, running away was never a part of any of them…" Knox said glaring.

"Well, seeing an army like ours tends to change a man…" she said refusing to back down.

Opening the door to his barracks slow, as if to cause tension, his men stood at attention like it was their biggest priority after it gave way. There were near a hundred of them, all dressed in commoner's clothes now instead of their usual soldiers' uniforms.

"You'll see we have plenty of troops at our disposal, take as many or as little as you need. You'll find they're trained well enough, at the very least they can absorb shots while you go for a clean kill." Knox half chuckled.

"Appreciated. But I was hoping we could talk about the artifact first…"

"You let me worry about the artifact!" Knox said with a sudden flare in his voice, "I brought you here to kill the man who stole it, understood?"

"Of course, sir…" she said with a combative smile.

"Do you know who that man is?"

"The fool they call Radish…"

"Precisely, I take it you've heard of him?"

"The Quicksilver Thief? Everyone on Forza's heard of him. Magnus offered a castle in the Seven Cities to the first man or woman that brought him his head. Him and the Rogue may be the only two people in the Five Isles that Magnus would allow me to leave the battlefield for."

"Well sounds like if you can get this done, him and I both will make you a very rich woman."

Alireza nodded, "Your prisoner back there, he mentioned a girl with blue and purple eyes?"

"Yes… She's what…" he paused, "She was taken from me, and I'd like very much to have her back. If you take nothing else from this conversation, take this, not a hair on her head is to be touched, dispose of Radish anyway you see fit, in fact the more painful the better. But she stays safe. I've got my own plan for her."

"If I might ask…what's so important about the girl?"

"You may not. Either way she's of little consequence to you. She's simply someone who could end up being very valuable to a man in my line of work."

"As you wish…"

The three of them marched through the barracks while Knox looked over his men with contempt, they continued until the dormitory walls slowly morphed back into cave. In front of them was a castle of a staircase with thousands of steps carved from the rock of the cave underneath. There were piles of smoke bellowing from the crevices in the walls to either side, as they ascended towards the top floor above them.

Crouching down he shook his gnarly wolf's giant mane,

"I hope Hugo isn't too much of a bother. Most people are frightened by him, I'm impressed you seem so unperturbed."

"Didn't think Grey Wolves could be tamed. Guess it's true what they say?" Alireza said with hesitation.

"What do they say?"

"About your… abilities?"

Alireza was startled when she heard a loud *CRACK* and saw light flash before her eyes. She was shocked to see Knox now at the very top of the stairs, so tiny now from her position at the bottom. In the blink of an eye, he had moved an *incredible* distance. Knox watched her carefully climb to the top for many minutes with a look of satisfaction on his face.

"Does this answer your question?"

"That's quite a feat Knox… any chance you'd teach me how to do that?"

"Let's focus on Radish first…" Knox said lowly.

"So it's true then?"

"Hmm?"

"You survived Allora?? I've known men that have ventured there and never returned... *good men*... how did you do it?"

"It sounds to me like you're not focusing on the task at hand. I do hope you didn't burn up all that Kristal getting here just to get to know me?"

"Never hurts to get to know who you're working for..." she said with more confidence than she should.

The nerve to question me with that smug look on her face. She thinks of me as an equal. the thought disgusted Knox, *I could make this cavern her grave and none would ever know... We can't kill her yet though... We still need her...*

The trio soon came to a long steel door vaulted into the crumbling stone walls of the cave with several guards posted in front. After opening a big hatch, the door gave way to a sprawling cavernous lagoon. The bowl shape of the space caused footsteps to echo loudly, Alireza had a look about her that said the space gave someone even as dark as her pause as the dimly lit torches haphazardly placed along the walls revealed the edges of its underground blackwater pond.

As they got deeper in, with all the beakers and vials scattered about the purpose of the room became abundantly clear. There were hundreds of steel cages scattered about the place, some stacked on top of one another, and others placed about the room randomly. The cages were filled with rats in various states of decay, some gnawing on their cages, others docile cowering in the corners.

"Welcome to my lab..." Knox sneered with a level of unseen enthusiasm.

"Friends of yours Knox?"

"You might say that..."

The many whiskers in cages reacted to them walking by, until they arrived at a series of five prison cells along the back wall. Tables, chairs, and bones were within, and there was a single captive in one of the cells, who looked too sickly to even stand, only meagerly looked up at them with the one eye he could manage to keep open.

"And what might his purpose be?" she said with a cruel curiosity.

"You did say you'd like to get to know me better, so I suppose a little information can't hurt. I worked out a little deal with some of the police in Kleppenwitz, as an accomplished smuggler, they figured I'd do a good job of getting the lowlifes off the streets, and get them onto another island. Make them someone else's problem. But I didn't do that. I've got bigger plans for them." he chuckled as he looked through her, "You know the sailors say there be monsters in the deep, shame they forget about the ones right beside them…"

Alireza cracked a smile, "You and the Comandante would be fast friends…."

"Magnus with his immaculate Seven Cities knows just as well as I do how much the sick, infirmed, and most especially the lazy can impact a population. Like a weed in a garden, if they aren't plucked out… and exterminated," his eyes narrowed, "Over time they'll kill the very garden they rely on for survival."

"I'm beginning to like you Knox…"

The brigadier continued pacing beside the cage gesturing for her to come closer.

"My powers come at a cost, and require a great deal of resources you see…"

"So this power can be bought then?" Alireza grunted.

"No no, what I have is not something that can be purchased… not with gold at least."

Tapping the cage flippantly like it held a goldfish, he said,

"Gust, say hello to our new guest."

"Ello Miss…" he said as he lay there, like his aim was to raise his arm and wave but couldn't muster the energy.

"And Gust, if you'd be so kind as to tell our new friend what our purpose is…"

"Evolution…" the prisoner said as if the words were tiny needles being thrust out of his throat.

"And how do we achieve that?"

"Through sacrifice sir…"

"You crossed the Black Gale through sacrifice?" Alireza's voice perked up as if she thought this would be very useful information for her movement.

"Evolution…" Know said ignoring her question, "A babe becomes a tot, a tot becomes a man. We all evolve, but most stop. I refused. Evolution is the very reason your Magnus sent you here to pry. Evolution is the reason the best bounty hunters in the Five Isles couldn't touch me for Kristal in pounds. And evolution is what's going to unlock my full potential. If you thought that stunt on the way here was something, stay tuned. Soon I'll have entire islands scared to cross me, just like my brothers a hundred years ago…"

Surprised he was onto her she muttered, "No one sent me here to spy on you Knox…"

"I don't need your pre-rehearsed story, I need that girl and I need that chest!!" he shouted, his calm face turning into ember unreasonably fast, "You do that. You do that for me, then maybe we discuss the Allorian Gale…" his face back to calm.

The two of them continued walking along the long cavern, inspecting the many vials and beakers. The echoes of the awkward movements within created an eeriness about the place, and Knox with his bizarre lurch only added to it.

"This evolution of yours, sounds like it's not complete? Didn't even know one could become a Mercurial, thought that they just… were…"

Knox itched his chin carefully as he looked over her, one of his boils had popped and liquid was pooling down his face, but it didn't seem to bother him in the slightest.

"There's a lot of things you don't know Alireza…"

Without ever breaking eye contact he pulled a dagger from his sash and put it to his wrist. She watched on in a twisted amusement as the dagger bent before his limb ever did.

"Ho-how'd you do that?!"

"I hope this will put to rest any doubts you had." Knox said as he beckoned for her to follow. "As I was saying, this is a matter of some urgency. Me and my own kind were never meant to be separated… It's time for you to be off…"

"Your own kind? You know where they went?!" she said fascinated.

"Allora was not without its secrets…" he said with a smile that was ever so slight.

"How did you…?"

"I believe I've said enough for now… return to your quarters, get some rest… you're going to need it. Trust me when I say that Radish is a clever man… he's not nearly as much as a fool as he might lead you to believe… deception is his greatest strength."

"As you wish…"

Carneld Knox looked her over again briefly,

"That's some ring you have…" he said gazing at it.

"This old thing? Stole it from some vagrant on the way here. Told him he could keep the ring or his life. Of course I wasn't being honest, I ended up taking both!" she laughed with an ever so subtle hint of nerves in her voice as she removed it and twirled it around her fingers like it wasn't important.

"I see… I do hope you wouldn't lie to me." he said with narrowed eyes and brushed his gangly blood-soaked hands across her cheek.

She recoiled with disgust but couldn't quite find a way out of his grasp, as her revolt thickened his pleasure only grew, thrilled to demonstrate the power he had over her.

"Will that be all sir?!" she stuttered, failing to hide her revulsion.

"Enjoy your stay..." he gave a wicked smile.

Alireza stormed off along the cavern and out through the big steel door at the entrance as Knox didn't once let his eyes off her.

After she got through one of Knox's guards came running towards him. The man was wearing a black feathered cap and scarf that hung to his knees with a long dusky red coat to conceal the body armor underneath.

"Ahh... just the person I was hoping to see." he said. "Please stand guard outside of Miss Alireza's room, keep an eye out for anything suspicious... understood?"

"Course sir! Sorry but couldn't help but overhear your conversation... you don't think we've told her too much?" he said nervously.

"Wouldn't worry about that.... if Radish doesn't manage to kill her, we'll finish the job ourselves... Take that pretty sunflower of hers for my own." he said bemused.

"Understood... there was one more thing..."

"Hmmm?"

"A guard from one of our patrols just approached me as you was speaking with the miss... they found something down by Pigs Port."

"What might that be?" he said looking him over.

"A woman... and a boy. One of our crews just spotted leaving that wooden shanty of theirs. Tried to hide their sashes, but he saw one hidden under the boy's belt..."

Chapter 9

<u>Below the Flagpole Market</u>

Jack gandered at the lawman with suspicion, wanting to speak but knowing full well the way his mother had her hand buried in his shoulder meant she had the situation under control.

Detective Konrad was dressed so well he looked like he was on the way to a wedding, with his policeman's badge pinned on his wool two-button overcoat and twin-pointed felt hat in full view, his hat a few inches taller than standard issues to make him appear bigger than he was. He looked over the pair carefully creating an uncomfortable silence as his lieutenants watched nervously from behind.

"Good evening detective!" Riley faked a polite smile, "Some weather we're having!"

"Enough with your pleasantries! I'm looking for a fugitive, and you know just where he is!"

"Sorry detective, but I believe you may have me mistaken with someone else..." Riley said pretending to be nervous, her tone of a higher pitch than normal.

"No... no I don't believe I'm mistaken at all." he said squinting, "You mean to tell me you're not a bounty hunter. That you didn't just come from a bounty hunter's cantina no less than a hundred feet from here?"

"Not me... no sir. Just going for a nice evening stroll with my son here. I'm a fish seller by trade if you want to know the truth."

Konrad gave her a tired look, "Funny I don't see any fish..." he took a long intense look at Riley and Jack Tripleleaf, specifically taking an interest in their clothing.

"Never known a fishmonger to wear body armor..." Konrad said sharply, "Even rarer to see a fishmonger with a pistol on their hip... A hook not work? The fish need lead now?"

"What can I say sir, can never be too safe in Kleppenwitz!" Riley said cheekily, she knew the jig was up, but her confidence didn't waver.

The detective began pacing in front of the two of them, "Let me be clear as Kristal when I say that aiding and abetting a fugitive is a crime in my city. One that carries a very... long sentence..." his eye's narrowed, "You've recently come into contact with a man named Radish, have you not?"

"Name may ring a bell..."

"And you *'Gibbons'* are harboring him are you not?"

"I wasn't aware it was a crime, or aiding and abetting as you call it, for a man to have a drink at a bar?"

"You and I both know the Gibbons are far removed from the dives that line every corner of this city, what sort of Butternut do you take me for?"

"Funny you mention that… because truth be told, the street is exactly where Radish came from. Uninvited and unannounced… then he left just as quickly as he came."

"Is that a fact?" Konrad's eyebrows raised.

"You can go ask the woman in charge Matilda Baum inside if you want to confirm it, though she'd probably just tell you to go back to the codswallop you crawl out of every morning."

Konrad's face was a visibly darker shade now, "I do fear you have no clue who you're dealing with… There may come a time in the not-so-distant future that you require our help. And when that time comes, I will keep this top-of-mind madame."

"Last I checked your organization wouldn't help us if we paid them. If you sir really expect me to believe that you can start with arresting the actual criminals in this town!"

The man bit his teeth so hard it looked like one may break off, "If it wasn't for the one good man I know in your little den of thieves the city would have shut it down by now. Keep that in mind would!"

"Ha! You're not shutting us down. Not in a million years. We'll happily swap locations if the city wants it that way. But the authorities can't kill an idea sir, nor can they get rid of the masses of people who believe strongly in that idea…" her eyes now narrowed to match his, "Now… am I under arrest?"

"I can make your life a living …"

She interrupted him, "AM I UNDER ARREST?!?!" she yelled with a moxie in her voice.

"No…" Konrad said barely able to get the word out.

"Then have a good day sir." Riley said as she started to walk by the crew of policemen.

"I'm not a man who's known for giving up madame, the next time I see you, you'll be lucky if I'm not handcuffing you…" he shouted furiously as she got further away.

"You'll need a lot more than four men to handcuff me detective!"

The pair kept walking in the opposite direction briskly, "Don't look back." Riley said with her head forward, "We're not in any danger... not yet at least."

"Surprised you were that vicious with him. Didn't think we wanted another group of crazies coming for us..."

"If we're going to be working with Radish running into him was just an eventuality. The man is a bully, plain and simple, and the only good way to deal with a bully is to fight back, show him we're not going to be pushed around like the poor defenseless folks he's used to harassing."

He nodded, her logic was sound even if a little unorthodox. Though he couldn't help but fixate on what Konrad had said, *If it wasn't for the one good man I know in your organization the city would have shut it down by now.*

Their moods brightened as the policemen were now out of sight, and they could finally take in the ambience of the city surrounding them.

They passed by a mismatched collection of stone cottages that had diverted enough canal seawater to make their very own moat of crystalline water with a stone drawbridge to accompany it. The cottages were equipped with enough pointy towers and stained-glass windows, one might've thought a family of wizards lived there. One portion of it had a cow out front eyeing passersby like he was a lazy guard dog, and the other had what seemed like a pet monkey perching on the light post out front that kept nodding off every couple of seconds.

Jack looked up at an old man asleep on a makeshift porch near the roof of one of the cottages and wondered what the man's life might be like, like who his family was, or how he made his living. Naturally he then wondered what his life may be like if he took a different path, if he took his mother's advice and became something safe like a schoolteacher, or bookkeeper if she was really feeling ambitious.

But when he looked down at the scar on his hand, his wonder evaporated, and he knew exactly why he chose his path. Shaped almost like an 'L' above his forearm, it was a daily reminder of his rocky school years. As if ridiculing him and calling him *'Deadhand'* all year wasn't enough, on the final day before they let out for the year, a few of the boys in his class waited until he was walking home from school, waited until Glasgo and Roy weren't there to help him.

Frozen with fear, nerves, and anxiety, and too young to know how to react all he could do was sit there and take their blows one by one, finally when his vision was too blurred to see straight the boy who was much bigger than him shoved him into a fence where a rusted nail caught his arm. If a nearby man with a hooked arm hadn't noticed the commotion and scared the boys off the damage could've been even worse.

Imprinted on his mind, as well as his arm, that was the day he decided he would rather die fighting than let something like that ever happen to him again. That was the day he decided to never leave the Cantina again with less than a dagger. That was the day he became a fighter.

Always on high alert outside the Cantina, and even more so now with Knox's men out scouring the Isle looking to kill any and all bounty hunters, Jack looked over to see Riley's eyes beading like billiards. Though on a night as clear and temperate as tonight's, he could see even she let her guard down, if only a little, to take it all in.

There was always vibrant energy in the streets of Kleppenwitz, every person that passed looked like they had at least something interesting about them. From artists with their feathered hats and colorful clothing, to stern looking businesspeople in their sharp wool jackets and knee-high stockings, the city was as diverse as it was electric.

"Can't believe I forgot to ask. Where did Chef Greene say we were going exactly?" Jack said itching his shaggy black hair.

"To the Flagpole Market, he told me to look under the broken trunk… whatever that means…"

"Like a tree trunk?"

"Believe so… there's hundreds of trees at the Flagpole Market, figure one of them has to be worn down enough to be considered broken… we find some way underneath and we find our man."

As they started getting closer to the Flagpole Market, they happened upon a crew of street performers mesmerizing the on-looking crowd with a fiery performance. The flicker of flames and rhythmic beat of their drums sent Jack into a daze, even Riley stopped looking around and watched them for a time.

The acrobats were incredible, backflipping with a spinning rope that looked like it was made of fire and jumping through emblazoned hoops effortlessly. The onlookers gasped as one spit fire so wide into the night sky for a moment it seemed like the sky itself had caught fire. The crowd erupted with applause as the fire belting off the drums started rhythmically dancing with flickering flames of the acrobat's fire ropes.

Jack and Riley both spotted a young child trying to grab the fire off one of the nearby drums as his mother grabbed him and scolded him.

"Reminds me of someone I know…" Riley laughed as Jack rolled his eyes.

As the crowd dispersed and the performers began pulling oil and fresh ropes from their wagon for their next show, he noticed a Clydesdale Horse at the head, mysteriously looking at him like they knew each othera. *When we take down Knox, I'll buy a stable of them* he thought, *One for Glasgo, Roy, Riley and Matilda too.*

After being briefly distracted by the incredible fire display, Riley had regained her focus and was rebuckling her wrist guards to make sure they were seated properly. Jack knew she wasn't in her comfort zone because she constantly double checked her arms and armor when she was nervous.

Riley's body armor was dull silver embroidered with sharpened obsidian edges. The make was Pregorian Steel, thick around the vital organs and light around the joints and midsection for speed and agility. You'd have to squint to be able to see it right, but each shoulder had a one-eyed monkey molded into the steel, a nod to the Cantina where she'd worked and lived for so long. She'd earned the steel working a job for a local armorsmith and had negotiated payment upfront in Pregorian Steel over doubloons, knowing full well that was the only way she could afford to have proper armor made for both herself and

Jack. At her request the armor had been sanded down from its usual glistening silver sheen, to now an old and dreary hue in order to mimic the look of a lesser more common armor.

Sitting above her armor hung glossy black hair along with a plain, even, and undecorated face. Unlike many of her contemporaries, she wore little in terms of jewelry, in her mind, sticking out was almost always a bad idea.

The pair was near the Flagpole Market as they approached a narrow street in between two red brick buildings. It was oddly quiet for a place so close to what was sure to be a packed marketplace. Two men were having a drink and a cigar ahead of them, one was stumbling over himself and looked like he needed to take a carriage home hours ago while the other laughed at his predicament.

The first man was tall and slender, with greasy white bespeckled hair and pale red skin, and was wearing a trench coat so long it kissed the ground.

The second man was fat in the face and slim in the waist, with a gray vest that came apart at the seams. The man clearly hadn't seen a barber in ages, his face was scarred from hairline to neck, and his eyes were a piercing green and bulging out in a way that was unsettling.

As the pair got closer something felt off about the men, their laughter seemed forced, and their posture too wooden to be genuine.

"I don't smell a drop of booze on them…" Riley whispered, panicked with her hand planted firmly on her hip.

When they had just passed the goons, she saw the unmistakable creases of body armor underneath their clothing…

"Jack! Run!!" she yelled at him as she grabbed his shoulder and took off along with him. "Duck!!" she cried even louder.

She watched what looked like a bolt of fire erupt from the fat-faced man's gun and glide straight towards Jack's back. Luckily Jack listened and it slid just over his back hitting a nearby wall and spattering bits of brick and dust all around them.

The debris had the lucky and unintended effect of hiding their silhouettes as they dove past the nearby corner which fed right into the Flagpole Market. Jack's heart sank as he saw just how busy the market was, so vibrant with colorful flags still swaying in the wind and set in motion by vendors in front of their makeshift stands showing off their wares.

"Pull your pistols!!" she said with fervor as she blasted off two shots of her own at the corner they just crossed. But Jack was way ahead of her as he shot in the same direction just after the words left her mouth, one of them looked like it'd grazed a leg of one of their pursuers.

Pandemonium erupted in the market as the people's pleasant evening was interrupted by a hail of gunfire. Screams echoed through the crowd as folks scattered every which way, fleeing into nearby buildings and alleyways.

There were more men now than just the two, at least four or five from what Riley could gather between potshots and reloading.

"We need cover!!" she yelled as they ran backwards down the market returning fire, "Over there!!"

Lucky enough to spot a section of the market dedicated to selling large ship parts she grabbed Jack and darted underneath a thick wooden slab of ship panel big enough for the two of them.

Pointing at two men on their flank hidden under a large kiosk filled with exotic candle lamps she yelled,

"Three, two, one…" right as she said it the two of them popped out from their cover shooting in unison. The lamps exploded like fireworks and sent each of their two targets to the ground lying motionless.

"Nice shot kid!!" Riley hollered, but the victory was all too brief, as there were so many shots zipping past their heads they could barely gather all their senses.

"There's too many of them!" Jack shouted as he popped up from his ducked position and shot ahead of him. What were five men seemed to have doubled in only a short time.

"You're standing too tall! Don't give them that big of a target!!" she said ramrod in hand, "We need to find this hideout soon or we're dead in the water!!"

The big wooden slab they hid behind had started to splinter as circular lead lumps began to spring out of its surface.

Jack looked around desperately for a tree trunk that was *'Broken'* as he heard it described but saw nothing. There were hundreds of them lining the left and right walls of the massive stretch of now empty street marketplace, but they all looked fresh as a daisy, like they'd just been planted.

The usual city sounds were completely deafened by the fire fight that now had been taking place for some time. Without thinking much of it, Jack stood up to shoot but as he did Riley watched in slow motion as a blast hit him in the chest. Her heart sank as she watched him violently hit the ground with the force of the blast. For a moment the boy's entire life flashed before her eyes, from the time he was a tyke all the way to now, nearly a man full grown.

Ears rang as his brief and dark world turned back to night. He felt Riley's hand tremble as she checked his body armor. He then felt that same hand hit his cheek when she realized the bullet was lodged in his steel armor.

"I told you not to stand up so tall!!" she said with an odd mix of anger and overwhelming relief.

"Think I got at least two of them…" he groaned as he held his chest.

"Thank heavens that hit steel! You have no idea how lucky you are! We're going to have a long talk about this later!! Now keep looking for that tree!!" she said as she started shooting again.

Their cover had almost split in two at this point and there was nothing else suitable nearby. Outmanned and outgunned with a position that was crumbling before their eyes, neither would say it, but this was the furthest thing from the meticulously planned and executed jobs they were used to. Soon more men would come from the alleyways to their sides or even worse from the distant stretch of market behind them and make this dogfight a foregone conclusion.

The two were covered in a haze of smoke and blasts that had made their eyes well and ears ring. Riley took one last look at Jack on the off chance it would be the last time she ever could, the situation seemed hopeless... hopeless until Jack saw something that ignited a spark.

A rusted, beat-up, and nearly broken in two chest that appeared to have been left out for the garbagemen was lying just a few hundred feet away in an alleyway that looked as old and rusty as the trunk itself.

"What if it wasn't a tree trunk Greene was talking about?!" he said happily while trying to forget the lump forming on his chest, "Look over there..."

Riley's mouth was open as she looked at a giant crack in the back of the rusty old trunk.

"Brilliant!" she said as she glanced over their cover, "You ok to make a run for it?!"

"Ready as I'll ever be..."

"Shoot at the brick walls, the lamps, anything that looks like it will explode and reduce visibility!"

A barrage of gunfire erupted as Knox's men were utterly confused to see the fire not coming towards them, but at the walls beside them. The men could be heard shouting and waving trying to see through the fumes of dust and debris that had just been created, but for a time they'd been rendered useless.

Now at the dusty old chest made of rotting wood and rusty metal Jack and Riley looked over the trunk searching desperately for an opening.

"Can't get it to budge!" Jack said as he heaved it upward with everything he had.

"Stand back..." Riley whispered.

One shot to the rusted keyhole and it flung open. Just as predicted there were no clothes or linens inside, but instead a wooden staircase cleverly hidden underneath, leading so far down they couldn't tell where it ended.

"After you…" Riley said hurriedly.

The desperation that had just ruled over them flooded into elation as the immense relief they shared could only be experienced after surviving something deadly. Riley slammed the trunk door down after them and jammed it shut with the lever of her pistol. Jack gave a half smile when he could still hear Knox's men outside shooting at empty smoke.

The wooden staircase creaked, as the old stone walls on either side looked worn to rubble from years of water seepage. There was a dampness in the air, along with a pungent odor that had both holding their noses.

"Well at least now we know where he got his smell from…" Jack gave a hearty chuckle, still in a rush from all the adrenaline pumping through his blood.

"Now is no time for jokes, while I appreciate you finding these sewers and saving my life back there, I'm still angry. Don't think I've forgotten about what happened. I told you if we do this, you listen to me no matter what. I've got half a mind to call this whole thing off, we've barely just started and you've already almost died!"

"It-it won't happen again, just got a little too excited in the heat of the moment is all…" he said genuinely.

"Well you could've been killed! Use your head. Your marks weren't that bad in school I know you've got a brain up there, if it was Knox shooting at us instead of his incompetent men we wouldn't have been so lucky." Riley said sternly. "I wouldn't give you up for all the pearls in the Sober Sea, remember that next time you're about to do something stupid!"

The two continued down a moldy old sewage way that was split by a slow stream of knee-high water. Stagnant, odorous and filled with debris, this water may've been the exact opposite of the clearwater canals they'd just passed on the surface. They stumbled along in the dark barely moving with their only guiding light moonlighting down from sparse cracks in the stones above their heads. Above they could still hear the soldiers marching angrily setting off echoing booms in the cavern.

"Where do you think they'll go next?" Jack said wearily.

"No clue," she said, "But I wouldn't feel safe anywhere but the Cantina right now."

As they continued for what felt like an eternity, eventually the passage led them to an old but secure looking wooden door covered in grey moss. The light from inside finally provided a small source of visibility as Jack looked over at his mother.

"Take out your pistol and be ready to use it..." she whispered hastily.

Jack nodded as she gave several knocks on the door with the butt of her pistol. But no one came as they sat there awkwardly.

"Dunno maybe try knocking normally?"

She tried again this time with her hand, and within an instant the old door opened.

Radish had a big grin on his face, as he stared at Riley with his one good blue eye, hardly noticing Jack. His trademark eyepatch covered red patchy skin, patchy beard, and pieces of his knotted hair. His suspenders still hung around his knees, but now his cotton undershirt was untucked, his leather britches looked damp, and his maroon sword was halfway out of its maroon scabbard, he'd somehow found a way to look even more unkempt than usual. The red scars on his face looked like they were beating along with his heart and moving in tandem with his awkward up and down manner of speech. Jack took particular note of the onion-like, nearly heart-shaped trinket around his neck that he couldn't turn away from back at the Cantina.

He fumbled about in the doorway almost as if he was having trouble standing. He had a peculiar way of walking and even standing he looked like some kind of mosquito caught inside a monsoon. Jack didn't know if he had some sort of ailment or if he was just inebriated, though he assumed inebriated.

"Hello friends!" Radish sneered.

"We aren't your friends..." Riley said with her gun pointed in his face, "Are you armed?"

"Well… not with a pistol… but I've been told a sharp wit is the most dangerous weapon of them…"

"Enough…" she cut him off while rolling her eyes, "Are you going to show us what we came here to see or are we already wasting our time?"

"Wasting your time? Well judgin by all the pistols I heard goin off upstairs you've got nowhere better to be!"

She couldn't argue with that as they walked with Radish through a small chamber that led to a much larger dormitory.

"Bang up to the elephant, eh?" he said touring them around his hideout. "It ain't no Forzian Kingdom, but I do hope it suits while we wait for our friends upstairs to bugger off."

It was a stark contrast coming from the murky sewer to now gandering over a sprawling decadent hideout. There were bits of milky Kristal and doubloons scattered about the messy drawers and cabinets, some of the coins were imprinted with the seal of Sullenmoon City with its giant sphere dome, some pressed with Vistan Crests, but most were minted in Kleppenwitz with its giant Laughing Monk as a print.

Hidden amongst shelves and pillars were ancient and oblong candles that just barely lit up portraits of old men and women Jack didn't recognize. The space was like an antique store, except it was the first Jack could ever remember that wasn't boring. There were two man-sized golden elephant statues with a confused expression, steel wheels and wooden walls that looked like a disassembled carriage, a safe without a door, a giant aquarium with no fish in it, and several dust covered mirrors that remarkably didn't show any reflection when they passed by them.

Depending on the time of night and how much rum Radish had consumed, he may tell you the place was the former hideout of a Vistan King come to the Boondocks to escape certain death from a rival kingdom, or if he'd had too much, he'd tell you the truth. That it was a former marketplace for illicit and stolen goods, with the perfect location right below the biggest legitimate market in Kleppenwitz. However a civil war or two in the thieves guild that operated the place had caused it to become all but abandoned.

"This where you hid the Quicksilver Radish?" Riley said sarcastically, "Couldn't imagine why you'd ever need gold again if the rumors of you stealing it are true…"

"Not here I'm afraid." he said with his hands clasped together, "Lost it gambling sadly at the Ran Down Moonbeams tavern near Port Stern not far from here, some picaroon sittin in a dive a mile away will be as happy as a three sheeted pirate when he finds out its worth!"

Riley looked at him bewildered, "What could possibly be worth putting up something as priceless as Quicksilver??"

"There's trinkets out there more valuable than you know Miss Tripleleaf, plus what good is bringing someone back from the dead if you have no plans on ever being dead?!" he said coyly.

She looked at him disbelievingly but continued exploring the cavernous hideout.

In the corner was another man sleeping on some oversized circular bed who was moving so little he might've expired.

"That there's Kersey… A man with salt in his veins" Radish pointed at the debatably sleeping man, "Best captain in the Five Isles…" he turned his head sideways and scrunched his face "ehhh… second best," he scrunched again, "He can usually get outta port at least…"

"Is… is he dead?" Jack said curiously.

"No mate he just smells like he is," he responded with a shoulder nudge.

"Where'd you get all this stuff? It must've taken you a lifetime?!" Jack said in awe while ignoring his mother's glares. His eyes darted from one shiny bauble next to some ancient jewel next to some mechanical oddity.

"Took me a while lad, but there can be no beauty without her rotten little partner frustration. As to where I got it? Can't tell you all the gory details I'm afraid. Would have even more men looking for me then…" Radish grabbed a small lamp off a nearby dresser, "You see this lamp mate? Found it near Alexandria while being shot at by some

Caldorian Bounty Hunters with black eyes… said to grant the owner one wish… if you know the magic words to activate it… which I don't…"

"Pretty sure that's a tea pot… and a stolen one at that…" Riley said patronizingly.

"Nothing wrong with a little chicanery love…"

"Don't tell me we came all the way out here and risked our lives for you to show us a tea pot you stole…"

"Perhaps when I do figure out the magic words, I'll wish that you were more polite…"

Arms still folded she continued, "You know we could've been killed up there, a little help would've been nice, I'm beginning to wonder whose side you're really on…"

"Miss Tripleleaf… you misjudge! I had no way of knowing that was you… If I had known me and my comatose friend here would've been up there lickety-spit, blasting away!"

Eyes arched Jack was beginning to think she may shoot him soon.

"I can assure you, I'm on the side with the big pot of doubloons waiting for me at the end of this marvelous rainbow of friendship!" he said smiling through his crusty yellow teeth.

"Well, you'd do well to remember you'll need both of us alive at the end of this if you want to see a single centime of that money, last I checked you aren't a Gibbon… You've got no way of collecting without us."

"Right you are!"

"Also, if anything suspicious were to happen to me or Jack, you'd have an army of highly trained bounty hunters looking to make this your final score. Oh, and now we know where your hideout is. Do keep that in mind, will you?"

He turned and looked to Jack, "Sure am glad she's on our side mate!" he said as he fidgeted with his necklace. "Is she always like this? Or do I just have that effect?"

Not meaning to, Jack completely ignored the question as he continued trying to get a better look at it. The crusty man's necklace glistened even in the shade, for a time Jack was in a trance and had to shake his head to snap out of it.

"What is that thing?" he pointed.

"The chain? Ahhh figured that's what had your eyes glazed. Wouldn't worry, tends to do that. It's Ghostmade lad... As Mercurial as Allorian Dirt!"

"Does it ... does it do anything?"

"Aye... it's a container of sorts..."

Riley interrupted with a loud laugh, "You mean to tell me you're the owner of a Mercurial Trinket? I'd sooner believe the Five Isles were ruled by monkeys!"

"Yes I understand there's a lot about me that's unbelievable."

"Next thing you're going to tell me is the Rogue gave it to you, hmm? Lend you his golden boots as well?"

"You're not too far off..." he said slyly, "If only he was fully here now, Knox wouldn't be nearly so brave."

"How did someone like the Rogue get mixed up with the likes of you anyhow? You extort him? Kidnap his family or something?"

Pausing for a second he took his hand off his necklace, "He came to me... doubt you'll believe that, but I'd put it on my honor..."

"Your honor?!" she cackled.

"Was long before all his accolades, he was just a boy sure not much older than our friend Jack here. Even as a boy there was somethin about him, call it a feelin or maybe it was the twinkle in his eye, but if you knew what to look for you could tell he was special the first time you shook his hand. A head like his with an arm to boot... didn't take me long to try and recruit'em. Shame we didn't take down more bounties together, coulda made a fortune him and I. But he fell for the classic mistake of letting his morals get in the way of doubloons. As for the rest, well I'm sure you've already heard it. Ran off to that hermit Jerrick Alamillo and barely heard from him again, mostly just heard tales of his exploits. But a man like that never truly leaves you," he said as he remembered fondly, "Lad had enough gusto in'em to leave a tattoo on even the simplest minds."

Jack was hanging on Radish's every word. When he was younger, he used to idolize the Rogue, hoping that one day he would grow up to be just like him. He used to beg Riley every night to tell him the story of the Rogue squashing the *Three Springs* uprising on Vista or how Magnus had doubled the bounty on his head once again.

"So do you believe the rumors then?" Jack got up the nerve to speak, "That he's run off? That he finally figured out even he couldn't match up against the Forzians, and ran off to the Kingsfall Islands?"

"No mate, I sure don't. If you believe those rag stories then I've got a lovely little beachside cottage on Allora I'd like to sell ya." he paused for an awkward amount of time, his voice grew quiet, and his eyes narrowed, "I'm a runner… if the two of yous had any sense you'd be runners. But if there's one thing I know certain… the Rogue ain't no runner."

The candles lining the walls seemed to grow quiet in unison along with Radish as the rustic red brick covering the hideout did the work of deafening any noises coming from the street above them.

"Well what *did* happen to him then?" Riley interjected.

He replied with squinted eyes and gave a half smile, "Where did the Rogue go? That I'm afraid I don't know… but I have found something, or rather someone I have reason to believe he was looking for… Which with any luck may give us a clue to his whereabouts."

Just as he spoke Jack heard a sound coming from one of the closed doors behind them, before he could blink Riley had one of her pistols on the door and the other pointed at Radish.

"You didn't tell me there was someone else here?!" she yelled.

"Not to worry dear, I can assure you she means you no harm!!" he said with hands up frightened of what she may do next.

"She?!"

The moldy door slowly began to open as a girl that couldn't have been much older than Jack anxiously crept out from behind it.

Jack couldn't take his eyes off the girl, and neither could Riley but for very different reasons. The girl was tall and slender and had golden nearly white hair. Her skin was so pale it looked like she hadn't stepped outside in years, her clothes unrecognizable, and she moved with such grace it was like she wasn't walking at all. There was an essence about her that struck Riley to the core, so much so she forgot she was still holding her pistol up at her.

Unable to stop looking in her eyes, she stared on awkwardly mouth open like a full moon, they were striking. One was sky-blue and the other a glowing purple.

"I recognize those eyes..." Riley whispered to herself, racking her brain to try and remember where.

Walking closer she softly said,

"Don't worry dear, you've got nothing to fear from either of us," putting her pistols back in their holster she again looked the girl in the eyes, "What's your name?" she said as delicately as she could muster.

"Can't talk I'm afraid!" Radish interrupted, "Me and sleeping beauty here tried everything from cold soup to boiled worms, even tried jumping from behind a desk and scaring her but all she did was kick me in the shin." he pointed down to a big red whelp below his knee, "But we haven't got a peep out of her. Only grunts angrily at us if we try and wake her up."

"Did you think of trying pen and paper?" Riley said annoyed.

"Course I have... just hadn't gotten around to tryin it yet. Been a little busy trackin down new partners, and makin sure that that berryhead doesn't find us and blow this place into rubble."

Riley ignored him and grabbed a quill off a nearby desk and a little

128

black book with it.

"What's your name dear?" she said with care.

The still very nervous-looking girl grabbed the pen and scratched down the letters that spelled,

"Apolline"

Chapter 10

<u>The Brave</u>

Cobwebs lined every corner of the walls and made for an odd backdrop for all the golden vases and silver chalices in their front. Two giant statues separated Apolline and the rest, one depicted a blindfolded woman in stone dress, arms crossed with pistols against each shoulder, and the other the famous Laughing Monk. The big miniature Brother Boondock, like the real one not too far above them, was still smiling, but he had his arms crossed instead of open.

Apolline stared at them suspiciously, even with a hint of a scowl.

"Are you alright?" Riley said as she looked at the mask her face showed, a mask she knew from using herself, "Your name's Apolline then?" she said lightly as she smiled and crossed her hands to the front, "What a beautiful name you've got. Do you know where you are Apolline? Do you know how you ended up in Kleppenwitz?"

The girl stared at Riley clutching her woven grass bracelet like it was her only lifeline when Radish butted in.

"Can't talk, she got ambrosia. Least that's what me and Kersey suspect. Thought about callin one of me *unofficial* doctor friends to find out though last I heard he poked out a man's eye when he was removin a wart on his neck."

"Uhh, better not. And amnesia you mean?!"

"Right that's the one!" Radish said as his eyes happily lit up like he'd just answered a question right on a test.

"Is that right?" Riley said to her, "You can't remember much?"

Looking a little more comfortable now she shook her head.

"These two men, are they being nice to you? You have everything you need here?"

Looking at Radish she nodded, but hesitantly this time.

Riley gave Radish a look sharper than a cutlass when Apolline approached, touched her shoulder and nodded again, this time assuredly.

"Think she's just mad about all the snoring from Kersey, girl keeps throwin random objects at the walls but that's not nearly enough to wake him up. If I still had all my hearing, I'd be mad too!"

Pointing at Radish, now annoyed, she feigned a loud snoring sound with her mouth.

"Wait! You're accusing me of snorin?? She's got some pearls hasn't she! You know I've never heard myself doing it then, so tell me how's that possible?"

Ignoring his bad joke Riley turned to her, "My name is Riley Tripleleaf, and this is my son Jack."

He'd gotten caught staring when he realized his name was called and consequently waved with a shakey hand. For some reason the lump on his chest from being shot earlier felt like it melted away and all he could focus on was the girl.

Extending his hand, while completely forgetting that it was his blackened right hand,

"Oh-uhhh…" Jack fumbled his words.

Without a second thought she grabbed it and shook it back. He was horrified when he realized what he'd done, but somehow, her face was just as it had been before like she didn't even notice.

I wouldn't dance with the deadhand! The words flashed across his mind as the memory hit him harder than the bullet his chest had taken earlier. The memory of what one of his old classmates had said when he asked her to the Ghost's Farewell Ball. She seemed to care very much, so why didn't Apolline?

There was something so striking about her, her skin so pale it almost matched her pearl white linen dress, but in a way that looked magnificent instead of unhealthy. Her long golden hair glistened even from a distance; whatever shade it was, it was not something Jack could recall ever seeing in any of his journeys around the Five Isles. The color somewhere between silver and gold, it was marched side by side as if each strand had been methodically patterned to fall in perfectly next to the strand beside it, without a single damaged or stray in the bunch.

Could this have been the new companion the monk was referring to? He continued telling himself that he was just a madman, and he could brush it off. But after Radish, and now Apolline suddenly appearing into his life out of nowhere, he wasn't so sure.

"Jack and I are a kind of bounty hunter, a very special kind of bounty hunter…"

Apolline was given a start when she heard the words.

"Don't worry dear. You see we're a part of an organization called the Jolly Gibbons. Where most bounty hunters can be quite nasty as it seems like you're aware," she glared at Radish, "We only go after murderers, kidnappers, and the like, people that deserve to spend the rest of their days in a cell."

Dropping her guard, if only a little, she nodded.

"Well Apolline, you've got nothing to fear from me or Jack, I don't know everything, but I do know that." Riley didn't know the girl well enough to make that call for a certainty, but she didn't need to when she could look into her eyes, "I've spent the better part of my life studying, hunting, and imprisoning the vile and corrupt, I know all too well who the predator and who the victim." pausing she looked over, "Radish, care to tell me how this poor girl ended up in your hideout with amnesia? I hope you've got a good story to tell, if kidnapping is what you've got up to down here, I'd just soon take the girl with us and leave you down here ten pounds lighter!"

"Kidnapping!?" he said not taking her as seriously as he should've, "Heroism more like it! Saved the poor girl I did, well Kersey helped too if you count fallin asleep at the ship wheel helping. Knox had her locked up in that big chest back there, you'll forgive me if I don't like to imagine why…"

She looked back at the massive chest in the sleeping quarters Apolline had come from. Rimmed with tarnished gold, with a deep blue color to its sections like the oceans of Vista, and intricate carvings of an undecipherable language.

"Can you confirm this, so I don't have to hurt the poor man? You were imprisoned in that trunk?"

Apolline smirked at the thought and nodded back.

"Tell me, is there anything you can remember? Like where you grew up? Who your parents are? Where your schoolhouse was? Even the smallest detail could be helpful!"

She looked at her uncomfortably for a while then looked down, shaking her head again in disappointment.

"I wouldn't worry too much. These things are often temporary. A little rest in a comfy bed and you'll be back in tip-top shape."

The girl took her black book and jotted down, *"I remember some things..."*

"What things?!"

"The dreams, every night." she wrote.

"What sorts of dreams?" she said hopefully like they may be getting somewhere.

'It's always me and my pet Francesca, exploring cities made of stars, never-ending lakes with no floor, with ships in them that can sail on air. And all the people there, they're so lovely, until, until the shadowy men come, until they come take me..."

"Do you know who the men were?!"

She shook her head again, shaking ever so slightly as she did.

"Hmmm... are you familiar with the name Carneld Knox? Most just call him Knox. He's a vile man, wanted on every sane island, tall bald and pale with a face covered in boils."

Just hearing the name made her shudder as she shook her head no.

"I see, well if you do ever happen to run into him, listen to this if you listen to nothing else. Run and hide, like your life depends on it, got that?"

Looking uncomfortable with the idea of having to run from anyone still she agreed and looked forward.

Riley sat there inquisitively for a time with her fist held under her chin, while the other three stared at her awkwardly.

"Welp, I hate to admit this, but this seems above my paygrade. I fear this isn't something I can just look up in the Monarch Library. But I may know someone who can help. You see we've got our headquarters, the Blackwater Cantina, not too far from here. With guest quarters to give you as much or as little space as you like, we've even got a library so big you couldn't finish every book in it if you spent the rest of your life in there!"

For the first time since Riley had met her, she saw a tinge of a smile on the young girl's face.

"And we've got a bookkeeper that may be able to help you, find out why you can't talk… why you can't remember. I'm sorry to be so quick about this, but I fear we're not safe here. Not nearly as safe as we could be in the Cantina. Would you like to come with us?"

She sprang up in her shoes enthusiastically looking like she very much wanted to get away from the smelly sewers.

After Apolline had the chance to look each of them over for a time, she seemed to settle in, and at least on some level accept that they were friendly enough not to put her back in the box she came from. She had followed Jack to the corner on the antique stool where he sat and had stolen his pistol, treating it flippantly like it was some sort of toy.

"Hey, be careful with that!" Jack said with eyes as big as walnuts. She was even more fascinated with it than Sarah Blitzen was earlier, peering her head down the barrel and fiddling with the hammers like they were something as innocent as piano keys.

While Jack was trying desperately to prevent Apolline from hurting herself or himself Riley quietly approached Radish.

"So she's the reason then? The reason Knox is on a killing spree right now? He wants her back that badly?"

"May have somefin to do with'it, that or he liked my pretty face so much he just had to sail down and get a second take!"

"Well it's lucky for you then, I had half a mind to hit you over the head with some blunt object and turn you in myself, have this whole thing finished before the nights out… But you're safe for now, again assuming nothing happens to the three of us…"

He retorted with a cheeky bow, like this wasn't coming as a surprise to him.

"What's the rub here then Radish? I'm positive you're not the type to save a defenseless girl unless there's something in it for yourself… If you'd be so kind as to enlighten me. What's in this for you?"

Bits of moonlight beamed down from the cracks in the ceiling above illuminating Radish's frayed eyepatch and made his blue eye shine like gold. Riley was happy to see his shirt now tucked and one of his suspenders hooked, his clothes could more accurately be described as rags, but at least it was an improvement from earlier.

Most bounty hunters would have body armor covering their chest and legs completely, but he only had bits and pieces. One slab covered his right knee while another plate of steel covered his left pectoral, and another on one wrist and elbow. He even had rusted chainmail under his shirt that Riley knew for a certainty wasn't going to stop any manner of gunfire. To top it all off he had one black leather sash draped from shoulder to waist that held lead and powder, and another that served as his belt and holster for both pistols, and more than likely handkerchief based off its dotty exterior.

"That Knox is ugly in both the ways, believe me we'll both be better off if he's kaput. Well would ya look at me? I sound just like a bloody welltodoer like yourself," he retorted. "They might even invite me to your little monkey parties with all my good deeds!"

"I said I wasn't going to turn you in, I didn't say that I wouldn't hurt you. It's all the same to me if you're missing an arm or another eye at the end of this. There's something in this for you, and if you want our help like you claimed you did, that's information I'm going to need."

"You see that fancy chest over there? It's Ghostmade, Mercurial, anointed with the nectar of the celestial deus, worth more than everythin in this room. Well... almost everything..."

"You want me to believe you tracked down the deadliest man within two isles of here, just for an empty chest??" Riley said in disbelief.

"Wasn't empty lass..." he winked, "And not sure if you're aware but unless the Mercurial poof back into existence as quickly as they poofed out of it, the goods they forgot to take are worth more than all the Kristal on Prego... Even somethin as dumb as an empty chest."

"So you do want the girl then? She's of some use to you?"

"Ain't exactly what I was hopin for... But who knows, maybe she proves useful."

136

Riley stared at his one good eye, trying her best to get a read on him. It was a skill she prided herself on and had saved her hide enough where she'd come to rely on it. Yet her instincts failed her, most would give a tell with the shake of their eye, a nervous twitch, or a touch of their hair, but Radish was cleverer than most. His face and arms, while bouncing about endlessly, revealed nothing.

"You said yourself the chest was Mercurial, maybe she's one they forgot. Maybe they weren't as perfect as the bookkeepers say. Surely that's worth something to you?" she said with a hint of snark as if to test him.

"If the girl was Mercurial, she would've removed all our eyeballs the second she walked out of that fanciful prison and zapped herself off to some distant world."

"That's a good answer Radish, just know if this is some ploy of yours to exploit her..."

"I know, I know miss. I'll be ten pounds lighter after your merry band of friends sends me to the mortuary. Fink they give a discount for the headless??"

"You're a quick learner, I'd still like to point out I'll be watching your every step. I get the sense you think you're smarter than us Gibbons but know I'm fully aware that you're hiding something. I knew it the minute I first saw you back in the Cantina. One wrong move and..."

"I do love it when you threaten me," he smiled making her wince, "But for now perhaps we should discuss matters of more importance."

"I'm not done with my questions yet." she snapped, "Let's say this chest is as valuable as you say. What use do you have for the bounty on Knox's head? You'd already have more money than you could spend in a lifetime..."

"Clever, clever, clever. Well... first... you ever hear of a rich man didn't want to be richer? Second, it's hard to find a buyer for these sorts of things. Would have to be some king or pirate lord to afford it. Last, it's not exactly easy to prove authenticity when that big oaf ofa chest don't allow you to move like a sailfish in open water like the others do..."

"I'm sure a man of your talents would have no trouble finding a buyer."

The noisome man flicked his eyebrows up, happy to have a complement as he sat himself at the nearby bar and began drinking out of something that looked closer to a vase than a cup.

"Last question then, you mentioned a weapon, something that could destroy Knox? You think this is Apolline?"

"Don't know, but it's possible. It don't take a gypsy to tell you there's somethin special about her…"

"You think you're dealing with a Butternut Radish? The girl is right fragile, looks like she may break a bone if she sat down too fast. You want me to believe she's a weapon??"

"I thought it was stupid myself. But I have reason to believe when the Rogue went missin, he was lookin for that very chest. And by extension that fragile girl. I can assure miss if the Rogue wants it, so do we. Hope that settles it, cause as of now you've got about as much information as I do."

"I see… well then not sure why you didn't start with that. You're not the first one I've heard talk of the Rogue seeking something on the Boondocks, which is good because I'm not about to take the word of a Picaroon…"

"Alright then. Sounds like we can agree for once. While I sincerely disagree this glorified librarian of yours will have anything at all to offer, safer there than it is here. And your band of charity workers is right odd, but at least the rums good. I know cause I already tested it."

About this time the pair heard a loud *CLACK* and ducked for cover, when they saw Apolline scurrying to pick up the pistol she'd just dropped and Jack taking cover behind a bench.

"Some weapon Radish…"

"Ha! You're preachin to a pirate, but give it time. She'll surprise you. That much I can promise, the Rogue doesn't miss, miss."

"What could it be? What is it about her??" Riley said with true curiosity as she took a seat at the oak bar beside him.

"That much we've got to figure out, I will say, it's the strangest thing. Haven't seen'er eat whatsoever since the day we found her in that box. Didn't even take a bite out of Kersey's famous rat-meat pie! And even stranger than that. She looks even plumper than the day we pulled her out. Spose she could be eatin when we slept, but if that's so, girls real good at hidin it."

"Gee, I can't imagine why she wouldn't eat that. After spending how long with her you still haven't gotten any information? Like her home island? Or if she's got siblings?"

"Steel trap that one, before today I didn't even know her name. Poor girls mostly only had Kersey and his awful snores to keep her company. Be honest with you today is the most we've gotten out of her. Perhaps she didn't trust us."

"Sounds like she's got a good head on her shoulders then." she said barely joking.

"Say what you will but not even so much as a fly has touched her head since she's been in my rescue! Can only hope that stays true with our friends outside."

"You think we're safe here then?"

"Did you close the trunk behind ya?"

"Yes."

"Then we're safe. For a time. Not forever though. Believe I can even hear carriages now. Police shoulda scared them off."

Slamming the bar table while gargling down a substance that looked like it could cut through steel, he spoke to her as if he was speaking to an audience.

"If they're not working with them. I heard through the grapevine Konrad and his men are quite fond of Knox cleaning up the streets. Even had a run in with him before we arrived here. You'll never guess who he was looking for."

"Konrad! The ole dog, how's he doin?! Now there's a face I hope to never see again."

"You know he's looking for you? Somehow he got information that you'd been at the Cantina."

"Course he is! Had to give'em the slip to check out a crime scene, bloke sure wasn't a bucket'o smiles after that, looked like he was seein about five shades of red. Funny his pal Knox had the same look last time I saw'em too." Radish chuckled.

"You've angered two of the nastiest men on the Boondocks enough to kill, and your response is to laugh? Have you gone mad?"

"I made rich and powerful men, less rich and less powerful. And with my winnings I mean to keep every taproom on this great island open for business. Some may call that takin from the rich and givin to the poor. You oughta be thankin me, just begging me to join your crew of dogooders! "

"You didn't think this information would've been useful back at the Cantina to share with the people you're partnering with? How many other powerful people want to see you dead?"

"Slipped my mind, apologies. As to how he found out I was in your lovely establishment fraid I'd have to direct that question back to you. If I was a bettin man, and I may be the biggest bettin man you ever met, I'd guess you've got a rat in your organization."

"Oh please, you were right out in the open in Hangman's Hall in front of what could've been over two-hundred people. There are plenty of places we don't allow outsiders, but the hall isn't one of them. That could've been anyone. You did manage to get in after all, not like opening a vault."

"Sure seemed like Gibbons to me, all I'm sayin is, careful who you make company with. Least while we're trying put over a man with the resources Knox has."

"I don't need you to worry about our matters," she said sharply, "What I do need you worrying about is how we're going to get a toe-tag on a living breathing god."

"Don't forget about his friends, not exactly slouches either!"

Riley shook her head and sighed, "What have you gotten us into? I'm starting to rethink this."

"Don't worry lass, I've got a plan!"

"A plan?!" she laughed. "What sort of plan could possibly help the four of us defeat an army?!"

"Plan's a strong word... perhaps concept of a plan would work a little better..."

Contemplating she looked around at all the dusty old tomes covering the walls with bits of Kristal between them as bookends and tried to ignore the sounds of Kersey sleeping.

She was used to planning every single meticulous detail for her missions, down to the number of footsteps she would take. Leaving nothing to chance, and success all but assured. But now she would have to give all that up and leave her life and all that she cared about in the arms of a bumbling madman.

At least she had time, she thought. Time to develop a plan that wasn't so haphazard and chaotic, though she'd have to find a way to fit Radish in, when it seemed like his very nature was chaotic.

What she needed to do now was get the others back to safety at the Cantina, where Peg the Bookkeeper would have information, and she would have the room she needed to reflect and figure out how to escape their deadly predicament.

Riley considered herself lucky to get a break from staring at Radish's brown-yellow teeth and approached Apolline who was sitting beside Jack, reading a book called *The Princess and the Pirate, A Forbidden Love*.

"What a fantastic choice!" she said warmly, "That was my favorite book when I was your age, must've read it a hundred times, when I was finally done with it the spine was so busted it was more pages than book..."

Head buried, the girl looked so interested she barely looked up at

Riley.

"Why don't you take that with us, give you something to read on the way to the Cantina. I'm quite certain a book is the last thing Radish will notice gone missing."

"Great idea Riley!" she beamed as she scribbled, *"I can't put it down, the princess with her furs and jeweled gowns sounds so lovely! Has Jack read it?"*

"You remembered our names! Look at your memory improving already!" Riley said, "Jack have you read it?"

"That the one with the pirate king and his ship crewed by monkeys?"

For an ever-brief moment she got caught up in her excitement and forgot about her predicament, she tried to say *yes* to him with her voice but all that came out was a high-pitched throat sound. Embarrassed and frustrated in a fit of anger she kicked over a wicker basket and turned away from them.

"Give us a moment Jack..." Riley said as she sat right beside her, she could hear her sobs even as she tried to hide them. *How incredibly frustrated she must feel,* Riley thought. Not remembering who she was or where she came from, not even able to speak a word.

Putting her arm around her shoulder she said, "Breathe dear, just breathe..." she inhaled and exhaled loudly along with her.

"We're going to get you help and find answers. The Gibbons have all the resources we need to cover the Five Isles up and down until we find out what's going on. May have to bend a few elbows and break a few toes to get there, but we'll get there."

Her face was still buried in her hands, but the sobs seemed to subside.

"The Pinwheels are bigger than you know, I can assure you someone out there knows exactly what's happened to you. And someone out there knows exactly how to fix it, just a matter of finding them. But you've got to keep a positive mind, it's everything when the situation gets bad."

Apolline looked up at her, looking directly into her eyes. She didn't need to say or write anything, Riley could see the appreciation in her countenance.

"Keep that black book on you sweet, don't ever feel shame for having to write something out. We don't mind at all if it takes you a little longer to put something down in words, we want to hear anything and everything you have to say. We're your friends, remember?"

She smiled back like a friend was all she needed at this moment.

"I'm not going to lie, there's some bad men who are after us. They want you for reasons we don't fully understand yet, but we're not going to let them hurt you again. Just follow my lead, stay close, and we'll get you through this."

The tears were drying now as if her words had helped them evaporate.

"Make sure and keep a journal in that book too, it'll help you gather your thoughts. Maybe even help your memory!"

Riley got up and noticed Radish giving Jack some advice on what appeared to be how to create a tiny, improvised grenade with a bit of Kristal and an empty jug of grog.

"Just met the guy and already he's trying to corrupt my son..." she sighed out loud.

As she walked over to give him every bit of her mind, she heard a loud **KNOCK KNOCK KNOCK** at the old mossy wooden door they had entered from.

With a racing heart she stared at the door until she realized this was probably just another one of Radish's cronies, come to get spirited late night.

"Expecting visitors?!" Riley laughed and looked towards Radish.

For the first time today, she could get a read on Radish. But even a tyke could have with what his eyes showed.

When she saw the fear welled up in him, she knew the answer was no. That this was no crony come to pay a friendly visit, but instead someone that meant to kill them.

Chapter 11

A Fool's Fool

Lucas Geist was redder than the stripes of his hair, standing in the last place he felt someone of his pedigree should stand.

"You tell anyone about this you'll be spending decades chained to a wall underneath the Cantina, got that??!" Geist said as he stood knee high in a mix of rotting food, old clothes, dirt and manure.

"Wouldn't dream of it sir!!" Jenkins was so deep in rubbish all Lucas could see of him was the black mop on his head he called hair. "Boy what a weird place to put a hideout! Though guess no one would think of checking in garbage. Part of his genius I suppose…"

"I'll worry about Radish boy; you worry about finding the entrance. Clear?"

"As Kristal sir!"

Lucas's normal pristine buckled leather black boots were covered in smudge, the stained black Pregorian Steel covering his legs and chest was now tarnished, and the ends of his cloak were threadbare. Even his usual well-kept blonde and auburn hair was loose and disheveled, which matched his demeanor near perfect.

He could still hear the dogs barking in the distance. Packs of them roaming the landfill, mangy and dirt-covered, half the size of a grown man and more than likely rabid. The black and gray hounds took turns trying to get close to them, trying their best to drive out the intruders. But they weren't quick enough. Lucas had fired six or seven shots but missed each time, cursing as he did.

Shame I have more important matters to attend to, or I'd gleefully rid this landfill of its mad dog problem.

"Find anything yet?!"

He couldn't see the boy's head anymore as he was diving beneath a pile of rotting vegetables and only heard muffled yells back. As he resurfaced, he responded,

"No entrance yet, but I did find what looks like a fossil here!"

"That's not a fossil, that's manure you Butternut!"

Piles of garbage the size of small buildings on Kleppenwitz surrounded them, and furious brown fumes were bellowing over top of them. There were mosquitoes and beetles the size of walnuts, dirty old possums that looked like they had won the dirty old possum lottery, and thousands of pigeons with peculiar beaks so hooked they curved back in on themselves.

The landfill had originally been founded by Marren the Apothecary, one of the original eight settlers, as a source of rich soil for the Municipal Park at the center of the city that housed the Laughing Monk. Referred to as just the 'Muni' by most on Kleppenwitz, the park had maintained its beautiful foliage and vibrant gardens as a direct result of the compost generated here.

The moonlight illuminated their way, which was common on the Boondocks. It was a rare night when at least some bit of moon couldn't poke through the clouds. Tonight, it was blood orange and out like the star of the show giving all the rubbish a coral hue.

"Find an opening yet?" he yelled indignantly at Jenkins past the point of losing patience.

The Gibbon's most unpopular manager had picked the spot directly in the center of the city of waste, figured this was the only spot where the levels of debris were low enough for Radish to dig out a hideaway.

"Nothing yet, but can't be much longer sir, not much ground left that hasn't got a hundred feet of garbage above it…"

His motivations for finding Knox were straightforward. The number of doubloons his head would bring in was staggering, and considering Radish had already foiled Knox once, surely he could assist him with doing it again.

A treasure's worth of doubloons was passed down by his father, and his father before him. But the kind of wealth he'd been given meant little to him. Enough to buy a cottage in the countryside and live out his days in a dull, uninspiring manner. Enough doubloons to fade into obscurity and nothingness. Nowhere near enough wealth to purchase what he truly craved. Power. Enough power to buy politicians to let him expand laws in his favor, enough wealth to bribe policemen to let him skirt regulations, perhaps even enough wealth to hire an army to expel Matilda and her band of rats from his once great Cantina.

They'd been at it all day, well before nightfall. Jenkins had crawled through every dirt pile in a fifty-foot radius and was so dirty he blended in with the waste near perfectly, as if he were a worm sifting through dirt. *So why hadn't they found anything yet?* Geist thought.

Lucas bit his lip so hard he could taste the pool of blood welling in his mouth when it came to him. He couldn't pinpoint what put the thought in his head, maybe it was the fact that Jenkins was similar in age to that deformed boy Jack or had the same hair color, or maybe it was the rotting fish heads reminding him of the Chef. Either way the thought entered his brain and wouldn't leave. He recalled vividly when he passed by the Acclaimatory earlier and saw the Chef laughing, sharing libations and pleasantries, and having a grand ole time with the hag Matilda, and the deplorable Tripleleafs.

On the other hand, he'd never known the Chef to be a liar, maybe the hag had put him up to it. Either way he had every intention of getting to the bottom of it when they returned. Tell the chef he could find another job if he didn't want to cooperate. That would get him talking.

It nearly drove him mad to admit defeat, but for now there was little other choice. If there was a hideout here, they would've found it by now.

"Jenkins! We're leaving!" he yelled.

"Already sir? But we haven't found anything?"

"It seems we've been duped, wash yourself off in the ocean near the carriage. I've got a change of clothes for you; I'll of course expect to be paid back for them."

"Thanks Geist!!"

The carriage was a short walk away, parked in a clear patch of grass between the giant trash piles. It was a standard four-person buggy, painted jet black with red stripes on either side. The undercarriage and lower halves were lined with painted black steel, enough to stop any standard fire, though the extra weight required Clydesdale horses to pull it at a reasonable speed. Lucas of course dreamed of something bigger, but it would have to wait until he claimed the bounty on Knox's head.

The interior was lined with bolted on portraits of decrepit old men who were part of the Geist Lineage and encased in glass spattered about the cabin walls were old tomes detailing the alleged heroism of the Geist Line.

Jenkins was forced to sit in the gunner's seat in the back behind the carriage because he still reeked no matter how many times Lucas told him to get back in the ocean for another wash.

The piles of rubbish got smaller and smaller as they oscillated towards Kleppenwitz, the Laughing Monk snuck into view along with the white cottages that looked from a distance like a winter forest swarmed by lightning bugs.

"So, how'd you wind up in the Cantina?" Lucas said opening the back window and breaking the silence, "Don't seem like a natural fit for a bounty hunter, how'd you convince her to give you work?"

"Saw me out there on the streets one day, guess she took pity on me is all, I'm sure I looked pittyable. And thank God she did, wasn't easy out there plus the rumors of people dissapearin…"

"She saved you and yet you betray her?!" Lucas didn't even try to stop his laughter, he couldn't believe what an idiot Mince was.

"I wouldn't call it that. She just refused to give me a shot like you did is all. Then she goes and lets a boy wonder around the Cantina like it was no big deal, already in a sash no less. Meanwhile I'm in the kitchen covered in fish guts and cooking oil, praying a day may come when she gives me the sash I deserve."

Lucas nodded approvingly, he recalled seeing Jack in Hangman's Hall as a tyke, knocking over glasses and falling over himself with his gimped leg. If Riley wasn't so good with a sword he would've lettered an orphanage.

"And that sanctimonious Riley running around thinkin' she's the best hunter, thinkin she's better than me and even you sir. Doesn't even have to say it, I see it all over her face. Just couldn't anymore sir…"

"Tell me have you ever seen her fight. Ever seen her swing a blade, or a fire a shot?"

"Uhh… no sir, sure hadn't…" he said sheepishly.

"I thought not. Your overconfidence will get you killed boy. I don't want to hear another word from you about who could beat who until you've been in a firefight yourself. I'll be happy to dump you back on the street if that's a problem!"

"Of course not sir, just thought you hated'em. Sorry, was out of line."

The spotted pigs of Port Pigly were now visible with hundreds of cargo ships behind them. Ships passed through the bay with coal on their decks stacked high as cottages and barrels of whale blubber stacked beside.

"You have any family Mince? Need to know who to take you to if you can't figure out how to keep your mouth shut."

"N-no sir, had a mom, haven't seen her since I was real small though. Can't really even remember her face, sad ain't it? Left me out on the streets before I had even lost all my teeth. Said she was sorry, but I cost her too much. It's alright though, didn't much care for her either." Jenkins said unconvincingly

For a moment he almost felt pity for the boy, until he heard the coachman yell they had arrived at their destination.

The stables were barely being held up by rotted wood and rusty nails, built so long ago no one alive in the Gibbons today could remember who built it. However, it was a stone's throw from the Blackwater Cantina, the convenience of which made the dilapidated appearance excusable.

"Remember what I said, tell no one of this. If anyone asks you got lost while men were trying to kill us and I was lucky enough to be passing by and rescue you."

"The perfect alibi sir, no one will suspect a thing!" Jenkins fiddled with his fingers nervously. As he got up from his back seat to leave he said, "Say sir, you think he stopped by yet? Has them all shakin in their boots? Just to see the look on those three's faces, haven't been able to stop thinkin about it."

"We'll see soon enough, and you may as well add that to the list of things you best not talk about."

The Blackwater Cantina's exterior towered above all the quirky cottages surrounding it like the wooden fortress that it was, with trees growing out many of its upper walls and a peculiar oblong structure that made many wonder how it had never toppled over on itself.

The interior was festive when they arrived through the great wooden doors. Somehow not even a madman trying to murder the whole lot of Gibbons could break their spirits.

He wasted no time heading straight for the kitchen, with Mince Jenkins close behind like a kitten following its mother.

Chef Greene was by himself in a kitchen that seemed far too large to have just one person inside of it. He was busy chopping off fish heads as Lucas approached,

"Chef!" he yelled violently, the anger he felt from earlier had crept back in, "A landfill? Really?! What kind of Butternut do you think I am? Think I'd fall for that?!"

Chef Greene shrugged without looking up.

"That all you've got to say?! Ignoring your superior?!"

He shrugged again and said, "Told you all I know, best lower your voice mon."

"Lower my voice?!" he was even more enraged, "You gave false information to a MANAGER!! I don't know how they do things where you're from on Prego, but on Otto we respect our superiors! You know the power I have here?! I could have you thrown out on the street tonight if I wanted!!"

"Go ahead, not like you pay good." he said in his low grumble as he kept chopping at the fish.

"I don't think you understand the gravity of the situa-!"

He was interrupted by Greene throwing a fish at his head.

Lucas looked down at the pistol holstered in his hip; he could barely stop himself from pulling it.

"Point dat thing at me and you'll have dis knife in your chest!"

Feeling a rare bit of courage, hearing this Jenkins sprung from behind Lucas and puffed up his chest at him,

"Dat goes for you too Jenkin." Greene said as he grabbed a second knife from the counter.

He knew Greene wouldn't be quick enough, and if not, his body armor would block the blow. It took every bit of his energy not to pull it, not to dish out vengeance. But even he knew the trouble this would cause him. He'd have to wait it out, bide his time until he could come up with a proper solution to his little rat problem.

"Don't ever lie to me again!!" he spouted awkward and flustered as he stormed off.

As he walked towards his dormitories, despite his best efforts the anger would not subside. *What happened to grandfather's celestial home, to my father's charming hideaway. Ruined by the likes of Matilda Baum, and dregs she brought in off the street. No need for poise, intelligence, decorum, or even so much as an interview, as far as she's concerned the Cantina's open to all.*

He thought about making it. The call he knew he could make at any time. One pigeon sent and he could have the whole Cantina shut down. It was a drastic measure, but one that may be necessary to restore the Cantina to what he knew it could be.

Chapter 12
Lead & Steel

Jack watched Radish pull out a glass vial of clear liquid from his pocket and rub it under the sleeping Kersey's nose while the loud **KNOCK KNOCK KNOCK** continued at the door. Within seconds the man woke with a start, while Radish grabbed his head and put his hand over his mouth to silence him.

With a mixture of fear, uncertainty, and bewilderment the four others in the room watched Radish furiously dig underneath the bed Kersey had just got up from, throwing all manner of crates and packages as quietly as he could.

"Where is it?!.... Where is it?! Knew I left it here somewhere!" he said frantically, "Let's see those are explosives... poison made on Prego... backscratcher... Aha! Got it!!" he whispered as he pulled out a brown leather sack that had what looked like golden letters poking out through the top, "Right this way!"

In the back of the dormitory where the blue chest still lay open and dormant, there was a portrait of a woman propped up against the dreary stone wall behind it. The painted woman was at least ten feet tall with a decisive unibrow, wore a ruffled black dress down to her ankles, with a white ruff around her neck that stretched out past her shoulders.

Cleverly hidden in the ruffles of the black dress was a slit in the painting that went up from the ground to right above where the woman's knee would've been. Jack was amazed when he saw it, the slit blended in so well with the black dress he wouldn't have seen it in a million years if it hadn't been pointed out to him.

"In ya go, in ya go!! Hurry through, whoevers at that door ain't here for tea!" Radish said waving his arms big in a circle.

Jack urged Apolline to go in first, and he quickly crawled in behind her.

It was a familiar setting to Jack as the crawlspace they'd just crept into on their elbows and knees had the same texture and smell as the sewers that led him here.

Riley and Kersey weren't far behind them, and when they looked back, they could see Radish in a prone position desperately trying to reseal the painting from its backside.

There was only a thin beam of light shining out from under the slit when Riley, Kersey, and Radish heard a sound they feared was coming. It sounded just like a cannon went off and the subsequent rumble of bits of wood and steel flying at lightspeeds confirmed it.

"Go...go!" Radish whispered urgently to Riley and Kersey ahead of him.

As he crawled forward, Jack heard a voice coming from the hideout he'd just escaped. A woman's echo that sounded like nails on a chalkboard.

"Candles are still burning, they can't have gone far. I want every single last man we've got creating a perimeter within one mile of here. Get a team posted out in every nook and cranny that exists in this sewer. Radish, my old friend... is a dead man..."

Hearing the woman from behind him Radish let out a bellow that sounded like a bullfrog as he crawled forward along with the rest of them, "Ugh... Not her!"

Elbows and knees were bruised and bloodied by the time all of them reached the end of the crawlspace. Radish was the last to crawl out to the four of them giving him a stare down.

"Come on give a hand gents!" he started pilling the tunnel he'd just crawled out of with piles of damp stones that'd fallen from the nearby walls and ceiling.

"Care to tell us what just happened?" Riley said half annoyed and half panicked.

After he'd felt like he piled enough stones on he replied, "Ah yes! So sorry forgot to mention him, our sleeping beauty has awakened. Everyone say hi to Kersey, Kersey say hi to our new friends and Apolline."

His captain gave a nervous wave looking like he was the most confused of any of them.

"Not exactly what I meant, I guess your hideout wasn't as hidden as you thought. Knox's men I assume? And what was that awful voice I heard back in the tunnel? It sounded like a woman?!" she said.

"Ah yes that... uhhh that..." he said quietly like he was hoping he was the only one that heard her, "Fraid I've got a bit of bad news. That awful voice you heard, was a woman named Alireza Bale..."

Dansen Kersey gasped while the rest just stared.

"Whose she?" Jack said squinching his eyes.

"Alireza is a Forzian General. Magnus's right-hand woman. As big a murderous psychopath as they come."

"Magnus, as in King Magnus?! Leader of an entire army?! What in the Five Isles would he want on the Boondocks?? Hasn't he got a war to fight on Prego?" Riley retorted.

"He does indeed miss. Must be something real important if he sent the Boiled Witch… It would appear whatever's happenin here, is much bigger than we coulda imagined."

"Whatever. At least we gave them the slip. Let's just focus on getting out of this sewer and back to the Cantina."

"About that…" Radish with an embarrassed look, "Wouldn't say we've given them the slip. This appears to be a bit of spring… a trap if you will. I'd guess we got about an hour until they find our little escape tunnel."

"Is there any good news?" she said sarcastically.

"Fraid not. Heard her say she wanted the men to create a one-mile perimeter. Which given the layout of these here tunnels, makes it high unlikely we get out unseen. If I had to guess, the only way we get out of this pickle is with lead and steel. If any of you lot gotta weapon, now's the time to pull it."

The stone walls of the sewer were crumbling and covered in a blackgreen algae, if it wasn't for the stream splitting the two ledges appearing higher in elevation, this side of the sewer was a spitting image of the one they walked in through, albeit a little less lonely this time around with three new companions.

With his maroon sword in front of him like it was some kind torch, Radish continued deeper and deeper into the tunnels, even though there was no source of light the tunnel seemed to grow darker and colder the further they went.

"Do hope you know where you're going!?" Riley hissed.

"Won't be much longer now! Keep a move on! You lot go any slower you'll have coral comin out your ears!"

Radish and Kersey were in the front having what looked to be an intense conversation, while Riley separated Apolline and Jack in the back.

For the very first time Jack noticed the rats Radish mentioned earlier, there were hundreds of them down here, especially near the water splitting the ledge they walked across. Most of them seemed to bead towards Apolline and Jack, like they were following their lead.

"Are you cold?" Jack said to Apolline, "You can take my cloak, should warm you up and keep any rain off."

With a frightful smirk she shook her head.

"You sure? It'll be a good disguise. You'll stick out like a white monkey wearing something that bright."

After some thought she took it and clasped it over herself. It was so big she now looked like she was wearing a potato sack.

"Excellent! You look much more like a commoner now. You hungry at all? I've still got some sea biscuits in my boot, they aren't the best but pretty good in a pinch when there's nothing else to eat."

She took one and gave it a big sniff, took a small nibble out of it, and then immediately spit it back out. *Can't blame her for that*, he'd had the same reaction the first time he tried one.

The tunnels continued, never stopping with every passing archway followed by another copy. Radish was humming some old cadet's tune and Jack was trying his best to ignore it. He took another look at Apolline, she looked solemn but certainly happier than she did when they first met.

"You holding up OK?" Jack said.

Apolline didn't even need to scribble anything down, he could see the terror all over her after hearing Alireza.

"I'm a little worried too." he admitted, "But all the money in the world couldn't afford you a better bodyguard than Riley. And she's at the cantina so you haven't met her yet, but Matilda might be my second pick. She's gonna love you, especially when she finds out she can talk enough for the both of you. Can be a little intimidating at first but once Riley says you're alright, she'll be the best and craziest friend you ever had…"

What looked like a glimmer of hope swept through her hopeless countenance.

"And I haven't seen Radish in a fight yet. But I doubt he's some greenhorn either, if the stories I hear are true, no man alive could pull off some of the things he's done without some serious skill."

"What about you? Are you as fearless as the pirate king from the story?" she scribbled as if she half expected it to be true.

Jack fidgeted, "Welp, to be completely honest. I've only brought in three bounties. And most wouldn't consider them particularly deadly bounties either. I can still shoot alright though so I wouldn't say I'm completely useless."

Seeing this wasn't helping the matter he continued,

"You see how we're all in a row right now? You and me will stick in the back like we are now when we get out. Just try and blend in and stick behind the people with guns and we'll be back to safety in no time."

Up ahead Radish was swinging his sword wildly into the dark, like he was composing a symphony in the night, while Kersey looked like he may blow a gasket trying to figure out what on earth could've caused Alireza Bale to venture all the way to the Boondocks.

"Monsoon's Mercy Rad! You sure that was her? She can't be the only with a voice like banshee. The Pinwheels are a big place…"

"Squawk like that… I'd rather have a banshee after me. That's her alright. Seven oceans and Five Isles, and she ends up on ours…"

"Just so hard to believe is all, eh? His top general? That girl must be somethin special…"

"The girl… Or Colombo. Though likely both…"

Captain Kersey was dressed in his old cadet's uniform he earned back when he was a commodore for the Freeboots on Vista. It was a camouflaged wool jumpsuit puffy on the bottom and narrow on the top with a host of rations, ammo, compasses, stationery, and other gizmos buckled to the front of it with oversized leather straps. The man didn't have enough hair on the top of his head and had much more than he needed on the outer edges of it. He was short, with a rich face, and had a belly that he had given up on, and always seemed to have a cough, almost like his gruffy voice was making him choke.

"You know back when I still had my hair eh, when I was a recruit in the Sailfish Fleet on Vista." Kersey said, "The generals, they used to pick the young guys to pilot the ships over the old-timers. Figured we'd had more experience, since we just left training an all. The old ones had never seen a fight in their whole career with the ghosts not long gone, they were right redundant, eh, the only thing they *had* gotten good at was sittin around an playin cards. Me and the boys used to laugh at them, now I'd give a ship to be one of'em…"

"You know what the monks say don't ya mate? M*ay you live whilst eagles fly.* Mayhaps we consider ourselves lucky, first inter-island war anyone alive remembers, and would you look at us, right gobbed in the middle of it!"

"You're a crackpot, you know that? As harebrained as they come!"

"Hair?! Rich comin from you!" Radish laughed.

Instead of a straightaway the tunnel had started to narrow, and the pungent sewage smell was becoming less pronounced like it was fighting a losing battle with fresh air. It didn't take long for traces of moonlight to illuminate the moldy stone walls, and it took even less time for them to see the rickety old ladder that led up to a manhole cover.

"Welp! Whose up first?!" Radish said cheekily.

"I can assure you Jack, Apolline, and myself will do no such thing." Riley said angrily, "Was this really your plan? Outsmart a Forzian General with a hidden ladder? You really believe this isn't the first place she'd look??"

"Guess we'll have to see then won't we?"

He looked each of them over and shook his head while swoshing drool in his mouth in preparation.

"This ain't gonna be for the faint of heart. If you're too frightened may as well take your chances down here. Maybe can build a little cottage and have all the rats you like to eat for the rest of your days. But if you plan on followin me, best brace yourselves..."

Radish paced back and forth like he was a general speaking to his army. He looked at Jack who still had his weapons holstered,

"Tell me boy, you ever killed a man?"

"I-I don't believe so..." he murmured.

"Oh how I envy you!" he tapped his sword at the pistol on Jack's hip, "Best you pull that out lad, today may be your lucky day!"

Not a second later and while still staring at Jack, Radish pulled one of his guns and shot some ten feet ahead of where the manhole cover was on the ceiling. Moonlight immediately shone through the hole in the ceiling and muddled voices of men could be heard above.

Weapon in mouth Radish beamed up the ladder with surprising agility. Slowly he lifted the cover, peaked at his targets, and shot two times switching pistols as the first was spent. From the top of the ladder he gave the signal for them to follow as he jumped out into the night.

"Remember the promise you made me Jack, you'll follow my lead no matter what. No more ignoring me and getting hit like you did back at the market..." Riley said like just thinking about it again set her off.

He felt the urge to argue back, to tell her again how he wasn't a child anymore, when he stopped suddenly. The lump in his throat blocked the words. The lump of nerves from the realization he was about to enter his second deadly encounter today. He'd never experienced yips this intense on any of his previous hunts, it seemed Riley was correct when she said getting shot tends to change someone.

When they got up Apolline had to cover her eyes after seeing the two men who were disguised as merchants lying motionless on the ground.

"They weren't friendly don't worry!" Radish scoffed, "Last I checked merchants don't carry rifles on their back."

"Not bad..." Riley said, "And here I thought you'd had too much rum to point and click."

"Got it backwards miss, the more I drunk the better I shoot! Now we need to move, someone will've heard those shots!"

It was nearly the break of dawn now, as the hustle of busy city sounds earlier had crept into an eerie quiet. The colorful buildings surrounding the alleyway seemed dimmer, the street torches had gone out, and any signs of life non-existent.

Outside the alleyway were twin red bricked government buildings on opposite sides of the cobblestones with their atypical, at least for this city, neatly manicured lawns and unblemished exteriors. The only way you could tell them apart was one had toothpick-like palms trees lining its gardens and the other had palm trees shaped like a fan and were barely big enough to reach the first-floor windows.

Ahead of them were a series of smaller box-shaped red brick buildings with crested roofs, the closest of which had a sidewall thick with ivy.

Thinking on his feet, Radish rushed over to the ivy and scurried up it like a monkey running for cover.

"Climb beside me, if you start to slip just grab my shoulder..." Jack said to Apolline as the crew scurried up.

Once on top Radish began hacking at ivy with his sword removing any chance for followers.

Jack looked over to see Apolline breathing in heavily, taking in every smell she could, and wide-eyed gazing over all the spectacular views of the hundreds of cottages around her and Big Brother Boondock in the distance. For all Jack knew, this could've been her first time even stepping outside.

"See that ruddy old wooden building in the distance with the ship at the top and one-eyed monkey flag?" he said to her, "That's the Cantina, I know it doesn't look so great on the outside, but that's by design. We just need to make it there and we're home free."

"It's like a castle, but with wood."

While many of the Blackwater Cantina facilities were underground, the dormitories were still high above ground. The building looked almost out of place, a haggard wooden behemoth amongst a sea of stone and whitewood cottages. It had seven giant spires at the top with various flags, and a few massive oak trees lined the upper deck that had somehow managed to survive after all the years up there sprawling out like a man yawning and with roots dangling off the side. There was even an abandoned ship still up there that a crew of pranksters put up one day before Jack, or even Riley, was alive, and had forgotten to take back down.

The youngest of bounty hunters took a break from staring at the building in the distance to scout out the building they were currently on top of. There was furniture, bits of roof jutting out, and even a few pet dogs and cats barking and scurrying about. For nearly half a mile the box buildings went on, and as luck would have it, they stretched towards the direction of the Cantina. Even luckier, there was only a few feet to jump between them, making it an ideal escape route.

Footsteps and the voices of men could now be heard from the street they'd just came from, Riley quickly grabbed a nearby rock and threw it far into the opposite direction.

"Is this what we're doing Radish? Escaping on roof tops? You know we've still got at least a mile to go when we get to the end right?!" she said.

"Aye, that's what the guns are for!" he shouted back.

As they jumped across the gaps, they could see men with rifles under most of them. The crew tried their hardest to jump silently over but even Jack knew it was only a matter of time.

Visibly shaking after seeing the Knox's men, Apolline clutched her grass bracelet like it would somehow make this all go away.

"Just stay back with me... remember?" Jack said, hoping his feigned calm would rub off.

"Are they going to hurt us?" her scribbles were barely legible with

how much her hand shook.

"Not even an army could stop us! Just wait till you see what they're capable of, you're in the best of hands right now."

They'd made it to the end of the row of buildings now, all poking their heads just barely down onto the streets below. The street was as wide as any on Kleppenwitz, with speakeasys, dine-ins, and pawners that hadn't opened up yet for the day. Soldiers disguised as patrons of said establishments were marching in pairs, circling back and forth with purpose.

"Count six of them." Kersey gruffed.

"Seven if you include the one behind the tree there." Radish pointed out.

"There's eight men, you missed the one crouching in the carriage." Riley said like she expected better of them.

"Guess that's two for each of yas, don't be shy, pull'em out then. Get ready. Count of three!" Radish whispered.

Riley noticed Apolline looking on and shaking and touched her shoulder gently,

"You don't have to watch this if you're not ready sweetie. This will all be over soon…"

As Radish counted the four of them had found their targets, in unison eight shots went out all a direct hit minus one. Jack's nerves had gotten the best of him and one of his shots had only skimmed his target. Riley and Radish immediately took a third shot downing the man, but not before he managed to shoot himself.

The sound it made was the scariest part, the sound of something coming at you so fast you couldn't comprehend. It was a direct hit on the brick pillar in front of them. One bit of brick grazed Riley's cheek leaving a trail of blood, another hit Radish's shoulder with so much force he dropped his pistol, and the other knocked Kersey over completely.

"I-I… I'm so sorry…" Jack said horrified.

"Nows not the time for sorries kid! Keep movin!" Radish ordered with the gusto of a wild tiger.

Without a second thought Radish leaped over the broken brick down onto a merchant's awning just below them. Like it was a trampoline he bounced up and then safely back onto the ground just below. One by one they repeated the process until Apolline had landed safely.

As they ran forward Jack's head was spinning with guilt. *I've made that shot a thousand times at the range. Calm down and just breathe...* he told himself. *I got lucky that time, another miss could get someone killed.*

"Best you lead eh?" Kersey murmured at Riley, "Boss could get lost on his way to the privy."

"That so?"

"Y'know he showed up at my door a few months ago, hadn't seen'em for years! Said get your things there's treasure to be had. Reckon that was a mistake as it usually is, Alireza bein here just confirms it."

They turned the corner to a wider than usual cobblestone street that looked like it had been ransacked. Several lampposts were in pieces on the ground, knocked over by an eight horsed carriage so big it took up half the cobblestone.

Shaped almost like a spider it had four arched wings bellowing out of its main cabin equipped with gunny holes and steel plating. It was a dull black with dark blue spotted sections on the wings and had a carriage door that was hanging wide open with a feint light poking through it.

"Guess we didn't outwit her..." Radish said with hope fading, "She didn't need to know where we were, just where we were going..."

The silhouette walked slowly down from the ramp onto the street below, cackling as she did.

"Alireza Bale..." Radish said mouth agape, "Might be the first woman I saw I didn't like..."

There wasn't one amongst them that didn't have shivers running down their spines.

"We've got to get out of here, run!" Riley cried, trying to find cover.

"Mom are you joking? There's only one of her and five of us!?"

"Trust me... We can make Stalker's Pass. No need for us to take this fight..."

Jack looked around at everyone agreeing with her, even Radish.

"Mom's right kid, she'd turn us all into goop by daybreak. Then put Apolline here in an even worse cage than the one she came from."

"Alright then after you..." Jack said frustrated as he readied his pistols.

Riley rushed them towards a back alleyway no more than four or five blocks away, they could still hear the echoes of her laughter as they ran.

There was a new series of houses they were running along the bottom of, a set of uniquely un-unique white cottages. The roofs were relatively flat, stood no farther off the ground than the ones they'd just ran across moments prior and unfortunately made for a great vantage point for someone looking to shoot down at them.

It didn't take long for a hail of fire to come raining down on them. It seemed as if an army were swooping down on their position, but when they looked up, they only saw one lone shooter, Alireza still laughing as she took aim. They could just barely make out her wiry hair and those awful cobweb veins surrounding her eyes.

The parties' ears were ringing, and time seemed to swirl into a dreamlike haze as chunks of sidewalk spattered every which way and left a trail of smoke and debris in their wake.

One after another they shot back almost as many shots as she fired off, but they'd all been absorbed by a railing just below her. The railing had been destroyed but she kept up right along with them.

Her shots continued relentlessly, a lead ball grazed Kersey's shoulder, one was absorbed by Jack's armor, and a bit of concrete slammed into

Radish's eye, after which he thanked the heavens it wasn't his good eye.

Still, they returned fire. And still inexplicably came up short. Dansen Kersey's gun jammed as he shot, Jack and Riley could've sworn they'd fired perfect shots but each of them seemed to groove right over her left and right shoulders, while Radish was firing wildly into the night as he had been temporarily blinded by all the debris. No matter what they did or how many times they fired they couldn't seem to get a clean shot.

Now approaching the alleyway that would get them in range of the backside of the Cantina, they paused and took a breath. Jack knew the alleyway well, him and Riley had used it many times when they needed to get into Cantina discreetly. Other Gibbons had dubbed it the Stalker's Pass, as they too used it to sneak themselves or a bounty in when an adversary was hot on their trail. With the white and wood homes still on their left, and brick siding on their right, the alleyway was just big enough to fit the five of them side by side.

As she looked up towards the rooftops, Riley noticed a patched wooden walkway along the rows of houses that would've made Alireza's life much easier.

"Shoot down the walkway!!" she yelled back as she began running down the pass.

With little fuss they took aim at the foundations, and each rung of the walkway came down with force and crash landed into dust as they ran further and further into the pass.

"That oughta slow her down!" Riley said with panting breath.

She looked over at Apolline who was bruised and bloodied like the rest of them, her lip was trembling. She grabbed her hand and gave it a couple of squeezes.

"Almost back!" she said trying her best to give an earnest smile and sound confident when she knew very well this could end badly.

For a time, it had grown oddly quiet, their hurried boots and Apolline's sandals pounding against pavement was the only hint of noise as dawn broke.

It didn't take long for the shooting to start again however, as Riley had to shove Jack and Apolline to the ground to avoid a shot that hit the brick just above them.

They noticed her atop a large section of pointed roofing using it as a sniper spot, once again when they returned fire misses, jams, and even a flock of birds got in their way. At the very least a few of the shots destroyed her perch, leaving her fumbling to keep up the chase.

"There's something unnatural happenin here, eh?! Never seen someone dodge that many shots!" Kersey said sialoquently while trying his best to reload one of his pistols.

"You didn't think killin a Forzian General would be easy did ya?" Radish laughed, "Oughta call it a miracle none of us is dead yet!"

For as terrible as the situation was, it was shaping up to be a lovely day on Kleppenwitz. The skies were clear save for a few massive clouds in the distance, the pigeons were singing in squawks, and you could even hear the echo of monkeys from the forests outside the city.

The five of them were nearly to the end of Stalker's Pass now when they heard the shot. The assassin had adapted, learned to shoot at the one without any armor.

Riley stopped in her tracks and pulled Apolline toward her so hard she nearly toppled over. The shot grazed Riley's ankle and took a chunk with it as it burst open pavement just in front of them. Her forward motion caused her to fall violently to the ground dropping her guns as she did.

Without even thinking Jack rushed to her aid, putting himself under her shoulder and carrying the two of them forward. Looking down at her foot he lost his breath when he could see a bit of bone sticking out her busted boot. He'd never in his life wanted to hurt someone as much as he did now. He tried to fight the tears but seeing his mother like this he couldn't manage it.

Radish and Kersey were firing blindly at every corner of rooftop they could see as Jack followed with his free arm. There were going to be some very angry homeowners when they woke up to see their roofs completely destroyed, but there was still no sign of Alireza.

"That's a bone alright!" Radish said wincing as he looked down at her foot, "Wouldn't worry too much kid, definitely not lethal. Just make sure she doesn't take another one!"

Riley, Dansen Kersey, Jack, and Radish had finally gotten to the end of the alleyway, and the backdoors of the Cantina were just barely in view. Being so busy trying to get Riley on her feet again, they never noticed that one of them was missing.

"Apolline!" Jack shouted, "Where is she?!"

Their worst fears were realized when they turned around and saw poor Apolline being held at gunpoint, with Alireza Bale's arm choked around her neck using the mute girl as a human shield.

"Now seems like a pretty good time for you to drop your weapons…" she said grinning like someone that needed to be put away.

Alireza looked even worse than Radish remembered, the cobweb veins surrounding her eyes seemed to take up her whole face now instead of just part of it. Her fingers were a decaying purple and green and looked like they'd been soaking in a bog. The only part of her that didn't look vile was her skin-tight black leather suit and her golden sunflower shaped ring, that shone brighter than one would've guessed with the dusk sun now bearing upon it.

"So good to see you again Radish. How long has it been?"

"Not long enough!" he said sharply.

"You can imagine how delighted I was when I got your scent back there in the sewers. Comandante Magnus will be so pleased when I drop off the Quicksilver you stole… as well as your moth-eaten head."

"Quicksilver's gone mate, lost it cave diving near Alexandria. Beautiful this time of year. Maybe let the girl go and have a look?"

She let out a laugh that could turn a spine, "Oh Radish, I'm sure I don't believe you. You know what I think? I think the Quicksilver is right there in that disgusting brown bag of yours. After you're lying on the ground, grasping for your last breath, I may just have a look…"

Apolline was quivering uncontrollably now, hardly able to breathe with the arm around her neck squeezing so tightly. She made muffled cries and looked at Radish, Jack, and Riley, anyone that could free her from the pain she was in.

"I'd like for all of you standing here to thank Radish for your untimely deaths. If he could manage to keep his paws out of places they don't belong, then none of you would be in this… unfortunate situation."

"Only one of us is dying here!" Riley said with a scowl on her face, trying desperately to ignore the pain in her foot.

"Oh?" Alireza grinned, "And how exactly do you plan on stopping me? Judging by your shooting, you all couldn't hit a ship if you were standing inside of it. And seeing as how none of you have tried to gun me down yet, I'd say my beautiful little shield here is doing her job wonderfully…"

Jack was boiling with rage; it took everything in his power to keep his guns pointed at the ground. He looked behind him, towards the Cantina, hoping that Matilda and her men had heard them and would come to their rescue. But there was no one, they were just out of range for anyone to see them.

For the first time in a very long time Riley didn't know what her next move was going to be. She attempted to signal Apolline back, give her some reassurance, but it felt hard to deliver a message she couldn't promise.

"I don't know why you all seem so upset," the assassin said, "Think of this as a contribution to a cause much greater than yourselves. Just look at this city of thieves around you, grown men begging for their food on street corners, a new bar on every corner for drunkards like Radish to stumble around like the waste they are. Look at how you squander your freedom. Someone's got to take care of it, bring peace, and order, no matter the cost."

She brushed Apolline's golden hair with the butt of her pistol.

"And don't worry too much, Knox is going to take very good care of our beautiful friend here. Just need to run a few tiny little experiments on her is all. Then she's free to go… if she can still walk." she howled.

Now in and out of a state of consciousness Apolline tried her best to stay coherent. She looked down at the ring on the woman's rotting fingers, it looked like a rose sitting on a throne of bones. It seemed to call her, like it was speaking right to her without needing words. It was pulsating up and down and down and up, each second growing bigger. She could hardly manage to take her eyes off it, when she finally did, she knew what she needed to do. Desperately, and with the biggest eyes she could muster, she stared at Radish and Riley trying to signal them.

Seeing this Radish took his pistol pointed it straight up into the air and fired a lone shot. The lead decayed into airborne nothingness just as quickly as it'd been launched.

Alireza howled again, "And just what was your plan there?! Plan on killing some birds?! Waste of a shot…"

"Never trust a scallywag miss…" he smirked.

As the words left his mouth Apolline ducked her head and with every bit of energy she could muster, and with every ounce of her body weight she grabbed the ring on Alireza's finger and flung herself to the ground holding on to the sunflower so hard she could feel it piercing skin.

It was all the opportunity Riley ever needed. The blast came from her pistol not even a second later, as Apolline still held on to the ring and Alireza's upper body was still upright and exposed.

The shot was a direct hit to her shoulder splattering bits of blood and bone all over Stalker's Pass and flung her back so ferociously she slammed into the back wall of the alley.

Apolline rushed into Riley's outstretched arms, looking like she had never known the relief she was feeling now.

"Heavens your hand is cut to bits!" she said, "Hold it against my shirt, not too hard, but firmly. We need to stop the bleeding. We'll get you all patched up when we get inside."

"Atta girl!!" Radish yelled as Jack and Kersey cheered along with him, "Just come outta a box and already took down one of Forzian's finest!!"

"Thought you were a goner eh, good work!!" Kersey gruffed and cheered.

"Brilliant! Would've never thought of that!" Jack said and gave her a high five.

Even Riley briefly joined in on the celebrations until she snapped out of it and got back to her usual focused self.

"Not time for a victory lap yet gentlemen, we need to move, Knox's men are still out here!"

"Right said." Radish replied, "Just need to finish the job, make sure she's not movin."

Stalker's pass looked like a hurricane had run through it. Bits of busted wood, brick, and cobblestone covered most of it, and the clouds of dust the debris left behind were still lingering.

The party had gotten so caught up in excitement and the dust clouds were still so thick they failed to notice the assassin's body was no longer in sight.

Alireza Bale was hobbling back through Stalker's Pass and had made it to a manhole cover, attempting to lift it up and escape back down into the sewers. Radish fired a shot that grazed her leg, but it wasn't enough to stop her.

"Come'on!" Radish yelled, "We don't take care'o her now, I can promise she'll be an even bigger problem next we see her. She's got no defenses, now's time to finish it!"

"We've got no time! I won't risk our safety any more than is necessary. You and Kersey go if you like, but we're going back to the Cantina." Riley replied adamantly.

"Aggghhh!" Radish yelled in frustration, "Fine then, we won't be long. Just make sure and leave the doors open for us."

"If me or mine's safety is jeopardized, I will do no such thing. I'll close the doors with or without you. So I suggest you make you make it quick."

As quickly as she could with a busted leg, she hobbled away from the pass with Apolline assisting under her shoulder, as Jack was split between them concentrated and determined. He looked at Kersey and Radish running towards the sewers and then looked back towards his mother. He made his choice and ran up to Riley and Apolline, putting his head underneath his mom's shoulder for support.

The huge wooden doors of the Cantina never looked so spectacular underneath the gruddy wooden structure towering above it, and the sign of the sleeping monkey just above the doors, had never been so welcoming. Finally, they were home, finally they were safe.

Obviously having heard the commotion from outside, Matilda was out front with around fifty men, wearing full body armor, and looking down on every man and woman there. She had a giant rifle hoisted over her shoulder so big two of her men couldn't have carried it, and so much body armor five of her men couldn't have carried it.

"Well well, if it ain't my two favorite people in these isles. We were just on the way to whatever firefight we heard." Matilda yelled with her bold voice as she saw them approach.

She walked up to Riley and gave her a big bear hug, lifting her up so high her feet were dangling near Apolline's head. She took the opportunity to grab Jack as well with her free hand, as the two of them together dangled above her giant knees politely grasping for air.

"Was worried sick about y'all! Just the thought of bein cooped up in here without my friends! It's enough to bring a tear to my eye!" she said as she rocked them back and forth with her eyes closed, doing some strange combination of humming and singing an unintelligible song.

"Thank you Matilda…" Riley groaned struggling to get out the words, "But we've had such a rough time of it today… if you wouldn't putting us down."

"You got it Riles! Say who's the new girl?" she said bending down past her waist to take a look.

"It's a long story, I'll tell you when we get inside. It still may not be safe out here."

Matilda had got so caught up in the excitement she barely noticed the shape they were in.

"Monsoon's Mercies Riles! What in the Five Isles happened to your foot?!"

"Alireza Bale happened… a Forzian General, in Kleppenwitz of all places…"

"Welp Dr. Ableton is gonna get woken real early this mornin, you need medical attention right now! Takin you straight to the medbay. Don't you try to argue me out of it either!"

Without a second thought she picked Riley up again, this time with her whole body in both arms.

"I'm fine! I can make it there on my own!"

Matilda wasn't having a word of it, she marched through the great wooden doors like a freight train as Riley looked like a bomb that might explode in any second.

The men marched in behind her as Jack and Apolline could finally take a moment to catch their breath.

"Some day huh?" Jack said still panting and flush with adrenaline.

Apolline nodded back in the most understanding way, looking like she could've slept right then and there on the dirty cobblestones below her feet.

As the two went to walk inside they could see Radish and Kersey screaming,

"Waitttttt!!!" in the distance.

He did as he was told, and safely ushered everyone in, feeling like this had been the longest day of his short life. He knew the road was going to be rocky, but experiencing the thin line between life and death firsthand was something else entirely.

Shoving a hand in front him, Jack went to close the big wooden doors behind him and took one final glance at Stalker's Pass. It was so far away, and he was so dizzy from the fighting, he couldn't be sure if it was a hallucination or not. But right at the entrance to the pass, he could just make out a bald man, in white linen robes, with a wolf almost as big as he was. And the cold stare he was giving made him feel like a cutlass had just slid down his spine.

Chapter 13

<u>Wormslayer</u>

A week had passed since Alireza Bale took a chunk out of Riley Tripleleaf's foot, and she in turn took her shoulder. Still holed up in the med bay, laid on her cot with a lumpy bandage on her leg, she felt like it was completely unnecessary for her to still be there, Jack knew this because she mentioned it every time he came to visit

Doctor Ableton stitched up what he could to get her ankle looking normal again and said the missing bone would repair on its own, or at least he thought it would. Apolline had gotten off easier, she was able to leave the med bay the same day after getting four or five stitches in her hand and neck.

Aside from the needle and bruised hand, Apolline had had a pretty good week. Jack had shown her most of Monarch Library including the empty, dark, and dungeonous lower floors which felt like they held more books than grains of sand at the beach, he showed her Hangman's Hall where she overate octopus eggs and enjoyed watching men climb up the rafters looking for Plunders the Parrot's stolen gold, and he showed her the shooting range which she seemed to enjoy so much she wanted to spend as much time in there as Jack did after he'd missed a crucial shot.

Today was Riley's last day in the med bay before the good doctor would let her leave. Jack and Apolline patiently slept beside her while she was still resting. Hanging out here had become a habit for them, over the past week they'd spent every day amongst the pine walls here and every night exploring the Cantina.

Like all hospitals, the med bay could be a very depressing place. Men who had their arms blown off in a fire fight on Vista, or needed a leg amputated from the Black Molder of Caldo were all located here warts and all, mostly hidden behind curtains, or given a room of their own if their condition was bad enough.

Riley's curtained room, as well as a few others, were covered in pinewood to mirror the look and feel of Hangman's Hall. It was certainly comforting, but the blinding lanterns in the center and surgeon's tools hanging about the walls were a glaring reminder you were still in a hospital.

"How's the ankle ma?" Jack said as he opened his eyes and stretched wide, looking over at her wide awake in her cot.

"Ugh, it's fine. These bandages always itch like you wouldn't believe, got half a mind to rip them right off. I could bloody tap dance right now if I wanted."

"You know the doctor said your wound needs to heal, it could get infected!"

Clearly having no desire to be chastised by her son, she turned her head,

"Apolline! Good morning sweet." she said with a much brighter tone,

"Have you enjoyed your time at the Cantina so far? Everyone treating you nicely? Did Jack show you everything?"

"Week has been great!" Apolline smiled back and wrote, *"Matilda let me climb inside the Bounty Board to see the gears inside, and Jack showed me the shooting range, the library, and Hangman's Hall with all the scary monkey statues!"*

"That's all?! He didn't take you to the hall museums? The secret dungeons underneath the actual dungeons? The Tarnished Vaults? Or the Hanging Gardens? Wish I could experience them all over again, you've still got much to see!" What's been your favorite spot?"

"The library!"

"I thought you might say that… it's mine too. Can get lost in the place. And I highly doubt there's one bigger on this whole island! There's also all sorts of hidden chambers that house some of the more *controversial* books that'll only open if you know where to nudge a shelf or which book to pull in." for a moment it looked like Riley forgot she was confined to a hospital bed as she dreamed of it.

The man they'd all been waiting on, Doctor Ableton, finally waltzed in while they were mid conversation, as he'd already done several times, like he'd been waiting just outside for the conversation to turn interesting so he could interrupt it. He had a wrinkled egg white robe with green linens underneath that harmonized well with his shaggy grey hair that looked like a bush, which looked even bushier than normal today.

He looked at them blank and confused for a time, like he hadn't already met them several times this week.

"Ahh if it isn't my favorite patient," he said while he checked his clipboard awkwardly, "And her name is- her name is… Ah!… the splendid Ms. Tripleleaf, of course, of course! So good to see you in such great spirits! And how's the arm?"

"The arm??!!"

"I meant the…" he checked his clipboard again, "The… ah yes… fractured lateral malleolus! How's the ankle doing??"

"My ankle is fine, even got up to move around yesterday without any pain whatsoever."

"And how's your head? Your mental health holding up? Oh how stressful it must be for you all constantly being shot at, chased down by all the ne'er-do-wells. Could be worse I guess… you know back in my day we didn't even use painkillers, not a lick of Kristalyn to knock them out. Though the pain usually did that just fine." he said in his crotchety old voice.

"I'd be a lot better if I wasn't chained down to this bed…" she said indignantly as she pushed herself upright in bed.

After examining her bandages for a time he said, "Don't see any blood, certainly a good sign. And tell me Ms. Tripleleaf, have you tried walking around on it yet?"

"Have you not listened to a word I've said, you must be joking?!"

"Oh I don't joke Ms. Tripleleaf, not when it comes to health. I'd recommend you remember that, maybe then you won't have to come back!" he chuckled by himself while Jack and Apolline stared unblinkingly

"Well then. If you are moving about, and there's not blood on that bandage. You're free to go. Just leave your robes in the bin and take your belongings on the way out. Oh and do make sure and drop by if you feel any pain and require Kristalyn to take care of it. Expensive stuff but well worth it!"

As the good doctor walked out of the room he turned around one last time,

"Oh, and one last thing Ms. Triplemint. If you wouldn't mind letting Matilda know I did a good job with your care! It'll be hard for you to believe but I've had some complaints in the past… last thing I need is to be looking for another job!"

Riley couldn't help but reinspect her wound to make sure everything looked OK given how this conversation went. But before long, she was finally up on her own two feet again, escorting Jack and Apolline to Hangman's Hall for an early lunch.

The fresh air of the Cantina compared to the stale funk and occasional groan of the med bay made the world seem a little brighter as they paused to look at what shenanigans Hangman's Hall would bring today.

The trio spotted two men hanging from the chandeliers attempting to jump several feet over and up onto the top of the Bounty Board. Quickly they stepped aside, making sure to avoid the spot of hardwood floor where the fools were about to crash land.

There were only two men sitting on the chandeliers today which meant the hall was quiet. More than ten up there, and a party was forming, and any more than twenty meant there was no better place to be on this island or the next.

It wasn't all fun and games however, Matilda had again doubled security at each entrance and exit after hearing of Alireza and her men nearly killing two, potentially even three, of her favorite people. She'd been circling Hangman's Hall constantly, looking like a tank in all her body armor, glaring at most with one eye bulging and the other squinted, and questioning every single person she didn't recognize.

"There she is!" she said as they were so busy taking in the tomfoolery they hadn't noticed her approach.

"Matilda!" Riley said happily, "You look like you're ready to take on Knox all by yourself!"

"If you'd let me I might just do that after what his little sidekick pulled last week."

In addition to her hundreds of pounds of body armor, today she was wearing her hair in four tight braids, that looked like they were pointing to each of the four cardinal directions.

"You got no clue how happy I am to see you up and walkin, last time I seen ya you were knocked out after surgery, sleepin like a dog." Matilda's said with the usual deep drawl in her voice as her eyes started looking watery, "Probably not sposed to say it, but for a minute there I feared the worst, n' let those bad thoughts creep in. Feel like a pot'o gold right now seein you back a-hundred." she attempted to wipe her eyes with a bit of her dress shoulder, but it was all covered by body armor, so she grabbed some of Riley's instead.

Riley attempted to console her, but she just held up her hand and said,

"Y'all hold tight… Sorry bout this… just give me a minute…"

After the crew stood there awkwardly for a time, like a light-switch Matilda was back to her normal grit.

"I can't thank you enough for looking out for me," Riley said, "If you hadn't carried me all the way to the med bay… then carried Doctor Ableton over your shoulder, out of his office kicking and screaming and into my room… well who knows, I may very well still be in that hospital bed!"

"Well I appreciate that Riles, and I'm sorry I didn't come to visit more…"

"You came every day!" she laughed.

"Well shoulda been more. But it's just that things have been so crazy this week, what with making sure nothin catches on fire down here, and tryin my best to hunt down Lucas and my supposed assistant."

"Oh boy, what did he do this time?" Riley said looking angrier by the second.

She turned her head a bit like she didn't want to say, but continued,

"I don't want to put more on your plate than you already got, so you let me handle this one. But rumor has it, ole Lucas and Jenkins didn't take too kindly to our little give the wrong address spoof, Chef Greene tells me Lucas was this close to pullin his gun on'em. Said he had to threaten'em both with a knife if they didn't back off."

"Monsoon's Mercy! How do we even allow him to stay here when he's pulling stunts like that??!"

"Believe me, if I was Queen of the Isles, he'd be on the first ship outta here to straight to Forza, heck maybe even Allora dependin on my mood! But unfortunately, that'd have to come down to a vote between me and the other managers. And I can't even find any of'em half the time, much less convince'em to vote out a man whose family has a lotta history amongst these halls and walls."

Matilda knew Riley well enough to see that the look on her face meant she was anything but pleased. "It's one thing to have an outsider like Knox coming for us, but having someone on the inside who hates us just as much feels even worse..."

"Listen Riles, I plan to put so much fear into that mustard head he may just leave on his own accord and take Jenkins with him. But if that don't smack sense into'em, I'll find the other managers one way or another and tell'em it's either him or me. Can't say if I mean that yet or not, but I'm happy to threaten it!"

"That's alright," she said quietly, "I don't think he means to kill us, least not yet. For now, we focus on getting Apolline help... and eliminating the man that *is* trying to kill us."

"Like I said... you let me worry about those two. I know you got the weight of Five Isles on your shoulders."

It wasn't a second later, Matilda spotted out of the corner of her eye a tuft of black hair and eerily slender frame creeping around the kitchen,

"Jenkins!!" she yelled angrily, and with that she was gone just as quickly as she had come, huffing towards the kitchen with the agility of someone much much smaller than herself.

Finally sat to table, tempers cooled as they were thinking about what they may order for lunch instead having to focus on Geist's antics.

Jack spotted Radish sleeping in one of the corner booths, drooling and puckering his lips like he was trying to kiss someone.

"He's been at it all week you know?" Jack said in bewilderment, "Matilda gave him a room in the Starboard Pods, a nice one too with a view of the Muni and Big Bill, but he just sleeps down here in the hall. Got pillows and everything..."

"It's because this is the quickest path to the bar," Riley laughed sarcastically, "Though I suppose he's earned it, that little trick he pulled shooting into the air, sure was useful for giving me an opening. Seems he wasn't lying when he said he roped us into this cause he wanted our help. Still don't trust him, and neither should you two, but it's certainly a step in the right direction."

About to put in an order at the bar, they kept being interrupted by a group of scoundrels sitting at the table next to them that looked like they'd been rolling around in mud and smelled so fowl it was creeping over to their table. With their hygiene and lack of social boundaries, Riley told the others she should've introduced them to Radish. One of the men even had a pet rat that kept peaking in and out of his jacket pocket hoping to steal a fallen bit of table scrap.

The men were in a heated argument, and had been ever since they sat down, shouting so loud Riley found herself yelling over them.

"Course monsters exist!! They're called Mercurial!" one of the men said between blackened teeth with spaces so big you could've fit a doubloon between each of them.

"Everyone knows Mercurial exist you unwarshed Butternut! I'm talkin about real monsters, not Mercurial that looked more human than you do. Like men with tentacles for arms, and the head of a tarantula! Just like in the old stories about the sea people..." the man with the pet rat said.

"You know for a lad don't know how to read or write you've got some imagination. If monsters like that are real, how come no one's ever seen one??"

"Cause they all hide is why. On Allora I heard, the caves there. It's a cursed isle, why wouldn't it have cursed creatures. Men dumb enough to go to that rock don't just up and disappear for no reason... the monsters eat them up, bones n' all..."

"You keep up that rubbish, and I'd be happy to drop you off there to see for yourself!"

Attempting to give them some leeway at least for a little while, Riley's patience was running out. She loudly cleared her throat, after which the men angrily looked at her then immediately away again upon realizing who she was, and got the message loud and clear.

"So   Apolline!"   Riley   said   cheerfully,   "How   are   your accommodations? Is your room big enough? Did Matilda give you one with a nice view?"

"She did! The monk is so big, and all the ships are so pretty! I love seeing all their colorful sails and cargo, it puts me right to sleep, even drew a picture. Do you want to see it?" she wrote in her little black book.

"Of course!!"

She had sketched a remarkably accurate scene of Big Brother Boondock with few man of war ships underneath at Pigly Port.

"That's incredible! This schooner looks better than the ones outside!" she said, "Did you just learn to do that?!"

Nodding she smiled showing her long row of pearly white teeth. She was wearing a hand-me-down floral dress Matilda had given her that could've housed three of her, but she'd found a way to make it work by sewing it up a bit.

"That's quite the talent. Keep it up! I always told Jack when your good at something, don't stop!"

Apolline smiled and ripped the drawing out of her black journal and handed it to Riley.

As Riley went to stuff the parchment in her sleeve, she noticed the girl attempting to keep her head down and not show scratches on her neck. Quickly her demeanor went from bright to concerned.

"How are you feeling Apolline? I'm really sorry you had to go through all that last week. Is everything ok?" she said with an uneasy voice.

Apolline looked uncomfortable being reminded of it as she brushed gold hair out of her eyes but nodded her head all the same.

"I'm not going to pretend like I know exactly what's going on, or why all these awful people are after you. But what I can promise is within these walls, no one's going to touch you ever again. In fact, I think it's best if you're in the Cantina under Matilda's protection while the rest of us put an end to Knox. I can't take back what happened to you, but I can certainly put down the people responsible, all while you're safe as can be in this crazy place."

Grasping at Riley's hand she smirked and squeezed it a few times, her way of thanking her.

Before they could finish their words, kitchen staff delivered their lunch. Since it was a port town, most meals in Kleppenwitz included some sort of seafood, and this was no exception. There were salmon fillets, breaded gravy, a spring mix with orange avocados imported from Prego, and an alfredo pasta that had the usual chicken replaced with fish eyeballs, considered by many to be a delicacy in the region.

Two nearby men wouldn't stop arguing over who got closer to the board in a dagger throwing competition, providing excellent tableside entertainment as each man attempted to tear the other's wig off.

Before Riley could look away and take a bite of her salad, she felt a tap on her plated shoulder and looked up to see an old friend.

"That the Pride of the Blackwater I see?!" the man said with his deep and silky-smooth voice.

"Stono the Caiman?" she said in disbelief, "Can't believe you're back?! Surprised you still remembered how to find the place!"

"I'd never forget the place that houses someone as lovely as yourself!" Stono said. Jack's eyes grew wide as doubloons when he could barely make out Riley starting to blush.

Stono the Caiman as he was nicknamed had a swarthy complexion with deep brown eyes and hair, and was wearing his usual faded turban, with steel rimmed goggles, a voodoo necklace brimming with miniature skulls to represent all his bounties, and a peculiar body armor that blended seamlessly between leather and steel, complemented by leather boots that wrapped up to his knees. Stono had an impressive track record and as such he was one of a handful of men in the Cantina that Riley respected.

His young son Glasgo was by his side as he usually was, and after having just arrived back from their most recent hunt the two of them looked just as bruised and battered as Riley, Jack, and Apolline had the week before.

"You two look like you ran into a thorn bushel!" Riley chortled,

"If it was easy, they wouldn't pay us. Round the Cantina I hear your crew had it worse than me. Alireza Bale?"

"You've heard of her?"

Stono pulled his collar to the side revealing a deep smile shaped scar across his near entire sternum. "She was kind enough to leave me this gift after attempting bring in one of her own. As it turns no man, nor woman, escapes the Bounty Board, not even Forzians. Ain't too many fights I wouldn't take again, but that was one of them."

"Well then you'll be happy to know I left her with a gift of my own. She got away, but was wounded pretty badly, doubt she could've survived the hit she took."

"Well gander at me red as a baboon's rear, though not the slightest bit surprised. Spose I oughtta thank you, that's one woman you *don't* want rememberin the day she ever met you."

After Glasgo had given Jack a slap on the back so big nearby patrons looked over, he'd gotten busy regaling him and Apolline on his most recent trip to Vista and all the trouble it entailed.

"First took a little detour to see the Black Gale or the Last Monsoon as the crewman called it, since I'd never seen it. Plus dad wanted to see if it had gotten any bigger like the sailors say. Then made port in Alexandria, here I thought Kleppenwitz had water. Not compared to this. Their waterfalls got waterfalls, seems almost every house we saw was built to avoid the water falling down into the cliffs an ocean below it. Built right into the rock underneath it too."

"Well sounds like a lovely vacation Glasgo." Jack laughed.

"Vacation he says, if I never see another marsh in my life it'll be too soon!"

"That where you mark was hiding?"

"Sure was, top ten on the board if ya can believe it. Prince of the Marshwolf they called'em. Sounds real nice till you hear he was robbin and killin folks dumb enough to step in his marsh. Spent a week covered in that foul mud so his ugly brown wolves couldn't track us. Had over a dozen of'em at his beckon call, as big as the Grey Wolves, but a fair bit dumber by my guess."

Glasgo heavily favored his father, albeit a much shorter, much more impulsive version. He had the same brown eyes as his dad with hair that was long and needed trimming and wore the same manor of leather and steel body armor. He had a fresh face, same as Jack, and a grin that rarely left.

Not something she'd ever admit, but Jack suspected Glasgo was half the reason Riley even agreed to let him chase bounties in the first place. Afterall she couldn't have him cramped up in the Cantina all the time while his mother *and* friends went off on exciting missions.

"Name's Glasgo Stono! But most just call me Glasgo to avoid confusion." he outstretched his hands towards Apolline, showing off all the golden bracelets on his wrist he preferred to keeping his gold in doubloons. "I taught Tripleleaf here everything he knows about bounty hunting!"

"The only thing you ever taught me was how to convince Matilda not to throw us in the dungeons when something wound up broken, I taught myself the rest." Jack laughed.

Apolline looked gloomy knowing full well she couldn't greet Glasgo back like a normal person.

"This here's Apolline" Jack said covering for her, "She got her throat a bit cut up after an injury a week ago, so she's trying to rest her vocal cords. Apolline Meet Glasgo, he's the one responsible for all the times mom wanted to ring my throat as a kid."

"Not all, just most! Remember getting lost in the hanging gardens? What an adventure!"

"Sleeping under a leaf with no water for two days is not my idea of an adventure…"

"There's no fun to be had when your life isn't at stake Tripleleaf. Man-eating plants, slumber spores making us delirious for half of it. Haven't had a better camp out since!"

186

"Mom wouldn't let me out of my room for weeks after we pulled that stunt, still don't think she's gotten over it…"

"So, how'd you get mixed up with Apolline then? She teachin you to play piano or something?" Glasgo said as he welcomed himself to a seat beside them.

"She's helping us take down Knox…" Jack said beating his fingers into the table confidently.

"Knox?! The Mercurial?? You're joking… A fishies got a better chance on Caldo. How exactly you plan on doing that?!"

"Well fortunately, or maybe unfortunately. We've brought in some help besides just Apolline. Guy that goes by the name Radish…"

"The Quicksilver Thief?! Monsoon's mercy Jack, what've you gotten yourself into!?"

"Believe me, I'm just as confused about what's going on as you are. You can go and talk to him if you like…" Jack said reluctantly and pointed at the still sleeping man.

"Fat chance. He'd slice my hand off just cause he thought I looked at'em sideways!" he said as he rocked back and forth in his chair with excitement.

"I think the tall tales might've gone to your head. Wait till tonight when he's awake, once he's had a few he'll tell you all the about his adventures with the Rogue."

"You know for a while there, I thought the Rogue was just some fairy tale the Freebooters made up so they didn't look so pitiful going to war with Magnus! But right over there is the man that can tell me all about'em! You really never know who will turn up in Hangman's Hall. So how exactly does he plan on killin a Mad Mercurial?"

"We're still working out the details on that to be honest…"

After Riley had finished talking Stono nearly had to carry Glasgo away to get him to stop asking about Knox and the father and son wondered towards their quarters, but not before Stono the Caiman took a curious, and awkwardly long look at Apolline's eyes.

"Well I was surprised to see Stono in such good spirits, haven't him like that in eons! Must've been a big bounty! By the way Jack, did you Radish ever say what happened to the assassin?" Riley said between bites, "Can only pray we won't have to deal with that demon woman a second time…"

"Haven't gotten a chance to speak to him to be honest. Came up once and asked where our pigeons were, then every other time I've seen him, he's been in here entertaining a crowd doing party tricks like he's the leader of a circus. Last time I saw him he had to have Kersey smother him with a blanket after he set his beard on fire doing some magic trick."

She chortled back, "Guess we'll add burnt hair to his list of… interesting smells. Did you get a chance to talk to the Bookkeeper then? After we get Apolline situated I'd love to get her take on how Alireza was able to dodge so many of our attacks."

"Peg? We were in the Monarch Library more than a few times, but never saw her. Figured she was in her back office consumed by some book bigger than my head. Didn't bother knocking, figured we'd wait for you."

"Good. We'll make visiting her a top priority. Just hope she hasn't buried herself in her office again."

It was still only midday, but it felt like midnight to Jack. Even though Pregorian Steel could block lead, the force behind it was still very much at play, the two blows Jack had taken had left large lumps on his chest and back that needed to heal. Riley mentioned she was tired and her bandaged leg needed rest and Apolline was also never one to turn down a mid-afternoon nap, so after some deliberation the crew decided to have a rest and meet back in Hangman's Hall for dinner.

The air was stale and dusty when Jack got back to his quarters, he noticed the last book he was reading *A Cutlass and a Cutthroat* still open on his bedside table beside a unmade bed, a saddle he got last he went riding with Glasgo and Roy, the Gibbon's Crest of a one-eyed monkey hanging above his bed, and his first cutlass bolted to the wall that was secretly sanded down after he scarred his chin practicing with it. All things that normally brought him joy, but not today.

Lying in bed he felt a pang of guilt for not being at the range, practicing as he had done every other day this week. He'd been having a recurring nightmare that the shot that narrowly missed them and hit the wall in front had instead hit Riley.

Perhaps it was because it was so recent, he could never remember another dream being as persistent or even as vivid as this one. He thought about his mom and how she always managed to be so cool under pressure, even Radish, as flawed as he was, didn't seem to struggle with any nerves. What he wouldn't give to have the same ability, he felt like the world's biggest imposter, only given a seat at the table because of who his mother was, not because of his own skill.

The thought was pinned into his brain, and had been eating at him all week, when he looked through his scopes back on top of that building it felt like his heart was pounding so hard it may beat out of his chest and knock the pistol right out of his hands.

Maybe Lucas was right when he said Morty wasn't a real bounty or maybe even Jenkins had him pinned when he said someone his age had no place in the Cantina.

As he took off his gloves he stared at his crippled and charred right hand, which only made things worse. He hated it so much even he could barely stand looking at it. It always brought back memories of the schoolchildren harassing him when he was younger.

I wouldn't dance with the deadhand! he whispered. Mirabel Voss was his crushes name, it took him all year to work up the courage to ask her to the Ghost's Farewell Ball, and on the last day before school let out for winter break, this was her response. She'd shouted in the mess hall where everyone could hear, and the name *deadhand* stuck like glue. All these years later and the memory still crept up, especially on days like today.

He should've been thrilled that he managed to even stay alive after encountering someone as deadly as Alireza, or smiling because Riley wasn't gravely injured, but the malaise wouldn't shake. It hit him so suddenly as bad emotion liked to do. Jack knew he was spiraling and how unproductive it was, but as was usually the case he was powerless to stop it.

Luckily, even the weight of the world that was weighing down on him wasn't enough to keep him up, his anguish cathartic in a way, and led him off into a deep slumber.

It must've been needed sleep, because by the time he woke up to the noise coming downstairs from Hangman's Hall, it was already nighttime. Seemingly by magic, his insecurities from earlier whisked away and he felt prepared to take on whatever challenges the crazy isles brought his way.

Really is nothing like the power of a good nap he muttered to himself.

By the time he dusted himself off, got a fresh change of clothes and moseyed down into the hall he found a very annoyed-looking Riley and intrigued Apolline standing behind the rest of a crowd that had gathered around Radish. He was atop a worn-out bar table retelling one of his tall stories while most of the patrons looked delighted, many of whom had taken to watching his tales over any band or speaker that was on stage that week.

Like he was conducting a symphony, his arms wiggled up and down with the beats of his story.

"Sandworm was just as tall as Big Billy out there, might be even taller!!" with glazed eyes he pointed toward the ceiling very nearly falling over as he did, "With eight rows of teeth each one as big as a galley!!"

"Couldn't just shoot it?" one of the onlookers shouted.

"You never left this island I take it?" Radish said gleeful to be holding information over someone else's head, "Sandworms got skin like Pregorian Steel, few of the tribes out there even use it as body armor on the off chance they find one rotting somewhere in that god forsaken desert."

"So how'd you kill it then? Even for you, don't seem possible..."

"A Caldorian Worm's skin can't be pierced, least not by any normal means. The only way to truly hurt them... is from inside!"

The crowd cheered as if he was starting to win them over.

"Colombo, or the Rogue as you know him, had the idea. We setup a pile of animal carcasses so high and so smelly we each nearly passed out and died of exposure before the worm could come and do that himself!"

"You mean to tell us you get eaten by a Caldorian Sandworm and lived to tell the tale?" another man said who was struggling to standup likely not because of how good the story was.

"That's exactly what happened sorty! Just as we about had enough, we hear a rumbling in the distance like the sound of a hundred storms closing in on us. We didn't see it comin, for somethin so big, the ugly piles of snot are stealthy as a fox. Not fifty feet away we see its rotted worm head pop outta the sand like a volcano erupted, few moments later it's towering above us thinkin he'd found his next meal."

"That how you lost your eye? That monster rip it out of ye?"

"No, that's a story for another night I'm afraid." Radish retorted, "I did almost lose it though, but the Rogue was smart enough to pull us towards the center of his disgusting mouth where none of his teeth could shred us to bits. The slime in his guts was so thick neither one of us could move more than an inch at a time, much less see the light of day we'd just cursed only a minute before. I already had my pistols drawn and was firing the whole way down its bile filled esophagus, the Rogue as clever as he is... or was..." the hall flooded with whispers as he said this, "He had his sword drawn and managed to cut a hole open so big we could finally see sunlight. Just as quickly as we went in, we fell out so high took seconds to reach ground, the belly slime and a patch of soft sand was lucky to break our fall."

The crowd cheered louder now with spirits flying as men clinked their glasses together and howled at the moon.

Jack could see Riley rolling her eyes and barely believed it himself. Still, he decided to join in with the rest of the crowd and shouted,

"So you killed a five-hundred-foot-tall monster for the fun of it??"

He eyed him like he was annoyed that someone had the audacity to poke holes in his story.

"Fun...? Partially. But there's a reason those things are so big and so deadly compared to any other animal. Some say the Mercurial themselves bred them for the same reason we breed dogs... protection. So, to answer your question let's just say they swallow a lot more than just carcasses..."

Radish hopped down from the table to a round of applause with bits of bread and spirits being tossed at him, face looking like he was the newly anointed king of Hangman's Hall.

He approached them beaming as the crowd behind shouted, "Wormslayer! Wormslayer! Wormslayer!"

"I've been trying to speak to you for an hour, was getting up there and telling our members some invented story really that important?!" she said as coldly and loudly as she could attempting to speak over the sounds of all the men yelling.

"Invented? I like the sound of that, makes it sound like I did somethin special stead of just lie!"

"Well now that you're finished and we have Jack here, in case you hadn't noticed, Peg Odswald is sitting in that booth right over there. Said she'd finally had some time to see us tonight..."

"A bookkeeper? They're glorified librarians miss, don't need to go anywhere, I already know what she'll tell us... the information we seek is in some book. Like a carpenter tellin me to use wood."

"Considering Peg isn't the one drinking herself into an early grave it's not a difficult choice for me to decide who to follow. Come with us or waste away in here, I don't care what you do!"

Chapter 14

An Isle's Wonder

"You know on parts of Caldo they nicknamed Mercurial the Snowy Owls instead of using our nickname Ghosts. Fascinating..." Jack and Radish could overhear Peg telling the girls many feet ahead.

"What's your real name?" Jack said as the two of them walked behind on the way through the library.

"Radish." Radish said back matter-of-factly.

"That can't be a real name. Your mum calls you that? What's your last name then?"

"Radish."

He couldn't help but laugh, "Your name's Radish Radish???"

"It's just Radish…" the man said squinting his eyes at him.

It took some time to finally arrive at Peg's office with how slow she walked and her habit of stopping when she thought of something interesting to talk about, like her favorite of Pre-Mercurial Forzian Wars or mating patterns of the Great Vistan Marshwolf.

"You know it's rumored one of the Otto Eight that settled this island built this place as one of their special projects." Peg said with a hunched back that became spryer the more excited she was to talk about some esoteric subject, "Nothing but a little stone and wood, but such craftsmanship… it still stands all these years later. Remarkable! I believe the builder was Melin the Miserly of course. She was the smartest of them, funny that didn't make the history books written by all those men, but if you know how to read between the lines it's clear. Other bookkeepers keep arguing in favor of Barian Meadows… fools if you ask me!"

Like most doors of the Cantina the door to Peg's office was thick and made of hardwood, it was somewhat unique however in that it had twenty or so different types of locks and levers painted gold and bolted to the edge.

As she went to open the office, she took a good look over Apolline for the first time,

"And who do I have the pleasure of meeting today?" Peg said sharply.

"This is Apolline, she's the one I wanted to talk to you about…" Riley responded for her.

"Ohh to be young and pretty again! Aren't you a little a dove. And with eyes like stars! You know it's quite rare in these Five Isles, to be given that gift, never seen it myself. A heterochromatic in our midst!" she said and paused for a moment, like she was wracking her brain for information.

The inside of the office was as cozy as it could be, partly because of how packed in all the furniture was, partly from the sound of the oversized fireplace embers crackling every few seconds, and partly from the pleasant aroma emanating off the thousands of beat-up books lining the walls. Above the walnut desk in the back of the room that looked way too big for Peg, suspended by glass and metal chains was a replica of the Five Isles floating up there with uncanny grace, a much smaller version of the same work in library hall they'd just walked past.

"So young Riley, what do I owe the pleasure? I understand this is something that couldn't wait? Let's not waste more time than we need, I've been graced with more work than I ever asked. Just received a pigeon this morning about a bookkeeper from the south arriving next week to have a debate on the age-old question of whether Mercurial are made or if they're born. Can't imagine the point, not like they left us much to go off! Nevertheless, I do enjoy a nice public flogging, so I must prepare..." Peg said with her snappy tone as she jumped into the throne-like chair at her desk.

"Hmhm," Riley cleared her throat, "I assume you've heard about the troubles at the Cantina as of late? Seen all the increased security, heard about Crowfeet?"

"I wouldn't be of much use around here if I didn't listen to at least some of the whispers of the rumor mill. A Mercurial, is it?"

She nodded, "Didn't know whether to believe it myself, then we had a run in with one of his assassins last week. Was the strangest thing, as if by magic every shot we took at her missed or our guns would randomly jam right before the killshot..."

Peg looked up at her then back down at her big tome, "Curious indeed. You know amongst other things it's still hotly debated amongst our order what could've possibly persuaded Mercurial to meddle in the affairs of mortals... preventing all those wars. I closed our last council with a line wishing for their return, never imagined the return would be like this..."

"So what do you think then? The reason we couldn't hit her was some sort of Mercurial... Magic? Some kind of invisible shield?"

"I know of no other sources for this type of sorcery, and especially no other sources that could cause Riley Tripleleaf to miss."

"You tellin me we marched all the way here, through mud and bore blood," Radish burped and grinned, "Riskin me poor sweet captain's life... for some ole bat to give us a pat on the back??"

Before Riley ever got the chance to snap at him Peg cracked back as if she was a snapping turtle, "It wasn't you I was congratulating my mildewed friend. I don't see any gun at your head sir, I seem to remember you taking the long walk here on your own volition, by all means... the door is there. I don't wish for more cleanup than I'll already have after you sullied the place with the rags on your shoulders." she said as she slammed one book closed and opened another.

Everyone in the room seemed quite pleased with her response minus Radish who rolled his eyes and sunk deeper into his armchair.

"Lucky for me I had my good chairs replaced this morning. Now, as I was saying, the power you describe is most certainly Mercurial, as to whether that power came from within her or some trinket the Mercurial left behind is anyone's guess."

"You mean a Ghostmade? Like the Rogue's golden boots?" Jack said.

"Exactly dear! In fact, I've got a few dusty old tomes right on the shelf behind me that could give you and Ms. Tripleleaf more information if your heart so desires!" Peg said excited he seemed just as interested as she was.

"Whaddid I tell ye, the answer we seek is in some dumb book!" Radish howled in his wobbly chair.

Calmy and with purpose Riley approached him, "You said these weren't your good chairs right Peg??"

Before she could even nod yes Riley kicked the legs right out from under his chair as he tumbled facedown onto the floor.

"Bet you didn't learn that trick in some dumb book..." he moaned holding a rib.

"Perhaps if you could read one you'd realize just how wrong you were..."

"Can't believe I left a proper party for this," he held his forehead and stumbled onto his feet toward the door, "Considerin I'm the one among us that knows how to have a good time, I'll get to it… adieux ladies… and Jack!"

The door shut to brief silence until Peg snorted, "The air smells sweeter already! At least the man's clever enough to know he's not clever enough for any library… took to Hangman's Hall like a fish on Vista I imagine. Not like you to get hung up with a man like that Tripleleaf, where in the world did you find such a type?"

"He found us," Riley sighed, "The man makes Lucas seem almost tolerable, believe me if it wasn't for Knox deciding to take arms against every bounty hunter on the Boondocks, I'd have put him in a cell the first time I set eyes on him. That's if I was feeling generous. He's not without his skills though, so for the time being we're stuck with him. By some cruel trick our fates seemed to be aligned… for now."

"Hmmm. Watch yourself around him dear. The years have taken much away from me, lucky I found most of it I didn't need, but in return they've gifted me with enough wisdom to know who to trust." she said cautiously, "And that sure as the seas turn is not a man I trust…"

"Thank you Peg, trust when I say our hands our forced here. I could add another book to your walls with the events of the past two weeks, unfortunately… for now it's better if I keep quiet."

Embers cracked from the fireplace as if they were waiting for a pause in conversation while Peg peered down at her shredded old tome between words. Jack and Apolline sat still beside one another nervously glancing about and listening on with peaked anticipation.

"Hmph, well then I wish I could be of more help, unfortunately my old bones won't do much good in the battles to come. Tea anyone?" she said grabbing the hot china on her table and pouring herself a glass, "It's Pregorian! Got the best minerals, only stands to reason the same applies to the tea!"

"Delicious!" Riley said as she poured a cup for herself.

"Mmmhmm, considering you're still here I assume there's more you still need from me?" she hunched back in her chair briefly, like a queen on her throne, "The girl. She's the main reason for your visit is she not?"

"How-how'd you know that?" Riley said with a rare bit of nervousness.

"The eyes give her away! There's something exceptional about this young one."

"And what might that be?"

"I have my suspicions... but want to be sure," she said thumbing through pages again, "Which is why I've been rudely burying my head in a book this whole time instead of focusing on my dear friends."

"Do you need some time?"

"Of course not!" she said with a sharp and wooden tone, "I'm a bookkeeper after all!"

More and more the fire crackled and the dusty aroma never felt so pungent as Riley put her arm around Apolline like they were awaiting test results.

"Do you know what a Brave is?" she murmured without looking up.

Biting her thumb, Riley tried to give an answer, but no words came.

"And what about you Apolline, dear child?"

Just hearing the word made something stir inside of her, though she shook her head no all the same.

"Ah... Yes. I thought not. Well then, perhaps it's easier if I just read the passage out loud to you. Ahem. From *The Allorian Chronicles: Volume Seven, Chapter Seventeen, Verse Seventeen*:

Not all who walked on Allora's sacred dirt and survived were Mercurial, however. A small portion of its inhabitants were at least in some part human, and in some part Mercurial. These individuals were known as the Brave. As the Mercurial were not known for their openness and have been gone for some time, no one can say for sure why they were allowed to coexist amongst them,"

Teeth clenched as tight as a vice Apolline held onto her every word.

"Some evidence suggest they were bricklayers and stonemasons," Peg Continued, *"While oddly enough other evidence suggests many were scholars, professionals, and even soldiers amongst their ranks. What all the evidence does agree on however, is that the main way to differentiate between the Brave and the Mercurial, was that the Braves all shared one single trait… Heterochromia or… unmatched eyes."*

"You're saying we're sitting in a room right now with a Mercurial??!!" Jack said trying and failing to keep his voice at a minimum.

"You're sitting in the room with a partial Mercurial. Yes, that's what I'm saying. The girl's a certified wonder of the isles." Peg drawled finally looking at each of them.

"How could that possibly be??" Riley said and gripped Apolline's shoulder tightly as she looked like she may feint. "They've been gone for nearly a hundred years… the girl can't be any older than eighteen? It doesn't add up!"

"I know it makes little sense to us humans, but as I understand time works very differently for their kind…"

"What in the heavens could be happening to cause two of them to appear out of nowhere? And in the same city no less!?"

"Sadly, I'm not an expert. I can only reveal what the text tells me, and I can assure you we're lucky to even have that. Wouldn't be shocked if the only other copy of that book was locked away in some Forzian Vault. As to your question, I would venture to guess you should consider yourselves lucky, purely speculation of course, but I'd imagine you'll need the help of a Mercurial, if only a partial one, to have any hope of destroying a full blown Mercurial like Knox."

"She'll do no such thing, she's already almost been killed once. She won't come close again, at least not on my watch." Riley said irritated at the presumption.

"Wasn't suggesting you do, as I said, just speculation dear."

"So does she have steel skin? Lightning feet? Allegiance with animals? Like-like the ones in the books? Is she just going to up and disappear on us like her ancestors did?" Jack interjected hastily.

"I hate to be the one to say it… but my knowledge on the subject has come to an end. I do wish I could be of more help, but as I said, I'm only repeating what the text tells me, and the rest of it is too worn to read, heavens half of its pages have been ripped out!" Peg held up the tome to show all holes and dried out water stains.

"There must be more than just that! She doesn't have a mom or dad to call on, and no place to call home. Heavens Peg she doesn't even remember who she is! You've got to have something!" Riley shouted her emotions getting the best of her.

For the first time in this whole conversation Peg's demeanor looked grim, "I'm afraid that's it. You're more than welcome to search every book in my office, if you think I've missed something. But believe me when I say that isn't something that happens often."

Riley looked hopeless, she had more than expected her to provide the answers they needed, just like she'd done so many times in the past.

"There is another option, albeit with the world outside as it is now, a likely incredibly dangerous one. I hesitate to even say it…"

"I'll take anything at this point." Riley said with a dash of hope.

"There's a dealer in this town, a purveyor of exceptionally rare 'antiquities', if you could even call them that. I believe with his reputation and line of work; he's likely the foremost expert on the Mercurial in all the Boondocks."

"His name?" she said eagerly.

"His nickname is Ghostmonger, but his real name is Jerrick Alamillo. Last I heard he lives in that castle right across from the Muni, the real skinny one…"

"The one that looks like a needle?" Jack said remembering it vividly from all his adventures in the park.

"Correct young Jack!" she croaked back.

"He was the Rogue's former accomplice, after Radish." she said mouth wide, as she remembered the scallywag talking about him back in the sewers.

"Oh, it wouldn't surprise me a bit dear, as I said the man does have quite the reputation."

"Do you know which part of the castle is Jerrick's?"

"It isn't a part love, he owns the whole building!" Peg chucked between a sip of tea.

****

His mind was on a distant island, or even more likely a distant planet as Jack thought about the events of the past couple of weeks. He'd thought capturing Morty the bombmaker was as much crazy as a he'd experience in a lifetime, but then he remembered receiving a harrowing prophecy from a crazed monk, and after that getting into a firefight alongside one of the Pinwheels most infamous thieves, to finally now where he was sitting right across from a partial Mercurial, or Brave as he now knew it to be called. History had written tomes about less. And another one would almost certainly be written about the events of late. There was something incredibly special happening here, that defied odds, coincidence and even the grandest of expectations. What exactly that was he hadn't the feintest idea, but somehow knew in his heart, with full confidence that the mystery would soon be revealed.

There were fists beating down on the dinner table rustling silverware and clanking the plates.

"*I don't have any powers!!*" Apolline jotted down wearing a scowl as she slid it over for the table to see.

"I understand this is coming as quite a shock, but Peg Odswald is as bright a mind as any I've met… And I've met a lot…" Riley said back as gently as she could manage.

In response she began prodding her arm with a dinner fork to show off the red marks it would leave.

"Please don't hurt yourself dear, and to your point, we know almost nothing about your condition, it could take years for steelskin to develop. Which is why we need information from this Jerrick fellow. I know you feel overwhelmed, but believe me we're just trying to help."

"Wouldn't worry bout nonna that Apo, you got nothin but time holed up in here to figure yourself out," Matilda said with a hunk of lettuce sticking out of her mouth, "Plus if you can't ever find your people, we're happy to be your backups! Just ask Riley!"

"You're not the backup!!" she laughed.

Hangman's Hall for perhaps the first time ever seemed a little less interesting after the news the four of them just received. A man wearing a bad wig was up on stage next to their table, playing some instrument that sounded like a mix between a mandolin and guitar, while patrons danced and skipped next to them, yet the whole table could focus on nothing but the Brave right beside them.

"What's it feel like to be a Brave? Can you see visions of the future or something??" Jack said earnestly.

"Y'know I heard before they up and left, they had buildins on Allora that made Kleppenwitz's look like mole hills! Maybe she can teach us how to build those here!" Matilda laughed.

"I AM NOT A BRAVE!!!" she furiously scribbled and got up out of her chair.

"We didn't mean noth-"

But it was too late, Apolline had darted off towards her quarters like she was ready to swear them all off as guilt swept each of their faces.

"Let's keep the Brave talk to a minimum with her, or anyone else for that matter." Riley said like she realized she made a mistake, "This is clearly coming as quite a shock to her, and she needs time to process. Put yourself in her shoes, imagine you didn't have the slightest clue as to who you were, and a bunch of people you just met wouldn't stop bringing up your identity."

"If I had known I never would've…"

"I know son, believe me all of us are just as fascinated by it as you are. But for now she needs to think on it, and we'll stay out of her way until she tells us she's ready."

"Understood."

"You got it Riles!"

"What a strong young woman," Riley said watching her storm away arms crossed hair swinging wildly, like it reminded her of her younger self, "No voice to communicate, no family to support her, and now this Brave ordeal… if it got out half the city would be asking for her autograph in the best case, and worst case every picaroon in the Pinwheels would be out looking to kidnap her. Not sure if I could have handled all that when I was her age…"

Their table was so close to the stage and by extension dance floor several people had already bumped into their seats, they could even see Radish occasionally on the floor when the patrons cleared, he was doing some odd dance where he planted his feet, shook his hips, and waved his arms in the air like they were snakes. The table had a big laugh when they saw him whisper something into a woman's ear and she in turn looked at him with disgust after pouring her drink all over his head.

Eventually, he approached them in a crooked line and pulled up a seat.

"I don't know what you said to make that woman dump out her drink, but I couldn't be more confident you deserved it." Riley couldn't stop sniggering after seeing him close up, covered in oozy red.

Whatever the drink was, it must've had plenty of fruit as Radish plucked bits of orange and strawberry off his shirt and into his mouth like some sort of drenched king and laid his leather boots up on the table.

"Waste of good rum… well… mostly a waste…." he said nonchalantly as he plucked a bit a fruit from his ear into his mouth, "Won't hear me apologizin for a rovin eye. Speakin of not apologizin, how'd your little book club end up? Surprised Riley didn't pitch a tent and decide to stay down there for good... Start up a much easier career as a librarian..."

"Maybe if there were less men like you in this world I could have..."

Jack sprung up in his seat as an awkward pause hushed the table, save for Radish who continued,

"Let me guess. Did the old book lady send us on some errand to find a book?"

"She wants us to go find'a friend of yours eyepatch," Matilda said crossly, "Heck we were all surprised you even had any of those!"

"Had some, but it's a dangerous game we play, most my friends end up dead." he grinned and winked at Matilda, "Cept Kersey... don't think the heavens or hells wanted him, so now I'm stuck with'em! Much as I need it right now don't leave me out to dry, what friend of mine did the book lady send you after??"

"Jerrick Alamillo, remember you talked about him back in the sewers?" Jack said.

"Alamillo..." Radish whispered his face completely turned and looked serious for once, "Well that just can't be..."

For a time, the table stared at him as he looked like he was solving a math problem in his head.

"I know'em alright. Never met him. But anyone that deals in, let's say, less-than-legal goods knows Alamillo. The Ghostmonger."

"He worked with the Rogue? After you did?" Jack said, having to scooch his chair in to avoid a patron that had crashed into the table next to them.

"Aye. He did. If I had to give one positive note, it's he's got an eye for talent. Just one little problem however..." with cold stare he looked them over, "Alamillo ain't here. Hasn't been for months. Last I heard he was bound for Prego, don't know what he was lookin for, but I'm sure it was Mercurial, otherwise he wouldn't be lookin."

"You're certain of this?" Riley said with disappointment.

"I'm certain I heard it..."

Riley lifted her shoulders and looked squarely into his eyes, "Tell me... do you know what a Brave is Radish?"

"A person who is strong in the face of perilous danger??" he said so overconfidently his eyebrows fluttered as feet went back up.

"That's someone who is brave not a Brave. Having a really difficult time telling if you're this stupid or just pretending... a Brave is a partial Mercurial. A group who lived on Allora alongside the Ghosts, were every bit a part of their society, and apparently disappeared right along with them. Disappeared until now at least..."

He began clapping his hands rapidly making his stained cotton shirt and glossy necklace wave back and forth, "Guess I'll have to eat my words then, old book woman came through! Apolline is a Brave then?? Certainly explains a lot..."

"You knew???" Riley sprang up in her seat with the rest of the table.

"I knew that no one of us could live in a chest with no air, then pop out lookin fresh as the day they left." he said tapping his upkicked boots together.

"A fair point for once." Riley said with calmer nerves, "Well then what do you make of it?"

"What do I make of it? Kings and queens would raze this place to the ground just to getta glimpse of her is what I make of it. Best we keep as quiet about this as we can. Oh... and kill the only other person that knows about her..."

"Knox?"

"Knox..."

"I don't think anyone here would disagree, but I want to speak to this Jerrick fellow first. After he tells us how to get Apolline's memories back, he may prove useful on the subject of how to kill a Mercurial."

While waving his hand through his salt and pepper hair he snorted, "Suit yurself lass, but he ain't gonna be there... Spose anythin beats havin to track down Knox though, and then findin a way to kill'em."

"Let's say we do manage to get what we need out of Jerrick. Do you even have an idea of where Knox is hiding? Would we just be wondering around in the dark looking for him?"

"Believe I know just where he is..." Radish said as he looked down at his trousers and pulled out a tiny orange crystal, "He's underground, not far from here I believe. But the trouble ain't findin'em, trouble's gettin past his defenses..."

The old wooden walls croaked, and the music blared on in the background as the four of them discussed how they would get inside Alamillo's castle across from the Muni. Riley's long black hair looked a bit loose compared to its normal orderly fashion, her skinny shoulders slouched, a good indicator of her heightened stress levels with all that had happened lately.

"Is it even safe to leave here? Won't Knox be watching the Cantina?" Jack said with a crack in his voice.

"Reckon we could just wait'em out? Ain't like we're pressed for time, and a heckuva lot safer in here..." Matilda said.

"Knox was watchin this place yesterday, today, and will tomorrow and every day to come until he gets what I, and now we, took from him. There's no waitin that man out, he's as mad as he is dedicated."

"Agree with Radish, no point in waiting," Riley said, "We'll leave early in the morning. I believe Matilda will have no trouble creating some sort of diversion for his guards to follow?"

She nodded and approvingly slapped the body armor on her shoulder a few times.

Riley continued, "Then I recommend we all get a good night's sleep. Even you Radish, maybe sleep in a bed for once, we'll need you at a hundred."

"If you don't like me now, you certainly wouldn't like me at a hundred! But as you say, I'll gather my pillows."

"Oh and more thing," she said, "You never told us what happened with Alireza… did you finish the job?"

"Sure hope so, I'd much prefer to only have one of the deadliest people on this Isle tryin to kill me" he paused and inhaled as if there was a flower in front him, "We saw her floating down the sewage river in the canals, pale and motionless, even shoulderless… that was a first. With the webs round her eyes never thought she'd look worse, but she sure did then. We saw her float off right before we could get a clean shot. Anyone else I'd say that's finito. But with her… well… hard to say."

Chapter 15

<u>The Auburn Woman</u>

Apolline sat on her bench and stared at a rainbow parrot that wouldn't stop checking her hands thinking they were some sort of magical device that every so often may release a snack. The hanging gardens were every bit as beautiful as Riley described. Just a few doors down from her room was a sprawling jungle sitting atop one of the Cantina's dormitories. The foliage at the front was a beautiful array of different shades of red and pink, then several feet behind that, shades of green, then blue, and so on.

Tonight the garden was set aglow by moonlight on the occasion it was able to sneak past the dense canopy along the walls. Even in the evening the bright foliage didn't dim, if anything it looked brighter, the space felt like a museum of plants instead of paintings.

As she lay there trying to calm, she thought about Riley Tripleleaf, and Matilda Baum, and how even though she was very frustrated with them currently, how lucky she was to have been taken in by them. Riley always seemed so strong, able to handle even the most dire of circumstances without losing her head, then there was Matilda who never failed to make her laugh and feared just about nothing, and even Jack had been a great companion to explore the Cantina with, though she didn't quite understand why he often seemed so nervous around her.

The park bench was cushioned and cozy, when put together with the chill breeze inside it would've made for the perfect place to sleep tonight. But sleep wouldn't come, it seldom did for her. She hated being alone, being left to her thoughts and the terrifying blank canvas that was her memory. She always had the urge to vent about it to Riley, but what would she think of her, when she was so pitiful and helpless, relying on others to protect her, couldn't even fire a gun, and Riley the Pride of the Blackwater, with all her strength, well she'd probably just think she was pathetic.

"M-m-m", she tried speaking using everything she had but it was like someone was poking her throat with mini darts and even through the pain the words wouldn't come, "Ma-ma-ma", again she failed. She slammed her fist against the bench at the thought of another person asking her a question, sitting there looking at her awkwardly, and being humiliated when the only thing she could give back was a pitiful little mumble.

Maybe it was the new environment, maybe it was her exhaustion, but eventually sleep did come, and easier than it had any night before at the Cantina.

A fuzzy haze drove into darkness, visions blurred, and a dream followed.

It had started off pleasantly enough, as Knox's boiled and cracked face was nowhere to be seen like in the others.

She was in a field covered for miles with matching brightly colored tulips. Whichever island it was, it was a foreign one, though with the smell of all the flowers and tiny critters passing by she could tell it was a friendly place. A woman was there with her weaving a bracelet out of nearby grass, with auburn hair so long it looked like it went down to her ankles, and eyes just like hers.

Apolline didn't know who the woman was, but when she lay her head in her lap, the look she returned said she could sit there looking into her eyes for eternity. It must've been some sort of family, because she had her same dimples and same smile that looked like it stretched from ear to ear.

Looking to her left, then right, she saw Jack and Riley there kicking some sort of ball, waving at her to join them.

Birds sang harmonious songs, and the sun drenched everything in sight, as she lay there laughing joyfully, wasting the day away with great company. Even speaking was easy in this place, and conversation flowed so effortlessly it made time pass by like a raging river. She wanted this moment to last forever… to spend the rest of her days in this fantasy. But she knew it couldn't last. Knowing all too well from her past that, somehow, someway, all silver must tarnish, and she had to savor every joyful moment until it inevitably came crashing down.

And then, slowly, just as predicted, the light flickered. And the darkness came.

When she opened her eyes the beautiful woman with auburn hair was gone, and all the tulips lay wilted, frozen in death. She could sense them coming. The men without faces.

As she closed her eyes and opened them again, a man with no nose, no eyes, and no mouth appeared in front of her. The man's face seemed to shift constantly, almost looking like someone she recognized, then shifting again to another right before she could put a finger on who it was.

The figure moved just like a man, even looked around like one, but he was something else, a hollow and darkened silhouette.

A deep and unsettling screech was originating from him, like it crawled out of his pores as he calmly exhaled. His hand was clasped around her neck and choking the life from her. Desperately she tried freeing herself from his grasp, but it was no use. He was far stronger.

Two other men had taken Jack and Riley too, torturing them as well, watching her as they did it, like they wanted her to see her friends dying.

The world grew cold, and her vision dimmed, as she accepted her fate. At least she'd gotten to spend her final day with loved ones, not even the men without faces could take that from her. When she opened her eyes one final time, she saw another silhouette. Except this shadow looked like it was made of light instead of darkness, shining so bright it was as if all the sunlight from earlier had been condensed into a single entity.

Something deep inside compelled her to stretch her arm towards his heart with a lifeless grasp. As if by magic, as she stretched towards the light's chest, her arm went right through it like it was air and she pulled the light right from where the man's heart had been. Glistening like a merry go round of sun beams she held it up to the dark man's face as it screamed a deep and terrible scream.

Like a snowman melting in the hot sun, the figures faded away, Riley and Jack faded away, and the last thing she saw before she woke was the auburn woman fading along with them, with her arms outstretched as if to try and keep her there.

Early morning moonlight invaded her eyes when she finally woke. The little parrot was still there, still hopping between her hands looking for food.

She must've slept well, because by the time she got back to her quarters her neatly made bed didn't look anywhere near as appetizing as it normally did.

What few dresses Matilda, and pants and tunics Riley was able to spare were stacked and folded neatly on top of the bed, beside an ivory hairbrush Jack was able to barter for in the hall for some old gear he'd outgrown. There was a boring old mirror left behind that she'd spruced up with some rose flowers from the hall and leaves leftover from pots out front, and beside it was a decorative vase she'd found where she kept what little belongings she had.

It's a start... she sighed as she looked from the colorful mirror she created to the dreary brown walls beside it.

As she went to try and measure the wall, hoping she may find something beautiful to hang up, the scar on her hand just barely poked through her bandage. Alireza's awful cackle rang through her ears as she noticed the scar had shrunk so much from only a week prior, it was barely still visible.

I've got to find Riley...

****

Jack latched his armor together, Prego Steel shining along its dull sanding like it wanted to escape.

Hangman's Hall looked like a command center instead of its usual mischievous self, with guards marching back and forth, and their superiors barking out orders while pouring over parchment city maps. Jack, Riley and Matilda were in full regalia looking like they were seconds away from marching out when they heard a door slam from the top of balcony.

"Where are you going?!" Apolline scribbled like her hand was on fire as she dashed towards them.

"Awww, I'm so sorry sweet. I should've come up to tell you goodbye and apologize for last night. It's just so early, I thought you'd still be sleeping."

"You're leaving me?! Here?!"

"I thought we agreed you'd stay here while we looked for Jerrick Alamillo? It's not safe out there, and I'm not going to risk having you get hurt again... Why not go see Peg again while we're out? I'm positive she'd be delighted to show you more of the Monarch Library, maybe even find some more information while you're at it!"

"I'm not going to see Peg. I saw them again, the men without faces.

All of you will die out there if I don't come with!"

"I-I don't understand??" Riley paused.

"Alireza Bale would've killed you all if not for me, I need to go with you, I must go with you!" she jotted hands still moving like a storm.

"What in heavens do you mean?" she said breathless, taking a shallow step back from her.

"Her ring was Mercurial. It's why you couldn't hit her. And I was the only one that could take it off, dampen it."

"I-I see," she said taken aback, sitting in silence while she mulled things over, "I meant what I said when I mentioned I wouldn't see you hurt again. I can assure you you're safe in here… I need you to tell me with absolute confidence you're ready to go in harm's way again before I see you leave."

"The dream felt too real, I need to do this. I need to go!" she wrote emphatically.

"Alright then," Riley hesitated like she wished she'd reconsider, "Same rules apply, stay behind me and Matilda at all times. Matilda has guards doing a patrol around the building, creating a diversion while we grab a carriage. Stay alert. And stay close. Understood?"

Jack smiled and Matilda gave her a pat on the back like they were happy to have her come along.

"You said you were the only one that could take her lucky ring off. Does this mean you're finally realizing how special you are?" Riley questioned.

"I don't know…" she wrote with a tentative look, *"I know I don't have powers though."*

"Take you one'a these…" Matilda said throwing a large brown cloak at her, "Keep it overr yur head till we get to that buggy!"

Waving her arms around like tumbleweeds, Matilda sent a group of guards who looked indistinguishable from one another with their matching brown cloaks, out the back exit, into the rickety tunnel that led outside.

As if he'd been standing with them the whole time Radish crept up behind and commented,

"Dressing the guards like potato sacks, interesting strategy…"

"Potato sack's a big improvement over whatever the heck you got on now!" Matilda said shoving a cloak into his chest so hard he kicked back a couple feet, "Now put it on yur pea-head, and don't take it off till I say!"

The five of them stood in a line, dressed the same but having very different statures, waiting for Matilda to give the signal to move out.

"Where's your captain??" Riley said glaring at Radish suspiciously.

"Kersey? Sent him out last night to scout the place out. Check if he saw any goons near the Muni…"

"Didn't want to fill us in? You know that's information most people would share with their partners? We are still partners, aren't we?" she eyed him, eyed the pistol on her hip, and eyed him again.

"I'm tellin ya now ain't I?" he said sarcastically.

"No more secrets… trust me you falling out of that chair was me being courteous." her suspicion didn't falter, but she could only sigh in frustration as there was no time to dig deeper.

A piercing whistle came from Matilda so loud the entire hall turned and looked at her. It took no time for them to get out of the tunnel, each huddled up in their disguises as if they were walking in a blizzard.

Still dark out, the pleasant spring morning was halted by the sound of fire that snapped off in the distance, crackling like a thunderstorm without the rain. But as the crew scurried off towards the old stables, it was clear it wasn't aimed at them. They'd just have to hope the Cantina Guards were the ones doing the firing not the other way around.

The stables that housed the Cantina's horses and carriages were just across the street in a dilapidated building that looked like it was built a hundred years ago and long abandoned.

Pistols Akimbo, Matilda kicked a wooden door open like it was made of straw, as they pushed forward with Apolline in the center, lightning still cracking off in the background.

"Three of y'all take them cloaks off and hop in the back." Matilda yelled as they got to the carriage, "Me an Riley'll sit up front with Dusty and keep a watch…"

Their carriage was a dusty old metal clunk, and the coachmen who was waiting for them might've been even dustier with more wrinkles than teeth, and a mustache that went east and west with an oversized top hat to finish it all off.

"Didn't I tell you to wear body armor?" Matilda shouted up at the man.

"Too old, don't need it." he snapped as he held the reins up in his hands as if to say they were taking too long to get in.

"Aight." she hesitated but then realized maybe he had a point.

The cabin's body was shaped square almost like a fence post, with two just as square doors along on either side that didn't look like much, but all the round dents in them proved they could at least stop some bit of fire coming their way. Referred to as the Fleetwood Model, the carriages were known for their no-frills features, a complete disregard for aesthetics, and their ability to outlast other brands in even the worst of conditions.

Finally, no longer hearing the sounds of gunfire, they could relax, they were en route, and thankful to see no other horses on their tail. For now they could focus on getting to the Muni without being seen.

Matilda and Riley sat outside behind the coachmen, while the rest of the crew bumped along in the orange velvet cabin. Helping himself, Radish threw the brown leather sack he always carried onto a whole row of seats and used it as a pillow as he lay down like he was having an afternoon nap.

"Already comfier than the Cantina." Radish said kicking one foot over the other.

"Would help if you used one the beds..." Jack said watching him rudely sprawl out like he was sunbathing as he took a seat next to Apolline in the second row, "Is your behavior what lost you that eye?" he couldn't help but commenting after he hogged so much space in the cabin.

"Which eye?"

"The one with the eyepatch over it???"

"Who says I lost it? Maybe it's still there an just givin it a rest..."

On the one hand, Jack was fascinated by Radish and his reputation, but on the other hand he could see why his mother told him not to trust him a thousand times.

"Are you actually here to help us?? Or are you just going to lampoon every chance you get?"

"Ugh," he groaned, "Whatd'ya want kid?"

"You saw me miss that shot back after the sewers." Jack said the question still burning on his mind, "How do you do it? How do you always shoot so perfectly, even when men are shooting back at you?"

"Ahhhh... The boy wants to learn... Spose I can help withat... but only cause we're partners." he grinned and snapped his fingers at him, "Shooting is the subtle art of caring without caring. First let all the air out your pipes, and realize we're all gonna die someday, what's it matter if that day's today. Then give your head a little shake to flush out the nerves, focus and take your shot. Seems simple, and stupid, cause it is stupid. But if somefins stupid and it works, well then how stupid is it really..."

The rugged carriage had the distinct smell of old steel and cloth that had been put away wet, and unlike many other carriages the only windows to be had were tiny little things along the two square doors and an additional window to the front, its porthole showing a hazy vision of Coachmen Dusty and his backseat with Riley and Matilda.

Up at the front, Riley yelled directions at Dusty to go towards the massive park just in front of them, she couldn't help but hear Matilda's leg clanking against the steel platform underneath their feet.

"Not like you to be nervous…" she said while reloading a few backup pistols she kept hidden away in her leather belt.

"Well it ain't everyday a man who could kill your whole team with a wave of his hand is after ya."

"I doubt we even see him. Looks like we made a pretty clean break back there."

The leg clanking continued.

"Still nervous? What's going on? You're not yourself?"

Matilda itched the whiskers on her chin in a rare loss for words, "I want you to keep quiet about this alright?" she said in a low voice.

"Not like you to keep quiet this well either…"

"It's bout somethin I seen last night. But you gotta promise this stays right here or I ain't sayin!"

"Whatever you want Matilda!" Riley said coyly.

"Like I said, keep it low." she took her voice to a whisper so Dusty couldn't hear over the sound of horses clopping and neighing, "Ole Plunders the Parrot saw some gold chain in a ladies wig last night, and up and decided to steal the whole thing off her head, squawkin like it was his own tiny little version ofa laugh as he flew away. He stashed the wig in the rafters like usual of course, in Hangman's Hall. Apparently, she was some important politician's wife, said she'd raise caine if we didn't get her wig back."

"This is what your nervous about?" Riley chuckled.

"It gets worse. Anyways as I'm crawlin up there, tryin not to fall to my doom over some dumb hairpiece, I could get a real good glimpse at some of those booths in the back with no lighting. And you'll never believe who I saw."

"Jenkins?"

"Close. Saw everyone's favorite manager Lucas Geist, having a grand ole' time with Detective Konrad." she said her voice even lower.

"You think he was trying to sell us out to the detective?" she said not even close to laughing now, "Finally get his precious Cantina free of the all the no-goods?"

"That ain't even the worst part." Matilda said with a thousand-yard stare, "There was someone else clinkin glasses right along with'em. Someone that's in this carriage right behind us."

"Radish?" she said, now shaking like a caged bull.

"Yup."

"He's a dead man…" Riley sprang up with her gun drawn, but Matilda grabbed her shoulder.

"Listen Riles we gotta be careful with this. Less he knows that we know. The better. We still need to know why that wooly booger decided to meet with Lucas and Konrad, and what their exact plan is. If they're gonna raid the Cantina, or plan on sendin us into some kinda trap, we need to know about it."

"You expect me to trust him around my son?! Around Apolline, the poor thing?!"

"We ain't gotta trust him. All we gotta do is watch him… carefully… till we get back to the Cantina tonight. We wait just a few more hours from now and he'll get all flowered up and loosen that leather around his hip. After that, it'll be the easiest thing in the Five Isles to toss'em in a cell and listen to him sing like a canary once the shakes hit."

Quietly she stewed, not wanting to look back at him and do something she may regret. She'd been disgusted by him when she first met him sleeping at the Cantina with his yellow teeth and rotted clothes, but this brought things to a whole new level.

"Bet Lucas's plan is to use Konrad's police force to kill Knox, probably even us while they're at it. One less share of the bounty to split." Riley said calming somewhat.

"Yeaaah I'd thought'a that too." Matilda grumbled, "Gotta give it to the guy, he's clever if nothin else…"

"This is the last time I ignore my gut, not sure how we expected anything other than betrayal working with a bloody mercenary."

The Municipal Park was so close its trees towered over them as big as the flags at the Flagpole Market. Like sand meeting sea, castles, oversized cottages, and sprawling red-bricked estates met the park's vibrant foliage only separated by a thin cobblestone road. There was so much happening within the park it might as well have been its own city. There were house sized statues of members of the eight stretched across its corners, museums and amphitheaters peeking through dense forest and foliage, and at the center lay a rainbow garden just as vibrant as the one at the Cantina. Finally, the park and all its inhabitants had a big brother looking over it. The Laughing Monk towered above everything else in view and bookended the northern corner.

"We're pretty darn close, you ready to get outta this wheelbarrow or you want to take a lap until you're cool enough not to shoot Radish." Matilda chuckled.

"Go ahead and park it. Not going to be easy but I think I can manage to steady my trigger finger for a few hours…"

After giving the signal, the Fleetwood Carriage came to a convincing stop as the brown, white and black horses snorted. They were on top of a grassy knoll patrons commonly picnicked in, luckily it was early enough there wasn't anyone laying about to get in their way.

"Best make it quick!" Matilda yelled back to the crew, "Pretty illegal to park there, so if you see a flatfoot just tell'em a wheel fell off or somethin, I don't know get creative…"

They rushed out and towards Jerrick Alamillo's high, thin and foreboding castle only a couple hundred yards away. Riley carefully walked in the back behind everyone, never holstering her pistol, and never taking an eye off Radish.

One of the many red-bricked walkways in the park they now dragged their boots across held a hulking oak tree with auburn leaves, and branches like spaghetti that flowed down to rest on the dirt below. It took Jack back to a simpler time, he remembered having the first birthday he could remember here, and how he broke his first bone falling when Glasgo had spotted him on one of the high branches playing hide and seek.

"Nervous?" Jack said looking at Apolline as they walked along the brick with pep in their step.

She nodded back as if transfixed on something behind him.

"Don't be. We got Knox off our trail, and there's answers up there I can feel it. By tonight we'll be celebrating in the Cantina with more food and good music than we know what to do with. Maybe even finally convince Radish to take a bath!"

Still staring at the auburn leaved tree behind him with a lonely look she wrote, *"Do you think there's others? Others like me?"*

"Of course there is! Mom's spent her life traveling back and forth through the Five Isles, and even she wouldn't claim to have seen half of it. Probably not even a quarter of it. Your people are out there somewhere, waiting for you, knowing exactly what's happened to your memory. We just gotta get this Alamillo fella to tell us where they're hiding! Even if we have to shake it out of him!" he laughed.

She grabbed his blackened hand and squeezed it while mouthing the words *'Thank you!'* as they ran by tall trees and blossoming flowers.

When they finally arrived, Jack looked the stone building up and down and up again, which given how tall it was took some time, once they passed the gargoyle lined steel gate that had been left open, the stone behemoth looked even more frightening up close. It had a dreary courtyard with a garden of black and grey roses, and not a horse or carriage in sight. The giant stone castle blocks appeared to be black instead of grey with swirls of marble whisking up the exterior, and every couple of feet were black windows you couldn't see through lined with steel bars in the shape of X's.

"Think I gotta shoot to open this place up??" Matilda said poking a lower window with her huge finger like it was some kind of fish tank.

"No need for that, doors open…" Radish said as plucked the pin he'd used to pick it back into his hair and waltzed inside.

The Gargoyle theme didn't stop once they walked into what looked like a grand ballroom designed for a vampire, with its grand spiraling staircase hugging the wall with floors just as black as the exterior, an unlit steel chandelier that branched out like a bat's wings, and portraits of unrecognizable pale men whose eyes seemed to move every time you looked at them.

"Thought we would've seen Kersey by now?" Riley said walking up the stairs and glaring at Radish, trying her best to keep her real emotions suppressed.

"You saw that pot belly of his, I'd bet a doubloon he's at a dive two blocks down. Good thing he can sail, not good for much else!." Radish said like he thought nothing of it.

The entirety of the second floor was polished with dust as if someone hadn't lived there in ages, with strange portraits of other worldly landscapes, suits of body armor, and endless candelabra. It was clear to Jack why the place didn't have any security, it was creepy enough on its own to scare off any unwanted visitors. Luckily being a bit higher up now he could see the Muni through the X-shaped windows, which helped alleviate the dark feeling the space brought.

It was still so early the sun hadn't risen, yet the stars still did an amazing job of illuminating the park as they walked up another flight of stairs.

With everything going on around them the walk-up felt short. At the top they come to a decorative wooden door with two grinning gargoyles hoisted above it and so big Matilda wouldn't even need to duck to get through it.

"Pistols drawn…" Riley announced as she went towards the door.

"Not with that leg," Matilda yelled, "Let Onion… or Radish. Whatever his name is kick it down…"

Jack put himself in front of Apolline with pistol locked ahead and held his breath as Radish kicked the door so hard wooden splinters flew like cannon shrapnel, making way to a very interesting but empty chamber.

"Told you no one was here…" Radish laughed.

"A wonder of the Five Isles your cockiness hasn't got you killed yet, we still have plenty left to search…" Riley said annoyed.

The rear wall was made up almost entirely of a translucent stained glass, giving a first-class view of the Municipal Park, as well as the Laughing Monk's backside. The remaining three walls were made of a deep brown oak, which gave off a strong but pleasant smell reminiscent of the Cantina, and on the back wall there was a winding staircase much smaller than the one they just came from. It appeared to lead to an upper floor and bent upwards in so many directions it hardly seemed structurally sound. Green and golden plants, some smaller than a finger, others bigger than the crew put together, covered most of the room, and beside the plants were museum-like glass enclosures that looked thick enough to stop a pistol shot.

Inside the enclosures were seemingly random objects, among them a necklace that looked similar to the one Radish wore, a decorative but weathered pair of boots with gold steel bottoms, a sparkling golden ring in the shape of a sunflower, a dagger made of silver and gold with a lion carved into the pommel, an ivory horn, a worn to yellow piece of parchment that looked important but was curiously left blank, a crown made of woven grass and wilted thorn flowers, and a tattered black compass with no guiding needle.

"What are these things?" Jack said too curious to even watch the volume of his voice.

"Given this is the home of a man known for dealing in Mercurial antiquity, I'd bet my trousers it's Mercurial antiquity." Radish said boldly.

"These are Ghostmades?!"

"That. Or with how easy it was to get in here. Ghostmade replicas…"

As they were looking along at all the museum like enclosures wondering what on earth they could be or represent, a man with grey pushed back hair walked quietly down the winding staircase, like he hadn't noticed five people had just broken into his home.

"Who are you?!" Riley said completely caught off guard and pointing her gun at the man.

"Me?" the man with grey hair said with a deep and slick voice, "I'm Jerrick Alamillo. Who are you?? And why are you in my home?!"

"Out of town, eh?" Riley said beaming a smile at a stunned Radish.

"Ghostmonger…" Jack whispered with excitement.

Chapter 16
Hover Fly

Jerrick Alamillo shoved one of the glistening strands of his grey hair back with the others as he stared at them eyebrows raised, waiting for an answer. His face looked too small for his head, like it'd been squished, and he wore cubic robes and gloves that Jack couldn't help but notice looked like it had just been cut from a fanciful window curtain behind them. The man's demeanor said unalarmed, cool and collected, as if their visit wasn't a surprise.

"So sorry for the intrusion sir," Riley said hesitantly, as if breaking into a law-abiding citizen's home made her uncomfortable, "You have nothing to worry about. We're not here to rob you, or worse... only looking for information. Drastic measures had to be taken, as we understand it, you're an impossibly difficult man to find."

"Heh, bounty hunters, is it?" Jerrick said looking at the one-eyed monkey crested atop Riley's armor, "Sure hope I haven't done anything to get on that board of yours…"

"Of course not sir! It's just that, well… we're in quite the predicament," she looked over at Apolline fumbling with her fingers, "And have been told you've got a very specialized knowledge in a field of great interest to us, or perhaps more accurately have been thrust right into the middle of."

"Heh! Well you're not wrong there, no doubt you've noticed all the displays. My life's work, lay bare… Go ahead, have a look!"

"Are these all Ghostmades?" Jack muttered unable to hold it in any longer.

"No, no, no. I'm afraid not. If these were real Ghostmades I'd own more wealth than the entirety of this city put together, instead of merely a building inside of it."

With closed eyes and mouth agape pointed towards the ceiling, Radish slumped himself against the nearest wall, while the rest of them stood directly behind Riley, excited for what an expert like Jerrick may have to offer.

"These are merely replicas, my boy, heh! But just because something isn't real doesn't mean it isn't valuable. Finding yourself in possession of even one of these objects is a life changing endeavor to say the least." Jerrick paced back and forth between the exhibits paying more attention to them than his guests, "Growing up every boy and girl on Kleppenwitz hears the tales of the Rogue and his Golden Boots of Speed, but none of those same boys and girls could tell you about the Starboard Dial, or what the Rose of Serendipity is capable of."

He paused studying them for a time and continued,

"I've spent my life studying these antiques, taken prisoner in the dungeons of Forza whilst searching for scrolls lost to time, even seen dear partners vanish to traps in Vistan Crypts, all in hopes of getting even the tiniest glimpse of one these treasures. Or most times would probably just settle for a drawing of one. Because in order to find a Ghostmade one must first know what they look like!"

"Where you think they're hidden then?"

"Heh! If I knew that I'd be on the first ship out of Pigly Port instead of wasting away in here... Always fun to speculate though I suppose. Lots of people have a Forzian Palace as their first guess, others say it's Allora where it's too cursed to even check. You can see why their reputation is an elusive one! I've made many friends in my travels, many of which up to and including myself, suspect Caldo may be a good dark horse candidate. Though if you imagine that necklace in the glass compared to the vastness of even Caldo's smallest desert, knowing which island one's on hardly narrows it down."

Noticing the man was unarmed Matilda glared at him while she holstered her pistol,

"You mentioned the Rogue didn't ya mister? Wouldn't happen to know where he is would ya?? We got us a little homicidal maniac problem, and we sure would like his help with that. Seein as how he was your protégé an all, thought you may have an idea as to why he up and vamoosed."

"Hmmm?! Protégé?? You must have me mistaken for another old man, heh!"

"Radish here has led us to believe the Rogue worked under you after him. Have we been misled?" Riley said squinting her eyes.

"That's the story I heard miss..." Radish said sleepily without moving from his post or opening his eyes.

The full sun hadn't quite made it up yet, but the tip was just starting to show, making Jack wonder why the curtains weren't drawn.

"Ahh yes, I remember now! Must've misheard you there, heh! My ears are as gray as my hair I'm afraid, aren't as sharp as they once were!" Jerrick said without any follow-up.

"Ok then... welp... uhhh... you gonna answer?" Matilda said with a face that looked like she'd just taken a bite out of her least favorite food.

"Ahhh... Erm... Unfortunately, I'm saddened to tell you I have not heard from the Rogue in some time. I did hear from some customers however, that he was seen on Kleppenwitz, and not too long ago, heh!"

"Ain't exactly breakin news mister, we heard that over a week ago... there's nothin else you could say about'em? Anythin could help."

"I could tell you he was exceptional, but you already knew that, heh! Could tell you how many years he set the Forzian invasion of Prego back with his maneuvers leading Vista. I could even tell you about the shame I feel that he obtained a Ghostmade before I ever could, but you knew that as well."

Jack's nerves cleared as he walked towards the Ghostmonger, he of course wanted to ask about the Brave, and by extension Apolline, but knew it was smarter to start broadly. Get him talking, so they could get all the information possible out of him.

"If you're not able to help with finding the Rogue, maybe you could tell us what you know about the Mercurial... Know where they went? Got the scoop on why they left?"

"To answer the where would be folly." he said pushing back another strand of hair, "Pure speculation, like fools gambling away their month's pay in the rat pits or flipping a doubloon in the air. But seeing as how you all are heavily armed and I am not, I better answer your questions best I can. I would guess they moved to an island so far away from here, all the Kristal on Prego wouldn't get you there!"

"And the why?" he murmured.

"Ahh yes, the why. We may be able to do a hair better than pure speculation, though still speculation. In my... journeys... I've come across some who believe the Mercurial were not fit the for the Five Isles, or Six Isles from their perspective. Sickly even. Something was making them ill, ill enough to want to leave the country islands they fought hard to protect, something drove them out... and did it quickly... as to what? Well it's one of the Pinwheel's biggest questions. Just happy I've got enough life in me to continue exploring for answers."

The sound of her body armor clanking together echoed across the high ceilings as Riley walked towards Jerrick who had seated himself in a patched leather chair,

"Tell me, Jerrick, in your travels, have you ever heard of a part Mercurial, part human?"

"Ahhh, a Brave you mean?"

"You know about them?!" Riley said with a hopeful excitement on her breath, "A bookkeeper told us only a handful of people even knew they existed."

"Heh! Well I suppose you're looking at one whose within said hand then..."

"Well, go on, what have you got?"

"I know that unlike the Mercurial... not all of the Brave have gone..."

Silence washed over each of them, as they put pieces together. A spark of hope welled up in Apolline's eyes, *'Not all of them have gone, does that mean there's others? Does he know of a place with fields of tulips, and women with auburn hair?'* she flung her book at Jack like she wanted him to ask.

"I also know…" Jerrick continued, "That men far scarier than myself think the Brave are the key to unlocking the power of the Mercurial. For all our sakes let's hope it's men like me who find their secrets before them!"

"I'm sure even Magnus from a half a world away would kill just to get a glimpse of her…" Riley muttered.

"Does that answer your questions or does this old brain of mine need further picking, heh!"

"Just how do you know they're still around, have you met one? Or even several? Know of any with auburn hair? Or did you just pick this up in some scroll?" Jack said.

"Let's say I've met one who has met one. And the others I spoke of, well you're smarter than you let on, the others I read about in scrolls. Heh! So I suppose to answer your question succinctly, no, no I've never met one… but all of that can change today if you'll allow it!" he said back to her with a devilish smile.

Riley jumped in her shoes as her suspicion reemerged, "I'm afraid I don't know what you mean sir?"

"I mean just what I said! All that could change today! All you've got to do is introduce me to the girl hiding behind the lad with black hair and broad shoulders and… boom… I'll have met a Brave. And in doing so come closer to the Ghosts than I've gotten in all my years of searching. That is the reason for your… surprise… visit, is it not?"

"Y-Yes…" Riley muttered, "B-but how could you have possibly known that??"

"Wouldn't be the Ghostmonger if I couldn't recognize Ghosts, or in her case partial Ghosts, heh! Her eyes give her away, none other in the Five Isles glisten quite like those…"

"Apolline!" she raised her voice, "If you're comfortable saying hello to this man, come on over. If not stay put. And don't worry if he tries anything I'll kill him."

She walked over trepidatiously, still wearing one of Matilda's floral dresses with a few scraps of body armor tacked on Jack had managed to find lying around.

There was an uncomfortable and covetous look in his eyes, one that told her to keep her distance.

For what was an odd amount of time Jerrick simply stared at Apolline in wide eyed amazement.

"Well don't just sit there with your mouth open, are you going to say anything to her?"

"Ugh, erm. Heh! Apologies for my unblinking eyes. I hope you'll understand, me meeting someone like you is like a captain's first time setting sail!" he said eyes still wide, "Apolline... what a lovely name that is! Where to begin, where to begin? I'm sure I could talk to you for weeks without running out questions. Tell me Apolline, do you remember Allora? Remember your people at all? Any information whatsoever you've got is more precious than gold."

Riley interjected, "Erm sorry to disappoint you Jerrick. That's kind of the reason we're here, hoping you can help us. Apolline has a severe case of Amnesia. Doesn't remember her childhood, who her parents are, or where she's even from. Really she just remembered her name. I'm sure a man as smart yourself can understand what a painful thing that is to have to go through."

He looked pensive in his leather chair but just nodded back.

"As you well predicted there's some awful men out there that want to exploit her, and I very much intend not to let that happen. We risked our necks getting here hoping you would be able to help. We helped you with being closer to the Ghosts than you've ever been, now help us."

"Fascinating! They must've wiped her memory…."

"Who wiped her memory?"

"Even as an expert I'm saddened to know so little, and can only offer conjecture based off prior dealings. But the who? Well… who else would it have been? The Mercurial of course… As to if they did it for their own protection, or for hers, I cannot say…"

"Well how do we get it back??" Jack said passionately.

"I'm sorry to tell you, I don't think there's any easy answers there. Give me one moment please…"

Grabbing a dusty book on the side table near his chair he began furiously combing through it, shoving it right up to his eyeballs,

"Let us see… Mercurial Architecture, no don't want that… farms, no again… Alloran Crags, not what we want! Hrmph! Suppose the passage I was thinking of was in a different book. Would you all mind excusing me while I go looking for it? Won't be long, rest assured." Jerrick said as he stood up and set the book back on its table.

"Go right ahead…" Riley waved him on as she watched him already darting up the ever-winding staircase.

"Bit of a strange man, isn't he?" she said looking back at Apolline, Jack, and Matilda.

"Pretty accommodating too, given we just broke in," Jack noted, "Most folks would be seeing red if you smashed their door to bits, but he almost looked happy to see us…"

The mischievous pigeons on the trees out front looked like they were spectators, watching them intently through the giant glass window, as other birds fluttered across their view and the folks down below walked past enjoying a cool early morning on Kleppenwitz.

"Jerrick sure doesn't dust much, looks like this place hasn't been cleaned in months..." Riley said to the crew as they were looking at one of the exhibits.

The casing was so dusty she carved a little *'J.T.'* and an *'Apo'* into the top of the glass as they looked through it. It held the Starboard Dial Jerrick had mentioned earlier, with its tattered leather sides and faded yellow stripes, the thing looked more like scrap leather than a proper compass.

Time passed at a snail's pace for them as they awaited Jerrick's return, looking over all the remaining exhibits and sculptures mounted to the walls, they even heard some commotion, a couple bumps and clanks, coming from upstairs which Jack interpreted as a good sign, he must've been throwing all kinds of books around looking for the one he needed.

"Can't believe he has the nerve to be sleeping right now after selling us out to Lucas and Konrad…" Jack overheard Riley whispering with Matilda.

"Something wrong?" he said warily, "Who sold us out??"

"Not now," she whispered looking over at Radish with vitriol, "We need to focus, I'll tell you when we get back…"

Taking a second pass of the museum, now with the knowledge that the pieces were merely replicas he took a closer look. Something felt very wrong when Jack decided to inspect the compass Jerrick was so fond of, crouching down looking at the bronze plaque at the bottom of the exhibit he said,

"This says Starbound Dial... didn't he call it the Starboard Dial??"

"One here says Sunflower of Serendipity... pretty darn sure he said Rose of Serendipity..." Matilda yelled back from a squatted position.

Suspicion crescendoed and didn't take long to escalate into something much darker.

"I get the feeling this man is not who he says he is..." Riley said as she picked up the book Jerrick had and read the title *'Vistan Monarchy: The Triumvirate's Tale Of Subterfuge and Betrayal'*

"Not about the Mercurial at all," she muttered.

"Something isn't adding up here…" Jack sput out.

"About eight things ain't addin up here!" Matilda shouted.

"Look alive folks, whoever this man is, he is not Jerrick Alamillo..." Riley said just loud enough where only the room could hear her.

"Told ya he wasn't here!" Radish laughed while yawning.

"So nice of you to finally join us. Sounds like this isn't coming as a surprise to you?"

He nodded as he stretched his arms and legs, "Knew he was full of it the first minute he started speakin..."

"You've got plenty of experience there, suppose you know just what to look for..."

"Back when Matilda clearly asked if he knew the Rogue, and he stumbled. Not a man, woman, nor child alive who meets the Rogue and forgets about it. Tuned out there, was all the information I needed..."

"Who do you suppose our convincing impostor is then?"

"Heaven knows. Maybe a burglar we caught in the act? If we really wanted to find out, could just waltz up there right now, put a gun in his face and watch the bloke sing..."

"Not a bad idea." Riley said coldly, "Jack you and Apo stick down here, keep watch while we find our friend."

"You think I'm gonna miss out on the action? Not a chance…"

"Ugh, fine. Keep Apolline behind you then, she doesn't have a full suit on."

Slowly, carefully, they crept up the winding steps that changed direction every few feet, with Riley and Matilda at the front, and Radish guarding the rear behind Jack and Apo. At the top there was a closed door, just like the one Radish had kicked down earlier, gargoyles and all.

"There's only one of him, so I don't expect too much trouble… still be ready for anything," Riley whispered as she went to open the door.

A small bell chimed that was bolted on the ceiling from the door being opened, and they looked upon a library much like the one in Peg's office, with the same walls made of books and rustic chairs and worn fireplaces. Unlike Peg's office, however, this one had unlit fires, and windows that looked like someone had painted over them with black finish. Save for a lone flickering candle in the middle fighting to stay aglow, the room was uncomfortably dark.

There was a curtain missing from one of the windowsills that faced the Muni, and across from it was another seemingly out of place dark green curtain that had been shut, obscuring any view of the room's final unexplored chamber behind it.

Apolline let out a scream so loud it was a shock none of the room's glass shattered. When she saw Jerrick there. When she saw the impostor Jerrick, mouth open and pooling blood… lying motionless, sitting in his worn leather chair that faced them, with a gold-hilted dagger sticking out of his heart.

"We aren't here alone!!" Riley bellowed ready for a fight.

Chapter 17

<u>Lantern's End</u>

The green curtain finally opened and revealed itself, giving way to a horrible sight. Poor Kersey sat in a wooden chair with hands and legs bound, bruised and bloodied looking only slightly better than impostor Jerrick. But unlike the impostor, he was lucky enough to still be breathing.

They first saw the Grey Wolf Hugo staring at them, snarling at them with his dagger-sized teeth, looking as if fear was not an emotion he possessed. The beast purposefully and unblinkingly inched ever closer to them, instinctively, as if they were just another meal, making it easy to miss the gangling man behind him.

Carneld Knox stared at them with the same unblinking eyes as his beast, with a look that showed contempt and satisfaction. The contempt was one he showed to most people, but even doubly so for them after they'd wasted so much of his time. The satisfaction was for having lured them here, lured them into the perfect trap.

Even from across the room they could see Knox's pores oozing water and blood, backdropped with such pale skin it looked just like red dye streaking down white canvas. His eyes were bulging and bloodshot, nearly twice the size of a normal set, and each of them looked a ways out of their socket, like they would've fallen out ages ago in any normal man.

A gold-hilted dagger identical to the one put through the impostor's chest was now held at Kersey's throat, as Knox gripped it from behind him and continued looking at them with a triumphant glare,

"I ssugest you drop your arms if this man's life is ssomething you value…" he said in his cold, snake-like voice.

"It isn't. Go ahead and try it though, I'll have four balls of lead in you by the time blade meets flesh." Riley said with fire in her eyes, as she pointed one of her pistols at him and the other at Hugo.

"Lad's just a Captain. An not a very good one at that. Real Butternut that one. Best let'em go, he's no good to you, or really anyone else for that matter." Radish added in an odd tone that was uncomfortably nervous.

The single candle in the middle of the room flickered, causing it to go dark and Knox's silhouette to vanish, if only for a moment.

He responded with a bizarre smile, that had no happiness or joy behind it, only a cruel fascination,

"It's a fight you want then? I wass hoping you'd say something like that. Truth be told I haven't had any real action in some time, most know better…"

The man in front of them didn't feel real to Jack, like he was a mirage in a dream, like the boogie man he'd spent his life seeing wanted posters of plastered on the city walls, decided to show up one day to confirm every awful story he'd ever been told.

Ready for anything he planted his feet to the ground, trying to pretend like the horrifying visage he was were facing hadn't shaken him to the core. Besides Radish, it was the first time any of the crew had gotten a good look at him, they'd heard all the stories of course, about how he was rotting away, but none of them did him the proper justice. Apolline couldn't even bare to look at Knox with all his sores, instead she just buried her face in Jack's shoulder, praying this would all be over soon.

The light flickered again, this time longer than before. When it reemerged, they could see the beast gnashing his teeth together, making a low and aggressive drawn-out grunt.

It felt so uncanny for him to see one in some building, a slave to captivity instead of roaming snowcapped plains hunting for rabbits and other small game. Jack had gone his whole life hearing of the famous Northern Grey Wolves as a fiercely independent breed, remaining true to their nature no matter if caged, tortured, or maimed. This one, however, was different. Obedient and loyal to an odd degree, as if somehow Knox could communicate with it without ever giving a command.

When the light flickered a third time, Matilda, who was closest, looked down to see Hugo's teeth bare and gnarling a mere few feet away, lunging towards her so fast she couldn't react. Shots fired from Riley and Jack, but the beast was too quick for even a seasoned bounty hunter. Violently he shook her wrist as he slammed her to the ground with the full force of his weight, shaking with enough power to easily break an arm. They tried to get more shots off, but there was never a clean open, the two kept switching back and forth, to Matilda on top trying to choke the thing, to Hugo pinning her down with his claws snapping his canines back and forth inches from her face. Seconds passed like hours as her companions jumped back and forth, and over, helplessly watching the brawl happening midfloor.

Just when Jack thought he saw an opening to stab the wolf with his sword, Matilda swooped to her feet, and with all her weight in her shoulders, threw her arm back, then forward, making the Grey Wolf fly. He let out an ear crunching yelp as he crashed into the nearest wall.

Hugo, however, was a clever beast and wasn't going to lie there and give them an opening. Before they could raise their arms, he dashed off back behind the green curtain, to the chamber behind that Knox was still guarding.

"Had worse..." Matilda said as she dusted herself off, ripped the mangled armguard from her wrist and threw it at Knox. She tried her best to hide it behind her sleeve, but the blood trickling down her arm and onto the floor made hiding impossible.

"Very impressive!" Knox said in his strange tone, "Poor Hugo will be upset he's not getting a morning snack. Serves him right though. He didn't earn it."

"Mind telling us what you want?" Riley said sharply, "Keep in mind there's five of us, and one of you. I like our odds."

"Five people... one Ghost... I don't"

He closed his eyes and took a deep breath like he was smelling a rose,

"What brought me here, is, you stole something from me. Something I worked very hard to acquire. And I'm here to get it back." he paused, "You know, I was told Gibbons weren't nearly as savage and idiotic as the average bounty hunter, yet here you are barking up my tree, about to die for some girl you just met. I must've been misled..."

"That 'thing' we stole is a living, breathing, human being with her own thoughts, pains, and struggle. You can't steal a person, because they don't belong to anyone other than themselves sir." she half-pleaded.

"Respectfully, I disssa-gree." he murmured, "Though maybe I should be thanking you. She was still in a box on that satellite of ours, of zero use. And one of you freed her, saving me more trouble than you know. May even allow you a quick death as compensation."

The light began flickering again, this time in quick succession.

"You brought a knife to a gun fight. You're mighty confident." Riley said with a hint of nervousness in her voice, it was slight, but not to Jack, and it sent shivers through him.

As the light flickered again, the darkness lasted only for a moment...

but it was all the time Knox needed.

When she saw Knox again, Riley gasped like the dagger in fake Jerrick's heart had just entered her own. He was no longer holding his knife to Kersey's throat but was now holding it to her son Jack's throat, sporting a rotten grin. He'd managed to travel an impossible distance in a split second, no person alive could be that fast, no person alive was even close to that fast.

It all happened so quickly. One moment he was looking at Knox through his scope, he blinked from the light flicker, and when he opened his eyes, he saw that disgusting arm half covered by a white robe, popping out of the shadows. This was the first time in Jack's young life he'd ever had a knife to his throat, and it was terrifying enough he prayed it would be his last. He tried his best to breathe, remain calm, but Knox's vice-like grip on his neck was making it difficult.

Jack didn't remember the last time he saw his mother having to fight back tears, but she was doing it now as she pointed both guns at Knox's big forehead. The hollow look she returned told him everything he needed to know about how dire their situation had become.

"I suppose this one you do care about?" Knox said looking directly into Riley's eyes. "I'll assk one more time before the boy dies, drop your arms..."

"Let him go, and I won't kill you..." Riley said with a trembling voice, "If he dies, then you do too…"

She wanted to believe the words that'd just come out of her mouth, that she was even capable of killing him. But she'd just watched the hideous man sprint across the room with superhuman speed. Stealth, positioning, subterfuge, all her normal tools meant nothing now, the look on her face showed what the rest knew already, she only had one option left.

Just by the angle of his hand, Jack could tell there was a substantial height difference between him and Knox, more than enough to give a skilled marksman an opening. He knew what had to be done. Either they handled this here and now or he would kill them all and take

Apolline for whatever cruel ends he had in mind.

"Take the shot..." he said nervously looking over them.

He was met with only silence as Riley and Apolline looked on horrified, Matilda with a beat red face, and Radish with a blank stare that couldn't even look at him, only fixated on a nearby corner instead.

"Take the shot!!" he yelled, pleading this time.

"Take the shot!!!!" he yelled again, even louder.

Looking like a bull about to charge, Matilda couldn't restrain herself any longer. Seeing the boy she'd watched grow up since he was a tyke, about to be killed was too much for her already strong emotion to process. As she planted her back foot, about to charge and caring very little what happened to her own life, something stopped her dead in her tracks.

Kersey began to move. He sprang up from his chair with his bloody face and even bloodier uniform, shrugging off the rope around his arms and legs like it'd never been tied at all... like it'd only been made to look like it was tied...

Unable to focus on anything else, other than the most precious thing in the world to her, Riley looked through her sights and steadied her hand. As painful as it was to ponder, Jack was right... she needed to take the shot. The high-pitched humming sound of ringing ears felt like it'd contaminated her brain, and then the rest of her along with it, her senses stricken down by all-encompassing emotion, only her sight and touch remained. She took a deep breath in, held her breath, and slowly started to squeeze the trigger.

She stopped just short of firing when she felt something hard and cold pressed into the back of her head.

"Wouldn't do that if I was you..." Radish said with his gun to her head.

With a look like she'd just been torn in half, she turned and faced him,

"Wh-what are you doing?!?!"

"I'm the Quicksilver Thief miss, not the Quicksilver Angel. The last lesson I'll be teachin you is… never trust a scallywag…" he said with a triumphant look, like everything was going as planned.

Chapter 18
The Grisly Underground

There was a sourness in the air now, a bitterness, and lack of understanding amongst them that could only be born from betrayal.

"Apologies love... nothing personal. You see our loyalty is negotiable, and you got outbid!" Radish said as he tapped his fingers on the way down her arm then snatched the silver pistol out of it faster than she could blink.

With his weapon focused on Matilda, Kersey approached them with the same rope that'd been falsely binding his limbs.

"Ahm!" he said through snotted cough, "Can't believe these idiots fell for that spring, eh boss? The goody two shoes were dumb enough to trust scoundrels afterall… That lovely Riley there had me half thinkin they wurn't as dumb as you said… heh! Guess I was wrong, Pride of the Blackwater'll soon be Pride of Carneld Knox's Dungeon!"

As he went to tie her arms together, she gave him a side strike with her still clenched fist, giving him another big welt on his face.

"Watch it…" Radish said nearly laughing his gun still drawn, "He's got enough lumps, don't need anymore…"

With a mix of shock and disbelief the crew watched on helplessly as their two former friends snatched their guns, knives, and swords away one by one rendering them as useless as an Allorian Deed.

"Pray…" Riley said, just louder than a whisper as Kersey finally managed to get rope around her arms, "Pray that Knox kills us quickly, if these ropes should slip for even a second, that's more time than I need to put you in the ground…"

"Best we double tie them ropes Kerz."

The small study that might've felt cozy with a lit fire and some paint now felt like coffin. A coffin whose walls were slowly closing in. The lone wax candle on the middle table now barely flickered, taunting them, as if it wanted to give a full view of their last moments.

The traitor approached his partner with spring in his step and took a good look at his face, "Knox banged you up pretty good didn't he? Dunno if we had to go that far. Not like this lot was on to us…"

"Wasn't even him!" he laughed, "Took a tumble the way up those dumb windin steps, n' bloodied my nose. After that just gave myself a few whacks with the pistol, closed my eyes and croaked like a frog when you entered… and voila!"

"And that's why I keep you around Captain!" he said with a triumphant glare until he happened to look back at Riley who was shaking with rage, "Aww don't be so mad, it's only business. I'm sure if you give Knox what he wants, he'll be real kind to you and yours…" he said with a clenched jaw and pursed lips that said otherwise.

Her bandaged knee still throbbed in pain even when she wasn't putting any pressure on it. She couldn't stop herself from shaking, her vision was hazy, she couldn't think, she could hardly even remember to breathe. The only other time Riley could remember feeling this bad was back there on that ship when she found Jack, starving and just barely able to hold on to consciousness. Except even then, she still had a weapon to defend herself, even then she could take her future and that of her loved ones into her own hands. Now all she could do was watch the world around her fade to black.

Peering over at Jack with his black hair ruffled and those small cheek freckles she was the only one to ever notice shining back at her like stars, for an ever-brief moment he looked like a kid again. He was the same kid now with those eyes as round as doubloons, the same kid he was on the day he came home from school crying because the kids nicknamed him *Deadhand,* and she had to explain to him that it was his decision whether he let words hurt him or not, and that if he returned sour words those other kids would quickly learn some manners. How she wished she had an answer now like she did back then.

The ringing of chain mail and body armor could be heard coming up from the winding steps, surely more of Knox's men come to assist, which he was going to need with the way Matilda was writhing around on the ground hands and legs bound trying to knee anything that got close.

Making for an odd juxtaposition but on brand for him, Radish seemed to be the only one in the room that was in a bright mood as he tip-toed towards Knox like he was in a field of bear traps.

"Happy to see you made it, sounds like my latest pigeon found you…"

"It did…" Knox said flatly with eyes elsewhere.

"Hope you're still not mad about that dumb chest, I trust you found it in my sewers and reappropriated it."

"The chest is back with me, and while part of me still wants to kill you, given the circumstances of you opening it for me, I'll forget it happened. Should you cross me again however, no hideout on Otto is clever enough to stop me from finding you."

"Then I'm all scubbers, call me crazy but for a moment there I thought this may be the last view of the Muni I ever get. Trust that's it then. There's your girl. And there's her friends. All without a shot fired. May as well've come with little silver bows on top of their heads."

"You've done your job to satisfaction..." he said ignoring Radish as if he was a nuisance and not taking eyes off Apolline.

Hands rubbing up and down he looked towards the exit and said, "Well, I can tell when I'm not wanted. Just the gold then and I'll leave the new acquaintances to become what I'm sure is dear friends..."

Picking up a dusty bauble that was lying next to them he eyed it closely, "Your gold issn't here. It's a large sum Radish, even for an operation like mine. You'll help escort our friends to my lab, keep quiet, give me a day or two, and you'll have your riches."

"Alright" he said with a hint of anxiety in his breath knowing full well he had no other choice, "Onward then capitan."

The skinny stone castle they were currently somewhere in the mid-section of seemed to almost wobble with the morning sea winds crashing against it. Tiny sun rays made it through ornate glass windows that'd been painted over and gave them a good look at all of Knox's men that were pouring into the chamber. Forty of them at least, if not more, clad in chainmail and boiled leathers they looked even more soap repellant than Radish did. Each carried unremarkable walnut pistols on their right hips and a cutlass on the other, many had beavered tricorne hats, others had missing teeth and patchy scarred beards, and many more had a dagger holstered on any spot of the body you could think of, but all of them looked at Knox like they were just as scared of him as everyone else in the room as they awaited their orders.

"Of mine own flesh," Knox said with a twitching wonder in his eyes as he approached Apolline.

Sprawled on the ground and looking over at her friends as if to say help, all they could do was watch on in horror, Riley instinctively pulled on her ropes until she couldn't feel her hands anymore, but it was of no use, they were tied too tight.

"Don't look away from me, I'm the only family you've got left. Don't look at them either, they can't help you now child. In fact, it is *you* who is going to help them..."

****

The journey to wherever they were being carried didn't take long. In fact, it was suspiciously short. Jack could tell they were underground by the change in temperature, and because the burlap sack they'd put over their heads had the smallest hole that when the soldier carrying him bumped up just right became visible.

As she always was, Riley was right about Radish when she said he'd sell his own mother for enough doubloons. But unfortunately, she was the only one that could see it. The men in the Cantina howling out victory cries of Wormslayer never saw it, Lucas Geist never saw it as he pleaded to not put him in chains back when he first showed up, and as much as he hated to admit it, he hadn't seen it either. The man had a weird charm about him that was an excellent mask for who he really was. Jack wanted to see the world as a decent place, with good-hearted people just trying to make their own way, but he was now beginning to understand why a bit of cynicism could go a long way.

The men carrying him must've been in the middle as they mostly kept their voices down, presumably to not be heard by their superior.

"Y'know he wadn't always this mad." One of Knox's men whispered to another, "But you wander in dark corners much as he does, and eventually the mind follows. My centimes say leave curses be."

"True what they say then. Power's a hunger that can't be sated. Knox can't be sated, meanwhile I'm over here never been fed!"

Jack couldn't help but chuckle when he heard one of them tell another to help with Matilda after she'd knocked one of their teeth loose, even when bound and blindfolded she was a force to be reckoned with.

"Useless. Seven men couldn't hold her... then put another seven on

Butternuts!" one of them yelled.

"Where we takin dem? Maybe boss'll let us have some fun with'em before he kills'em!" another guard said with a deep and cracking voice as he walked down the narrow cave slope.

"Y'know he told me specially put them in the lower dungeons, and don't touch'em. Unless you want to see his fire keep your hands where they belong. Not till he gives us the go at least. The girls goin with him though, said he had plans for her."

Though the Gibbons, save for Jack, couldn't see it with their burlaped hats, they were being carried on shoulders down a spiraling and deceptively steep rock walkway that given one wrong step would've ended in certain death in the orange hot pools below. The entranceway to Knox's hideout was too big to be called a cave, more like a cavern it could've fit a fleet of galleons all stacked on top of one another and still had room for all the bats sleeping at the top. With strange insects scurrying about the ground and black algae covering most of the rock that fed off the traces of light coming from above, the place seemed to have its own ecosystem. The walk down it had already taken far longer than the walk to get there and judging by the guard's grumbles there was more to go.

"An Isle's Wonder how dis place hadn't collapsed yet with that big holy flub on top of us." the deep voiced guard hacked out of breath as he continued ever downward.

"We got the girl now, that's what he wanted. Y'know another week we'll have our pay and never have to set foot in this tomb again. Y'know have us enough for a crew to steal a ship and start our own little pirate business. No waitin round for a handout like sods, and no boss that's like to kill us cause his breakfast was served cold."

"A pirate?!" the guard laughed, "I seen scarier jars of mayonnaise. You don't even frighten the rats down here, how you expect to frighten sailors?"

"Same way as all the rest. With a cannon almost as big as your two front teeth!"

The sound of Jackboots squashing beetles rang loud as the two chatty guards looked over at Radish and Kersey who were passing by on their way down the chamber, looking like they were very much not in the mood to make friends.

"Last I saw you, you was waving like a daisy sailin away with Knox's treasure. Might be the first in history to pull one over on Carneld and still be alive. You're pretty clever, I'll give that." the deep voiced man said indignantly. "Your name's Radish ain't it? Like the fruit??"

"It's a vegetable Butternut." he replied, eyes forward like he hardly noticed the man.

"I'd be careful how I talk round these boys, boss gave us orders not to hurt the prisoners. Didn't say a peep about you two though..."

"Funny, he didn't mention you either." Radish said back with a confrontational smile.

Grimacing as if he wanted to clap back but couldn't he said, "We're to escort you two to your quarters after putting them in the cells. Yor not to leave for any reason until we've got the gold ready. There's a stonewalled privy in there, two cots, plenty of books though by the looks of ya that's not your cup of tea, we even had a chef ship over Codwater octopus eggs, mash potatoes, and the finest roasted duck in Kleppenwitz."

"That duck is the best you'll ever have." the other guard chipped in eagerly.

"Fowl for the foul! Let's crack on then before me and my captain lose our appetites. You'll have to forgive my testiness, Captain Kersey and I got a date with the Kingsfall Islands, get away from all this mess, least for a time. Didn't expect a holdup..." Radish said trying to sound convincing but with enough suspicion Jack could pick up on it even while being carried like a rag doll over a big man's shoulder.

Still unable to see but they could hear the giant sound of a door opening. Steel bolts snapped like lightning as rock bowed to steel. This wasn't a standard door at all, in fact it sounded like a bank vault opening with its giant crack, and considering the shivering echo it sent about the cavern it must've been massive.

The torches along each wall made their presence heard as they fought back against cave winds. A sprawling cavern now a rock tunnel a mere fraction of the size, they could hear the guards splitting off at tunnel forks, preparing to go about their usual duties.

It wasn't much longer until Jack heard the sound of a different door closing, a cell door. The darkness was abated if only a little, when the same two guards they overheard on the way down lifted their burlap covers. Still bound at hands, knees, and now at the waist tied to a boulder that almost looked like an owl. He looked around to see a dank moldy prison cell, tighter than plausible and surrounded by rock. The only light inside came from under an exit door and its peephole at the top, that must've led to the rest of the hideout. It was a good thing they were all dear friends, because the cage's center they inhabited had them packed on top of one another with ropes so tight it was a struggle to draw breathe.

"You all sit tight…" the deep voiced guard said, "If you get hungry, don't worry what's left of your poor little souls. Plenty of our whiskered friends scurryin about that'll do the job. Heavens know I had plenty in my day. I'll be right outside those doors, and if I hear any of yous trying to fiddle with a cage or your harnesses, well, let's just say Knox didn't hire me for my people skills."

With a beat red face and her rage making her completely forget she had the ability to speak English; Matilda was still furiously trying to kick at the two guards even from halfway across the room.

The man with the two massive front teeth unsheathed his pistol, and cracked her over the head with it, hit so hard blood immediately began pooling down her forehead as she went limp from the blow.

"Ha! Would ya look at that, the beast does feel pain. More where that came from if you can't sit still!"

With an eerie quiet in her voice Riley looked up at the man and said, "You're going to die for that. You mark these words"

"Heh! I'd give you a little bump too," he said as he dug a heel into the bandages covering her foot. Hiding the pain was the easy part, hiding her flush face and sweat oozing out of every pore, however, was impossible. "but there's a special plan for you, you little pearl. An old friend of yours made her way back here, and she's none too happy about what you did to her shoulder. Don't worry, she'll be along shortly."

As the men waddled off and shut the door behind them, the grim reality started to set in. Time stood still as the three of them sat there silently, struggling for words that may help.

"Are you ok Matilda?" she said trying to bend and contort her head enough to get a good luck at her.

"Ya I'm fine. Takes a lot more than that to hurt me..." she said voice barely a whisper.

"Apo's gone..." Riley sulked looking up at the cave walls as if she foolishly thought they'd provide some help to their situation.

"I'll find a way out of these ropes, we're gonna get her back and find a way out here!" Jack said attempting to keep his voice down. Perhaps now the most incensed of them all, he put all the pressure he could on the ropes binding his hands to the point where they'd started bleeding.

The door leading out of the prison was made of wood and wouldn't have been too much trouble to kick down. The iron bars surrounding them, however, were a different story. The crew could see the orange torch flame lighting up rock from outside the cast iron peephole but could not see the guard that just left.

"I think he might've gone to take Radish to his quarters!" Riley said with hope in her voice. "On the count of three push out with your arms and legs with everything you've got... one... two..."

With the hope of being free from their prison breathing second life into them they heaved until their bindings started to ever so slightly splinter.

Again they pushed as the pressure built, and built, and built until the hemp ropes looked ready to snap.

It wasn't until they heard a KNOCK KNOCK KNOCK on the door that all hope faded.

"I HEAR YOU IN THERE. IF I COME IN AGAIN IT'LL BE

251

FINGERS I TAKE INSTEAD CRACKING SKULLS!!" the booming deep voice of the guard echoed through the prison.

****

Apolline was horrified. The skeleton who shared her cell looked away from her, huddled up in the corner like he didn't want to be seen, with the unloaded flintlock pistol dangling from his hand. Trying to distance herself from him as much as possible she positioned herself in the opposite corner, though it did little to relieve her anxiety. She looked over the other cells with more skeletons that'd met an equally grim fate and shuddered, looking away at the stone chamber outside her prison. It was shaped like a frying pan, with a sprawling bowl like center and long narrow passageway leading to the only vaulted steel door exit, with a red wooden door opposite it leading to Knox's quarters. The small pond at the center was almost peaceful, like it belonged at the base of picturesque mountain ridgelines, like it didn't belong in this dark place.

She could see him across the way, sitting contently at some tiny wooden desk, scribbling in an old tome and lit by only a few frail candles. Candles that showed eyes that looked like they'd never known rest.

The four guards beside him, along with the other twenty some odd posted along the walls of the cavern, looked wooden and expressionless. Without their leather jackets you could see their ruffled white linen shirts as well as enough guns between them to start their own battalion. A couple of the patrols were inspecting two golden man-sized elephant statues Apolline recognized from Radish's hideout under the sewers.

That wasn't all they'd stolen from Radish's sewer palace however, when she looked around the cavern she could see the disassembled carriage parts along the stone pillars that held space up, she saw the sealed safe with no unlocking mechanism, even the lamp and the books and bookshelves were there, it seemed they'd gotten absolutely everything, including that glowing hunk of wood and steel that gave her pause just looking at it. Only a stone's throw from her cage was the chest where she'd slept for so long. She had to wonder if Knox had put it so close to torment her, forcing her to look out at the cage she'd come from, from inside the one she'd just been thrust into.

Scattered amongst the hideout rubbish were a series of log tables overflowing with glass beakers capped with corked tops. Ranging from small mildewed brown beakers to long skinny and neon, the substances inside looked poisonous even from her cell and the dead rats below confirmed it. Hundreds of cast iron cages stacked below the tables, and sometimes beside and above, held the whiskered test subjects, some dead, others hiding away feebly in the corner, and alarmingly some were baring teeth and gnawing on the gates or rabidly pawing at anything that stirred with a blood crazed visage.

With his white linen robes dusting the stone floors and jewelry clanking like chainmail he got up from his desk and glided towards her gracefully, going so slow it appeared like his feet never lifted from the ground.

"Welcome to your new home…" he said with unblinking eyes.

Even in Alireza's death grip she hadn't been this frightened. Even the men without faces seemed like a spring shower compared to Carneld Knox. Ugly in both ways as Radish had said, and for once he wasn't lying.

"Are you ready to get started child? I'm sure you're every bit as eager as I am to get this done with…"

She shook her head no with a fire that said helping him was the last thing she'd ever do.

"Ah, disappointing. I suppose we'll have to go about this in a bloodier manner than I'd hoped."

'Go ahead and kill me, I'd die before helping you' she wrote as sparkles flowed from her multi-colored eyes.

"Yess… yes… yess," he said almost toying with her, "I figured you may say as much. And what of your friendss? Are you willing to watch each of them die?" he said as he beckoned over one of his guards. "I saw the young man was the first you turned to back in the castle, think we'll start with him…"

'What do you want? Why are you doing this to me?!'

"Why?!" he said almost as if he was happy to get a chance to explain himself, "As powerful as I am. I'm not immortal. There are forces in this world, not many mind you, that may be able to harm even me. I know you're just waking up to this place, and may be the only one on this island that hasn't heard of him, but a man goes by the name Magnus, with an army of a size that hasn't been seen in a century. And not only that he has the power of our people in the trinkets he keeps. Ghostmades as you may have heard them called."

'What has that got to do with me??? I'm not immortal either, cut me if you like and see the same blood as anyone else.' she scribbled while prancing up her eyes at him and shoving her notebook at the cage wall.

"No, no. You're not immortal, nor will you ever be child. But that doesn't mean that blood of yours doesn't have power. A power your young mind could never fully appreciate. We've just got to find a way to unlock it."

She had no words for him, a cold persistent hopelessness was all she could feel, going back in that chest would've been a better option than this.

"So, time's turning. What will it be then? Cooperate today, or cooperate in many months after each one of your friends has met the same unfortunate fate as your cellmate over there?"

The sound of the still water pond in the backdrop whistling through the cracks of cave was all she could hear as he stared at her never breaking and never blinking.

"I see. We'll send for them then. I suggest you enjoy the time you've got left with them, as you still know them." he said as he signaled his guards and walked back towards his desk.

Chapter 19
A Torch to the Cantina

Detective Konrad looked over the brown wooden behemoth with contempt, with its jagged corners and uneven top crowned with an eyesore of a rotting galleon, a far cry from the square and uniform government buildings he called home.

The mostly white and slate roofed cottages in the vicinity spun around the cobblestones and faced the Cantina as if they were kneeling to it, bowing down to pay homage, and a good portion of the residents found themselves out front in their gardens, looking like they'd love to know what so many men were doing here and with so much weaponry.

"Ready for a raid boss?" Nuster said curling up his nose like it was his very own hard forged battle cry.

"These creatures have caused us more trouble than they're worth. Now a stain on my good city. That all ends today." Konrad said with unfaltering confidence back to the twenty or so men behind him.

Rifles hung over their blue wool overcoats and badges, with pistols clasped tightly in their hands, the policemen knew full well a fight was on the horizon. Some looked nervous enough to ralph, others looked prepared, jolly even, as they stacked behind Konrad like soldiers ready to clash.

Glaring at his gold pocket watch like staring at it would give a different result Konrad said, "Where is he?! He was supposed to meet us out front at seven sharp."

"It's only six-fifty sir!" Nuster chortled back to an annoyed detective.

"Yes, I'm aware. Suppose I thought a man of his caliber would be early."

Built to sit on top of a natural rock formation, the front entrance to the Cantina had two draw bridges sitting atop a double wide section of the city's clearwater canals that acted as a natural barrier against any of her enemies. Dense black sea foliage and sea sponges that tended to grow in this segment coupled with the shade a building as large as the Cantina created, often made the water out front appear to be black, and so it came to be known the Blackwater Cantina.

"Have you gone over all the plans?" he said to his subordinate.

"Course I'have, got the blueprints to map the place out down to how many toilets they got. There's more dungeons down there than we got at the station. But we got the men. They can hide from one of us, but good luck hidin from twenty."

"And how do we know it won't be locked down tight? We both know security in there would rival any bank on Kleppenwitz."

"Spose we'll have to trust the plan. Trust that it'll be disabled like he said."

"Did you bring the explosives just in case?"

"Lucas is takin care of that, said they still had a prisoner that made bombs like you wouldn't believe."

"Good…"

Two worn marble statues that depicted stone monkeys decorated the front vista and were comparable in size to the wooden entrance doors behind them. The first had a mischievous smirk and one eye squinted as he aimed a pistol at the other, and the second had a frown as he pointed a cutlass up at his counterpart.

Made of stone, hemp and red oak as ancient as the Cantina itself, the drawbridge felt anything but stable as Konrad and his men crossed. Looking down into flowing waters below the men saw waterlogged chests lodging schools of small glitterfish, cannonballs piled on top of one another, and rusty scimitars that'd likely been thrown in when they lost their edge. Many speculated the same men who put the ship on top of the building might've also been the ones that glued the planked handles of the bridge with silver pieces of eight, now causing Nuster to have a fit, attempting to get his men to stop trying to pick them up. And likely knowing all about it because this prank had already worked on him a time or two.

Instead of a lion, or a pig like other doors in the city, the black ironed knocker depicted a mandrill baring teeth. It was almost a struggle for Konrad to lift with its size, but as soon as he did, with the sound and force of a boulder flying down a mountain, the doors gave way.

The dozen or so men staring back at them were in polished steel that looked like it was still hot from the forge, wrapped around their shoulders, elbows, and wrists. On their chest and legs sat leather fine enough to stop small arms, complemented with bronze daggers tucked into their burgundy sashes and gold stocked pistols holstered above guarding the ribs.

"Back to the kitchen boy, there's fish guts need cleaning!!" Konrad's crew heard a man shouting, "You don't have the spine for this, you'll only slow us down!!"

Emerging from behind the line a man stepped forward with flowing blonde hair that accentuated a bigger than average forehead, with the same garb as his soldiers only his steel was gold instead of silver.

"Mmmm, Detective Konrad," Lucas said beaming with an outstretched hand, "I'm ashamed to say I've never had the pleasure of fighting alongside you. Happy that ends today."

A motley crew of policemen and bounty hunters stared at each other like old friends from their respective lines as their commanders drew into whispering distance.

"And I'm ashamed I couldn't come to your aid sooner. As I'm sure you're painfully aware, a city like this keeps a police force busy enough to break…"

"You know we aren't so different sir, we both risk our lives taking out the trash around here. Of course we've got different methodologies, different rules, and different quarters, but the end result is the same. We get to enjoy a city free from urchins."

"Wise man Geist. You know I still remember back years ago when I was on patrol and happened upon you throwing that beggar into the canal right behind me. What a treat that was!"

"Came into the building asking for handouts, I told him the only thing he'd get for free around here is a shower!"

The detective howled at the jest like a grandpa and his men followed suit as if to support their superior.

"After seeing that I knew you were a man worthy of my respect, all the years have done is confirmed my initial inspiration." Konrad said back like he was in love, "Speaking of, perhaps you can be my next recruit? Could skip the line, I could get you a sergeant's salary starting out. Security, a pension, the respect of anyone around here worthwhile, and I've even developed some methods for taking home a little extra. What with all the danger we put ourselves through, it's the least we deserve. How does that sound? Get you away free and clear from this den of thieves."

Even Nuster looked like he was having a hard time stomaching all the self-congratulations that we're happening, though he kept quiet all the same.

"Mmm, I'm afraid that would be difficult." he said pondering the thought, "You see this place has been a part of my family for generations, my father and grandfather helped build it up to glory. Only to have it all come crashing down after they died. I do not wish to see it destroyed, only repaired."

Just beyond them, through double doors lay Hangman's Hall. It was still early, so Chef Greene, his staff, a bartender, and a few barmaids might've been the only thing in there moving as anyone familiar with this foyer could've confirmed simply from the unusual lack of noise.

"About this plan…" Lucas's face finally turned from jovial to more serious. "Do you really think this is a man we can trust?"

"I wouldn't trust him for all the Kristal on Prego, but I've weighed all our options. And unfortunately, going with him makes the most sense."

"Agreed. Shall we get on with it then?"

Our chariots await sir. We'll go over more details on the ride over."

As the party marched away from the Cantina, guns still in hand with nearby townspeople still rubbernecking, they heard a man approaching from the rear.

"Where you think you're going?!" he said.

"Stono!" Lucas said in disbelief, trying and failing to look at him through the eyes of his goggles.

Along with him was his son Glasgo, Chef Greene in body armor that looked like he'd fashioned them from the kitchen's pots and pans, Marcus A. hiding in the back, and a small crew of Stono the Caiman's most loyal men.

"Think you'd get to have all the fun without us, did ya?" Stono said with a smirk.

Chapter 20
The Pugilists

Jack watched the rats scurry around his feet, debating if it made sense to try and capture a few to stockpile in case they tried starving them out. It was alarming what a few hours like this could do to the psyche. Hours passed and he was ashamed to admit they still didn't have a plan. The ropes binding him, Riley and Matilda were just as strong as they were before, and the guard outside liked to whistle every couple of minutes to remind them of their predicament.

"I see some rocks in the corner," Jack whispered, "Maybe if I could get to them, and when the guard comes back, kick it just right…"

"Too risky," Riley responded, "We need to get these ropes off if we want to be anything but useless."

"THAT BETTER BE THE RATS I HEAR IN THERE AND NOT WHISPERS!" the guards yell boomed through the tiny prison.

Stunned into silence, and frustrated into panic, they looked around at one another with a new level of despair.

"No more talking. Not until the whistles stop. Not until he's asleep." Riley said below a whisper, almost mouthing the words out.

The light coming from the peephole and under the door was the only real thing to look at as it illuminated the occasional bug, critter and rat. As time went on, panic turned to dread, all they could do now was wait and hope the guard fell asleep before someone came to replace him. *As worthless a plan as there ever was,* Jack thought, *If Riley taught him anything, it's that hope would get you killed.*

The sound of what seemed to be a chair falling over crept its way into the cavern and momentarily spooked them out of depression. Not long after, with bellies full of air, they watched the doorknob turn.

This is it. Knox here to finish the job. And he'll have easy time of it too, all because I couldn't see Radish for scoundrel that he was.

But it wasn't Knox, and it wasn't his men. And it wasn't Alireza either. It was the Quicksilver Thief and his snotty captain.

Waltzing in like it was his room at home, he looked them over and chuckled. Piecemeal body armor still on, his flowing salt and pepper hair almost made him look put together until you took a single look at the rest of him.

"What good would the Quicksilver Thief be if he couldn't open a lock…" Radish said to Kersey very impressed with himself as if he was finishing a previous conversation. "Adieu." he said finally noticing them and flicking his eyepatch as if it was a salute, "Here I thought our accommodations were bad…"

Crouching down to meet her at eye level, he pulled out what looked like a chunk of roasted duck from the sack on his back and watched the rats scurry to eat it, within seconds the tiny creature's stomachs were facing the ceiling.

"You're a fool to have trusted him." Riley said half laughing half enraged.

"Who says I trusted'em?"

Looking amused he pulled out a bone dagger from under his white linen shirt as Kersey watched the door.

"You're a fool without morals, but not a monster like Knox. And I doubt you have a stomach torture." she continued, "If you're here to kill us, go on with it already. And let me turn my head first so that face isn't the last one I see…"

"A fool? What kind of fool kills their partners, partners that are about to make them rich… I'd say the real fool in this situation is the one insultin her rescuers…"

Smiling as if to show off his grisly molars he placed the dagger in her bound hands.

"Go on. Cut yourselves free. Knox ain't dead yet, so I'd make it fast if you ever want to breathe open air again."

It was the strangest feeling Jack had ever known, having the one who betrayed them now become their salvation. Elation, confusion, and hatred fought a skirmish in his head, though now that Riley had cut them loose and they could stand to stretch, the scales seemed to be tipping towards elation.

"Why-why do this to us?" realizing she had a dagger now Riley's captive mentality snapped back into her usual full confidence,

"Cuz before we were not in Knox's hideout and we did not know where he was…" he said one word tiptoeing to the next, "Now we are in Knox's hideout and know just where he is. Plus I may've learned a thing or two about this Knox, and his… *powers*."

As they stared at him his words took time to process, after all betrayal for the greater good still felt like betrayal. Jack looked at him with bewilderment, like his young years had never prepared him for a situation like this, while Matilda stretched her arms out wide barely paying anyone any mind.

"You don't like my face?" Radish said almost serious.

"Give me your gun Butternut."

"Aww c'mon Tripleleaf, is that really necces-"

"Now!"

Once he'd handed it over, she immediately pointed at him, as he rolled his eyes looking back unsurprised, like this wasn't the first, or second, or third time he'd had a pistol pointed at his head.

"Didn't think it would be wise to let your partners in on this little plan of yours?"

"Mercurial would come waltzin back by the time you agreed to that!"

"Mmhmm…" she'd never show it, but he did have a point.

As Kersey gruffed and looked around to see what was going on Radish turned and shooed him off, indicating he should still watch the door. As he turned around again Riley reared back and jabbed him in the nose with the butt of her palm.

"That's for lying to your friends. I'm not one to keep making empty promises, don't let it happen again! Mind I'm going easy on you because at least your little plan hasn't got us killed yet."

"Ahh the sweet embrace of recognition!" he said as he held his bloody nose.

"There's five of us here, going up against likely over fifty men. With those numbers they'd beat us if all they had was wooden swords."

"Now what kind of thief would I be if I hadn't thought of that…"

"Here's your stupid gun, take us to ours…"

It felt amazing not having just the door's peephole to look out of anymore, without the bags on their heads they could finally see and not just hear the cavern around them.

The first thing the team saw as it was impossible to miss was the giant vault door no less than a hundred feet away. With its size there was no longer any mystery as to what made the ear shattering sound on the way into the hideout. Opposite the vault the cavern sunk to tunnel small enough Matilda would have to duck to get through, with at least three torch lit and ghostly tunnels sprawling out in opposite directions. Lasty, on the wall beside the prison door there was a waterlogged chest green with algae and big enough to fit a human. Inside of the chest was their guns and steel, and lying unconscious on top of the chest was the guard from earlier who had assaulted Matilda.

Dumping the man off with indifference, she began handing each their holsters back and checking to make sure her arms were reloaded and in working order.

The shove must've awakened the man as he lay on the cold ground, defenseless now and with eyes half open he pointed at each of them,

"I wish I was there to see it…" he said fading in and out, voice more slobber than words, "To see what Knox does to you. Huhuhuh, you've made'em mad enough, he'll get creative, that much I know."

Looking again over the gash and dried blood draping Matilda's face, it was all the information she needed to make her decision. He'd shown her just who he was.

"What's your name sir?"

"Roger."

"Goodbye Roger." quick as a cat's paw her dagger was in and out, leaving barely any trace with a small entrance and exit. Peacefully the man slumped back down into his eternal slumber.

Almost forgetting Jack was beside her, she put a hand on his shoulder, "Sorry you had to see me like that…"

"If you hadn't, I would've! You saw what he did!"

"I know you're mad, and I am too. But don't ever celebrate death son, it's what separates us from them." she said as she eyed Radish.

"Why wouldn't I celebrate?! He deserved to die, he made his choice when he signed up to work for a lunatic!"

"I didn't say he didn't deserve it. I said don't celebrate it. Lest you lose sight of who you are, what we are... That man was an innocent boy just like you were at one point, then this world turned him into a monster..."

The larger than average torches hung beside the vault made it glisten like it was out in the sun, as their shadows made its wheel like hinges appear to be moving. Along with the door their arms and armor shone by torchlight, and an air of tentativeness rolled over them, preparing for what would surely be an unfair fight given their lack of manpower

Matilda glared at Radish understandably suspicious with hand itching head, "There's more he ain't tellin us..."

"That I can believe!" Riley chirped.

"You mind explainin to us what your little pow wow with Lucas and Detective Konrad was all about. You know there ain't much happenin in the Cantina I don't hear about!"

"Why don't you ask them yourself..."

"Maybe you thought Riles over there was bein mean when she gave you that little palm bunch. That ain't mean. I can show ya mean. This your plan all along? Play games with us? Lampoonin?"

"No... my plan is to sit right here and wait for the calvary to arrive..." he said as he took a seat on the chest, slumped back, and yawned.

Like clockwork one of the vault's hinges shot off fast as bullet letting out an echo that rattled the whole chamber.

"What was that?!" Matilda shouted.

"The calvary..."

****

One by one they piled into the chamber through the small port that had been opened thanks to Radish disabling the door's security system. Armed as well as any soldier could be they formed ranks and stared ahead at the three forked tunnels in case any of Knox's guard had heard the ruckus. Riley, Jack, and Matilda's hearts sprang when they saw a few familiar faces shimmy through the door, Stono, Glasgo, Marcus and Chef Greene with pots and panned armor clanking against the vault door had made for an exceptional surprise.

"Never thought I'd have the pleasure of working with you again Ms. Tripleleaf." Stono approached and said with a smirk, like he was the least frightened man there.

As Jack watched soldiers file in forming a line facing Riley like she was a general, he had to give Radish some credit, even if Knox was the deadliest man on Kleppenwitz, now with numbers, at least they stood a chance.

"Pleasure's all mine Stono, cannot thank you enough for coming. But I do hope you know what you're getting into..." she said.

"You know all too well me and Glasgo dream of days like this."

Second up Marcus A. lined up beside Stono like a soldier with his fresh-looking bandana, "I aint livin in fear no more miss, we'll show this sod why you don't want monkeys on your back! Ole Crowfeet was a friend of mine, I owe'em this much at least."

"I owe you one Marcus!"

Lasty was Chef Greene who beat the frying pan over his chest like a battle cry, a battle cry that said he'd been ready for a fight ever since he left the Cantina.

"How did you hear about this?" she said to them, "I almost can't believe you all are here in front of me."

"Word got round the Cantina this mornin about a deal your partner made with Lucas. Not trusting him I figured I better come check myself." Stono said.

Lucas and Konrad were the last to shimmy through the vault doors, striding with high shoulders as they commanded from the back.

"No thanks necessary for saving you and yours rear's." Lucas said as he closed in making sure to keep his distance from Chef Greene, as if still embarrassed, "Our cut of the gold will do that just fine…"

"The cut?" she said suspiciously, like she knew this was coming.

"Mmmm, Of course. Don't think I work for free, do you? We'll have my cut, Detective Konrad and his brave soldier's cut, Radish's cut for being wise enough to enlist our help, the Stonos… I suppose, and whatever's left you and Matilda can do with as you like…"

Under normal circumstances she would've laughed Lucas all the way back up to the surface, but these weren't normal circumstances, she needed the help, and he knew it, "I accept your terms. Much as I'd love to chat like we're back at the Cantina there's no time. A patrol will surely be along shortly, a patrol we do not want alerting Knox."

Never once expecting to be the leader of this small army she looked over all of them, Chef Greene, Marcus A., Radish, Kersey, Lucas and his men, Konrad and his police force, and finally Jack and Matilda, all stared at her like she was a general, like even if many of them would never admit it, they knew intuitively following her command was the likeliest way they'd survive this ordeal.

"Listen up!!" she yelled as low as she could, "There's three forks over there, so we're going to need to split if we want any shot of finding Knox before he finds us. My group will take the first, the detective and his squad in the second, and Lucas and his men, along with Stono and his, take the third. That should be more than enough skilled fighters in each tunnel to offer resistance in case you need to turn back. Any questions…?"

The small army of eyes still stared at her unblinking, like they waited on every word.

"If you hit a dead end turn back and follow another crew's fork. If you run into trouble turn back and follow another crew's fork or go out the exit if it makes more sense. If you listen to nothing else, listen to this. Should you encounter Knox, run immediately, like your lives depend on it, because they do. None of us are strong enough to take him alone.

You stay smart, you stay alive."

"A plan that's like to get us killed…" Lucas muttered to one of his men.

"Excuse me?!" Riley scolded

"I said I'd be thrilled! Now can we get on with this? After I deal with Knox personally, I'd like to still have enough time for my afternoon tea…"

Always impressed with her lack of stuttering or stammering, how she delivered her speech so flawlessly even with little time to prepare, Jack watched his mom file in with them as the other two crews whisked off into the darkness down their respective tunnels.

Radish led the vanguard of the first tunnel, with Matilda, Jack, and Riley at the rear and Kersey puddling around somewhere in the middle.

While he had time to get away from Radish, Kersey tapped Riley on the shoulder with a face that looked near tears, "I'm real sorry miss, bout all those mean things I said back in that awful castle. Makin comments on your looks, it's j-just awful. I just had to sell it is all… I-I don't think yo-you're stupid. You or yo-your crew."

"That's alright Kersey, I understand. And I apologize for giving you that welt on your head. We can talk more about this later, but for now I need you to toughen up, OK? If we're going to get Apolline out of here safe, I need you at one hundred. Heaven knows she needs all the help she can get right now."

He nodded still looking as guilty as a dog who'd stolen the leftovers.

For as a life-threatening situation as this was, the tunnels they walked and crawled through were a bore. Only alabaster stone tunnel, after alabaster stone tunnel, that after a time all seemed to meld together, with the only novelty being some new bug or critter lit up by the same dull torches. The boredom quickly came to an end, however, when they heard the feint howls echoing in the distance behind them.

"There he is…" Radish whispered back.

"There's who?" Matilda said while using the butt of her pistol to itch at her braids.

"Hugo..."

"That dumb wolf? Loved to see him try that little biting maneuver again when I got twenty feet of distance between us..."

"Not in his instincts to strike from a distance, he'll wait till we're nice and cornered..."

The tunnels got warmer the further they got, and the draft that somehow managed to find its way in blew hot air on their faces. Unwinding became impossible with the constant patter of paws behind them and what sounded like the feint echo of swords clashing behind them.

"What is this place?" Jack said breaking up the silence. "Are we really right underneath Big Bill?"

"That's the spot. Sure lucky for us Konrad don't own mugs, cause when he gets spirited, an isle's wonder how he sings." Radish grinned, "This dear Jack, is an old mining operation, owned by the city, and rented out in backroom deals the mayor don't know about."

"You're joking?" Riley said.

"Ain't even the half of it. As it turns out, Knox has been forgetting to pay. Hence why Konrad was so happy to lend a hand. Now what's a man with his kinda power got money problems for? Which led me to fink even further, what's he doin dealin in poisons? He should be able crack my neck and be back in bed before his coffee cools."

"You're saying we shouldn't be worried right now?"

"Nope. I'm sayin you should be more worried about guns and soldiers than Ghosts..."

"You know I'm beginning to think you tried some of that duck... The way he moved was not of this world. I don't care if he is ripping off Konrad, or how he chooses to torture you. I know what I saw back in Jerrick's Castle." Riley said annoyed.

"Do you?" Radish winked.

The space only grew warmer and narrower as they marched deeper into the earth. It was clear this wasn't going to be a quick trip, as to how long it had taken was anyone's guess with no sun to guide them.

A square door of thick steel stood ahead, just like a miniature version of the one Radish had disabled. Except this one, with its intricate series of steel hinges as thick as the door itself, had no handle, no pulley to open it, and no hidden lock to reveal its contents. Just a door half hidden by boulders with no method of opening. They were at the tunnel's end now, a dead end, and were officially cornered.

****

Lucas had found a nice nook to hide in, crouching behind some gunpowder wood barrels with a fanciful pistol and dagger in either hand. He didn't dare lead the charge, after all why should he. He was their commander, *may as well be a king* he thought, *and a king always leads from the back ranks.*

The fighting began almost immediately, they were lucky enough to catch the first of Knox's men by surprise, many still sleeping in the dorms. But surely that wouldn't last, even a deaf man could have heard the sounds of steel biting steel echoing down the tunnel.

Jumping out of his jackboots every time a shot fired, he tried his best to stay hidden as the battle raged on around him. Somehow summoning up some courage, he poked his head up, and he witnessed a man still in his mogul's crawling right by his nook with a cutlass in his back. Knowing it wasn't one of his by the clothes, he poked his head out a second time to get a better look as the man expired.

Waiting a few minutes after the movement had stopped, in a dashed crawl Lucas scurried over, snatched the pistol out of his cold hands, and crawled back faster than he'd moved all day. *Mmmhmm. Disarmed a pitiless assassin looking to sneak up behind my soldiers, the folks over at the Cantina will hear all about this act of bravery tonight.*

He cheered his men on from the quiet comfort of his hideout when they pushed forward and cursed the day he met them when he saw others fleeing. The shouts of men at war seemed to shake the rock at his back, and with all the fire his ears were well past ringing.

A serious debate was taking place in his head that had been going on for some time,

"Hard as wood, tough as steel, a figurehead of the Blackwater Cantina, and a bounty that hunter sends marks fleeing at the very whisper of my name. I should be out there. My soldiers need me out there!" he whispered to himself.

"But what would they do without a leader? If something should happen to me out there?? Where would they go? They'd never find another like me, another who inspires them, motivates them, and who gets their best! They'd be lost and purposeless, like a ship without a heading."

"Well, I suppose that settles it. I'll stay put." he whispered again as if he was trying to convince himself this was the most difficult decision he ever had to make.

So deep in the very trenches of his own mind, he failed to notice the man that just crept beside him.

"Back! Stay back fool!!" Lucas said as he sprang to his feet, gun shaking with nerves as he attempted to put it on target.

"Put that gun down! I'm on your side!" Stono yelled with a voice like fire raining down from the heavens.

"Mmmm. The Caiman." he felt like all the air had left his body, "You've really got to do a better job of announcing yourself."

Near laughter he replied with his buttery voice, "Quite the hiding spot you've found Lucas…"

"I wasn't hiding!! You see a king always leads from the back ra-"

"Save it. You at least kill that one behind me? With steel in his back?"

"Of course I did! Caught him trying to sneak up on you all, and um, well, you know. I-I put him down! Like the dog he was! Even took his gun, see!"

Stono was officially laughing now, "He's got a cutlass in his back, and yours is in its scabbard!"

"I-I found this s-steel in my nook! It was quicker to grab, and quieter too than pulling mine own." his voice shook, he dare not talk back to Stono the same way he would Riley.

"Well then, got some good news for ya. You can come out of hiding," he said still bruised and dripping with blood from the fighting, "The battle is won. Least for the path we took…"

"Splendid work Stono! As always." he said trying his best to hide the balloon of relief that just popped inside him, "What happened in there?"

"The men all fled, the ones that survived at least. Right after their leader did."

"Knox?!" he said as if it was too good to be true.

"Fraid not. He's still around somewhere. Alireza ain't though. Was smart enough to tuck tail and run, but not before I could give her a scar big as the one she left me!"

****

Detective Konrad opened a rickety door half hidden by a protruding rock and had to lurch his stomach to stop himself from vomiting when he saw inside. Men, women, and some children lie in a dozen or so bunk beds in various states of decay.

Puss and boils covered the faces and hands that poked out of white linen robes, some were barely moving, others didn't move a muscle, making it impossible for Konrad to tell how many were still alive.

"What's got you near hurlin??" Nuster jeered as Konrad slammed the door shut.

"A hospice. And a week from now it'll be a mausoleum…"

Fumbling with his fingers locked in his chest, Nuster mirrored his superior's seriousness and followed him deeper into the tunnel.

Guided by two flatfoot at the front, Konrad had instructed them to keep a cutlass in their dominant hand, and a pistol in the other, hoping to sneak their way in, instead of guns blazing.

The strategy turned out to be an effective one, a patrol of two guards wearing tattered trench coats long enough to scrape the ground were quickly taken down and hidden behind a pile of food barrels.

The cavern twisted and turned and opened up to crystal lakes and closed again to piles of stalagmites oozing steam. It got darker the further they went as the torchlights got fewer, Konrad ducked and bobbed his head with pistol outstretched, knowing full well a deadly clash was imminent. But the further they got, the more astonished he was that clash never came.

They passed another couple of rickety doors on the way forward, Konrad didn't even need to open them to know what was inside, the smell coming from the door was more than enough.

Konrad almost felt guilty. *That cheat Knox will pay for what he's done to these good people!* he told himself, as if the irony that his force failed to protect them was lost on him.

The tunnel opened up to a final chamber, for once well-lit and shaped like a fishbowl made of stone. There were more stone owls in this room, with wings in various states of flight, that seemed to all be looking towards the back of the room.

Barrels piled on top of one another, some with medical supplies like syringes, and others contained carrots, potatoes, dried meat, and sea biscuits. One barrel in particular caught his eye after seeing 'PREGO' stamped in big black letters on the side.

Using his dagger to pry it open, Konrad started pulling out mounds of hay that'd be used as packaging. Finally, towards the bottom he found a sheet of steel as thin as paper and long as a cutlass.

"That's Pregorian Steel…" he murmured as he tried and failed to poke his dagger through it. Even after he reared back and put all his force into the thing, the sheet seemed to bend his dagger more than the other way around.

"I'd hold on to that cap, worth a fortune!" Nuster said with his hands still in his chest. "Isle's wonder why he'd keep that buried in here, instead of on one of his soldiers. If the force ever bought us that kind of protection, instead of this rust on my back, all my worries would be departed!"

Towards the back of the room there was a rock section that the lights couldn't quite reach. Konrad instructed Nuster to follow as he grabbed a torch off the wall to explore the last chamber.

There wasn't nearly as much in this nook as there was in the chamber before, only a lone chain hanging from the wall with a circular handle at its bottom. Upholstered by a steel plate the rusted iron chain nearly touched the floor and dangled with the warm cave winds.

"Well, that looks important." Nuster said as he went over to get a closer look.

"Don't touch it! We don't know what it does!" Konrad shouted at Nuster, but it was too late.

A sound just like an anchor's chain being dropped in open water came from behind the rock, as the friction of the handle hitting the steel plate guard created a small cloud of dust.

Konrad glared at his underling like he could've killed him.

"Uh, sorry cap, it-it just felt right…"

****

274

Jack pointed his gun at the beast, unable to look behind and inspect the steel door that was now making a ruckus. Hugo had parked himself between two giant rocks only a few feet in front of them and wasn't the slightest bit shy about returning a monstrous smile.

"He'll sit there till nightfall if we let'em." Radish said nonchalantly.

"After you then..." Riley lampooned.

"Think I'll sit tight, I like my havin all my fingers. Luckily, I got a plan. And what good is a thief without a plan."

Rummaging around in his stained sack he pulled out a piece of duck bigger than his fist. Taking one look at Matilda's arm he handed it to her.

"Only right I let you do the honors..."

"Really think this'll work??" she said as she snatched it and lobbed the breast down the hall they'd just come from.

"A beast is a beast..."

At first, he sat back staring like he hadn't even noticed. But the smell must have suddenly hit him. Hugo could not deny his instincts, faster than the bats that inhabited the cave he took off after it.

"Didn't expect it to be that easy..." Radish chuckled.

Focusing so seriously on the deadly beast that'd come in and now out of their lives, none of them had yet noticed that the steel door blocking their path from earlier was now hanging wide open.

As they turned and investigated the room Riley gasped, and Jack nearly dropped his pistol. Sitting there blindfolded and bound at the edge of the lake was Apolline, teetering back and forth on a wobbly chair that looked like it may plunge into the pond at any moment.

"Buckle your boots, this'll get interesting..." Radish said serious for once, "Don't take a bookkeeper to tell you he's in there..."

Bending down to meet Jack at eye level Riley grabbed his shoulder,

"It's not too late to turn back now. There's no shame in it. If we walk in there, there's a very good chance that one of us, or even both of us won't walk out alive. It doesn't make sense for one of your first missions to be this deadly. The exit's still open, and the path should be clear. I can meet you back at the Cantina tonight with Apolline in tow, and we can finally put this crazy chapter behind us."

The visage of that terrifying monk inexplicably popped into his mind as if he were looking down on him from a stone tower. It seemed like so long ago now that he told him to follow his new companion. He'd followed Apolline this far and hadn't been killed yet, it seemed the monk may've had a point.

"I wouldn't back out of this for every pearl in the Sober Sea..." Jack smiled back at her.

Chapter 21

La Derniere Valse

Something about the cave didn't feel right. It was quiet. A quiet unlike the previous chamber. Like it was designed.

They'd positioned themselves behind a large stalagmite and stone pillar at the long hallway in the beginning of the chamber. Looking around for any sign of life besides Apolline they saw nothing, only a large collection of Radish's things like the golden elephants, the strange safe, and carriage parts. Elsewhere they spotted a tiny desk in the far corner beside a mysterious red door, an army of rock pillars and stalagmites that lined the chamber, and finally a grim looking collection of prison cells cascaded along the back wall.

"Should we just go grab her?!" Jack whispered.

"Not unless you wanna get caught in your second trap of the day..." Radish said keeping his pistol pointed ahead.

A pair of bats looked down at them from the nest they'd carved out of a stalactite above, glaring at them like they were none too pleased about having their morning sleep interrupted.

"We're not going to have choice. If we wait too long she's gonna fall and drown!"

"Wouldn't worry there... There's reason she's still alive. But... I suppose we best kick things off, no sense in waitin..."

Standing up tall and well out of his cover as the rest looked at him like he'd gone crazier, Radish shouted,

"You can come out now Knox! Tell your men to drop their arms and I'll see if I can convince my angry friends here to take ya in alive!"

Still there was quiet, no sound, no reply, and the only stirring came from the vibrations of the pond in front of them moving along with the echoes of his voice.

"Your chicanery is at an end Knox!" he yelled again, "If you were going to hurt her, youd've done it by now. You need her alive, you know it and I know it..."

Just after the words left his mouth a figure appeared from the shadows at Apolline's side.

"Is this a betrayal Radish? Not like you to give up that much gold over some girl..." Knox said clearly mocking him. He was nearly a hundred feet away, but his words echoed over like he was right beside them.

"That gold's about as real as your powers..."

His mocking face immediately morphed to scowl as his eyes shot darts at the thief.

"Carneld Knox, the Mad Mercurial they call you on all those posters. Well, they got one of those parts right. You know I'm plum chuffed we're getting to chat like this, had a few questions burnin in me mind, if you'd be so kind as to oblige, then we can get on with it."

Silence came back into the cavern as all eyes were on him.

"Might be cause I had to stare at fresh boils that long walk down, but I sure did lose my appetite. But you'll be happy to know none of your exquisite food went to waste, that Hugo is a big fan of duck…" Radish snapped his finger and continued, "On to my first thought. Most curious thing. Back at that crime scene by the Cantina, got a wild hair and tasted some of your pet's… well former pet's furs. Tasted an odd bitterness in there, a bitterness I could only compare to paint. Now what's an untamable Northern Grey Wolf doin with paint in his furs?? Or… or… perhaps… it wasn't an untamable Grey Wolf. Perhaps it was a very tamable Vistan Marshwolf painted to look like one…"

By now Knox looked like a pot of water ready to boil over.

"And what of poor Crowfeet? We all heard the story, how he thrust his blade into your back, and it shattered to bits. The stone skin of the Mercurial! But you know what else may have that effect?" he said smirking with his hands telling his story in front of his face, "Pregorian Steel. And wouldn't you know it… I happened upon some of that steel right down here in some caches I'm sure you thought were well hidden. Carved'em thin too, easy to hide behind a cloak or… say… white robe?"

"If you can get past my guards, you'll see what I'm capable of soon enough. You and your friends are fools for not escaping when you had the chance, all this over a girl you don't know and will never be able to understand!"

"Don't forget about that big bounty on your head. Last question. Where are they Knox?" Radish glared at him like the battle to come was already won, "Where you hidin'em?"

"The guards? Well, I'm so glad you asked…" he whistled and one by one well-armed men wearing trench coats and stained silk coats that hung down to the knees came from behind the stone pillars at the back of the room.

"I didn't mean them… And I think you know that. I mean your

brothers. Must be here somewhere. You'd need to keep 'em close."

The sickly rats in their bird cages all along the walls hissed as if they were an audience applauding, most impressed with Radish's detective work.

"Enough!! You've gotten farther than you ever should've I'll admit. But if you were half as clever as you thought your little plan would've included killing me!" he shouted.

"Plan ain't over. You fooled everyone else, but everyone else wasn't payin attention. Must admit it was clever, the last bit I couldn't figure. But when I saw a shadow move in that corner at Jerrick's Castle right before you grabbed poor Jack here by the throat, well, I finally had it. There's more than one of you ugly nonces, an doin a switch is the only way you could pull off moving so fast."

None of them could believe what they were hearing as the information he revealed seemed to make their heads expand. But it all made far too much sense to just be another one of his tall tales.

After hearing his name for so long, and fearing the day he ever encountered him, Jack was kicking himself for not seeing it sooner. All it came down to was soldiers, enough gold, and a couple of simple parlor tricks to fool the whole town into whispering his name instead of yelling.

The first shot came whirling past their heads as they ducked for cover, looking out they could see it was Knox who fired it, and his men wasted no time following right along. A half a second slower and the shot would have more than likely killed one of them, maybe Knox wasn't a Ghost, but it was clear he was still a skilled marksman.

A cacophonous orchestra of gunfire rained down on their position, slowly biting away at their rock cover and causing the air to grow dusty with all the exploding shrapnel from the walls behind them taking fire.

Riley's veins might've burst open with all the ice in them, she had her weapon back this turn. And now it was time to go to work. Two shots rang out and two men dropped as she tossed the spent pistols to her feet while Matilda scurried to start reloading them.

Face crumpled with tongue poking out just barely squeezing through teeth Matilda was quick when it came to reloading. A guard managed to sneak by their line and thinking fast she took one of the unloaded pistols and launched it at the man's head, after which the man hit the ground so hard a dust cloud erupted upwards from his body.

"Bullseye! Don't even need the gunpowder for these dummies!"

Another two men had moved up to the elephant statues in front of them, eyeing Jack, Riley counted three… two… one with her fingers and shot at the men's feet poking out while Jack finished the rest.

Kersey and Radish had moved up to a wooden carriage wheel, as Kersey was firing wildly with arms flailing and yelling gruffy obscenities at the attackers, while Radish was trying his best to belittle Knox from afar,

"You all call each other Knox one and Knox two?! Or were the others lucky enough to get a name not so stupid as Carneld?!"

Sprinting and sliding into the right leg of the elephant, Riley tucked herself in, not making the mistake the guards lying in front of her did as she surveyed the room.

"Twenty of them, at least!" she yelled back at her companions, "Knox keeps moving pillars but he's there too. Don't take your eyes off him!"

A big ball of lead whirled over her boot revealing her big toe and buried itself in the dirt causing smoke to pour out of the chamber it made. She returned fire at the man who sent it, and unlike him, didn't miss.

Following up, Matilda did her best shot-put impression with a nearby rock Jack was certain he wouldn't have been able to lift past his knees as she lobbed it over the safe two guards had snuck behind. When it hit both targets, she heartily flexed for her companions, forgetting for a moment she still needed to take cover.

Advancing up along with her, much closer to Apolline now, Kersey and Radish hid behind the second elephant statue, and Jack and Matilda were crouched behind the wall of a carriage that'd been put up against a jagged rocky pillar.

"I think we're close enough where I can get to her!" Jack yelled.

"Not yet!" Riley shouted back, reloading while not needing to look away from the battle, "Wait till we're all loaded up, then we'll cover you…"

Taking his sweet time to finish putting lead to gun, Radish gave them a wink like he was ready, as Riley counted down with her fingers again.

Quicker than a mouse whose den had just been uncovered Jack jutted off towards Apolline, ducking, diving and sliding the whole way. It was hard to see straight with the tiny explosions happening at his feet, but his eyes eventually adjusted. It didn't take long for the fire to deafen, as he looked back, he saw his crew lighting up the cave, with Matilda finally using her weapon as intended, Riley tracking a man down like a sniper with the steel monkey on her shoulder shining back at him looking just as serious as she was, and Kersey and Radish firing wildly with the recoil of their weapons making it look like they were cracking whips.

Jack wasn't aware he could be so nimble on his feet and better yet his knife, when he got over to her, he cut through the ropes like they were made of butter. Dashing as fast as his beating heart would allow, he made his way back behind the carriage wall cover with Apolline, only seeing a couple of shots hit ground on the way.

"Ar-are you alright?" Jack said out of breath while Matilda helped dust her off.

She nodded back yes with untidy hair and dirt covering her face, for once not looking so put together.

The fifty pound stones of anxiety on their shoulders faded into dust now that they had Apolline back, most especially Riley who looked like she wanted nothing more than to embrace the poor girl, but between all the dodging and weaving and shooting she was preoccupied with, it would've been impossible.

Feeling something warm along his glove, Jack looked down to see blood oozing from his charred right hand. He'd been lucky, while the bleeding was immense, the cut wasn't deep and had just barely opened his glove enough where he could see the gash on his fingertip.

Rubbing the blood off on his breeches he pulled a pistol from the back of his sash and handed it to Apolline,

"Have you ever used one of these?"

Confused and near tears she shook her head no.

"It's easy. If you see anyone at all that isn't one of us. You point and click. Ok? If that doesn't work, you run right out of that tunnel behind us until you can see sunshine…"

The battle seemed to be going in their favor, by anyone's count there was now no more than thirteen or fourteen of Knox's guards left with the other half lying on the ground motionless. Knox was on the backfoot now, taking less shots and looking more and more nervous, though still just as deadly. Each of them had learned fast to duck under cover whenever Knox left his, after his shots kept ripping in frighteningly close.

"Stay the course!" Riley yelled still weaving, "We'll widdle his men down until there's none left to protect him. That's when we strike!"

"Look out!" Jack said, struggling to pull in his next breath. One of Knox's men was right behind her in prime position, with a knife in his hand so big some might've called it a cutlass. He must've snuck by while the team was providing cover fire for him and Apolline.

Holding his pistol up he could feel his hand start to shake again, he was clamming up like he did back on top of that building. At the Cantina's shooting range, this would've been an easy shot, but in the moment, it was anything but. It didn't help his nerves to see everyone else focusing towards Knox, they wouldn't have been in time to save her.

Let the wind out of your pipes, stop caring, give your head a shake to flush the nerves, the only thing that exists is you and your mark, focus and shoot he told himself

As silly as the advice he'd been given was, it was effective. He hit his target only just left of center, more than good enough to have the desired effect.

Turning to look at what had happened, she smiled back at him with a smile that said *I love you* better than words ever could, then got right back into the fray.

Ten soldiers and Knox was running, barely even coming out to shoot now. From being hopelessly outnumbered to now having comparable numbers, things were looking up, and there was hope in the dusty air.

But if something seems too good to be true, it's because it is. A whistle let out through the chamber almost as loud as the gunshots. It had to have been Knox. The mysterious red door across the way on the opposite side of the lake finally opened, and more soldiers came pouring out.

Their hats all tipped with black feathers, it was obvious from their shooting patterns, these weren't just some pirates picked up in a back alley. They fought in the war zone for no more than a few minutes and already Jack could look around and see blood on each of his companions from all the shrapnel flying off his carriage wall, Riley's elephant, and Radish's second gold elephant.

The burning suspicions of Radish became confirmations when the final two men came from the red door. Mirror images of Knox, with the same robe, the same boils and scars, and the same hatred were now tucked behind the many stone pillars and joining in the fray, with faces that said they'd been looking forward to this all day.

"Ha! What'd I tell you lot!? Bad enough lookin at one of'em, now there's three!!"

"Will you shut up and focus??!" Riley yelled back at Radish having just taken down the first black feathered soldier.

Most likely because he, or rather they, hated him the most Radish had to keep ducking back into cover every time he went to shoot, long before he could fire himself. He was completely pinned and for now would have to rely on the others to get any information on the battle at all. Even Jack was having a difficult time of it, shooting from the top of his cover and then switching sporadically to the sides wasn't coming close to working anymore, the new soldiers had begun doing a very good job of predicting where he'd pop out.

Steel rang like a gong after lead hit Riley's shoulder armor and exploded into bits in the hallway behind them. She was blasting away as quickly as she could hoping to stop their advance, but they moved too fast, too stealthily, and parried each of her shots in a way that made them impossible to pin down.

Much further than the original backwall, now on the ground on either side of the pond's midpoint, hidden behind pillars, the safe, and even more carriage parts, the Knox Brothers and the rest of their men were advancing fast, faster than any of them could keep up with.

"Was this part of your plan Radish?!" Riley yelled, "Come all the way down here, save Apolline, then get ourselves killed?!"

"To tell the truth, I wasn't being completely honest with Knox earlier when I said the plan ain't done. This is bout as far as I got!" he yelled while ducking his head in and out of his position like he was some sort of owl.

The elephant statues that guarded two thirds of them had started to bend and crinkle and looked like they may give way at any moment, while Knox's crew looked frenzied with feet set, like they were preparing for their second and final advance.

Realizing it was more effective than her rifle, Matilda had gone back to hurling the rocks at her feet, trying to oval them over the enemy positions. When she finally ran out of rocks, she saw Jack sitting prone looking for a mark, and Apolline in the corner by her feet, shaking frighteningly, holding on to her grass band for dear life. Trying to comfort her as best as someone like herself could figure, she put her enormous hand over her tiny hand and said,

"Don't worry sweetpea, these knuckleheads couldn't beat us on their best day! Give oh, thirty minutes, an hour, and we'll be back in the Cantina eatin like the queens that we are!"

Her words seemed to help relieve Apolline's fears until Riley shouted,

"I can't hold them back much longer! Get your cutlasses ready!"

The guards had taken notice of the effectiveness of Matilda's rock throwing technique and began throwing some of their own, each of the crew now had their backs pinned into their spots so hard it was painful.

Quickly diving Jack dodged the ones sent his way, looked to his left and saw Riley tucked away pistols pointed up waiting patiently, while Radish and Kersey were doing the same while scrunched up into some kind of ball. But when he poked his head out again, he gazed in astonishment at a midair rock coming right towards his mother's best friend, looking like it was the perfect throw and too far along for any warning.

As Matilda ducked over Jack and Apolline like a mother goose, the back of her head was just sticking out of their rock pillar and carriage cover. He tried to grab her leg and pull her down but there wasn't near enough time. The sound it made when it hit was deep and hollow, and loud enough to send out an awful echo.

Furiously Jack rushed to her side to check on her, a lump as big as the rock that hit her was in his throat when he saw her sprawled out on the ground.

"Is she alright??!" Riley screamed sounding nervous for the first time in the whole fight.

"Yeah," he said taking his fingers off her throat, "Still breathing, but she's out cold… "

Like her anger was guiding the bullets themselves, she took down two more men, again with only two shots as they tried and failed to advance.

"I can see the whites of their eyes now. And they aren't looking for a place to shoot anymore, they're looking for a place to ambush. Get ready. They're about to charge…" Riley said low enough where only her crew could hear, "Finish reloading, and don't fire again. We'll have an opportunity when they charge, don't waste your shot unless it's a kill shot…"

Like the guards read her lips, what was at least fourteen men followed by the Knox Brothers, left their cover in a rage and stampeded towards them like bats out of the underworld.

"Wait… wait… wait…" she whispered, "Now!!!"

Popping out in unison Riley, Jack, Radish and Kersey spent every shot they had left as the men at the front were sitting ducks and now lying on the ground as the rest continued their charge.

Cutlasses rang from sheath, their echoes replacing the sounds of gunpowder, as the firefight became a swordfight.

Splitting up to fight each group, Radish and Kersey had one Knox and three of the men with black feathered caps, Riley was a whirlwind behind the elephant statue with the other two Knox Brothers, and the remaining two guards attacked Jack as he put himself between them and Apolline.

At first, Riley was far too much for the two brothers to handle, raining down sword upon them that had each staggering backwards in a way that proved they'd underestimated her.

Staying on the offensive so they couldn't mount one of their own, gracefully on the balls of her feet she hacked broadly towards their heads, spun around slashing at torsos, and kicked at their shins while keeping her eyes up to distract them. With each passing blow she could feel their parries become a little weaker, their thrusts slower, and ripostes off target.

"One-hundred years the Mercurial are gone, and now that one has returned you want to hide her away from world? Hide her greatness!"

"I want her to do whatever she decides to do," she said with cutlass en garde, "Not see her become your slave…"

"Leave this place now, leave the girl, and maybe you'll get out before the rest of my guards can find you!"

"The rest of your guards are dead, just like the Knox Lineage and all its lies will soon be." Riley said with cold composure, anger refueled after taking a glimpse back at Matilda.

However outmatched by there being two of them and one of her, she felt a little joy as she was starting to think she could win this. When she finally landed her first blow, right above the right Knox's elbow…

that hope faded. The steel cutlass in her hand vibrated enough to make her arm shake with pain, she knew this sensation because she'd felt it before. It was what happened every time a sword met Pregorian Steel.

Jack grimaced at the men with beards that made a fuzzy loop around their chins, cleaner in appearance than any of the others Jack had seen up close, the men held their swords up to him smirking like they thought killing a boy as young as him would be easy pickings.

Pinned almost into a corner Jack made sure to keep himself between the two black feathered men, Apolline, and the still sleeping Matilda. The pain in his finger from it being grazed by a bullet earlier didn't seem like a big deal at the time, but now that he had to grip his sword tightly his hand felt like it was on fire.

Thinking back to the wooden posts in the Cantina's shooting range with makeshift faces painted on and two-by-fours for arms, he recalled Riley behind them, sword in hand yelling *Parry, Riposte, Lunge!!* He never considered himself a swordsman, always preferring a pistol or rifle in his hands, but with men right on top of you hacking and slashing there was no other option. He'd have to become one, and do it quickly.

Holding a defensive position with feet planted firmly he held his sword sideways as their blows struck from the top. He was up early, when after parrying a blow, he ducked, spun and slashed. Hitting one of the men's calves and hamstringing him. *That wasn't so hard* he thought, *a few more hits like that and they'll be done.* But his good fortune didn't last, as he stood up the other man who still had two good legs took one of them a hammered it into his chest.

The first thing he saw as he flew backwards was his cutlass launching up into the air, well away from reach. The second was his vision blur as the hard cave wall he'd been punted to stabbed his back. And the third, was both men rushing towards him, swords in hand as he looked on too dazed to react.

Radish was somehow having a good time, even as Knox's last thrust nearly took off his nose.

"Your pretend Mercurial friends teach you how to fight like that??" he said mocking Knox while making a thrust of his own right after.

"I won't need their help to put an end to you!"

"If you're so confident why not take all that fancy armor off and we can have a real fight…"

Diving between and around the elephant statue that was now riddled with bullet holes, Radish kept him as annoyed as one could possibly be as Knox gave chase around the structure like a fox chasing a rabbit in and out if its hiding hole.

Keeping a careful eye on Kersey who was busy with the other three men, he looked like someone had just poured a bucket of water on him, drenched in sweat and just barely dodging all the blows coming his way.

The moment he turned back towards Knox was when he simultaneously saw and felt the blade piercing his forearm. It was enough to make him writhe in pain but not enough to disable him completely.

As he ducked under the statue to the other side once again, he saw Kersey fall to the ground after one of the men had landed a blow to his torso, ripping a hole right through his vest.

Desperately he dashed towards his captain and thrust his sword into the back of the man who'd wounded him.

"Fall back!!" he shouted as he picked him up by the vest and waved his sword at the approaching men.

Riley felt like she was fighting the steel vault door they'd come in through instead of a man. Six or seven blows she'd landed against the two brothers, to the legs, torso, and upper body, and each bounced right off, causing her more harm than him.

The pain in her ankle from being shot by Alireza a week prior was causing severe discomfort, at the beginning of the fight it was easy enough for her to ignore, but now that the duel had gone on for some time, she could feel herself losing a step because of it. Not only just the ankle, but the rest of her was also starting to slow down, she could only swing at Pregorian Steel so many times before it started to wear her down entirely.

For the entirety of their skirmish the Knox Brothers were on the defensive, letting her swing at them almost as if that was the outcome they were looking for. But the tides had turned. She found herself on the backfoot now, parrying their flurries with her back mashed painfully into the statue.

The fighter in her knew it was foolish to take her eyes off her opponent, but the mother in her couldn't help itself. She felt her cutlass leave her hands after she spotted Jack running for his weapon out of the corner of her eye.

Jack scurried towards his sword on all fours until he could finally get on his feet again, running towards it after it'd been launched when he took a kick to the chest. He could hear the wrathful footsteps of a man following after him but didn't dare look back and waste time.

His despair halted when he snatched his weapon back from the cold ground. Finally turning around, he saw only one of the two men he'd been fighting, and he was right on top of him. The soldier's cutlass was already on the downswing, about to deliver a blow that would surely be fatal. No amount of agility could've saved him, in less than half a second, the man's cutlass would slice right through him like fresh bread.

The first shot since the swordfight began echoed through the chamber, Jack watched the air leave the would-be assassin's body as he hit the ground hard as a stone.

Looking over he saw Apolline remove her hand from her double shaded eyes, the gun he'd given her still smoking and pointed towards its target.

Expecting the other man to be right behind him he swung his sword up around his head, but his heart sank when he saw the second man rush over to the now defenseless Apolline, and still unconscious Matilda.

"Drop it!!" he shouted knife at the Brave's throat and cutlass in the other hand at Matilda's waist.

Stunned into inaction all he could do was stare back at the man, eyes wide with horror and frozen as a maple tree. If he gave up his weapon this long journey would come to a close, and in the worst case possible. On the other hand, if he refused, one of them wouldn't make it out of this cave alive.

"Now boy!!" the man shouted again furiously, taking his knife and slicing a thin cut into Apolline's palm.

Even from a few feet away he could see the trickle of blood pooling onto the ground, slowly dripping from her hand. It was all he needed to see as the blade loosed from his hand and hit the ground with a silencing roar.

The three Knox Brothers and their four black feathered elite that managed to survive looked proud of themselves as they stacked their new prisoners on their knees beside the sleeping Matilda. Riley had no choice but to surrender after Jack dropped his blade.

With a sword at each of their throats, Jack, Riley, and Apolline knew they had lost. Radish and Kersey had managed to sneak away towards the entrance of the room, but with an easy exit so close, not a one amongst them thought they would stay and fight.

"Give it up Radish, your partners lost, you lost." one of the Knox Brothers shouted across the cavern, "Give up now and save your friends from a gruesome death…"

"Not friends, partners!" he shouted back, "Be doin me a favor to be honest, one more cut for me and my fine captain!"

Hearing these words Jack wanted him dead as much as Knox but couldn't say he was surprised. As he lay on his knees watching all that he loved in the world in such an awful shape, he thought about Stono, and even Lucas. Hoping there may be some sort of salvation. But he knew how long it'd taken them to get through the tunnels, and that the others more than likely had battles of their own to deal with. It had all happened too fast to put together, one moment he had two men peeling away from his sword feeling confident their crew was winning, to now battered, bruised and defeated with a sword at his neck nearly drawing blood.

"You may be right Radish. Maybe you don't care if they live or die. Or you could be lying as you always do." he said with dead eyes and a cold fiery voice as he lifted Jack's neck with the tip of his blade, "But. Since it costs me so very little to test, I think I know a fine way to tell for a certainty…"

Having to glare up from on his knees Jack looked across the way and could see the panic in Radish's eyes as he felt Knox's cutlass digging into his neck. Trying to stay conscious, the sounds of his mother's screams were somehow the worst thing he'd heard all day, they pierced just as well as Knox's blade. He spotted Radish searching for extra shot, but come up empty, then dive to the ground looking for stones to throw, but again, nothing. Matilda must've used them all up earlier.

As his vision blurred to near nothingness, through the fog he could see Radish's pendant cut through it clear as day. Almost like its golden cage was holding back a glowing sapphire. The panic riddling the man's face earlier now looked hopeful, as Jack watched him rip the pendant from his neck and throw it right towards them.

The necklace hung in the air for what seemed like an enormous amount of time as every eyeball in the stone bowl darted towards it.

Jack was the first one to reach for it, but it just barely slipped out of his hand and quietly rolled to the floor behind them.

"Was this your plan Radish?!?" Knox howled as his brothers jeered along with him, "Trying to take us out with a bit of jewelry?? If this really is the Quicksilver Thief in front of me, I must admit I'm dissapointed…"

"Ok ok, you win Knox! Just put that blade down and we'll give ourselves up…" he said feigning like he was frightened as he carefully watched behind them and walked out from under cover with hands up.

After laying down his cutlass he was shoved to the ground as Knox's men carried him and Kersey like dead animals and threw them into the pile with the others.

"Good boy Radish." he said quietly, but he stopped only for a moment and turned his sword back to Jack with a cruel look in his eyes.

Perhaps it was because Knox's Crew thought she was the last one to be a threat to them, as they lay on their knees solemnly in their final moments, one of them was able to slip away.

She didn't know why she wanted it so badly, it was like the heart-shaped necklace was whispering her name. Demanding she come and take it. Apolline was holding it up like it was her prized possession when Knox finally noticed and made a dash towards her.

The golden caged pendant was glowing bright blue now and growing and growing. What was previously the size of a walnut was now bigger than her hand. Before long the gold cage that surrounded the jewel burst open and revealed a magnificent sapphire with two prominent jagged edges in the form of a heart.

"Caldo's Corazon…" Jack whispered in awe barely able to find even these words.

The sapphire didn't stop growing, by now it was the same size and color of the chest in the corner Apolline had exited. As if by magic, the glass surrounding the structure burst into a million tiny pieces sending a shockwave so loud every one of them keeled over and grabbed their ears.

When they looked up again, they saw a man with dusty hair and a jaw like an iceberg lying down where the jewel had been, wearing steel so fine it couldn't have been anything other than Pregorian, and sporting golden boots that were somehow even more magnificent.

"The Rogue…" one of the Knox's cried, cried like he knew these were the last words he'd ever speak.

"Morning Knox…" he said with a happy calm as he looked down at his scabbard and pulled out a pearl-tipped dagger, "Don't look scared now… don't waste your final moments…"

The crew could barely see all the men being taken down, only seeing the result of them groaning and falling over dead. Like lightning in the night, he cut men down as if he were a scythe meeting blades of grass.

Each of the three Knox Brothers had a dagger in them before the crew could even process what was happening. They barely had time to blink much less time enough to realize that their sure deaths had just turned into a sure victory.

The once raucous battlefield now lay silent, as the clouds of dust stagnated then settled, and their savior looked them over like a distant friend. A cheeky applause was the first sound coming from the silence as Radish looked at his former colleague with glowing eyes.

"There he is! Welcome in Colombo! Fantastic work! I think we had it of course but appreciate the help!"

"Ahhh Raidsh," he smiled back just as cheekily, "Don't think I've forgotten it was you who trapped me in that thing!"

"Well… not on purpose. And don't forget it was me who got you out." with eyes perched he wagged his finger in full confidence, "And that's gotta count for somethin!"

"It doesn't…"

The Rogue was built like he wouldn't have even needed his Mercurial Boots to take out Knox, broad shouldered, and with muscles that jutted along like mountain ranges. He hadn't even broken a sweat eliminating the Boondock's deadliest outlaw, his armor looked just as fresh now as it did when he burst out of Caldo's Corazon.

The crew was bloodied and beat to pieces but overall ecstatic to still be alive, even Matilda had woken up looking like she'd pull through just fine, though she went right back to sleep the second she laid eyes on the Rogue.

It all felt like a dream to Jack, seeing every boy's hero on Kleppenwitz right there in front of him, and every bit as impressive as the stories told.

"Thank you, sir… for saving us…" he said through a cracking voice.

"You did me the favor of finding him, which played its part just as well as my dagger. Go on and collect your bounties, you earned it. All I ask is when the time comes to pick sides you pick the right one." he said with his mountainous voice as he flashed a look towards Apolline. "The Gale Cometh, as we say."

A sudden whisper croaked from the ground at their feet, startling the survivors as they looked down.

"You killed a false god only to beget a true god." Knox mumbled in amusement, eyes down unable to grasp the energy needed to look up at them, "Alireza isn't here which means she fled. Soon Magnus will know all your names and know exactly who harbors the object of his desire." again he croaked like a dying frog, "This world is a prison, one I'll soon be free of. Finally see our friends… finally know their power…"

As if to finish the job the Rogue calmly walked over to him, but his steps were wasted. Knox's final words had already been said. With a last gasp he laid flat, finally him and his brother's tortured souls could rest.

"Ignore his threats, don't forget in the end his greatest tool was manipulation. Manipulation through fear…" the Rogue said undisturbed, "The *'Comandante'* Magnus is far too busy dealing my men on Prego to worry about the happenings in Kleppenwitz…"

"Well… uhh… I suppose that wraps it all up then…" Radish said nervously like he had somewhere to be, "We'll just go an collect our gold, have us a little party tonight, and you can get back to your big war on Prego!"

"Oh no no no…" the Rogue said with a fiendish smile, "The others can do as they like of course. But not you old friend. You've single-handedly set the Freeboots Campaign back months, and you're going to pay me back for every bit of that lost time. I suggest you have fun tonight, as it'll be your last night of fun for some time. I've got a very special mission just for you, and we leave in the morning…"

Chapter 22
A Celebration, A Revelation!

The hundreds of monkey statues in Hangman's Hall as still as they were, always looked like they were up to something.

"Twenty assassins, dare I even say thirty Knox sent after me. The man was no fool, he knew he needed to take care of me first if he sought a victory." Riley could overhear Geist loudly boasting to a crew of patrons with a chalice in his hand big enough for a king, "But I struck them all down with sword and dagger fast enough to make the Rogue jealous!!!"

The band's fingers blurred as they generated an electricity in the room and there wasn't a still foot in the house. It was the loudest Riley could ever remember, and the shear amount of people in Hangman's Hall for tonight's celebration party might've been even louder.

There were so many men on the chandeliers you could barely even see them anymore, as Riley made sure not to walk underneath them and took her seat at a rickety wooden table beside Matilda.

"Weird isn't it?" Riley said as she laid back, took a load off, and tried to speak over the roaring crowd, "Not seeing Knox's name at the top of board anymore?"

"Ain't as weird as the Rogue over there, right inside my Cantina, dancin up a storm like he's some normal guy. Like he ain't the biggest deal on this island or the next!"

"I don't know about you, but I feel a lot better knowing he's not missing anymore…"

Riley had a hundred reasons to admire Matilda, but somewhere at the top of the list would've been her grit. She'd been bitten, bludgeoned, and bouldered, and aside from a few bandages, with her jolly attitude one could hardly tell what a crazy day she'd just been through

"I never got a chance to thank you, for coming along on this unreal journey. If it wasn't for you wrestling down Hugo, or that pistol and all those rocks you threw, well… I-I don't think we would've made it." she paused and looked her in the eyes, "I only ever started this to protect Jack; it was never my intention to drag you in…"

"You kiddin me??! Id'a come even without all those doubloons we just got. Not sure what I'd do without ya here. Can't keep this place in check all by myself!"

"Well just know if there ever comes a time in the future where you need to back out of this mess. I won't hold it against you."

"I'm with ya till the end girl! If you'll have me…"

"Gladly!" she couldn't hold back her smile and had to quickly strain to keep her eyes appearing normal.

It was one of those nights no one in the building wanted to end as time passed by quicker than anyone would've liked. There were so many lanterns hung off rope from the ceiling that the shady back booths lit up like a sunny day, the band fed off the crowd's energy playing and dancing along with them like it was their last show, spirits were being flung in revelry so frequently one was lucky to still have dry clothes, and the massive wooden corridor of Hangman's Hall felt like it was rocking back and forth like a boat with all the patrons stomping and skipping around the place.

"Figured out what yur gonna do with your share yet?" Matilda said as she slid a drink over to her so big she knew she'd never finish.

"Catchup on my backlog of books, then take a loooong vacation!" she laughed looking over the golden roses Matilda's assistant had just brought over, "Maybe along the way we'll get some information on where this Jerrick fellow is hiding. Finally get poor Apolline some answers…"

The pair shared a big laugh as they watched Radish scurry around the dance floor running from a band member whose banjo he'd stolen. For running at a good speed, he played the instrument well, until he tripped over someone's foot and came crashing down.

Right behind the now writhing in pain Radish, in front of the giant fireplace in his oversized beaver-lined top hat was the mayor of Kleppenwitz, clapping and kicking his legs up high like he hadn't let loose for months. He'd come tonight to hand deliver their bounty and personally congratulate them for a job well done ridding Kleppenwitz of Knox's cruel regime.

"Drinks on the cities' tab for the Jolly Gibbons!!" they could hear him shouting sounding almost as gruffy as Kersey, "The city owes this establishment a debt that can only be repaid by taxpayer funded libations!!"

With so many people in the place, Plunders the Parrot was having a record night. Swooping, flapping, and diving looking about as happy as a parrot thief could possibly look.

As she was starting to wonder where Jack had gone off to since she spotted his friends Glasgo, Roy and Sarah in the crowd, she watched Plunders bead in on that disgusting sack Radish always carried around with him after he spotted something gold poking out of the top.

Swooping in with more cunning than the Quicksilver Thief himself, Plunders pried it open with his beak and flapped away with a golden letter.

It'd taken him a while to notice, but as he flew towards the rafters, eventually he *did* notice a scrolled-up letter dyed gold wasn't anywhere near as valuable as the actual gold he was trained to plunder.

With this realization, he dropped it like it was a soggy cracker, as it floated down like a feather towards the ground at Riley's feet.

If it had belonged to anyone else, she wouldn't have gone near it, but for someone as ill-mannered as Radish, Riley gave no pause picking it up and opening it.

Sir Radish,

I'm not in Kleppenwitz, nor will I be for some time. I'm afraid the wonder of the Mercurial never ceases, but if I keep on these chancy hunts of mine, I'm liable to lose my other hand!

I've infiltrated a Forzian Crew bound for a location I cannot discuss. But I believe I may still be of herculean assistance.

As to your first enquiry, unfortunately I have reason to believe the treasure you seek is in the custody of a man who is deadly as deadly gets and has a small army of his own you'll need to deal with. The sir goes by the name Carneld Knox.

As for your second, and yet just as interesting question, there's a collection of bounty hunters who reside in a misshapen wooden leviathan called the Blackwater Cantina, since you've spent a great deal of time in Kleppenwitz, I'm sure you're familiar. They refer to themselves as the Jolly Gibbons, and make no mistake, are just as dangerous as Knox.

The boy you've sought for so long resides within that Cantina. Goes by the name Jack Tripleleaf.

That's all I can say for now, one way or another, I trust we'll meet again soon.

Signed,

Ghostmonger, Jerrick Alamillo

The term racing heart wasn't near strong enough to describe what she was feeling as she was on her feet with pistol in hand before Matilda had time to look up.

"Where's Jack?!?!" she shouted in a fury desperately looking around the room.

****

Jack Tripleleaf watched a snowy owl dance across the night sky as he looked up at the gaudy stars.

He looked down at the red sash around his hips with the crazy looking monkey as its buckle. It was now one shade darker. Still solidly red, but a big improvement over the near pink he'd been given before.

Though he could hardly believe it himself, Riley had been the one to give it to him, while Matilda, The Stonos, Sarah Blitzen, Chef Greene, Roy and others emptied their glasses on his head in celebration. He was, at least in the Gibbon's eyes, a full-fledged bounty hunter now. He could go where he liked, take his own missions, and take orders from no one.

It wasn't me who saved the day, Jack thought, *The Rogue did that just as easily as someone else would put on shoes in the morning. But I made the shot I needed to make… when it counted. And even if mom refuses part of my cut, hers will be more than enough to pay her back after she blew her savings on my leg.*

Just the thought made him feel ten feet taller.

I wouldn't dance with the deadhand! The words of his old classmate Mirabel Voss flashed across his mind as they often did, but tonight not even these cruel words could put a dent in his spirit.

Still soaking from the rum baptism, he sat on a bench in the Hanging Gardens eyes still glued to the stars. As big as Kleppenwitz was, he'd never known another place as spectacular to watch them.

While glaring at what he could've sworn was a second owl he heard something rustle in the distance.

"Jack..." a young woman said as she approached him.

He nearly heaved when he saw who said it.

Even though her voice was quivering, he barely noticed. It was like it was made of Kristal. Like she'd spent a thousand lifetimes perfecting the craft of harmony.

"Jack!!" Apolline said a second time, taking a seat beside him.

None of it felt real, he closed his eyes and bit down on his lip as hard as was reasonable just to check if he was dreaming.

Embarrassed when all he could taste was a trickle of blood, he finally got the courage to open his eyes again, and there she was still staring at him like an old friend.

"I-I'm sorry if I scared you, I just, just had something I needed to tell you..."

Looking at the wells in her eyes, it felt like he was trying to lift a boulder to stop the ones in his, until he felt a glimmer on his cheek and realized her tears were just a response to his own.

"The first thing Radish did when I climbed out of that box was put his necklace in my hands..." Apolline said wearily.

Jack was drifting in and out of lucidity, like he was floating amongst the stars he'd just been watching, gazing at Apolline up so close as if she was miles away.

"I couldn't have been the one to open it..."

Feeling weightless, and craving something, anything to snap him back into reality, he looked down at his hand. Surely his blackened, scarred, and disfigured right hand would do the trick. But when he looked down, still quivering, there were no scars, no sores, and no disfigurement, only two perfectly normal, matching hands.

Afterword

Dear Reader,

I hope you enjoyed reading the first iteration of Boondock Bounty as much as I enjoyed writing it. The book has been a passion project and labor of love for me for many years, and I'm thrilled to finally be able to share it with you. After this long, I'm dedicated to making it as good as it can be. If you have any thoughts, questions or concerns, please don't hesitate to reach out to me at MorganGeller7@gmail.com. Additionally, if you'd like to receive future updates on Boondock Bounty the series, reach out to the aforementioned email (Even if it's something small like "Hi!" or "Add me!"), and I'll add you to the email list.

I cannot express enough gratitude that you took time to purchase, read, and enjoy this book, and hope to hear from you. Lastly, if you have any interest in going one step further, leaving an Amazon review is the best way to propel a small indie book like mine forward in today's crazy market.

Can't wait to see what the future holds for Jack, Riley, Matilda, Apolline and even Radish, and look forward to continuing with you down the winding path of this crazy adventure!

-Morgan Geller

Stay tuned for the second book in the series Boondock Bounty: **The Stormsong and the Pirate Lords**